Lily Quinn

• VOLUME I •

NATALIE & ERIC SEVERINE

LOOSE LEAF
STORIES

Wanted UNDEAD OR ALIVE

*For Erika Moen
and Lexi Maxxwell*

*For inspiration, courage,
and so much fun*

Chapter
ONE

I had a vampire to catch and the guy behind the front desk of Golden Touch Auto sure as hell wasn't going to give me what I needed to do it. He never managed to raise his eyes above my shoulders, so I stared at his chest right back. The name tag there read *Ted*.

"Hey, Ted. I'm here to see Max," I said. "Can you go get him?"

"Max...?" Ted asked.

He looked like he was trying to get my shirt to pop a button by will alone. I considered granting his wish, but then this was going to take all day.

"Maxwell Ferguson," I said, enunciating carefully. "Big shoulders, short blond hair, nice ass? He's been working here for like five years."

"Uh..."

"Just tell Max that Lily needs to see him. I'll be waiting out behind the shop."

I made Ted repeat the message back to me – twice – in case the poor guy didn't have any blood left in his head and then I went outside, leaving him to stare at the tire rack instead of my rack. I circled around the bland little concrete cube of a building to the parking lot in the back, where the GTA guys stored the cars that still needed work, or whose owners had skipped out on the bill.

The Golden Touch Auto garage chain had to field a dozen or more complaints about the name – in case you don't get out much, GTA also stands for *grand theft auto* – but someone up in the corporate office didn't seem to think it was worth the paperwork to change. Or maybe they thought it was funny.

Probably not, though. Suits, in my experience, had a tendency to smother one's sense of humor. Another good reason to get anybody wearing a suit undressed quickly.

Outside the garage, the breeze off the bay was cool and damp. The water was too far away to see, but close enough that I smelled salt. I leaned against the sun-warmed concrete of the auto shop and pulled out my phone while I waited. I opened the notes I had taken on my new bounty and scrolled through them. It doesn't hurt to check over information in my profession. Missing a single detail might get me killed.

But then Max came out of the battered steel rear door and I pocketed my phone again. He never kept me waiting long. Unless I asked him to.

"Hey there," I said.

Max wrapped his thick, muscular arms around my waist and gave me a tight hug. He smelled like sweat, engine grease and that strong orange soap they use for cleaning up the really nasty oil and shit. Max had thoughtfully washed his hands before coming out to meet me.

"Did you bust up your car again?" he asked.

"Nope," I answered. "The 110 is fine. But I'm working tonight."

There was that mix of worry, pride and pleasure on Max's face that I saw every time I had a job. He always looked like that when I told him about a new mark, his blond head lowered and studying me with dark blue eyes, his mouth caught somewhere between a smile and a frown.

"So what is the world's sexiest bounty hunter chasing down tonight?" Max asked.

Not that he had ever met any of the other hunters. Although in my opinion, Max wasn't wrong about me being the sexiest.

"A vampire," I said.

"Vampire?"

One of Max's eyebrows rose a little. He knew what I did and the world I lived in, but sometimes he still had a hard time believing it. Just between you and me, I do occasionally exaggerate for effect. It makes Max smile, and I adore his dimples.

"You've hunted them before, right?" he asked.

"A few times," I said. "Don't worry, I know how to deal with a bloodsucker."

"Where are you going?"

"There was a sighting at a club downtown called Midnight, apparently. The College thought it was a solid enough lead to post a bounty on the bastard. There's a decent price on his head and it gets better if I can find his maker."

"Are vampires dangerous?"

"Nothing I can't handle. Besides, I'm just checking the guy out tonight." I grinned at Max and winked. "A stake out."

He laughed at my lame joke. Ah, there were the dimples.

"Alright, Lil. What do you need?" Max asked.

"Your cock in my mouth."

I smirked and dropped to my knees, undoing Max's zipper as I went down. I felt his long dick already half hard in his well-worn and oil-stained jeans. I freed his length quickly, before it could reach full size and become impossible to maneuver with anything like grace. Hey, I'm a professional. I take this shit seriously.

I leaned in close to inhale the masculine scent that was so Max: sweat and musk, oil and orange. His cock was hot and heavy in my hands. Now that I had his dick out in the open, I pumped it a few times and licked my lips as it grew rapidly in my grasp.

"Uh... do we really have to do this behind the garage, Lil?" Max protested.

Only Max uses that nickname. Everyone else calls me Lily. Except at the College, where they insist on using my whole name – Lilith Quinn. Names are powerful magic, they say.

Whatever. I prefer sex.

Max was still modest, even after all these years, but a long, low groan considerably undermined his complaint. I could have dragged him inside, I supposed, back into the GTA garage to ride him on top of one of those rolling boards they use to get under the cars, but I thought Max might object for real. Instead, I answered with a little moan of my own as I closed my mouth around his cock.

Max rose swiftly to full hardness between my lips and I went to work on him with my tongue, getting his dick nice and wet. I could already feel it building inside me, that hot tension that I can only describe as bright golden energy. Pure power. Fuck, it was good. It always did and I wondered if normal human girls felt like this, too.

Without releasing him from my mouth, I grabbed Max's hips and shoved him back against the concrete wall. I held him there while I worked my lips up his shaft. Deep-throating a guy like Max isn't for the faint of heart, but I'm a veteran little cocksucker.

His dick slid past my tongue and down my throat. I swallowed against Max's length and would have smiled as he groaned louder, except my mouth was distorted into a perfect pink O around him. He wasn't complaining *now*, was he?

I took Max's hand and pulled it over to the top of my head until he got the idea, curling his strong fingers into my red hair. I pressed my palms flat against his tensed, muscular thighs and concentrated on bobbing my head up and down over him. Fuck, I loved sucking cock. The feel of silky skin over hardness beneath made my heart and pulse pound, stoking the fire inside me.

Max guided me along his thick shaft and I was more than happy to let him set the pace. He never pulled my hair and always seemed to know when I needed to breathe. Or when I wanted to be gagged with his dick.

I let Max fuck my mouth. Saliva ran down his length and left dark wet spots on his jeans. Max leaned against the wall with his head back and his nice square jaw clenched to stifle any excessive noise. It might not have seemed like it to the casual observer – and I wondered if there were any of those around – but I was actually the one using Max right then. The lust boiled off him in waves and joined the hot, rising flood inside me. I felt it filling my body, felt the burning flush in my cheeks and between my legs.

The peak was coming. Max pushed his cock faster into my mouth, shoving the big blunt head deep down my throat. His warm scent was growing stronger and I smelled the tangier notes of my pussy soaking through my panties. I could hear Max's heart pounding even against the backbeat of power tools from inside and someone blasting Mastodon from the garage stereo.

I opened one of my eyes just a slit and could pick out the thread count of Max's jeans. My senses were becoming better, sharper – far beyond that of any human. Just what I needed to spot a vampire through a thick crowd or even follow the bastard by scent, if I had to.

Max removed his hand from my hair and I gave him a long, slow suck from root to tip, then pulled my lips off his dick with a loud and satisfyingly wet smack of sound. I grabbed his slippery cock and started stroking.

"Come on, Max," I purred up at him. "Fill my mouth with your creamy cum. I need it."

"Yes, Lil," he grunted.

I opened my mouth and stuck out my tongue as Max groaned in pleasure and relief. I pointed him at my lips, but didn't bother to make sure it all went in. Semen gushed from his cock and pooled on my tongue. It splashed all across my lower lip, too, and dripped down my chin. By the time Max was done, my cheeks were streaked in white and my mouth was full to overflowing. I looked up at Max and showed him my mouthful of thick, sticky spunk before swallowing it all.

Max sagged back against the concrete, panting hard. I wiped my face with my fingers and sucked them clean, then glanced down at my shirt. The black fabric was wet and sticky with the mess that had missed my mouth, so I unbuttoned the shirt and pulled it off. Luckily, I had thought ahead to wear a tank top beneath. It usually paid to dress in layers in case of unexpected weather and cum-stains.

I stood again and raised my arms over my head, stretching. The energy flowed through me and I felt fucking amazing, ready for anything.

Max tucked away his slowly softening cock – I was tempted to suck another load out of him for the fun of it – and zipped his jeans closed. Is it just me or is a guy zipping up his pants *really* hot?

"Thanks," I told him.

Max smacked my butt smartly. "Do you need any more, Lil?"

"No, I'm great," I said. "Tonight, I'm only watching. I don't have to throw a car... yet. That was just what I needed."

"Any time, Lil." Max gave me another hug and then turned back toward the auto shop, waving. "What are friends for?"

Chapter TWO

I had taken a picture of the bounty from the College notice board. An email would have been a hell of a lot easier, but the wizards of the College still use parchment for pretty much everything. Not paper, but actual parchment. I don't even know the difference, but they sure do. I was just lucky that any of the wizards were willing to use a telephone.

There wasn't much on the College wanted poster besides the name of the nightclub – *Midnight* – and a description of my suspected vampire – tall, dark and handsome. Not terribly helpful, but I had caught worse with less.

I parked my silver i10 across the street from Midnight and settled back in the driver's seat to watch the doors of the club as the sun disappeared behind the glass towers. Sunlight gave way to red neon and the flickering yellow glare of the arc-sodium streetlights. But the College's description of my suspect could have been almost any one of the men queuing up behind the velvet ropes and staring pensively down the line at the big slab of Midnight's bouncer. So I reviewed what I knew about vampires for something useful in finding one.

It starts with demons, like so much bad shit does. They can't come to our world without being summoned. Not anymore, at least. Even when called up from the Nether by a sorcerer worth their silver salts, demons require a lot of binding and power to keep around for long. But a demon can feed some of their blood to a human and *voila*, they have an agent in the mortal realm. Specifically, a vampire.

That vampire could give their blood to another mortal and create a new vampire, who could do the same. The power grows more diluted with each generation, but even a vampire four or five times removed from their original demonic blood donor can lift a full-grown man in one hand and set a new shot put record.

But vampires are voracious. The tainted blood that gives them their speed, strength and immortality eats through the vampire, paradoxically killing them. So they need to drink more and more blood to fuel the power burning through their undead bodies. Blood from a demon is ideal, of course, but enough human blood will do the trick.

Personally, I still prefer how I get my powers... Although they do say that a vampire's bite is better than a hit of the best Ecstasy in the world. But I'd never tried it and experimentation didn't seem like a smart idea. The College comes down like a ton of bricks on demon summoners with damned good reason. And as real-world agents of the demons, vampires are high on the College's hit list. A well-paying hit list, I might add.

I didn't give the club much attention until the sun went down – I came early for the parking space – and not just because only losers show up before nine o'clock. The stories about vampires burning in the sun are true. I don't know why. One of the College wizards could tell you... if you've got a few hours to waste. But even though the forest of skyscrapers had long since plunged all of downtown into a premature twilight, no vampire could rise until the sun had set over his resting place. And then he still had to get himself all dolled up for clubbing.

My dashboard clock read 9:32 in cool blue slashes of light by the time the bouncer even started letting people past the velvet chain. Midnight was – unsurprisingly – a goth club. Everyone was dressed in black leather, black vinyl, black lace, and more black. There was white pancake makeup, too, and a fuckload of eye shadow in a wider array of colors. Some of the more moneyed goths showed off custom porcelain fangs, too, just to make my job that much harder. I had to watch closely, but that blowjob I gave Max had sharpened my eyesight to roughly that of a golden eagle.

Most of the fanged men shuffling slowly through the line outside Midnight were too pink-skinned and breathed too convincingly to be the real thing. But I snapped a few photos of guys whose pallor didn't appear to be makeup or whose chests rose only shallowly. After a few hours, I'd built up a list of about twenty men who fit the rough description of my vampire. I was going to have to narrow that down considerably before kicking some ass.

Somewhere around two in the morning, I spotted a familiar face exiting Midnight. Again? I swiped through my saved photos and there he was – a tall, dark-haired guy leaving the club with his arm around a girl in black lace. The timestamp was 10:44 pm. There was another one from about midnight of him going back inside. Now he was on his way out once again, this time with a blonde in a vinyl dress that she must have painted on.

Someone had quite an appetite. But was it for pussy or blood? I needed to know for sure. I wasn't about to put a stake through some poor human guy's ribs just because he had struck out with his first date.

He took the girl back to his car – a slick black Ferrari like an obsidian spear-point with an eight-cylinder engine jammed inside. I noted the license plate as he walked around to climb into the driver's side. I threw my car into gear and pulled out behind him. Thanks to my enhanced eyesight, I could follow the Ferrari almost a block away without losing him. I got stuck on the wrong end of a red light once, but quickly picked his plates out of the late-night traffic and resumed my tail.

He pulled into the garage of a glass spire of upscale condos, not unlike the one I called home. I parked my i10 behind an empty Prius and made sure I had a good view of the building. I wanted to watch the place for a while to see if my suspect left again. And if the girl did.

As it turned out, I was both luckier and unluckier than that.

I spotted him up on the third story, in a corner loft lined with floor-to-ceiling windows. He didn't bother to close the blinds. He probably didn't think he needed to and I had to admit that the view outside had to be nice. The streetlights below reflected off the glass and would have made it hard for most people to see anything inside, even with binoculars.

But not me.

My potential vampire led the girl into his living room and wasted no time in peeling her out of her shiny black dress, leaving her wearing nothing but shoes and lacy red panties. She swayed a little on her platforms, which meant she was either drunk or an amateur – a pro can run down a werewolf in four-inch high heels. Guess which one I am.

I couldn't fault her enthusiasm, though. She swiftly stripped the guy out of his black silk shirt, then went for the front of his tight leather pants. My breath caught when she went down to her knees and unzipped them to let his hard cock spring free. The girl licked her very red, very shiny lips as she caressed his growing length. My angle wasn't the best, but it was good enough to kindle wet heat between my legs.

My suspect pulled the girl up after only a few strokes. Her technique didn't look bad, but he seemed impatient to get to the main course. He yanked off her crimson underwear and thrust one hand between her legs, fingers swiftly finding and entering her eager, wet pussy. He twisted them inside her, then slipped them out. They were glistening and shiny wet.

He lifted the girl up as though she weighed no more than a paper doll. She was shorter than him by a head, but had plenty of softly sensual curves and a pair of full, blushing breasts. Not a large woman, but not a tiny one, either.

Abnormal strength – vampire warning sign number one. Max could have picked the girl up like that, but what about this guy? He was tall, long and lean under that pale skin. Was he just wiry, or was it something more? It wasn't enough for me to go kicking down his door.

The maybe-vampire pressed his beautiful blonde conquest against the window with her legs wrapped around his waist and slid his cock up into her. Despite only a short bout of foreplay, she was dripping wet. Though to be fair, so was I. The guy was damned sexy in that lanky, gothic way.

The girl's head fell back and pale curls flew around her shoulders. I couldn't hear anything – the condo's soundproofing must have been great, because my hearing was every bit as good as my vision – but her red lips were parted in what had to be a loud moan as he began to pump himself deep into her. My suspect held her up against the window, fucking her brains out with the city and her legs spread out before him.

I couldn't stand watching anymore, but neither could I stop. Not yet. I needed more information.

So I unbuttoned my jeans and kicked the driver's seat back a little. The lowered angle let me slide one eager hand down my pants, and incidentally gave me a better line of sight on the girl's round ass pressed against the window. She left glinting smudges of sweat and wetness every time her pale lover slammed his dick up between her legs.

My pussy was achingly hot and waiting for my hand, so I didn't make it wait long. Damn, I was wet. I had soaked right through my panties, so I shoved two fingers down between my legs and got to work. They had a head start there in the loft and I felt like I needed to catch up.

I matched the guy's pace as he leaned into the blonde, driving his cock in deep and fast. My slicked pussy tightened and I gasped in pleasure. None of that searing energy like with Max, though. It takes two, as they say, to tango. I can't charge up off my own fingers, but I still had plenty of energy from sucking Max off, enough to keep my senses honed to a razor edge and pick out every dripping, thrusting detail of the show going on above.

What I needed now was to get off or I was going to go crazy. As the blonde woman's head fell forward against the guy's shoulder, her mouth open and eyes squeezed shut in bliss, I pulled slippery fingers from my pussy and attacked my clit.

"Oh, fuck," I moaned as I came.

I really hoped a police officer didn't come by right then to notice that I hadn't fed the parking meter. I didn't mind the casual observer cruising by on a bike even at this hour, but a cop tapping on the car window was going to ruin my fun. Unless they were cute.

I writhed and my hips rose up off the driver's seat as I rode the bright, sweet waves of orgasm rippling out from my core. The pleasure surged again and I shivered to see white spunk oozing down the window where the girl's round ass was jammed against it. My suspect still held her suspended off the floor. When he had finished pumping his load into her, he brushed back her honey-blonde hair and nuzzled her shoulder. A little post-coital necking?

Even with my perfect vision, I caught only a brief flash of white fangs before he was sinking those sharp points into the girl's neck. A spray of crimson painted the glass.

"Oh, fuck!" I shouted. I bolted upright in my car and yanked my hand out of my pants.

He was a neat eater, but the jugular pumps a lot of blood, especially when you've just been well fucked by a vampire. He closed his lips over the wound swiftly and the girl twitched. One of her high heels had fallen off and her toes curled in helpless ecstasy at his bite.

I grabbed the door handle and began to fumble through my glove box, searching for the nine-millimeter pistol I kept there. But then I stopped. Jugular bleed-out takes about three seconds. Four if you're a big guy. Maybe ten if a vampire is drinking down the blood and slowing the flow. By the time I could get up into the condo, the girl would be long dead.

At least her death was a pleasant one, though I couldn't feel very good about that. The girl's head lay back against the window. Her arms had fallen from around the vampire's neck and dangled limply at her sides. She was already gone.

"Fuck," I sighed.

I made myself release the door handle and sat back. Why didn't I have some sort of stake-launcher? Not that I thought a piece of wood could have pierced modern tempered glass, but for a moment, I cursed my lack of James Bond-style toys.

I zipped my jeans closed and drew a deep breath. Okay, I knew I had the right guy, and that meant his ass was mine. I snapped a few more pictures while the vampire pulled his pants back on and then scrubbed the window clean, but my phone's camera didn't have sex-powered eagle-vision and the photos were utter shit.

Oh, well. I pocketed my phone. I had gotten a good enough look to pick the bloodsucker out of a crowd the next time he went hunting. And his demonic thirst would compel the bastard to hunt again soon.

Not tonight, though. My vampire pulled the curtains closed and didn't leave again, but I remained until dawn just to be sure.

A two human a night habit suggested that this guy was pretty high up the vampiric food chain. So how was I going to get him?

Storming his apartment by day was one option, but not my favorite. When I was all charged up, I could kick down even a heavily reinforced front door with no problem. Big, messy public break-ins were harder to clean up, though, even for the College wizards.

But maybe I could get invited into the vampire's condo.

Chapter THREE

The next day, I pulled the dust cover off my Alfa Romeo and found the keys in the bottom of a drawer. I didn't want someone to recognize my 110 and get suspicious. I doubted anyone had noticed me the night before, but it didn't pay to be careless. Careless vampires and bounty hunters both got weeded out pretty quickly by the College. My vampire mark had probably been around for a while, and I intended to do the same.

I drove out to Midnight early again and parked across the street. Once more, I remained in the car long enough to start getting restless and fuck around pointlessly with my phone as I wondered. What if my vampire went somewhere else to hunt tonight? He would pick up some other mortal girl who had no idea those fangs weren't for show.

The night was growing dark and a thick, damp fog rolled in off the bay to blanket the streets in gray. The power Max gave me had burned off hours ago. It only lasts about a day. Less if I have to use a lot of it. No more super senses or strength for me, at least not until I got laid.

I knew that I could have accosted Max at work again or picked up some random guy – which was never difficult – but I was saving myself for someone special. I wanted to use my vampire's own sensuality against him. It was the least I could do for the countless girls he had seduced and killed.

Still, I was beginning to worry that I had missed something important. But then I spotted the slick black Ferrari sliding through the mist like a prowling panther. I let out a relieved breath. There he was.

While my vampire cruised down the street in search of a place to park, I climbed out of the Alfa Romeo. Now that I was certain my target was on the hunt, I wanted to be inside and in position by the time he arrived.

I stalked down the long line of made-up goths waiting outside Midnight like a row of black cornstalks. I had made sure to fit right in, wearing a tiny vinyl skirt so shiny that it reflected the red neon lights of the nightclub and so short that it barely managed to cover my ass. My matching corset wasn't comfortable, but it cinched my waist nicely and shoved my tits together into some truly impressive cleavage. I'd applied black eyeliner and smoky charcoal eyeshadow, along with deep red lipstick the color of dark cherries.

My boots were knee-high leather and buckles, with thick heels that added a few inches to my height. I'd left my hair down and it fell almost to my waist. It was going to be a bitch to comb later, but I was willing to bet that it looked damned impressive streaming out behind me like a red banner.

The same big, muscular bouncer was on duty that I saw the night before. He held up a hand the size of my head before I even got close and tried to wave me off.

"Back of the line is that way," he told me in a basso rumble.

I didn't retreat. I sauntered right up to the bouncer and smiled when his eyes drifted down into my cleavage and then stuck there. I leaned across the rope and brushed my hair back over one shoulder to make sure it didn't fall down and conceal anything I might need.

"I'm on the list," I said.

I gestured to his clipboard and moved in closer, pretending to look over it. My breasts grazed the bouncer's thick arm and I pointed to the bottom of the page.

"See, I'm right here," I told him.

Here was a discreet but firm squeeze of the bouncer's crotch right through his dark jeans. I liked the feel of the impressive bulge there, but I was here on business, not pleasure. Though I'll admit that I can sometimes have trouble telling the two apart.

The bouncer's desire gave me a warm little jolt of power. I was going to need a lot more than that before the night was over, but it still felt good.

"Oh... yeah," he said with a tight edge to his voice. "Yeah, there you are. Go ahead."

He unhooked the rope and – to a chorus of groans and protests from the club-goers still waiting in line – waved me forward. I gave the bouncer a well-deserved wink, then stepped through the shiny black glass doors and into Midnight.

Inside, the nightclub was a vortex of strobing lights and scented smoke stirred by the twisting and swirling of black-clad bodies. The Midnight bar was a slab of dark glass under contorting lines of red and purple neon. A DJ with violet streaks in her hair and flowing lace sleeves stood between banks of speakers pounding out a mix of Switchblade Symphony turned up so loud that maybe some dogs down the street were enjoying the lyrics, but the patrons of Midnight – which now included yours truly – were left with only the throbbing bass.

I swung my hips with the beat a little – not really dancing, but I had to admit that the driving tempo *was* infectious – and made my way to the bar. Dancing is fun and all, but the bar is where hearts are broken and mended and then broken again. It was where I did a lot of my work, too. I ordered a vodka cranberry, since half the club seemed to be drinking them. But I had only taken a couple of sips when three different men asked to buy my next one.

"Make her a Black Widow," the tallest one called over the bar. He had long, curly brown hair that had a distinctly tortured artist look to it.

"Don't let the name fool you," said the man on my left. This one was shorter, but more muscular, with bare arms covered in a thick jungle of tattoos. "A Black Widow's pretty much just grape juice."

"That's what you say about wine, too," Tortured Artist said with a disdainful sniff.

"It's *true* about wine," Tat Sleeves insisted. He tapped the glass counter for the bartender's attention. "Two manhattans."

"That's kind of a heavy drink for so early in the evening," I said. Not that I don't like whiskey, but I was working.

The guy with the tattoos looked me up and down, then gave me a confident grin. "You seem like the kind of girl who can handle her alcohol."

Liar. I mean, I *can* handle more than a few beers, but I doubted that Tat Sleeves actually thought so. He was just trying to get under my skirt. Even if I didn't already have other plans, I would have blown him off. Any man who tries to get a girl drunk just so he can fuck her doesn't deserve her time. But the third guy, this one with dark skin and gold eyeliner accenting his cat-like eyes, slid up next to me with a charming Cheshire smile.

"This could get pretty messy," he said. "You're going to have guys fighting over you all night."

"It happens," I told him with a shrug. It did.

The newcomer laughed and said something I couldn't hear over the pounding music, then leaned close to repeat himself when I didn't immediately answer.

"You're going to need a few more vodka crans to make it through the night," he said into my ear. "And I'd be happy to do the honors. My name is Raven."

"Don't you have class tomorrow, kid?" Tat Sleeves asked a little too pointedly.

Raven flushed a bit, but he didn't back down. He wanted me too much to be put off that easily. I felt the smoldering heat of his lust, and that of the other two men. Another little perk of being Lily Quinn. I'm not a telepath – I couldn't tell you who in Midnight was feeling guilty or had a secret or anything, but I can pick out any spark of desire. It only works when that lust is directed at me, though. If you want someone else, all it tells me is that you need your eyes examined.

All three men simmered with desire, along with a dozen others who hadn't worked up the courage to approach me yet. So much for trying to keep myself available... I was used to it, though, and would just have to hope that my vampire was aggressive enough to wade through rival suitors to get at me. And that he wouldn't settle for easier but far less hot prey. Vampires are powerful and arrogant, but they're also predators – they want their hunts to end in success.

"Care to dance?"

The question came from the guy with the nice smile, Raven. I considered accepting his invitation, if only because I might be more visible on the dance floor and I had some moves that would tempt even the dead. Trust me – I've done it.

But I didn't need to. My vampire sat at the end of the bar with a full drink in his hand. He was already watching me. When had he arrived? He wore a black silk shirt unbuttoned to display an ornate crucifix lying against his pale chest.

Before you ask: no, crosses don't bother vampires. Their demon masters were around long before Christ got nailed to one and the symbol means absolutely nothing to them. Now, if you can get your hand on an actual piece of that cross, give me a call.

I dropped my gaze before the vampire could catch my eye and looked away. No seductive lip licking or sucking suggestively on my straw. Tonight, I was playing the part of prey, not predator.

"Care to dance?" Raven asked again.

"I've had too much to drink," I answered.

I hadn't, of course, but their demonic blood means that vampires have the same sort of sharpened senses as I do when I'm all pumped up on sex. I was pretty sure my target was listening to every word, even through the pounding music.

Tat Sleeves stepped in. "Want to get out of here, then?"

I gave the vampire a shy sidelong glance and smiled, biting my lower lip. The vampire's dark eyes were still fixed on me. Good. Tat Sleeves caught my look and followed it to the other end of the bar. He straightened and scowled. Cracking an impressive set of knuckles, Tat Sleeves stalked down Midnight's bar toward the vampire. I took another sip and watched over the rim of my glass.

Tat Sleeves said something that I couldn't hear and gestured back toward me. He waited a moment, and then his face went red and he seemed to repeat himself with more force. I wondered if the guy was really going to start a fight over me.

The vampire finally looked away from me and turned slowly to Tat Sleeves without saying a word. His pale face was hard, his eyes very dark. All he did was stare.

It took only seconds for Tat Sleeves to feel it. Humans always do, though each of their reactions differ. Some are drawn to the power, even if their brains are screaming at them that it's dangerous. For them, that only makes the draw more powerful. That's usually how people react to me.

But Tat Sleeves wasn't turned on anymore. He felt the presence of a predator, that unknown monster out in the darkness that cavemen built up big fires to keep at bay. He gave me a last sorrowful glance and then spun away to slink off across the club. I made sure I wasn't looking when the vampire returned those dangerous dark eyes to me. Raven and Tortured Artist had vanished off into the strobing lights and perfumed fog, too.

Smart boys.

I ordered another drink. It didn't take long to mix some vodka and cranberry juice, then the bartender placed the red cocktail in front of me. A pale, long-fingered hand slid a bill across the shiny black glass of the bar.

"It's on me."

I felt the heat of his desire kindling. The sexual energy comes later, but I could taste the lust like precum on my tongue before tasty spunk fills my mouth.

The vampire leaned over my shoulder and I caught a scent like cold, wet stone. Like a graveyard statue after the rain. I didn't smell any blood, though, so I didn't think that he had fed yet tonight. I was to be his first. And last, if I had any say in the matter.

"Thanks," I said, finally looking up into his eyes. They weren't brown or blue, but a deep, unnatural red-purple color that wasn't contact lenses. "Who are you?"

"You can call me Incubus."

A demon of lust. It had to be a fake name, but I doubted Raven had given me the name on his driver's license, either. Everyone here had some kind of dramatic, gothic sobriquet. It was part of the game. I smiled and covered it with a sip of my new drink.

"My name's Lilith," I said. He would probably assume my name was just as fake as his. "Thanks for the drink, Incubus."

I dropped my voice a bit when I said his name, let it come out a little breathless. Incubus leaned against the bar beside me, his back to the shelf of bottles. He was tall and long-limbed, his skin pale and as smooth as porcelain. His thick black hair was long enough to lie on his shoulders. Incubus looked out across the seething, indistinct mass of the club crowd.

"It's a pity you aren't dancing," he said. "I suspect that you're amazing."

"I'm pretty wobbly," I lied to the vampire. "If I go out there, I'll just make a fool of myself."

"I doubt that."

I tugged on a lock of my bright red hair in an uncertain gesture and gently bit my lower lip again to make it look like I was thinking.

"I... It's these shoes," I protested weakly. "They aren't much good for dancing."

Incubus smiled to display blindingly white teeth. His fangs were small and sharp. The vampire's tongue flicked out over them. I squeezed my thighs together and felt heat there. Sometimes being the prey was a lot of fun.

"You could take them off," Incubus suggested.

"I like it with my boots on," I said.

I couldn't quite manufacture a blush, but I did duck my head in nearly sincere embarrassment. I really didn't want to take the boots off. Incubus laughed softly, a sound like rustling velvet, and leaned in close so he didn't have to shout over the music. He brushed my long hair away from my ear so he could speak into it and I shivered when he did.

"I like your boots, too," he said. "You know they call those *fuck-me shoes*, don't you?"

"They do?" I whispered back.

"Do you want to be fucked, Lilith?"

Yes. Yes, I did. My pussy pulsed with liquid heat.

"Is it that obvious?" I asked.

"It is to me."

Incubus took my hand and I let him lace his fingers through mine. He pulled me off my barstool and led me across the dance floor, toward the door. The air smelled like sweet sandalwood and sweat. Dancers melted aside to let us pass. I leaned close against Incubus, maintaining the pretense that I'd had a few drinks.

"Your hand is cold," I said. It would have been stupid not to say something.

The vampire waited until we had passed through the doors and outside before answering. The bouncer watched us go. I think he might have been disappointed, but he didn't interfere with Incubus. I doubted that the vampire had stood in line, either.

"It's a cold night," Incubus said at last.

We had been inside the club long enough for that not to matter, but I laughed like it was funny. I was supposed to be a little drunk, after all, and shivered for effect. Well, mostly for effect. It really was cold outside and my outfit didn't cover much.

"Warm me up," I said.

I paused at the curb and tugged Incubus' hand to stop him, too. I pressed myself against him and turned my face expectantly upward. My vampire did not disappoint.

His lips were cool and his teeth were hard. I opened my mouth and flicked my tongue across them, lingering over the sharp points of his fangs. Incubus' breath was cold and fresh, no oxygen sucked out of the air by his dead lungs, but his tongue was lively as it met mine. He bit my lower lip and held it with his fangs. My heart pounded. Incubus was a good kisser, but for a second, I worried he was going to bite me right here on the mist-shrouded street.

The vampire broke our kiss after a moment and inhaled deeply. He was smart enough to be able to fake the need for air. Then he smiled at me and revealed his fangs again. They were longer now, ready to feed. I totally gave him a fang-on.

"Where's your car?" I whispered.

I pulled impatiently at Incubus until he led me in the right direction. My skirt did nothing to block the chilly air as it hit the wetness that drenched my panties, making me feel feverish as the night sucked away my heat.

Incubus led me down the hill to his Ferrari and unlocked it with the click of a button as we approached. He opened the passenger door for me with deliberate care and I wondered how old he was, if the monster that called himself Incubus was from one of those bygone generations that so easily mixed their chivalry with casual sexism.

When I had climbed in, Incubus slid into the driver's seat on the other side. He turned the engine over and it purred like a contented tiger as he pulled out into the night. Thoughtfully, Incubus cranked up the heater and my cold leather seat warmed swiftly. I squirmed around to watch the vampire as he drove. I already knew where he lived, anyway.

"So would you think I was a total slut if I took off my panties?" I asked.

Incubus smirked and glanced at me out of the corner of his eye. I spread my legs as much as my tight vinyl skirt would allow.

"Yes," he said.

"Good. I wouldn't want you to get the wrong idea about me."

I unbuckled my seat belt and lifted my ass. I hiked my skirt up high enough to reach the lacy waistband of my thong and slipped it off down my long legs. The scrap of underwear got hung up for a second on the heel of one of my boots, but then I pulled the cloth free and brandished it triumphantly. The lace was dripping wet. I held the thong out toward Incubus and his smile widened into a hungry predator's grin. He obligingly took a deep breath and gave me a satisfying groan of pleasure.

I touched my wet panties briefly to Incubus' lips and he licked them hungrily. I slid the wet fabric down his chest until I got to the waist of his tight leather pants, then tugged on his belt and shoved my thong inside. His cock was as hard as a steel rod, but there wasn't enough room to stroke him. I tucked the damp thong around his dick.

"*Please* tell me we're almost to your place," I said.

Incubus ignored a red light and threw the car into a sharp turn that made me squeak in surprise. He chuckled as I stared. We raced down a ramp into the parking garage, green-yellow lights flickering overhead, and then glided smoothly to a stop in a numbered space.

My deadly date helped me up out of his car and then led me through the garage to the patterned steel doors of an elevator. I slid my hand down his back to grab his ass, but Incubus had to pull away to retrieve his wallet. He removed a keycard and unlocked the elevator. When the doors chimed and parted, I stepped inside and retreated to the corner of the elevator to clasp my hands in front of me, chastened. I became a perfectly demure little goth waif again, waiting to be pounced upon by my pale, dangerous hunter.

And Incubus pounced on me. My back hit the cool mirrored wall of the elevator – vampires do have reflections, by the way – and I thought of the girl he had fucked up against the window the night before. I remembered his cum dripping down the glass, and then her blood. Incubus wasn't going to get another chance. This was his last fuck.

A three-story elevator ride didn't leave time for much more than a deep, desperate kiss. Incubus grabbed my ass possessively and pinned me close against his hard, cold body. I didn't stop him and I'd be lying if I said I wanted to.

The elevator chimed once more and opened onto a nice hallway. Our footfalls were whisper-quiet on the soft gray carpet. Incubus held me close again, his cold hand cupping my ass beneath my skirt and brushing long fingers over my hot skin.

He led me to a slick black-finished door that he unlocked with a keypad. I made sure not to watch his fingers. I didn't want to make Incubus suspicious. Instead, I busied myself running my hands over the lean muscles of his chest.

The door clicked and then Incubus was pushing me through. I caught only a few brief glimpses of the place, but I guessed that the furnishings alone were worth half a million dollars. There was a stylish gold and amber Klimt painting – an original, not a print – tastefully lit behind thick UV protection glass on the wall. I had the distinct feeling that Incubus had bought it new.

"Beautiful," the vampire said, drawing back just enough to inspect me by the colorful city light glowing through the windows.

I turned a slow circle for Incubus and felt his eyes raking over my body: hot, predatory and possessive. He seized my hips and pulled me to him, then raced his hand up my back to unlace my corset and free my breasts. I stretched my arms up over my head, displaying my naked chest and hard pink nipples. I stayed like that, posing for the vampire, and waited. Incubus' fangs were even longer now and he unzipped my skirt so fast he almost tore the vinyl in half. I gasped, but didn't cover myself.

"Leave the boots on," Incubus said.

I moved my hands down and ran them over my shoulders, tits and belly, but stopped with an effort just before reaching my pussy. The lips were shining in the dim light and I ached to be touched.

"My turn?" I asked.

Incubus nodded, his dark purple eyes riveted to my naked body. I grabbed his shirt and yanked it open. Buttons flew across the tasteful carpet and his eyes widened a little, but he didn't protest. I raked my nails down his chest with a throaty purr of pleasure and his cold white skin didn't redden at all under my fingernails. I removed the crucifix necklace and dropped it to the floor.

The vampire answered my purr with a growl and shoved me down to my knees. I knew what he wanted and was happy to give it. I attacked his belt and pants. Finishing what I had begun in the car, I pulled Incubus' straining dick free as his clothes pooled on the floor, and he gave a small groan of satisfaction in response. Incubus' cock was just as long and hard as the rest of him.

My thong was still tangled around him. I wrapped my fingers through it and stroked the wet lace up and down Incubus' dick. It took only seconds to coax another low growl from the vampire. I smiled and sucked the crown between my lips. I tasted my pussy on his smooth skin and felt a thin veneer of heat from my touch, but beneath that, Incubus was like cold, pale marble.

Playing with ice cubes is for amateurs – for a real thrill, try a cool vampire cock on your hot tongue.

My whole body throbbed with hot desire and the power was building inside me now, just like with Max. I wanted Incubus and he wanted me. Desperately. I licked my way down his dick and up again, following my caressing tongue by stroking my sopping wet panties along his length. His balls were tight between his long legs, and were full and heavy when I massaged them.

"Not yet," Incubus said when I felt the lust peaking inside him, as sharp as his long fangs. "You told me you wanted to be fucked."

He grabbed my wrist and effortlessly pulled me to my feet. His dick trailed down between my breasts and then along my belly as I rose. Incubus kicked his pants away and led me over to an expensive-looking couch upholstered in a dark wine red color. Too bad we were going to make a mess all over it.

The vampire shoved me down, facing away with my knees on the edge of the couch. I clutched the back and my ass thrust out behind me, right at cock level. Incubus seized one of my boots, pulling and spreading my legs apart to stare at my bare, dripping pussy. But he wasn't fucking me yet. I arched my spine and raised my hips imploringly. I wanted him inside me. I needed him to feed the hot, powerful pleasure building between my legs.

Incubus tossed my thong away and grabbed my hips. His hands were strong and he held me still, unmoving. I let out a long sigh as he pressed the tip of his cock to my slit and pushed slowly inside me. He was hard and cool against the feverish, wet heat of my pussy and I had to grip the back of the couch tightly to keep from shoving myself into Incubus, to let him remain in control.

It seemed to take a sweet, agonizing eternity before Incubus was entirely inside me, his balls heavy against my clit. I rocked gently, trying to play the passive pet, but I *needed* this. Incubus wound one of his hands through my red hair and began matching my thrusts, pumping his hips against my ass as our bodies came together again and again. Our rhythm built like feeding a fire. The sexual energy built, too, welling up and pouring through me.

I screamed as I came and bucked harder than I intended to. If Incubus hadn't been holding my hip and hair, I might have writhed right off the couch. He pulled me back and held me close against his alabaster chest as I rode the wild waves of my orgasm.

Incubus released me when I came down from the peak and I pulled myself up off his cock, then stood on shaky legs. I may have been trembling, but I didn't feel weak. The lust coursed through me, into every part of me. It wasn't the orgasm, precisely, that empowered me. The energy I get out of sex isn't from how many times I cum, or even how many times my partner does. I can get off with a practiced lover, but still receive only half the power that I do from a fumbling but truly enthusiastic virgin. It's about what they give me, what they put into the sexual act even when my pussy isn't full of dick.

Incubus wasn't at all bad. He was *very* good at this, in fact, but I was dinner first and a fuck second. I needed more.

"May I ride you?" I asked as shyly as I could manage when stark naked, with sweat and wetness running down my legs to streak my buckled black boots.

Gracefully, Incubus arranged himself on the couch with the pale marble pillar of his cock thrusting up from his lap. I climbed over his hard thighs and spread my legs astride him. I reached down between us and guided his thick, slippery shaft into my pussy. Incubus wrapped his arms around my waist and settled his hands on my ass. He lifted me and set me down again, guiding me as I bounced on top of him. I gasped and wound my arms around him, riding the vampire.

Incubus leaned forward to suck my nipple into his mouth, but I pulled back. I had to stay away from those fangs. I was curious about what the wizards said, about how good that bite felt, but not curious enough to bet my life on it. I arched my back and braced my hands against Incubus' chest instead, using him for leverage to work my hips up and down.

"You're going to make me cum," I moaned as the pleasure built again. "Make me cum. Make my pussy gush for you!"

The vampire grabbed my hips and rammed me hard onto his dick. I didn't even need to bounce – Incubus lifted me easily up and then slammed me down until my thighs tensed and I writhed on his cock.

"Yes!" I screamed. "Oh, fuck!"

My whole body quivered like a plucked harp string and Incubus groaned. His balls went tight against my buttocks each time he pulled me down and his cock twitched inside of me. And then it throbbed and pulsed like a second heartbeat. Thick heat flooded into me – the only heat I had felt from Incubus all night. He held me in an iron grip, his dick buried as deep inside me as it would go, and filled me.

The vampire's load oozed from my body, running over our skin in white tracks like wax dripped from a candle. I panted happily and struggled to catch my breath. Incubus hooked a finger under my chin and looked at me with dark red eyes.

"Come here," he whispered.

Incubus pulled me closer into what might have been a kiss. But his fangs were bared and long, like those of a rattlesnake about to strike.

Chapter FOUR

"Oh no you don't," I said.

Incubus was pulling me down toward those deadly white fangs. How many freshly fucked girls had melted into that embrace? No more.

I planted my hands in the center of the vampire's pale chest and drew back. Incubus wrapped his arms around me and tried to pull me close again, but I didn't move. His supernatural strength was impressive, but my own strength coursed through me now and he couldn't overpower me.

"What the hell?" Incubus asked.

I reached down into my left boot. The great thing about those chunky, buckle-covered goth boots is that there's plenty of room to hide important shit in them – like a sharp wooden stake. I yanked it free and Incubus' dark eyes went wide. He tried to throw me off, but I clamped my knees around his waist and held on.

Incubus bared his fangs and let out a feral hiss, like the most pissed-off Halloween cat you've ever seen. I pointed the stake at him and the fucking vampire hit me. His stone-hard fist slammed right into my temple and rocked my head to one side. It hurt, but not as much as it would have a human woman, who probably would have been trying to scoop her brains up off the floor about then. I'm not that easy to stop, not when I'm all charged up.

Incubus' punch opened a gash beneath my left eye, but no sooner had it begun to bleed than I felt the wound closing and the pain fading. Incubus' eyes grew even bigger and he tried to backhand me, but I caught his wrist and bent it backward.

"A gentleman never hits a lady," I told him.

The brittle snapping sound informed me that I had broken the vampire's wrist, and he yowled in pain. Incubus' bones shifted and tried to knit under my fingers, so I tightened my grip. I raised the stake again.

"Shut your fucking mouth, vampire," I told him. "Or I put this through your cold, shriveled little heart right now."

Incubus stopped screeching.

"What the fuck are you?" he gasped instead.

"I'm the bitch who can pull your cock off with my pussy if you don't answer my questions. What's your name?"

He hesitated and I gave him a warning squeeze down below. I didn't really know if I could yank a guy's dick off with my Kegels, but let's just say that my vampire wasn't getting his piece back until I gave him permission.

"Chris," he groaned. "Chris Miller."

"Not that one. Your *real* name. The one that you were born with, whenever that was."

His mouth fell open to display his fangs, but they were slender needle points once again. The poor vampire couldn't get his fangs up anymore and I doubted there was a pill for that.

"Jacob Milliner," he answered at last.

"Good boy." I eased the pressure on his cock and wrist a bit. "How many have you made? How many of your bloodsucking offspring do I need to kill?"

"I..." Jacob gasped. "I shared my blood three times, but..."

"But what?"

"The damned wizards. Bounty hunters killed them all twenty years ago."

That was before my time. I gave Jacob another squeeze to be sure, but he repeated the same answer. That was convenient. I liked convenient, but I had another question.

"Now, who made you?" I asked.

No answer. I tightened up again and Jacob Milliner let out another shriek. I released his wrist and grabbed him by the throat, then leaned in close.

"You tell me or I'm going to tie your dick up like a fucking balloon animal, Jacob Milliner," I hissed.

"No," he wheezed. "I... I will not betray my master!"

Another hard squeeze and I pulled the vampire's face up right to mine.

"Fine," I said. "Do you want a poodle or a silly hat?"

Jacob writhed in my grip, but I had him by the metaphorical balls. And the literal ones, too. I didn't know how old Jacob was, but old enough that he was far more used to being the predator than the prey. He couldn't hold out forever.

"...Conrad Whitaker, the first of our line. Directly blooded," he said at last.

I frowned. The name seemed familiar, though I couldn't place it. But Jacob wasn't done. He laughed, the sound strained and frayed.

"I don't know who or what you are, you crazy bitch," he snarled. "But my maker is far too powerful for you. Conrad will rip out your throat if you harm me. He's going to—"

I slammed the stake up between Jacob's ribs, into his heart with enough force that the sharpened tip punched out of his back and into the expensive couch. I told you that we were going to make a mess. I stood.

Jacob Milliner sagged forward, staring at the shaft of wood driven through his chest with glassy eyes. Then his pale skin began to turn gray and crumble to dust. Within seconds, there was nothing left of the vampire but a man-shaped heap of ash.

I wasn't finished just yet. There had to be something around here that would help me find Jacob's creator, Conrad. I took a moment to shower in the dead vampire's expansive bathroom and then looked through his medicine cabinet while I dried off. Just cologne, bath salts and some massage oil. I wrapped the fluffy black towel around me and went into the bedroom to check the nightstand. Jacob didn't even keep any condoms there. Inconsiderate bastard.

A further search of the bedroom only revealed some more luxurious furniture and another Klimt painting behind a half-inch of glass. There were nice clothes in the closet, plenty of it nightclub goth attire, but also several expensive suits. Some fancy watches on the dresser and a pair of diamond cufflinks, too. They were nice, but I was a bounty hunter, not a thief.

Nothing useful yet. I tried the computer sitting on a stylish desk in one corner of the living room, but it prompted me for a password. I'm no hacker, not even the shitty kind. I tore open the computer and removed the hard disk, just in case I needed it later. I doubted that the drive contained anything sensitive, though. Jacob was just like the wizards of the College – old fashioned.

The desk drawers were locked, and I didn't like the clank inside as I jiggled them. They were too heavy, even for a desk of that size. My senses were amped up all to fuck by the sex and I smelled gunpowder. I didn't have a key to get past whatever Jacob had rigged up in there, so I pulled the desk away from the wall and ripped off the thick oak backing. One of the drawers slid free from behind and the sawed-off shotgun inside boomed. Most of the desk disintegrated into splinters. I leapt back.

"Holy shit!" I gasped.

Booby trap. I preferred my boobs to be the trap, thank you very much. I winced and rubbed my ears until they stopped ringing. Even without my sharpened hearing, that would have hurt. Luckily, the improved healing that comes with my sex-fueled powers also handles tinnitus pretty well.

But that was my signal to wrap things up and get moving. The soundproofing on Jacob's condo was good, but I didn't know if it was *that* good. I would have loved to explain all this to the cops – I'm a sucker for a guy or girl in uniform – but the College makes it pretty damned clear that we're never allowed to reveal things like vampires to the mortal world.

For some reason, they think it might upset people and the wizards go to great lengths to keep that from happening.

So I snatched a few yellowing envelopes scattered around the room by the shotgun blast, ones that looked thick or important. A hundred years of snail-mail, I guessed. I stepped back into my skirt and hastily tightened the corset into place.

I snapped some pictures with my phone, then grabbed a plastic bag and hand-broom from under the kitchen sink. I returned to the couch and swept as much of the powdery black ash that had been Jacob Milliner into the bag as I could. I wiped down everything I had touched with the kitchen towel, then wrapped it around the plastic bag and headed out the door. I remembered my discarded thong just before it closed and ran inside again. My underwear was behind the couch and I tucked them into the bundle of goodies under my arm, then sprinted out of Jacob's condominium.

I heard the elevator cables hissing and wondered if it carried neighbors or a curious property manager. Either way, I didn't want to stick around for introductions, so I headed for the stairs and made my way back down to street level on foot. Luckily, the doors weren't locked from the inside. I stepped out into the dark, foggy night and used my cell phone to call up a cab.

One vampire down and I had a solid lead on his maker, Conrad Whitaker. If what Jacob told me was true, then his creator had taken blood directly from a demon. He would be a powerful man, one worth a ton of money. I still couldn't recall where I might have heard Conrad's name, but it was a good start.

Chapter
FIVE

The first order of business when I got home was to get some sleep. I had spent all of the previous night on my stakeout and then most of tonight baiting, fucking and killing a vampire. Not that it wasn't fun, but I was more than a little behind on sleep.

Twelve blissfully unconscious hours later, I was well rested, though most of the sex power I built up fucking Incubus-slash-Chris-slash-Jacob had dissipated. But I didn't need to throw small cars or spot mice from low orbit just yet, so I figured I would settle for some coffee.

I sat up in my bed and stretched. My condo had a beautiful view of 12th Street. On a good day, I could even make out the red spires of the bridge, but this morning, I had the blinds all closed so the sun wouldn't wake me. I kicked my way out from under the fluffy down comforter and wrapped my naked self in a little red silk robe.

My bag of ex-vampire still sat on the kitchen counter, half covered by the dishtowel. Dead monsters aren't a great view over breakfast – even bagged up – so I retrieved Jacob's hard drive and his letters from where I had dropped them onto the couch last night. I was pretty sure the drive would be useless and deposited it on my dining room table to deal with later.

The letters, though...

I carried them to the kitchen and pulled open the envelopes as I absently shoved a mocha k-cup into the coffee machine. I grabbed a white box of takeout from the fridge without checking to see what it was and started shoveling cold chow mein into my mouth. I'm usually starving after I use my powers and I'm not quite sure why that is. If they're supernatural, then why am I always scarfing down the calories afterward?

Mysteries for another time. I sucked up a stray noodle, laid the open letters out across my granite countertop and began reading. I hadn't been able to collect them all before leaving Jacob's place, but it looked like I had managed to grab a fair sampling.

Jackpot.

Exactly as I hoped, the letters were all correspondences from Jacob's creator. They appeared to go back about a century. Jacob wasn't an ancient vampire, but I guessed that his maker was much, much older.

The two men seemed close, despite the somewhat stuffy language of the antique letters, and I suspected that Jacob was right about how pissed Conrad would be that his progeny was dead. Not that I was going to be the one to tell the guy.

There were a couple of photographs, too, old-fashioned sepia-toned pictures of Jacob in dark suits with stiff, starched collars. I guess he liked black even then. My quarry of the night before wasn't alone in most of the photos and his most frequent co-star was a striking man with slightly lighter hair than Jacob's. He looked about ten years older, and even through the faded pictures, the man oozed power and confidence. Conrad, according to the name printed on the back of the photos in neat handwriting.

The two vampires' haircuts and beards changed with the times, but neither Jacob Milliner nor Conrad Whitaker had aged a day in the last century. Not even in the most recent pictures, which were about five years old. These newest photographs were attached to newspaper clippings.

Newspapers... I told you vampires were old-fashioned.

While the letters all used Conrad and Jacob's real names, the news captions called them by several different ones. They didn't have much to say about Conrad, though, usually mentioning him just as the guy on the right shaking the hand of some tycoon or foreign noble. He was rich, influential, and reclusive.

The machine must have pinged while I was distracted because my coffee was lukewarm by the time I retrieved it, but I shrugged and gulped it down anyway.

Hey, I don't get *all* my energy from sex.

My new target's latest alias was Conrad Whitson. I said vampires are old-fashioned, not imaginative. I grabbed the silver laptop off of my desk and Googled the name.

I *knew* I'd heard it before. Conrad Whitson was more public than any of the elder vampire's previous identities – though I was willing to bet that it had more to do with the prominence of the internet and social media than Conrad coming out of his dusty-ass old shell. But it was the return address printed in impeccable handwriting on each envelope that gave me Conrad's location. No wonder Jacob had kept these locked up in a trapped desk. He didn't want anyone to see the letters but him.

I pulled up the location online and scowled in frustration. So much for being clever... I wasn't the only one who knew Conrad Whitson's address. It was posted along with photos on a number of social media and gossip sites. I consoled myself that none of *them* knew Conrad was a vampire.

His house was a huge mansion rather than a downtown loft like Jacob's, but I remembered the shotgun in the desk. If Jacob protected a drawer full of letters with traps like that, what was the elder vampire's house going to be like?

I had unpleasant visions of security cameras, infrared lasers and impenetrable steel-walled panic rooms. Getting to Conrad Whitaker was going to be nearly impossible.

Maybe... An invitation had worked with Jacob. Perhaps it would get me close to his maker, too. I clicked through my browser tabs until I found the gossip page again.

Perfect. I checked the date and called Max.

"Are you off tomorrow?" I asked when he answered the phone.

"I can be. What's up, Lil?"

"I need a hand," I told Max. "And a cock."

———

The next afternoon, I was sitting on my couch in comfy yoga pants and studying a tedious collection of finance articles when there was a knock on my front door. I didn't bother answering it; the doorman on my building knows to ring Max right up. He didn't even need to knock, but that's Max. Always such a polite boy.

The lock clicked open. Max was one of two people in the world I trusted with a spare key to my condo. He's my best friend. Remember what I said about the College wanting to keep supernatural shit like vampires a secret from the public? That would include wiping Max's memory, if they ever knew about him. But they didn't know and I intended to keep it that way.

Evaine was the other person I would have given a key to... if she had any use for one. Evaine wasn't quite like Max, but I trusted her with my life. I'll have to tell you about her sometime.

I closed my laptop and moved my bowl of popcorn to the coffee table as Max came in. He was still dressed in threadbare jeans and a red t-shirt with the yellow GTA logo embroidered on the chest. Max's hands were clean, but there was a dark grease smudge on his elbow and another along his jaw where he must have rubbed his face before washing his hands.

I stood and stretched up onto my tiptoes to put my arms around Max's neck, then gave him a kiss hello.

"Did you just come from work?" I asked.

He nodded. "Sorry, I couldn't get the day off."

"Then what the hell are you doing here? You're going to get into trouble one of these days," I warned, then gestured to the couch. "Well, you're here now."

Max looked at my white leather couch, then down at his clothes and remained standing. "Uh, want me to shower first?"

"No, don't."

I pulled on Max's shirt, untucked it from his jeans and yanked it up to reveal his well-formed chest and abs. Once I got his clothes off, we wouldn't have to worry about the furniture – at least, motor oil wasn't going to be the problem. I didn't mind a little sweat and grease on myself. The black smudge on Max's face was cute. Sexy, in a rugged sort of way, and my nipples peaked swiftly to points in the lace of my bra.

"How did it go with the vampire?" Max asked.

"Picked him up and put him down," I reported. "Easy-peasy. And I got the name of his maker, the first of his line. Ever heard of Conrad Whitson?"

Max shook his head. "No, I don't think so. Should I have?"

"He's the financial backer for a bunch of start-ups in the valley. They made him rich," I said. "Well, richer."

"But that's not the vampire you killed the other night?"

Helpfully, Max lifted his arms so I could pull off his shirt. I dropped it to the floor and he reached for the hem of mine. Max peeled it up slowly, smiling as he gradually revealed my belly and cleavage. I slithered out of the sleeves and Max discarded my empty shirt on top of his across the glass end table.

My turn again. I ran my hands along Max's rippled stomach and then over his chest. There was a light scattering of golden hair over the muscles there that tickled my fingertips. My hands moved south once more to his jeans. I unbuttoned Max's pants and pulled them down, along with his boxers.

"Nope. Conrad is the original demon blood drinker," I said. I removed Max's shoes to help with the pants-taking-off part and gestured with one of them toward my laptop. "He's going to be a tough job."

"How old is this guy?" Max asked. He kicked away his jeans, then knelt so he could slide my yoga pants off down my legs.

"At least a hundred years that I'm aware of. Probably even older than that."

Max whistled. I grinned at him.

"Was that for me or the vampire?" I asked.

"You, of course," said Max. That's why he's my best friend. "How are you going to take him?"

"Maybe doggy-style."

Conrad Whitaker was one of those brooding, seriously hand-some older guys. He radiated confidence and control even in pic-tures. It was only going to be more impressive in person. Conrad would be dangerous, though. He was the first vampire of his line and the power of the demonic blood was strongest in him. Plus, he had been around long enough to get nice and wily.

I stepped out of my pants and posed for Max in my pink thong and matching bra. His bared cock swelled at the sight.

"Conrad's holding a massive launch party tonight for one of his investments. Some new computer processor," I said. "I don't under-stand the tech at all, but it's supposed to be big and fast."

"Big and fast?" Max repeated with a grin. "Sounds like your kind of party to me."

I giggled and took one of Max's hands. His skin should have been roughened by all of the car work and harsh soaps, but Max always moisturizes for me. I pulled him through the door and into my bedroom. The blinds were open now; I lived up considerably higher than Jacob had and wasn't worried about anyone watching.

My open windows looked out across the dense crystal crown of downtown skyscrapers, all shiny and polished in their silver mid-morning glory, then the pewter mirror of the bay and red bridge spires in the distance.

"I'm going to show up, separate Conrad from the crowd and then stake him," I said. "That's where you come in."

"You want me to put a stake into an ancient vampire's heart?" Max asked.

He grinned, showing me his dimples and I slugged him in the arm. I wasn't strong enough for it to hurt... yet. I shoved Max in the direction of my bed.

"No, dummy. I need you to put this–" I grabbed his lengthening cock. "–inside me."

"You're such a shy, delicate little flower," Max said dryly.

"They don't call me Lily for nothing."

Max laughed and scooped me up into his arms. He carried me the final steps to the bed, then smirked and dropped me down into the tangle of sheets and blankets. I hadn't made my bed when I woke up. Why bother? We were just going to ruin it again.

I yelped when I landed, but Max was already there to soothe my injured pride. He knelt at the edge of my bed like a knight pre-senting some trophy, then slid his strong hands over my calves and gently along the inside of my thighs.

"Let me lick your pussy, Lil," he said.

I've told Max before – and more than once – that he doesn't have to get me off in order for me to charge up. It's just about the sexual energy, which is... well, I don't know. I'm no scientist or wizard, so I can't quite explain it.

But fuck, do I ever *feel* it.

Max didn't need to get me to orgasm to do the job. One time, he was taking a shower, just soaping himself up all sexy for me, and I got so excited that I accidentally snapped the towel rack right off the wall.

There are rules to what I can do, but they're pretty loose and fast. As long as it's lust, it's directed at me and we're both into it – or all of us, if there are more than two people involved – I get what I need. The gender of my partner doesn't matter one bit, or how many times either of us does or does not orgasm. All that matters is the lust that comes boiling up from us.

Those are *my* rules, but Max has his own. He always makes me cum. Is your best friend that awesome?

I twined my fingers through Max's thick blond hair and pulled him close, then leaned back into the sheets and shivered in pleasure as his hands slid over my legs to cup my ass. Max hooked my damp panties to one side and his warm breath caressed me. He licked along the length of my pussy, tasting me, and planted a soft kiss between my legs that sent another shudder up my spine.

Gently, Max parted my slick folds and then traced them with his tongue. He licked delicate circles that spiraled in and in, then penetrated me. I inhaled deeply, taking in Max's scent as well as his energy. Don't worry, this harvesting doesn't hurt anyone that I'm fucking. I'm no vampire. What powers me is the sexual energies we generate, not my lovers' life-force or anything creepy like that.

I wasn't taking anything from Max that he didn't give freely and it couldn't kill him. I would never do that to Max. I could fuck him all day and the worst he'd get is chapped. I would do *that* to him. And have.

I grabbed handfuls of the sheets and was already threatening to rip the fabric with the power coursing through me when Max moved his talented mouth up to my clit and started doing incredible things to it with his tongue.

"Fuck!" I gasped. "More, Max. Lick me!"

I clung to the bed as the sensation he stirred up between my legs seemed to escape the bounds of my pussy and course through my whole body. I cried out and pushed my ass into Max's face, grinding my spasming slit against his mouth. When I bought that condo, I paid extra for really good soundproofing. Now I put it to the test and just screamed my heart out. Max held on tight and urged me on through the orgasm.

Ecstasy stole my sense of time, but to guess by the way I collapsed panting into the bed after, it must have been a couple of minutes. Sometimes, I think Max tries to spoil my concentration on purpose. But the power and the pleasure were already building to dizzying heights, so I didn't really try to stop him.

"You shouldn't be so good at that," I groaned. "I'm pretty sure there's a level of orgasm that's dangerous."

"Maybe you could conduct some experiments," Max suggested. "In the name of science."

I sat and slithered further up the bed, leaving wet drops in the sheets in my wake. "I'm a magical sex-powered bounty hunter. Fuck science."

My thong tried to slide back into place, so I slipped it off and threw it away into a corner of my bedroom. Max whistled again in appreciation. I'd give him something even better to appreciate soon enough.

"Get up here," I said.

Max stood and climbed obediently onto my bed. His cock was still unflaggingly long and hard, in desperate need of attention after the licking he had just given me. I pushed Max back into the blankets. My human friend let himself be shoved into position – not that he could have stopped me very effectively anymore. He put his arms behind his head, which does some really great things to the muscles of his arms and chest. So I straddled his legs to take in the view as I sucked his dick between my lips.

I relished the feel of Max's big cock filling my mouth, growing even longer until the head was pushing into the back of my throat. I eased my lips up to the crown and circled it with my tongue while I grabbed Max's shaft. It took both hands. He was hot against my lips and fingers, such a contrast to the vampire the other night.

Max leaned back on one elbow, watching me work his cock. It twitched against my tongue. I rubbed his dick over my lips simply to feel the silky skin and blazing hardness under that.

I wanted more. I pivoted and turned around atop Max without ever taking my hungry mouth off his beautiful prick. Just one of my many talents. But facing away from him, I finally had to pull my lips off to position Max's big, wet cock against my pussy. He was long enough that I had to get up off my knees and balance on the balls of my feet to maneuver him beneath me.

I sank down onto Max with a low moan of satisfaction. His dick forced me open and pushed into my body. He held me steady with strong hands around my waist and helped me fall slowly. I gasped as each inch filled me. We didn't have to take it so slow – Max is big, but I've handled gigantic – but I savored the hot, tight sensation of him entering and stretching me.

At long last, my ass came down to rest against Max's stomach. I leaned forward to make sure he got a good view of my spread cheeks and his length buried in my pussy, then braced my hands on his thighs and rolled my hips. Max groaned as I twisted myself around on his thick cock to look over my shoulder. He lay with his fingers laced behind his head again, watching and trying to keep his breathing deep and even. Trying to hold back.

I reached behind me to unhook my bra and threw it off the bed. I winked at Max and ran my fingers through my hair. I arched my spine and began to bounce up and down on top of him. In the mirror on my dresser, I saw myself: my legs spread, my thighs flushed rosily and my open pussy stuffed full of Max's cock. My breasts bobbed with every movement and my hair tossed around my head like a flaming red halo.

Evidently, Max liked the view from his side, too. I saw the flash of motion in the mirror, but I still gasped when he spanked his hand across my left buttock. He curled his fingers into the stinging pink flesh and pulled me onto his long cock again. I pushed my ass back and his other hand came down. *Crack!* Max's hips rose off the sheets and he thrust his big dick up between my legs, holding my waist so he could pump himself into me.

I rode my best friend like a seasoned porn star, grateful for his strong hands on me as another orgasm rolled through my body like waves of sweet fire. I seared with sensation and strength. I grabbed my bouncing tits and flicked my thumbs over my nipples. My pussy was gushing along Max's length and our thighs were slippery as I tried to hold my position.

Finally, I fell forward and caught myself with my palms planted on Max's knees, trying to get my quivering under control. I lifted my hips off of him, but Max tightened his grip and pulled me down once more.

"You're a bad boy," I murmured.

I didn't manage to sound very indignant about it. My toes were still curling with pleasure and Max's cock was no less hard and hot inside me. His big hands ran over my ass and then came down in another sharp spank. I let out a cry.

"The bad boy is the one who's supposed to get spanked," I said over my shoulder.

"And what do bad girls get?" asked Max with a dimpled smile.

"Whatever you want to give them," I said.

"Do you have enough power to take on an ancient vampire in his own home?"

Hell yeah. Or a herd of angry wildebeests. Maybe an army of zombies.

"No," I said. It came out as a whimper.

"Liar."

But Max smirked and pulled me up off of him, then rolled me gently over onto my back. I fell into the sheets and he descended on my tits. He grabbed the soft mounds and squeezed them together so he could flick his tongue back and forth between them. My spine arched involuntarily as Max sucked one nipple into his mouth and then the other, enclosing them in fervent heat. I wrapped my arms around his neck and held him while I caught my breath.

"Come here," I gasped.

I pulled on Max until he moved between my thighs. I reached down, grabbed his slippery cock and lined it up with my pussy. Now that I had some of my wind back, I was ready for more. So I wound my legs around Max's waist and dug my heels into his flexing buttocks.

"My turn to make you cum," I said.

Max groaned and began working his cock in and out of my slick pink pussy. I locked my arms around his neck with full sex-powered strength, holding him trapped against my body. I gripped Max tight inside me, like I had with Jacob. Max was a good deal thicker and I squeezed him hard. But it wasn't a threat this time.

"Damn, Lil," Max panted.

"Don't stop fucking me," I breathed into his ear.

I gave Max a light prod with my heels to keep him going. I've had to learn to be careful with all the power I get from sex. The first time I felt that rush, I kicked the tailgate off a pickup truck.

Shut up. Like you've never knocked over a lamp while you were cumming your brains out.

But like an obedient stallion, Max pounded his way deep into my tightness. He was grunting with the effort of fucking me and I bit his ear triumphantly. His balls were getting heavier and hotter against my ass with every thrust, and his dick grew even thicker. If a werewolf barged into my apartment right then, I could have fought it off just with Max's hard cock.

"Are you going to cum?" I asked with his ear still between my teeth.

Max managed a long groan as he struggled to hold it off. And failed. "Shit, I can't–"

"Pull out. Give me your cum!"

I let go with arms and legs and pussy, suddenly releasing Max.

He groaned and propped himself up above me, releasing himself, too. His cock slid from my quivering body and bobbed over my stomach. I reached out and wrapped my fingers around him. They couldn't quite touch around Max's girth, but his dick was dripping with my wetness and my hand slipped smoothly over him.

Max was almost there and it only took a few strokes to force him over the edge. He struggled to keep his eyes open, to watch, and they squeezed into slits that burned with helpless pleasure. Good, I wanted him to see this. I arched my back and thrust my tits up as his cock pulsed and white semen gushed over me. Sticky ropes of spunk splashed my chest and ran in pale streaks down my stomach.

I pumped Max until he gave me every last drop and then wiped the oozing head of his cock with my forefinger to make sure I got it all. I stuck my gooey finger in my mouth and sucked it clean.

"Holy fuck, Lil," Max panted. He sat back heavily on the corner of the bed. "Are you ready to take on that vampire now?"

I considered lying again. I knew I could get Max to cum a second time, and probably even more than that... but I was going to need a serious shower to scrub off the mess he had just painted all over me. And I still had to get cleaned up for Conrad's launch party tonight. I smiled and leaned in to kiss the black smudge along Max's jaw.

"Yeah, I'm ready. I'll kick his head off," I said. "And in my dress, that will be quite a sight."

Chapter SIX

It wasn't hard to find Conrad Whitaker's huge manor house. Grand opening-style searchlights stood like great glowing kettledrums on the well-manicured lawn, sweeping dramatically through the veil of silver fog crawling off the bay. Expensive high-performance cars and limousines were queued up and down the long drive like it was the Oscars, not a microprocessor launch party. Men and women in tuxedos and evening gowns made their way along a bright red carpet toward the house.

No photographers, though. Good thing. Don't get me wrong, I'm not camera-shy by any stretch of the imagination, but photos placing me at the scene would only make my job harder further down the road.

A small army of valets waited outside the sprawling mansion. I climbed out of my i10 and tossed the key fob to one of them with a wink. The valet flushed, handed me a ticket, and I joined the stream of people in expensive clothes flowing into the mansion.

I received more than a few stares. My strapless blue dress was a hell of a lot shorter than any of the other evening gowns and a pair of black stilettos lengthened my already long legs. I wouldn't say I cut a swath through the crowd, but only because I'm modest.

I quickly found myself near the front of a line winding its way between the red velvet ropes and into a marble-floored foyer almost the size of my entire condo. Which cost me over four million bucks, thank you very much. City prices.

Up ahead, people who all had a lot more tech industry ties than I did were stepping through a set of huge ballroom doors. They spread out to mingle, admire the string quartet playing in one corner, or graze at a runway strip disguised as a banquet table full of caviar and overpriced champagne. But at the open double doors, each guest passed through the gauntlet – a pair of liveried ushers accepting their tastefully printed invitations.

Show time.

I approached the door and the usher on the right smiled at me. He was young and dark-haired – probably working his way through college for a degree in computer science or engineering and hoping to make a few connections tonight.

"Good evening, miss," he said. He held out his hand, too polite to actually ask for my non-existent invitation.

I smiled back and reached to my side where a purse would have dangled, but my hand came down on nothing. I tried my other side. Still nothing. I looked at the usher and made my eyes go wide in feigned horror.

"My purse!" I said. "Oh god, I have no idea where it is. I don't even have anywhere to put this."

I waved the stub of my valet ticket under his nose, then sighed dramatically and tucked it into my cleavage. Booby trap. The young usher's eyes followed the lucky scrap of paper and bulged a little. So did his pants.

"I can't believe this. I'm so embarrassed." I spoke faster and edged my voice over into mild panic. "My first big party and I don't even know where I forgot my purse. And... and now I'm holding up everyone else. You must think I'm so stupid... Shit, I should just get out of here before I make a scene!"

I pressed my hands to my heaving chest, where my hyperventilation was making my tits struggle valiantly to escape my dress. The young man at the door stared and I wondered if I could summon up a few tears, but I didn't want to ruin my makeup. Luckily, the usher took pity on me before that became necessary.

"It's alright, miss," he assured me. "Go on inside. Your purse is probably just in your car. I'll have someone go check on it for you."

"Really?" I sighed in theatrical relief.

"Of course, miss. If I could borrow that valet ticket?"

I didn't really want to give it to him, but there were a hundred or more cars parked out there. So I fished the little scrap of paper from my cleavage while the usher watched with eager eyes.

"Thanks," I said in a low voice. "I owe you one."

In my high heels, I didn't need to get up on tiptoes to kiss him. I planted my lips on the usher's cheek and left a heart-shaped red mark there as I pressed the valet ticket into his hand. Then I hurried through the doors before the blood from his cock could return to his brain and change his mind.

No one was going to find my purse, not in my car or anywhere else. I hadn't even bothered to pack one. In addition to letting me pull the old *my-wallet's-in-my-other-pants* routine, the purses that go with a dress like mine can just about hold a pack of cigarettes. If you fold them in half. There was no room for a gun, gear or a wooden stake. I couldn't hide much of anything in my tiny blue dress, either.

I wasn't too worried about the lack of a stake, though. I would have liked one of my own, but most houses are full of wood – even one owned by a vampire. Less than half of a percent of the world's population is supernatural and even most of those couldn't pound a stake through a vampire's tough flesh. I doubt that vampires look around their houses and see a forest of potential death.

But I do. That's my job. A piece of picture frame or bedpost would kill Conrad Whitaker just fine. If I could find him…

I moved swiftly through the crowd, watching the guests – especially the big men with earbud cords snaking up from their tuxedo collars. It was easy to pick them out with my sex-sharpened senses and I steered well clear. If something went wrong, I was sure that I could toss any of them through one of the crystal windows if I had to, but that would have ruined the party.

I didn't see Conrad anywhere yet, but the sun had only set a little while ago and our vampiric host was probably still getting dressed. But I kept my eyes open for anyone else with pale skin and sharp teeth. Conrad had created at least one vampire and might have made more, though I didn't see any.

Fine by me.

Vampires are the advance scouts for their demonic masters. You don't want to know how bad the soldiers are. Vampires work in our world to do... something. I wasn't really sure what, but when I killed Conrad, I was going to put an end to it. And collect a nice payday from the College for doing so.

Conrad's guests didn't seem to mind his absence much. That might have had a little to do with the champagne. Conrad wouldn't be showing up until he had already fed, I suspected. Hunting and killing among his own people was a *terrible* way to stay rich. This was his home and his party, so luring him away would be harder. Well, what's life without challenge?

Challenge was right. Conrad's late arrival was giving me time to worry. He was an elder vampire, the first of his bloodline and the direct link to whatever demon had offered him a devil's bargain. Even pumped up on Max's lust, Conrad was going to be dangerous and difficult to take down.

If I even made it that far. In addition to ducking a few date requests, I was doing my best to tactfully avoid any conversation that might reveal I had absolutely no business at a tech launch party. But the new processor and how much money it was going to make were just about the only things anyone was talking about. It wasn't long before I found myself cornered by a man with slicked white-blond hair and a thick Scandinavian accent telling me about teraflops or something.

I responded with vague enthusiasm, but then I spotted the trio of big, bulky men in suits moving through the crowd and my stomach did a teraflop. Were they looking for me? Two of the security goons held fingers to their ears as they listened to their radios. Thanks to Max, I could hear every word.

"...Caucasian female in her mid-twenties. Red hair."

"That describes at least fifteen women in here, Linden," one of them said in a low voice.

"Hazel eyes," came the answer over his radio. "Stan says she's got the shortest dress and the greatest legs he's ever seen."

Shit. Yeah, that was me. I should have known my little stunt at the front door wasn't going to buy me much time. Security here was too good for that. They had checked my car – just as promised – and not only found no invitation, but no purse at all. Conrad's late entrance was going to fuck up my entire plan. I simply had to cross my fingers and hope that no one had discovered the spare keys in the door. I was going to need those later.

Or sooner, unless I could pull a rabbit out of my proverbial hat and stick around long enough to do my job. I finished stuffing a caviar-covered cracker into my mouth, swallowed and ran my tongue over my teeth. Smiling at Conrad's hired muscle with a mouth full of fish eggs was *not* going to do the trick.

"Excuse me," I said to the pale-haired man now trying to get my phone number. "I really need to go."

I left him staring and moved away as swiftly as I could without breaking into a run. Now what? I had to buy myself some time to think.

I wove my way quickly through the ballroom toward the front, where the string quartet was set up on a small stage. The crowd was thickest there and Conrad's men didn't have any reason to believe I was more than an annoying party crasher yet, so they were still being subtle in their attempts to find and remove me.

But how long until they caught up? I wasn't worried about the guards hurting me. I could take any one or dozen of them in a fight, but then my cover would be blown and I would never get anywhere near Conrad.

I reached the edge of the crowd. There was nowhere left to go now except up onto the stage so everyone could watch me being grabbed and hauled out of their nice expensive party. There was a microphone with no one behind it. Maybe I could pretend to be a singer...? Even if I had a teaspoon of musical talent, that might fool the guests. But security was already on to me.

There was a stir on one side of the ballroom and the guests began to murmur. Now I heard something new over the guards' earbuds: "Mister Whitson is arriving by the east entrance."

Conrad strode into the party from an interior door. The east one, I supposed. Yeah, *strode* was definitely the right word. Conrad Whitaker – or Whitson, as this crowd knew him – appeared to be in his forties, not a day older than the most archaic photos I could find in his letters to Jacob. He had lush mahogany hair touched faintly at the temples with silver, a strong jaw and pale eyes the color of serpentine.

Our host wore an elegant black suit that wasn't a tuxedo, but which nonetheless managed to make every tux in the room seem shabby by comparison. Conrad took the rich, handsome executive look to a whole new level. He looked like a king – all he needed was a crown.

The string quartet fell quickly and gracefully silent as applause rippled through the ballroom. Conrad cut his way through the party crowd like a razor. His dazzling smile displayed the points of his fangs, but no one appeared to notice. The same magnetic power that Jacob had used at Midnight to attract women and repel competition served Conrad well among his investors.

Conrad stepped up onto the stage and stopped behind the microphone. Everyone in the ballroom drew together and I found myself shoulder-to-shoulder with men and women all staring at Conrad Whitaker in almost drooling admiration. I glanced back at the security guys. They were a few yards away, but couldn't get any closer to me without making a fuss. And they weren't about to do that while their boss was giving a speech.

"Thank you for coming and welcome to my home," Conrad said into the microphone. His voice was smooth and deep, baroque with some old-world accent I couldn't quite identify.

"I won't take much of your time," he went on. "It's not simply an investment we are here to celebrate, but innovation itself. This technology will push our world forward into a new age. Better and faster computers will empower our schools, our laboratories and hospitals to better do the *real* work of raising up and protecting humanity. You are all to be applauded for your many contributions to such a worthy endeavor."

Conrad nodded and then stood back from the microphone. His speech had been short and vague, but the crowd didn't care. Applause thundered through the ballroom and even a few loud cheers that would have been more fitting at a rock concert. Conrad's dark glamour was *powerful*. He had the whole party metaphorically eating out of his hand. Though I was sure that if the vampire asked, that could have become literal.

I straightened my back and lifted my chin. Time to get him eating out of my pussy.

The elder vampire stepped down from the stage and into his adoring crowd, his pale green eyes scanning over them all as he searched for someone. Jacob, perhaps? I remembered the diamond cufflinks set out in the younger vampire's bedroom. But Conrad wasn't going to find his creation at this party.

With their boss' speech over, security was closing in on me again. Everyone wanted to be close to Conrad, though, and it was still hard to move more than a few feet in any direction. If I could get to Conrad and start a conversation, his guards wouldn't pull me off his arm... I hoped.

I had already been at the front of the crowd when Conrad arrived. As he searched the party for Jacob, his eyes lit on me and I felt the flare of his desire, like striking a match. Conrad was definitely hot for me, even at first glance. Good. I had no idea what I would have done if the guy were gay.

But as I moved closer to Conrad, his security grew more desperate to intercept. One of them was even pulling a bird-like older woman out of his way, eliciting an indignant squawk from her and a deep scowl from her wife. I was running out of time.

I only needed a few more minutes, so I trotted out another oldie but goodie. I tripped, let out a cry and fell toward Conrad. He broke off a conversation midsentence with a pair of younger Japanese businessmen – although around a vampire, *younger* doesn't really mean much. Conrad caught my wrist and pulled me easily upright.

"Thank you, Mister Whitson," I gasped.

"Are you alright, my dear?" he asked in that cultured voice.

"Yes, I'm fine," I assured him. "Please, don't let me keep you."

Conrad still held my wrist in long white fingers that were cold enough to raise goosebumps across my skin. He lifted my hand to his lips and kissed it gently. Conrad smiled at me and I couldn't help noticing that his fangs had grown just a bit longer.

"It's my pleasure to come to the rescue of such a lovely young woman," he said, finally releasing my hand from his. I was slow to draw it back. "Forgive me, but I don't recognize you. If we had ever met, I'm certain I would remember such a beauty."

It was an old line, but totally worked with the hand-kissing and polite charm. Soft heat kindled between my legs. Hey, just because Conrad was dangerous didn't mean that he wasn't damned sexy.

The lead security guy finally burst through the tight ring of partygoers. He glanced between Conrad and me, then reached for my shoulder. Conrad gave an almost imperceptible shake of his head and his man drew back again.

"Mister Whitson, she–" he began.

"I'll take care of..." Conrad looked at me. "What is your name, my dear?"

"Lily Davis," I answered.

This wasn't the venue for gothic pseudonyms, but there was no sense risking that Conrad might recognize the name *Lilith Quinn*. I had hunted down other vampires – maybe even some of Conrad's other offspring – and the demons who create them get pretty pissed when you do that.

"Charmed," Conrad murmured. "And are you enjoying yourself, Miss Davis?"

He took a glass of champagne from a passing woman in a white jacket and offered it to me. I accepted with a small incline of my head and took a sip. The big suited security officer frowned for a moment, but then retreated back into the crowd to notify the other two that their services would not be needed.

I barely stifled a sigh of relief. I was safe... from security, at least. But Conrad watched me with inhumanly pale eyes. He was waiting for an answer.

"The party's been just lovely. But I'm afraid I don't know much about the technology," I ventured. "I'm more of a money girl."

"Really?" said Conrad.

I was speaking his language now. Even old-fashioned men loved their money. The Japanese businessmen were trying to get Conrad's attention again – as were a half dozen others – but he ignored them.

"I represent the Alcott financial institutions," I said, dropping one of the names I had read while waiting for Max to show up. I gave Conrad my best radiant smile. "I realize we might be a little late to this party, but we would be quite interested in becoming par-tners. To get in bed together on this venture, so to speak."

"Would you?" Conrad asked.

"Oh, very much," I purred. "Maybe you'd like to discuss some figures?"

Conrad graced me with a fully fanged smile. He may have already eaten, but no one refuses dessert when it's offered. The vampire looked me up and down, and I returned the favor. Conrad wasn't as tall as Jacob or Max, but his shoulders were broad and he filled out his perfectly tailored suit handsomely. Such a shame, I thought, since he was just going to end up as a bag of ashes.

But not yet. I took Conrad's cool hand in mine and he led me toward the ballroom door, the one he had entered by. He nodded to another security goon and we walked unhindered out into the hallway. We passed a bathroom and the door opened. A dark-haired woman in a burgundy velvet dress emerged, inspecting her nails, and beamed when she saw Conrad.

"Mister Whitson! I was *so* hoping that I would run into you," she said. Gushed, really.

To be fair, I did too. Just not from my mouth.

"It's a pleasure to see you, too," Conrad answered smoothly. "But we will have to speak later, Miss Eddenhaus. I have promised this young lady a moment of my time to discuss an important business matter."

Sure, business. Like a cock consultation. The other woman caught my eye to give me a knowing – and jealous – look, then left without further comment. Apparently, I wasn't the only money-grubber on the prowl tonight. The difference between us was that my gold would come from the College bounty.

Conrad continued down the hallway, but this time, I led the way. We only went a few yards further, just past a suit of polished armor that for all I knew, Conrad wore during tourneys back in his mortal days. Right now, though, I wanted him thinking about a different kind of lance.

I pushed him back against the wall behind the armor display. If Conrad had fought me, it would have taken all of the strength Max gave me in bed to force the issue. But luckily, Conrad had no interest in stopping me.

The suit of platemail blocked us from view. Mostly. Anyone who looked along the hall for more than a second or two would see us. And we were still close enough to the party that even without my improved hearing, I would have been able to make out the murmur of conversation and music just down the hallway.

"Really, Lily dear? My guests might see us," said Conrad.

"You've never had your dick sucked in public?" I asked. I sank down to my knees and set my champagne glass on the armor stand. "Then you're in for a treat."

I ran my hands up along Conrad's thighs, over his pants and teasingly close... then raked my fingers down again, drawing it out. Every minute increased the risk of someone stepping into the hallway and catching me with one of the richest men in the country up against the wall.

My fingers slid over the front of Conrad's pants and the growing bulge there. The guy was rich, handsome, and he had a nice cock, too. No one was *that* lucky. If I didn't already know that Conrad was a vampire, I would have assumed he made some kind of deal with the devil. Which wasn't far from the truth.

I unzipped Conrad's expensive black slacks and then worked his dick free. It wasn't particularly long, but it was thick and heavy in my hands. The skin was smooth, pale, and the large crown was flushed, but only slightly – nowhere near the deep blushing color of a human man's cock. And it was cool, almost cold to the touch. I sucked the head between my lips and moved as slowly as I could down his length.

The sounds of the nearby party were just as distinct to Conrad as they were to me. Vampire ears are every bit as good as mine at their powered-up best. So when my red-painted lips reached the root of his hard cock and the bathroom door opened, I knew that Conrad heard it, too.

One of his legitimate guests was only a dozen paces away. I didn't look up from my work, but I heard a woman's breath catch and felt eyes on the back of my bare shoulders, watching my red hair sway as I began to stroke Conrad's dick with my lips. The footsteps turned away and clicked a hasty retreat, but no one said a word.

My panties just couldn't keep up anymore and I felt wetness drip down between my thighs. I popped my lips from Conrad's glistening cock and licked at the broad crown like it was a lollipop. I looked up at the vampire through my eyelashes. He regarded me from his position of utter authority and power, hair still perfectly coiffed and handsome face entirely composed. Not even a groan? We would just see about that.

"I'm going to suck your cock and drink your cum," I said. My lips brushed the head of Conrad's dick with each word. "Then I'm going to give you the fucking of your life."

And considering the length of his life – which I could only guess at – that was really saying something.

Conrad's cold, sexy smile remained in place as I plunged his cock into my mouth again, but I saw the points of his fangs pressed against his bottom lip. I let his shaft get nice and wet so that my mouth made loud, slutty sucking noises. Conrad finally let out a low growl, deep in the back of his throat. He seemed to swell against my tongue and even warm a few degrees.

I would have smirked if my mouth weren't so full of cold, hard cock. Conrad watched with glittering, pale green eyes as I fluttered my skilled tongue along his length. I tore my lips from him, gasping loudly, and then replaced them with my fingers. My hand glided up and down his slick cock in a blur.

I gave Conrad a sultry wink and grabbed my champagne flute off the armor stand. There was still a little foam of bubbly golden wine at the bottom. I put the glass under the blunt, lightly flushed head of Conrad's swollen dick just as he began to spurt.

The vampire's dark eyebrows shot up. I guess even after a few centuries of unlife, he had never seen this before. I milked his cock expertly, coaxing a couple of bright white teaspoons of my prize into the glass. Delicately, I used the fine crystal rim to collect the final oozing white drops and swirled them in with my champagne.

"To you, Mister Whitson," I said.

I rose to my feet, toasting Conrad and tipped back the wineglass, drinking his champagne and his cum in one long, sensuous swallow. The musky cream slid over my tongue and then down my throat, tingling with the last effervescent bubbles of wine. It was delicious.

Another door opened, the one leading to the ballroom. An older gentleman in a tuxedo and gold cufflinks walked through, talking into a cell phone. He glanced across the hall and did a double take of me standing beside the suit of armor, licking my lips clean. Deftly, Conrad stashed his cock back into his pants and stepped out from behind the antique display. He took my hand again in an unnaturally strong grip.

Conrad nodded once to his guest and I raised my empty glass, grinning. He might have just missed the good part, but it couldn't be hard to put together what we were up to. I put some extra swing into my hips as Conrad pulled me down the hall, away from the party and in the direction of a curving staircase.

Chapter
SEVEN

Conrad Whitaker led me up the stairs, then down another long hall full of priceless antiques and closed mahogany doors. Sweat slicked my hand not clasped in the ancient vampire's icy steel grasp.

The further we got from his launch party, the deeper we ventured into the darkened, private recesses of Conrad's vast home. And with each step, my chances of encountering weapons, traps or safe rooms increased. I remembered the shotgun in Jacob's desk all too well.

Besides, I was growing impatient to see what it would be like to fuck an elder vampire.

"I can't wait anymore," I told Conrad with a gasp that I didn't even have to fake.

I chose a door at random and shoved Conrad in that direction. I couldn't use my powered-up strength without tipping my hand, so it was a bit like trying to shove a mountain. But the vampire wanted the same thing I did and he turned the shiny brass doorknob – so I guessed this room was safely trap-free – and let me pull him into a large office lined in bookshelves.

"If you don't fuck me right now," I panted, "I'll go crazy."

I hooked my fingers through my dripping panties and yanked them down my legs, then kicked them away. Conrad watched me intently, but did not immediately move.

I went to the huge mahogany desk and swept everything off the top. There wasn't much – just a blotter and an old-style Rolodex that showed some of Conrad's age. I jumped onto the edge of the desk, feeling the polished wood against my ass. I leaned back and thrust my legs up into the air, then let them fall slowly open to reveal my wet, eager pussy.

"Come here and shove your fucking cock into me," I said. "Let me show you how good I can make you feel."

I squeezed my breasts through the cloth of my tiny blue dress. I badly wanted Conrad to grab them in those cold, strong hands. His icy eyes raked over my body, down my legs and then finally between them.

With careful, deliberate motions, Conrad removed his jacket and draped it over the arm of the leather-cushioned office chair. Not taking his stern gaze off me for an instant, he undid his cufflinks and set them aside. Next, the vampire unknotted his black tie and then opened his shirt one button at a time.

I ran a hand down my belly and then under my dress to the dripping wetness of my pussy. I rubbed trembling fingers against my clitoris. The little nub felt hard enough to cut glass. Jacob had been hot, but his creator radiated power like few creatures I had ever met. Conrad Whitaker was taking his time, maintaining control over the situation.

Over me.

The vampire shrugged out of his shirt. His stomach was toned and flat enough to iron that shirt on. The dusting of brown and silver hair across his chest made Conrad's skin seem even paler, as white as paper. I'm generally immune to the charms of the supernatural world, but Conrad was old and powerful. His magnetism was definitely working, even on me.

I slid two fingers into myself and started thrusting them desperately. My hips rocked on the edge of the desk and the smooth surface grew wet as I dripped all over it.

At last, Conrad folded his pants with creases as sharp as knives and set them aside. Beneath were slithery, fine black silk boxers. Conrad probably spent more on underwear than some people did on their best suit. He removed these, too, and stood naked before me. There was nothing at all vulnerable about the vampire's nudity. No, there was something inexplicably *dark* about him, despite his white skin, pale eyes and silver-shot hair. Not a halo or aura or anything – if those exist at all, I can't see them – but a presence that was as cold and unyieldingly hard as the dick pointed between my legs.

I squirmed on the desk, but I was already perched precariously on the edge and couldn't get any closer to Conrad without falling.

"Please fuck me," I begged. "Fill me with that thick cock!"

I pulled my fingers from my slick opening and parted my flushed labia with them. Conrad seized my ankles and spread my legs apart as he pressed the head of his dick against me.

"Do it," I moaned. "Fuck me!"

I thrust my wet fingers into my mouth. The taste of my pussy was sharp and mingled amazingly with the lingering flavors of Conrad's salty cum and fine champagne.

Silently, the vampire tightened his grasp around my ankles and held my legs open. So slowly that it made me want to scream, Conrad pushed his cock into me. His coldness made my pussy blaze in contrast.

Conrad forced my legs apart until my heels were nearly at the corners of his desk. I'm pretty damned flexible and the elder vampire put it to full use. He held my long legs spread open and then slammed himself into me with authority. Conrad would have fucked me right off the far side of the desk if he weren't holding my ankles in that unbreakable grip. His girth stretched me almost painfully and pressed into every sensitive spot inside me with each hammering thrust.

Conrad only had to work himself inside me for a moment, pounding and filling my pussy completely, before I was moaning and crying out. The vampire didn't stop, didn't relent at all as he forced the sweet, deep pleasure through me. I reached over my head and grabbed the edge of the desk. Sexual energy flowed from Conrad to me in a measured stream.

The vampire was strong. Conrad held me effortlessly even as he slammed into me and we inched his heavy desk across the office floor. I'd fought vampires, but not one like this. Not the progenitor of an entire line. My lust-fed power grew and burned, joining the large reserves Max had given me. I hoped it would be enough.

"Shit, I'm going to cum!" I cried.

Conrad's pale eyes locked with mine. He moved faster inside me, skillfully stoking the bonfire of pleasure. Ecstasy crested and broke within me like a molten wave. It roared up from my core and seized my every muscle. My back arched off the smooth wood beneath me and I parted my lips to scream, but Conrad's hand came down over my mouth. He muffled my sharp cries brutally as I thrashed on top of his desk.

Finally, Conrad withdrew his cock and stood back, releasing my ankle and my mouth. He seized my shoulder and yanked me upright. I sagged on watery knees and nearly fell. Conrad was... amazing. I couldn't remember the last time I had desired a man this much. I almost didn't want to kill the vampire.

"Let me see all of you," Conrad commanded.

His antique European accent remained cultured, but had shed most of the polite edge. It was an order delivered only with a hint of courtesy because Conrad knew that he would get *exactly* what he wanted.

I turned around and swept my flaming hair over my shoulder, baring my back. I reached up behind myself – flexible, remember?

– and found the zipper of my dress. I dragged it slowly down, matching the pace at which Conrad had unbuttoned his shirt as best my overeager hands could manage.

I twirled toward the vampire again. He loomed over me, as hard and still as a statue in a museum. I raised both arms above my head. I swiveled my hips in a sinuous circle and worked my dress gradually down my body with only the hypnotic action of my hips until the blue fabric pooled around my feet. I stepped out of it, now only wearing my high heels.

"Beautiful," Conrad growled through long fangs.

He grabbed my shoulder and turned me away from him, then shoved me swiftly down over his desk. He impaled me on his dick with a single hard, unforgiving thrust. I pressed my face against the slick wood and moaned.

Conrad traced my spine with fingers like ice and came to rest cupping my ass. His thumbs spread my cheeks. One digit slid inward and I couldn't help lifting my hips invitingly. Gently, he caressed my asshole with the blunt tip of one thumb.

"Yes," I begged. "Please!"

I raised my ass higher so Conrad could slowly push his thumb into my tight pink confines. The tiny opening stretched for him and the sense of fullness inside me doubled. I couldn't breathe with the pleasure and stars danced around the edge of my vision.

Conrad's cock moved in and out of my pussy while his thumb rubbed at his hardness through the sensitive barrier of flesh inside me. He grabbed the crest of my hip in his other hand and guided me back and forth on his dick, directing me like a maestro conducting a symphony.

"Fuck," I whimpered. "I love feeling you in both my hungry little holes."

At first, Conrad fingered my ass in rhythm so I could feel his dick and his thumb entering me together, but the elder vampire kept me balanced on the blade edge of pleasure. Conrad shoved his thumb in as I rocked forward to the head of his cock and drew it away when I pushed back against him. The swelling tide of sensation was merciless. Even when his dick was sliding out of my pussy, his finger was pressing in.

"Oh, fuck!" I screamed. "I'm cumming!"

Conrad was relentless. He had to stifle my cries with his hand again while I came all over his cock and hand. Only when my body couldn't keep up anymore did Conrad pull his thumb from my ass with a slutty popping sound and let me sag forward across his desk, panting and shaking. Every fiber of my being burned with power and desire.

On the other side of his desk was the large wood and leather chair that held Conrad's neatly arranged clothes. This was no modern roller, but a heavy oak thing with a high back, almost like a throne. Trembling, I reached across the desk to hold on to the far edge, close enough to touch the chair.

One solid blow to shatter it and then a swift thrust to put the sharpest piece through Conrad's heart. That's all it would take to end this...

But Conrad wasn't done with me yet. After centuries of unlife, the vampire had strength and stamina I could only guess at. Before I could grab his desk chair, the vampire pulled me up to seize my breasts, yanking me away.

His cool hands cupped my tits and quickly found my nipples. Conrad twisted them expertly between his fingers and brought them to stiff pink points. Little jolts of sweet pain like burning sparks shot through the churning ecstasy of his cock driving into me. I squeezed my eyes desperately shut as another orgasm welled up and then exploded between my thighs, drenching Conrad's balls in gushing pleasure.

I strained forward against the vampire's grasp, trying to stretch sinuously across his desk and toward the chair again. But Conrad held me up straighter against him and kept me speared on the cold, hard length of his cock. I braced myself with my palms flat on the surface of the desk. Maybe... maybe I could just break off a piece of the top. That would do the job.

"Which investor did you say you represented?" Conrad asked. His breath was icy along the back of my neck and I shivered.

"Al... Alcott," I said.

No, I *whimpered*. Was that fear there in my voice? Need? Even I couldn't be sure anymore. Everything inside me was a storm of hot and cold and scorching desire.

"Interesting," said Conrad. He trailed chilly kisses down along my shoulder. "Miss Eddenhaus didn't recognize you. You remember her, don't you?"

Vaguely, through the blizzard of ecstasy, I did: the woman downstairs who had tried to talk with Conrad. Warnings screamed in my head, but I was frozen in place, overwhelmed by the pleasure and the power of the vampire's presence.

"I extended an invitation to the Alcott group." Conrad's lips brushed my ear and I shuddered in the grip of helpless need. "To Miss Eddenhaus. You, my dear, are a liar."

Conrad sank his fangs into my neck. There was a moment of bright, crisp pain and then the most exquisite sensation of penetration. I moaned. My throat tingled with ice where Conrad's sharp teeth punctured me, but I wasn't numb. It was pure bliss that flowed through me, filled me. I felt each burning drop of my blood as it welled up from Conrad's bite and dripped across my skin. His cold lips were over the wound and his tongue licked at my hot flesh, drinking down my blood as it rushed from my body.

His fingers dug into the softness of my breasts. Conrad pinched my nipples between thumb and forefinger. I whimpered. The jolts his touch sent through me were no longer sparks, but jagged lightning bolts. His dick was an icicle inside me, relentless and unmelting. There should have been steam boiling up from the merciless thrusting of icy cock deep into white-hot wetness.

My climax welled up from the bleeding bites as much as from my full pussy. It swelled and then receded. The pleasure rose again and then faded once more. It was rhythmic, like a heartbeat. *My heartbeat.* Each wave of ecstasy was stronger than the one before, but longer and slower. Because my heart was slowing... and soon, it would stop.

But I couldn't bring myself to care. The pleasure grew bigger and bigger, filling me even as Conrad drained me of life. Eventually, it would stop entirely and that would be the end, but I ground my ass weakly against Conrad, desperately trying to take him deeper, trying to reach that last peak of perfect sensation. I was a willing participant in my own death.

Conrad tore his mouth off of me and I actually moaned in protest. Warm blood trickled down my back. The vampire raised his hand to his lips and staggered away from me. He stared at the smear of blood on his fingers.

"I know this taste," he hissed. "Demon's blood!"

I was slow, weakened. Only seconds had passed since Conrad bit me, but he had drained me swiftly. The sexual power I had built up with Max and then Conrad struggled to heal the swift blood loss. I could barely move, but with the vampire's fangs and cock out of my body, at least I could think again.

It was all I could do to lunge across the desk and seize the desk chair by one arm. I turned, swinging it with all of my remaining strength and flinging Conrad's clothes in every direction. The vampire still stared at me in uncomprehending shock, his eyes and mouth open wide as the heavy oak chair smashed into his head and shoulders, flying to pieces. It didn't leave a single cut or even bruise Conrad's white marble flesh. But he stumbled back another step and I was left holding the chair's arm, snapped off into a rough point at the far end. Perfect.

I slid off the desk and jumped at Conrad, but my weakened legs wobbled and gave out under me. I fell. Not as perfect.

"I don't know why you taste of demon's blood," Conrad snarled like a rumble of thunder. "But I will wring your mysteries from your corpse."

His cold white hand lashed out and grabbed me by the throat, lifting me up. My feet left the ground and Conrad began to squeeze. I choked and thrashed in his grasp. This was not going to be the peaceful, pleasant death of his fangs.

Because I wasn't going to die.

"I'm a fucking succubus," I gasped.

I almost screamed with the effort as I twisted and rammed my splintered piece of wood into the vampire's chest, right through his heart. Together, Conrad and I fell to the floor, but only one of us sat up again. I panted hard as his body turned gray and crumbled away to ash.

"Well, half succubus," I amended. Not that Conrad cared much about the distinction anymore. "Nice to meet you."

Chapter
EIGHT

Despite its name, the College isn't actually a college. It's a sprawling mansion, along with a couple of huge outbuildings that are pretty much just slightly smaller mansions, including the verdigrised metal dome of an observatory. The whole College is gated off and set far back from the nearest road. To be honest, I didn't know what went on in most of those buildings – I wasn't allowed inside. Something about being half demon...

But being a bounty hunter for the College meant that they had to give me access to the main house, Dresden Hall. Which is named after an ancient Mayan book, not the fictional wizard. But I would totally bang Harry Dresden if he were real.

I parked the 110 in front of Dresden Hall, in the shade of a vast, overgrown old oak tree. No valets here or sweeping searchlights. The College was all old red brick covered in a hundred years' worth of ivy. The wizards of the College work a little too hard at keeping the mortal world free of monsters to concern themselves much with... anything else. Convincing them that I wasn't one of those monsters hadn't been easy.

I climbed out of the car and grabbed a satchel from my passenger seat. The big weathered front doors of Dresden Hall swung themselves open at my approach. There may not have been valets or butlers at the College, but some weird shit goes on there. Not that it was any of my business. My job for the College wasn't drawing arcane circles or mixing up potions in a sanctum – it was out in the city, kicking ass and getting paid.

I walked down a wide, arched hallway finished in wood and lined along one side with suits of armor not unlike the set I had sucked Conrad off behind. Each empty set of platemail held a shield emblazoned with a pair of dragons locked in combat – one white, the other red. The insignia of Arthur. You know, King of the Britons, protégé of Merlin and the master of Excalibur? Yeah, that guy.

But of far more interest to me was the opposite wall, which was dominated by an old-fashioned corkboard covered in notices. Some of them I couldn't read – whatever language the College uses for its secret notes, it's not one I ever learned in school – but plenty more were in English. This was the bounty board, where the College posted information and rewards for the capture of all the monsters that threaten our world.

I stopped and scanned the curling rows of parchment. Remember what I said about the College? Fucking parchment.

Crawling along the dusty top of the board was a small clay figure, no bigger than my hand – one of Sabra's homunculi. Sabra is another bounty hunter.

There are eight of us in the city and besides me, all of them are wizards from the College.

I found the scroll I was looking for, the one listing the vampire sighting at Midnight, and ripped it down. I held up the bounty to Sabra's homunculus and stuck my tongue out at the little construct. It turned on its tiny clay heels and scampered off to find its mistress. There was Stefano's spell-card tucked into the corner of the bounty board, too, covered in coppery hand-drawn sigils that would alert him if anything changed.

I had no idea if Stefano could see me through it, but I brandished my bounty posting triumphantly, just in case. His specialty was werewolves, but I could still gloat.

On my way out, I would check for new bounties – which I actually had to do with my eyes, since my powers don't include homunculi or scrying and wizards haven't figured out social media yet. But right now, I wanted to finish my job and get paid.

So I made my way deeper into the ancient manse and stopped in front of a stern-looking wooden door with a knocker shaped like a gargoyle. Its iron eyes swiveled up to look at me while I waited, but the door creaked open after only a few moments.

Inside, the ranking mages of the College sat gathered around a huge circular table, all wearing archaic robes and serious expressions. I resisted the impish urge to wave at them. Barely.

The round table had no head or foot, but the chair with the tallest back and most detailed carvings belonged to High Magus Vincent Myrdon. His long hair was the shiny gray of bullets and his deep widow's peak was sharp enough to cut parchment. Only his goatee still had streaks of darker color.

The High Magus of the College scowled magnificently at me through the open door. I really did want to wave – and maybe blow a kiss – but Vincent Myrdon isn't a man any sane woman makes an enemy of, half-demon or not. *Especially* a half-demon, perhaps. I was glad my business wasn't with him.

One of the other wizards, Dorian Vandi, looked up from the books laid out across the table and smiled at me. He was even older than the High Magus, but a lot more friendly. If he were fifty years younger, I would have been all over him.

Dorian excused himself from the meeting with a nod to Vincent and the rest of the council, then trotted out into the hall.

"Hi, Dorian," I said.

The old wizard closed the door carefully behind him and made sure his robes didn't get caught.

"Good morning, Lilith. Which one did you catch?" he asked.

"That vampire downtown. And his creator, the head of the bloodline," I answered. Rather modestly, I thought. "His house might be up for sale soon, if the College is looking for room to expand."

Dorian arched his bushy eyebrows in pleased surprise. I held out the satchel I was carrying, which I'd stuffed full of Conrad's letters and a few printouts of my research. Some of the wizards can manage an email if you put a gun to their skull – which I really don't recommend trying – but proof of capture usually came down to physical evidence. Sometimes that was photos or a prisoner or the occasional severed head. Getting my printer to work was annoying, but it was better than body parts.

"Are they in there?" Dorian asked.

I nodded and withdrew the two bags of ashy vampiric remains. I had swept up as much of Conrad Whitaker as I could manage before jumping out a window and leaving his party. I handed over the bag containing Jacob. Dorian opened it and pinched out a tiny bit of dark gray dust. He weighed it in his hand and peered at it closely.

"I'll test it for our records," said Dorian. "But I can do that later so you don't have to wait."

"Thanks."

I hugged Dorian, mashing my tits into his bearded face. I released him after a second, before the old guy could have a heart attack. Dorian straightened his spectacles and coughed, blushing.

"Er... you're quite welcome, Lilith," he stammered. "Does anyone know they're gone? Do you need a cleanup?"

What Dorian was talking about weren't guys in latex gloves, or hackers to erase DMV and police records. No, what the College did was far more arcane and effective. I didn't really know exactly what was involved, but I knew that I had never been arrested. Well, not for any of the work I did for the College, at least. But it was sure expensive...

I sighed. The other hunters could manage their own magical cleanup and memory wipes, but as you might have noticed, I'm not a wizard.

"Yeah," I said. "There were some witnesses at the party who saw me with Conrad and could probably identify me. And Jacob was a regular at Midnight. We don't want anyone remembering that."

Dorian nodded. "We can take care of it for the usual fee. Let's head down to the vaults."

He led me deep beneath Dresden Hall, into the basement and then to a massive steel door carved with runes – a lot more of them than on Stefano's little card upstairs.

I waited outside. I wasn't allowed into the vaults. For all I knew, my half-demon blood meant I *couldn't* go inside, but I peered down the cavernous stone hallway lined in more enchanted metal doors and wondered what the College kept in there. Well, I knew one thing and that was enough for me.

Dorian returned a few minutes later carrying a cloth-wrapped bundle. He set it on a table and removed my payment: a double stack of gleaming six-ounce gold bars, each one about the size and shape of a section of Kit Kat bar. Maybe that's even what they used to be. Turning lead and other stuff into gold was something the College mastered a long time ago. It made paying the bills easy, but I suspected that there were strict rules to control inflation. Wizards are big on rules.

"Five for the younger vampire," Dorian counted out. "Twelve for his maker. One each for the vampire ashes. We were almost out, so thank you. Minus three for the cost of cleanup. Sorry, Lilith."

"It's fine," I assured Dorian. It was a hell of a lot cheaper and less complicated than going to trial for murdering two vampires.

I unpacked the ashes and the rest of the proof of my kills, then filled my satchel with gold. The bars weren't large, but they were heavy for their size. I estimated that I'd just earned enough to buy a couple of new cars.

"Do you have any plans for that, Lilith?" Dorian asked, nodding at my bag. "We have our own specialized accountants, if you'd like to make some investments without attracting IRS attention."

I shrugged. Not yet. Perhaps not ever. I've been a hunter for the College since I was nineteen and cashed in a lot of bounties over the last eight years. I didn't do it for the money anymore. But I'm a half-succubus. What better job is there for a girl like me?

I winked at Dorian, threw my sack of gold over one shoulder and headed upstairs to check the board for my next job.

All's fae in LOVE AND WAR

Chapter ONE

I slammed my laptop shut and hurled it across the couch, but it just bounced harmlessly and not very satisfyingly across the white leather cushions. Nothing! Well, nothing *useful*. The internet was full of historical fairy tales and Disney-sanitized versions, or stories smutted up in bad erotic fiction. Those were fun reading, but none of it was going to help me get the job done.

Damn it.

At the College, the wizards had access to the real thing: vast libraries of arcane books, bound in wyvern hide and full of secret magical knowledge. At least, I assumed so. It wasn't like I'd ever seen them. My employers are a cabal of mages sworn to keep demons and other supernatural dangers out of our world. So my being half succubus means that they don't trust me too well. And that meant I didn't exactly get a College library card.

That left me the internet and my good looks. But since my stupid laptop was immune to my charms, I gave it a kick that wedged the machine further into the couch. Take that.

I stood and smoothed out my short red silk robe, determined not to let the internet get me all worked up. It was still early and the hardwood floor of my condo was cold, so I slid my feet into a pair of fluffy white bunny slippers. They had been a Christmas present from my best friend, Max.

I paced back and forth across the living room a few times, thinking and staring out the window. I lived up high enough that the big floor-to-ceiling windows of my condo had a great view of downtown, and even a slice of the bay. Water and glass sparkled silver in the sunlight, streaked in white where a few stubborn tendrils of morning fog clung to them.

Idea! I grabbed my cell phone from between a few cartons of Chinese takeout on the kitchen counter and scrolled through my contacts until I found the number. I hadn't called that phone number in a long time. I really should more often.

Two rings and then voicemail picked up, as usual, with an automated message that gave no name.

"Hey, it's Lily," I said after the beep. "The College posted a job that I... Well, I'm not sure what I'm getting into. If you've got a minute, I could really use some advice. Thanks."

I ended the call and stowed my previous night's dinner in the refrigerator. When I was finished, I figured that the morning's lack of work called for another cup of coffee. I brewed up a mug of vanilla-flavored heaven and carried it back to the living room.

All my windows were closed, but I smelled the smooth tang of fresh water just before I saw her. Evaine stood in the middle of the room and I jumped, nearly dropping my coffee. I've never gotten used to how she does that. Maybe I would if she came by more often, but it's not only me who doesn't keep in touch. Sometimes Evaine vanished for months at a time and not even the College could contact her, no matter how important it was. But it was good to see her.

Evaine wore a soft gray sweater and a knee-length white skirt that flowed around her slender legs. Her hair was long, curly and very pale – a true platinum blonde that you just can't get out of a bottle. Unless it was a djinn's bottle, I suppose.

"Evaine!" I said.

I might have squealed her name a bit. I practically threw my coffee down on the end table and ran to my teacher. She opened her arms and hugged me close. I'm not a short woman, but Evaine was at least six inches taller than me and my cheek rested comfortably in the hollow of her shoulder.

"Lily," Evaine said. "It's good to see you again."

Her accent was British and a touch of something else, maybe Welsh or Scottish. I was never sure, but it was always gentle and soothing. I turned my face up to Evaine's and kissed her. She smelled like sun-warmed grass and stone.

"It's been too long," I said. "We have a lot of catching up to do."

Evaine smiled at me and kissed me again. Her lips were soft and a light pink. They tasted like something sweet and very alive – it was like kissing a flower. I wanted more.

I wound my arms around Evaine and she let me tug her back into my bedroom. The curtains and blinds there were thrown open to let in the morning sunlight and it sparkled through the tiny droplets of water in Evaine's hair. I pressed myself hungrily against her.

I pulled her sweater up slowly, exposing her smooth, pale skin one creamy inch at a time. Then the gray hem lifted high enough to reveal Evaine's small breasts. She wasn't wearing a bra – Evaine never wore underwear at all. I'm not sure why. If she bothered with clothes, why not all of them? It was just one of Evaine's many mysteries that I really didn't give a shit about right now. It felt so good to hold her, to touch her again after so long.

Evaine slipped her sweater off over her head and shook out her cascade of hair. It fell past her waist in white-blonde ringlets that I couldn't help but caress. I ran my fingers through those silky silver curls as I bent to suck one of Evaine's perfect strawberry nipples into my mouth. If there was anyone in this city hotter than me, it was Evaine.

Lightly, she stroked my loose red hair. It wasn't as long as hers, but still impressive. A shiver slithered down my spine. I flicked my tongue over her nipple and was pleased to feel it hardening in my mouth.

"Is this why you called me, Lily?" Evaine asked in her lilting voice. "I thought you had questions about a bounty...?"

I kissed my way back up the soft flesh of her chest to her neck, and then further until I stood on my toes and gave Evaine's ear a small, playful nip.

"I do have questions," I whispered. "But I missed you."

Evaine slid her hands through my hair again and pulled me up to face her. Her eyes were as deep and aqua as the ocean. No one in the world has eyes like Evaine.

"I missed you, too," she said.

Evaine kissed me. My lips parted before her with a little groan of pleasure as she tasted me. Her fingers worked swiftly at the sash of my robe, pushing it open and I leaned in to feel her bare breasts pressed into mine. I twisted my tongue against hers, wet and warm. Evaine grabbed my shoulders as I rubbed my tits back and forth, teasing her nipples with my own.

The warm golden glow of lust and power was already building inside me, fed by Evaine's desire and my own. I wasn't saving up to bench-press semi trucks or anything, but it's not something I can control. This power is just a part of who, of *what* I am. When I'm with a lover, my body drinks in the sexual energy they give and makes me stronger, faster and even sharpens my senses. You know the rush you get after a good fuck? It's like that times a billion.

I let go of Evaine just long enough for her to tug the robe off my shoulders. The silk rippling down my back and legs made tiny goosebumps rise all across my skin. I returned the favor, pulling Evaine's skirt down into a puddle of cloth around her bare feet.

With no underwear or shoes in my way, Evaine was naked to my ravenous gaze. It had been a couple of years since the last time I saw her, but my teacher didn't look a day older. She appeared, as always, to be in her late twenties or early thirties. Her body was long and slim, her skin as milky white as though she never spent any time in the sun. I'm a pretty pale girl – we redheads don't exactly tan well, though I do pick up a few freckles during the summer – but I was positively swarthy by comparison.

Evaine looked down at my remaining clothes: a pair of lace panties so wet that I could clearly see the pink of my pussy through them, and my fuzzy bunny slippers. Evaine raised one platinum eyebrow and gave me a small, mysterious smile.

I stuck out my tongue and pulled her toward the bed. Evaine let herself be led – believe me when I say that she could have stopped me if she wanted to – and I pushed her down into the tangle of my sheets. Evaine leaned back slowly and stretched her arms across my bed, her soft breasts thrust up into the air to display the perfect pink peaks of her nipples.

Kneeling at the edge of the bed, between Evaine's long, slender legs, I brushed my cheek against her inner thigh as I moved in to trace my lips over her shell-pink pussy. She was so wet that her delicate labia made me think of flower petals dotted with morning dew. I'm not really prone to fits of poetry, but with Evaine, I can't help myself.

I kissed lightly between her spread legs, just flicking my tongue along her slit and tasting the sweet juices there, like drinking from a high mountain stream. Evaine drew a sharp breath. The sound made my heart flutter and I deepened the kiss, enveloping my tongue in tight heat. Evaine's hips rose a little and I felt her pushing into me.

"Lily... that feels wonderful," she sighed.

I disengaged my mouth for a moment and licked my lips. "You taught me everything I know."

"So I did. And very well, it seems."

"Damn right."

Evaine's fingers twined through my hair again, ringing them in coppery red, and I slid my tongue inside her once more. She was dripping, streaming wetness down my chin. Evaine's always been a gusher, especially when I do her right.

She writhed gracefully on the bed. Her pale hair fanned out across my sheets and shone like sunlight on water. I slipped my hands under the smooth curve of Evaine's ass and held her close as I licked her. My teacher's skin was soft and cool against my fingertips.

I lapped my way up along Evaine's silky pussy to close eager lips around the hard pink pearl of her clitoris. When Evaine gasped, I moved my hand up between her legs and then slipped one finger into her slick sex.

Evaine's gasp turned into a soft moan. She was tight even around a single finger and wetness ran down my wrist. I stroked her from inside, just the way Evaine had taught me, and her clit became a stiff little bud under my tongue.

I tingled in sympathetic pleasure and almost came too as Evaine moaned her orgasm. Her cry was musical and her porcelain face was a mask of perfect ecstasy. Evaine's smooth ass rose off the bed and she spread her long legs wide as her spine arched. Perfect. I pumped my finger in and out of her pussy and my teacher began to squirt. Hot, slippery juices sprayed my cheeks and mouth. I grinned at the warm wetness on my skin.

When I sat back, my tits were streaked and shining. I licked my lips and let Evaine entice me up onto the bed. There, she pulled me into her arms and kissed me, tasting herself on my tongue. I let my excited hands wander all over her willowy body, exploring her slender hips and soft breasts. Evaine's hands were all over me, too, teasing little whimpers from my lips as she caressed my nipples or brushed skillfully over my slick pussy. I just about came when she finally hooked a finger through the waist of my soaked panties and pulled them off.

Evaine slid smoothly against me, down the bed until she could intertwine our legs and press the velvety warmth of her pussy to mine. She rolled her hips in slow circles, grinding our bodies together in a slow, sensual dance.

I leaned back with a moan and braced myself against the bed to work my hips in tandem with hers. The heat of desire and power filled me like a building electrical charge. My toes curled in my bunny slippers and jolts of sensation arced through my whole body. I don't need orgasms to fuel me – just passion – but they were certainly a sweet, welcome bonus.

And Evaine was working me quickly toward that peak. Her slim, firm body pressed between my legs, smooth and slick against my clitoris. Evaine was so wet and hot. Her silky labia slid over mine, a soft caress of pure ecstasy that had me shivering and gasping in seconds. Every inch of me was taut and knotted in pleasure as the orgasm took hold. Unless I'm fucking a target that I intend to take down anyway, I usually have to restrain myself in bed. Being able to pulverize my lover's pelvis with my sex-fueled strength isn't exactly a turn on for most people. But not with Evaine. With her, I could just relax, be myself, and maybe snap the occasional headboard in half.

Despite my supernatural strength, Evaine's slender legs gripped me tightly, guiding me through my rise and release. Her pussy kissed against mine and shudders racked my body. As the driving crest of orgasm began to fade, Evaine slid one long-fingered hand down between us to rub at the tight pearl of my clit and sent me soaring right back into bliss. Evaine's climax sounded musical, almost like a song, but I moaned like a whore as I writhed between her legs. My vision went fuzzy and the world spun out of control.

Chapter TWO

When the bedroom finally came back into focus, I lay panting and sweating in a knot of twisted sheets. There were some new dents in my metal bedposts in the shape of my fingertips. Evaine pillowed my head against her flushed chest, stroking the sweaty red tangles of my hair.

"Wow," I said. My voice was still rough around the edges. "You haven't lost your touch."

I was used to being the sex goddess and I liked it, but being with Evaine always made me feel like a schoolgirl again. Hmm... Maybe I should slip into my pleated skirt and knee socks for her.

"You keep me sharp, Lily," Evaine said. "And you've taught me as much as I ever taught you."

I laughed breathlessly and doubted that was true. But it was still nice to hear. I kissed Evaine. I really had missed her.

"How is Max?" she asked in her posh accent.

"Pretty well. Still working for Golden Touch Auto, even though he's way too good for them."

"Max will find his true path. He's a fine young man."

"Should I give him a call?" I asked. "I'm sure Max would love to come join us."

"It's been a while," Evaine admitted. "But perhaps another time. Ask me your questions, Lily."

She made no move to get up or put on clothes. The bed sheets were quite damp, but if she didn't mind, neither did I. My face was snuggled comfortably against the hollow of her shoulder and I had a great view along my teacher's body, from her small, round breasts, down her long legs and to her delicate feet. It was one of the world's finer views.

"Sure," I sighed. I managed to tear my eyes from Evaine's lovely body and leaned up on one elbow to look into her equally lovely eyes. "It's about a job."

"What is the job?" Evaine asked.

I could just listen to her talk all day. I have, actually, though I was too young and stupid to properly appreciate it at the time. It was a good thing Evaine was about as patient as a mountain – I wasn't always the best student. But she never gave up on me, which is why I'm here today.

"Some super important book was stolen from the College library and the wizards are seriously pissed about it," I said.

Evaine nodded. She didn't look surprised, but her soft pink lips lost their post-coital smile.

"*The Gates of Avalon,*" said Evaine.

She had heard of it, of course. I'm not sure there's anything in the world Evaine doesn't know about. Which was why I had called her in the first place.

"There are apparently dozens of partial copies floating around the various magical institutions of the world," I said. "But this was the original manuscript, on loan from the Castle."

The Castle was the European branch of the College. Well, I suppose it was the other way around – the Castle was the largest and oldest organization of sorcerers in Europe. They established the College over a thousand years later in America to extend their reach into the New World.

But now Evaine actually frowned at me. "The original *Gates of Avalon*?"

I nodded. "The bounty on the book's return is pretty impressive, even by my standards. And there's a big-ass bonus if I can bring them the thief, too. The College apparently has some questions to ask them."

"I'm not surprised," Evaine said... unsurprisingly. "*The Gates of Avalon* was penned by Merlin himself when he founded the Castle. He wrote the book to pass along vital lore to his magi. It's an important piece of their history."

I trailed my fingers up and down over Evaine's pale belly, tracing thoughtful circles around her navel.

"Stefano told me that the other hunters are trying to shake some leads from the wards all over the library and the book," I said. "But none of them were tripped, though."

"And how did you get one of the College hunters to tell you that?" Evaine asked. "You bounty hunters are a notoriously competitive lot."

"I might have flirted with him a bit."

"Ah," Evaine said with a laugh like a crystal bell. "I see. And what else did Stefano Rossi tell you?"

"He didn't have much. There were no hits on the scry network and no one at the College saw or heard anything unusual."

"How did the wizards discover the theft?" asked Evaine.

"Vincent Myrdon. Stefano says that the High Magus wanted some late-night reading material, but when he went to the library, the book was gone," I said and then snorted at Evaine. I jabbed one finger gently into her smooth belly. "But you already knew all of this, didn't you?"

"I had some... concerns," Evaine admitted. "I heard that *The Gates of Avalon* was missing and suspected you had taken on the task of finding it."

"That's why you came so quickly when I called," I said, pouting.

So it wasn't because she missed me or anything. "Is this stupid book really that important?"

"It may be."

"There were a dozen magical locks on the campus gates and library doors, and wards on the book. And the College keeps up the most comprehensive network of scry spells outside the Castle."

Evian nodded.

"So who or what the hell could have gotten through all of that without leaving so much as a fingerprint?" I asked with a sigh. "Well, no clues that Stefano told me about, at least. And I'm not allowed into the library to look for my own leads. The other hunters are all wizards and have a serious head start on me."

Evaine sat up and gazed out the window. The sun was high in the sky now and made the glass skyscrapers outside blaze with pale golden light. Sailboats and windsurfers danced across the waves in the bay like playful birds.

"So... have you got any information for me?" I asked.

"There many creatures in the world who might wish to possess *The Gates of Avalon*," said Evaine. "But few capable of walking into and then out of the College without alerting the wizards. Or flying, as the case may be."

"Flying?" I repeated.

This was more like it. Evaine was worth a thousand libraries and came with much sexier perks. Maybe if I dressed up like a schoolgirl, I could get Evaine to play the strict librarian. And we all know that I'm not very good at being quiet, so I was going to require some... discipline.

I shook my head, trying to clear it.

"Alright, what am I looking for?" I asked. "Wyvern? Angel? Gargoyle? One of the djinni could do it, right?"

Evaine turned back to look at me. The sun streaming through the windows outlined her perfect body and silvery ringlets in warm sunlight.

"I don't think that the djinni would risk violating the border agreement for a book, even one as valuable as *The Gates of Avalon*," Evaine said. Then she smiled at me. "You will enjoy this hunt, Lily. I can think of only a single man both able and willing to do the job in this part of the world."

"I'm interested already. Who are we talking about?" I asked.

"He is called Kalen Silverwind," Evaine said.

"Nice name. Is it for real or does he just read a lot of fantasy books?"

"Kalen is an Unseelie fairy," Evaine told me. "And one with an impressively long career as a thief. It is said that Kalen Silverwind is as handsome as Oberon and as mischievous as Puck."

I grinned. Evaine was right. I really was going to enjoy this hunt.

Chapter THREE

I've been hunting, capturing and killing the nasty things that scurry through the shadows of our world for eight years. It's the only job I've ever had. The supernatural underworld wasn't where I did my shopping, though, so I had never visited the fairy market before. But Evaine said Kalen Silverwind was usually there, selling the treasures he stole, hiring himself out at a steep price, or just being a generally suave pain in the ass.

I had no idea what to wear for meeting an Unseelie fairy thief. There are all kinds of fairies everywhere in the world, but most of them keep their heads down and their mischief innocuous enough that the College didn't worry too much about it. Besides, maintaining a working relationship with the fairies was helpful to the wizards. Where else were they going to buy real nightshade, the stuff grown out of actual night?

But Evaine said that Kalen wasn't fae royalty or anything – they have their own king and queen, you know – so I figured comfortable and rugged would be good enough. Useful in case I needed to run or fight. And also easily removable, just on general principle.

So I pulled on my favorite leather jacket over a t-shirt and pair of jeans. The jacket was getting pretty scuffed up, but I'd had it since high school, so a certain amount of wear was to be expected. My ten-year reunion was coming up soon and I wondered what I would say when someone asked what I did for a living.

After a moment's consideration, I decided against bringing a weapon. My half-succubus powers don't last forever and I didn't want to get caught without protection, but I was still pretty pumped up from my tumble in the sheets with Evaine.

Following my teacher's directions, I drove down to Francis Port. It was early in the evening on a Friday, so parking might not cost an *entire* arm and leg, but at least a couple of fingers. I showed the only finger that mattered to the automated ticket machine and parked as close to the waterfront as I could manage.

Francis Port used to be a major shipping center, but that was a long time ago. Between trains and airplanes, the old bay just didn't do the transport business that it used to. The southern end of the bay – imaginatively named Southport – housed all that was left of the operational wharves and warehouses.

The Quay covers pretty much the rest of the bayside property. It was repurposed and renovated back in the sixties and now it's mostly made up of restaurants, bookstores and shops, with the occasional wharf that has withstood the test of time. During the day, they're full of fishermen and seagulls bickering with the tourists hoping for a glimpse of a sea lion. In the evening, they are prime makeout spots.

Tonight, the Quay was full of city natives and tourists alike. There was at least one bachelor party going on at Donovan's, and several college pre-graduation classes running up and down the old wharves. Twenty-somethings and drunken men congratulated one another loudly, shouting to be heard over the screech of seagulls and the wash of the tide rolling out under the pilings. The air smelled of cold water, salt and trash.

I briefly considered returning another night, when there would be less of a crowd, but the College *really* wanted their book back.

Besides, I doubted that the other hunters were taking the night off. If I intended to beat them to the prize – and I did – then I had to keep moving. So I ignored a few invitations shouted from the patio seating of the restaurants that served cheap alcohol and got to work following Evaine's instructions.

There were a lot of old brick buildings along the length of the Quay. I checked them all, though, jumping fences when no one was looking and heaving dumpsters away from back walls to search behind them. Plenty of graffiti, from cartoon cocks, phone numbers and initials enclosed in hearts to serious gang tags and more than a few urine stains, but no sign of what I was searching for.

It was growing late and I was nearly in Southport. Nice restaurants and tourist traps had given way to some truly seedy bars and the stores down here all had grilles bolted over the windows. I hadn't reached the warehouses just yet, but I was checking the map on my cell phone to see how many more blocks until I did when something shiny caught my eye.

I wasn't ready to cheer just yet, but I slipped between a strip club and a liquor store and there it was, scrawled in silver paint across the back of the store beneath a rusting, flickering fluorescent light. The mark looked something like a four-leaf clover, if you assembled one out of curving scimitar blades. The shining paint was as bright as a mirror, not sun-bleached or peeling away like the rest of the graffiti.

I knocked my knuckles against the spray-painted bricks. The wall felt solid enough under my fist, but the sound echoed like a stone falling down a deep well. There was a moment of silence and nothing happened. Evaine said that the fairy market moved all along the waterfront. Was this an old location? But I jumped a little as the brick wall went black and then faded away into emptiness, leaving behind only the silver clover mark floating like an ornate shaft of moonlight.

Very Harry Potter. Very fae, I supposed.

My eyes were still sharp enough from sex with Evaine to pick out the staircase winding through the darkness. Even though the liquor store was only a single shabby story, the stairs led steeply upward. I climbed them into the shadows until I stood on a landing that seemed to float in the endless black. There was nowhere else to go from here – no other doors or stairs, just jagged edges of crumbling brick.

But the landing wasn't empty. A pair of fairies stood in the center like guards in a fantasy novel or bouncers at a super-exclusive club. They were some weird bouncers, though.

The one on the left was nearly twice my height and had shoulders like a monster truck. He was wearing a pair of pants made of what looked like elephant hide, and no shirt. His bare skin was a dark jade green with a pebbled texture stretched over what had to be five hundred pounds of corded muscle. His jaw was wide and square, but his nose was small and flat between two lidless black eyes. There wasn't a single hair on his head or chest. I was curious if there were any to be found elsewhere.

The other bouncer was no bigger than my hand. She had colorful butterfly wings spotted in red and gold, but wore a black leather outfit like a badass Biker Barbie. Her hair was twisted up into little spikes that I wasn't entirely sure were decorative.

In addition to her tiny chains and shit-kicker boots, the winged pixie wore a deep frown identical to that of her big green partner. I wondered which one of them I was going to have to fuck to get into the fairy market. Both had fun possibilities...

Evaine had taught me a bit about fairies and their magic, but it largely amounted to knowing that I would never know enough. There were a thousand kinds of fairies, though they all fell into two very broad categories that had more to do with temperament than species.

There were the Seelie fairies. Those were the ones who made shoes for cobblers or cleaned houses while the humans inside slept.

I would hire some of them if I could, but fairy deals don't work that way. The College wizards preferred to deal with the Seelie court, if they can, and have managed to maintain good relations throughout the centuries.

And then there were the Unseelie fae. Those were the ones who led you off into the foggy moors until you slipped and drowned in a bog or invited mortals to dance themselves to death at their parties. The Unseelie fairies weren't at war with the College or anything, but neither did they care very much for the human mages who controlled this part of the world.

The big fairy – I think he was a troll – crouched down and the pixie flew over on swiftly beating wings to inspect me. She hovered a few feet in front of my face. I felt the embers of lust from both of them, but the heat was faint. They had a job to do.

"You a wizard?" Her voice was squeaky and high, but perfectly understandable.

"Would you know if I lied?" I asked.

The troll snorted and the pixie gave me a tiny but effective stink eye, still waiting for an answer. I shrugged.

"No," I said. "I'm not a wizard. I'm just looking for a guy."

"You're no regular," noted the pixie. "And I smell demon on you. You going to be a problem, lady?"

"I'm not a vampire or a werewolf, if that's what you're asking."

Werewolves carried a demonic curse and vampires gained their power from drinking demon blood. I had demonic blood in me, sure, but I had been born with it. And as to making trouble... well, that was entirely up to Kalen Silverwind.

The pixie buzzed over to the troll's ear and practically landed inside it to whisper to him. Then she flew a few inches away and he whispered back in a surprisingly quiet voice. I still had enough sexual energy to hear like a bat, but the two fairies weren't speaking any language I knew. It alternated between smoothly lyrical and popping like radio static. At last, the pair looked at me again.

"If you're not a wizard, how did you hear about the market?" the little one asked.

"A friend told me," I answered.

"What else did this friend tell you?"

Evaine had mentioned a fee. Well, she called it a *gift*, but I knew a cover charge when I saw it. This one was a bit weird, though. I didn't doubt Evaine often, but I hesitated before reaching into my pocket.

"She uh... told me you would want this," I said.

The troll held out a huge green hand. I pulled out the sock – just one, with a hole in the toe – and pressed it into his big, rough fingers. It had taken some serious digging around through boxes still sealed and shoved into the back of my closet to find this thing. The troll held up my sock before his large black eyes. His nose might have been small, but his sense of smell seemed no less sharp for it. The troll inhaled deeply.

"This one has been on a long journey." His voice was deep and as rough as his skin, but there was a smoothly musical note to it, too. "Across the emerald fields and back, carrying the prize. An orb lost, sometimes given up, but always reclaimed. But now this one has been left alone and longs for its companion."

The leather-clad pixie looked at me. I shrugged.

"I was on the soccer team for a year in high school," I said, a little dismayed.

Had I somehow misunderstood Evaine's instructions? I was back to wondering who to fuck. The pixie pointed over my shoulder, down the stairs I had climbed.

"Go on, then," she piped.

I frowned. Really? Kicked out already? What bouncer didn't at least *try* to trade entry for my phone number or a quick handjob? Nothing I'd ever learned about fairies suggested they were immune to lust. While I lack the supernatural allure of my full-blooded demon kin, I was still half succubus and damned hot.

But the tiny biker pixie motioned me impatiently back the way I had come.

I turned slowly toward the stairs, wondering if I could bribe either of them with something better than a sock. Did the fae deal in mortal money? I had plenty of gold, too – payment from the College for my work – but it was heavy. I'd left it all in my condo, locked up in a safe, and I wasn't sure if a promise of the shiny stuff would be enough. But when I looked down the deeply shadowed stairs, I found that they didn't lead out to the flickering light of the alleyway anymore.

Nice trick. I glanced back at the bouncers. The troll stuck a pipe into his wide mouth – I didn't catch where he had been keeping it in those skin-tight hide pants – while his pixie friend sat on the curved stem and lit it for him with a snap of her fingers.

"Watch yourself, demon girl," said the pixie. The fire between her toothpick fingers flared for a second before vanishing.

I nodded and descended the stairs. The darkness was closer now, colder than before and I heard the gentle scraping of the sea. I kept going down until I was well below street level and the stairs opened up into arched tunnels. They must have been inlets that ran under the old waterfront, but if I expected dank and dripping, I was surprised.

There was water, but it ran in channels along the center of the tunnel, all stained white by salt. The floor and ceiling were built of interlocking bricks old enough that the red had turned nearly black with age, but shot through with more pale, salty veins so that it was like walking through arches of midnight marble.

Not that it was dark. There were shadows, but lights of all sorts, too. Strings of Christmas lights in every color hung alongside a hundred paper lanterns. There were candles and oil lamps, as well, though many of the flames burned not just in yellow and orange, but blue and green and violet. I'm pretty sure I heard one of the fires laughing, giggling like an excited child. I saw several glowing orbs floating through the air and even sigils of light inscribed along the tunnel wall. Radiance sparkled off the salt veins and made them glitter like slender streams of starfire.

The market was full of fairies and their wares. One fairy with slick gray skin and a blowhole like a dolphin sold rosemary, marijuana and herbs I couldn't identify – and not just because I can't cook worth a damn – in plastic bags and crystal vials. Next to her stall, a hairy little man dressed in what looked like a stained leopard print toga squatted on a blanket heaped with costume jewelry all mixed with diamonds and platinum. A small group of slender elves with leaves braided into their hair picked through a knot of necklaces and seemed to be arguing over a jade pendant.

Further down the tunnel, a selkie with hair nearly as pale as Evaine's danced her fingers over the strings of a small Celtic harp, playing along with the old boom box at her feet that screamed 80s-era Metallica. A tall man in leather biker chaps and a tailored suit jacket stopped to listen, head-banging enthusiastically to the music. When the song ended, he gave the selkie harpist a thumbs-up and tossed her a couple shiny wooden coins. The selkie snatched them out of the air with a feral hiss and tucked them into a sleek sealskin draped across the back of her folding lawn chair.

A pack of bogans had tapped into one of the old gas mains and set up a forge under the rusting pipes. Swords and barbed arrowheads crafted of iridescent blue-black metal were for sale alongside horseshoes and hinges. A troll a little shorter than the bouncer out front and with paler emerald-green skin barked the bogans' wares. Literally barked, baring his teeth and growling menacingly when a pair of blue-skinned nyad girls ignored him. When the troll caught sight of me, he howled like a wolf. I wasn't sure if that was an invitation or a warning.

Or maybe that howl was meant for the dead sexy indigo-haired man who brushed past me, bopping his head along to whatever was playing in his headphones from the iPod floating over his shoulder like a helium balloon. He winked at me before vanishing into the market crowd. By the time I winked back, a group of tall, hauntingly beautiful women in black dresses belted with diamond chains were swishing past. One of them looked offended at my wink, but two of the others grinned at me, displaying mouths full of dagger-pointed teeth.

I followed the stream of fairies through their market. A teenage girl with floppy dog ears and a shredded *Rush* t-shirt sold some kind of skewered meat that looked like snake and smelled like bacon. The stall next to hers showed off rows of iridescent white candy, each wrapped in a small twist of lace. My mouth watered, but I'd already eaten and there was work to do.

Where to start? I stopped in front of a beach blanket piled high with DVDs, most of them still shrink-wrapped and bearing price tags from local chain stores. I flashed a smile to a man with looping lines across his skin – I wasn't sure if they were tattoos or natural markings – and feathery antennae who sat in a lotus pose on the edge of the blanket.

"Got any porn?" I asked.

"Sorry," he said in a whispery voice. "But come back next week and I should have something good for you."

"Sure. Do you know a guy called Kalen Silverwind? I'm supposed to meet him somewhere around here."

"Sorry," the fairy merchant said again.

I moved on through the market. I asked a few more sellers about Kalen, but if any of them knew the guy, they weren't saying so. Why would they? I was an outsider and not even a fairy. They might even realize that I was a bounty hunter. If Kalen Silverwind was as talented a thief as Evaine suggested, he hadn't ducked the College this long by making himself easy to find.

It was after midnight and I wasn't getting anywhere. I circled back to the bacon-snake vendor. She didn't want a sock, but was willing to accept my grocery store club card in exchange for two skewers. I sat down on a carved stone bench that looked like something smuggled out of Rivendell and ate. The meat was a little rubbery, but tasted pretty good – a lot like bacon, but with an aftertaste like apples. It would have gone great on some pizza.

I watched the crowd. Airports have nothing on the fairy market for people watching. But how was I going to find Kalen in all of this? Assuming that the fairy thief was even here tonight. For all I knew, Kalen Silverwind was celebrating his successful theft by snorting pixie dust off the backs of hot vampire girls on the other side of the world.

Or maybe another world entirely.

I glared sullenly down at my remaining snake-bacon kebab when a short little fairy halfway between a hedgehog and a garden gnome hopped up onto the bench beside me. He clutched a bag of peanuts and began crunching loudly on them, feeding them one at a time into his furry snout.

"Hey," I said in a limp sort of greeting.

The fairy's long nose twitched and he turned beady black eyes up toward me.

"Hey yourself," he said in a high, crackling voice. "I don't think I've seen you around here before."

"My first visit," I answered.

And probably my last – at least on this hunt. If I didn't make some progress soon, Stefano or one of the others was going to steal Kalen right out from under me.

The little hedgehog man grinned, displaying chisel-pointed teeth with bits of peanut shell stuck between them. "What brings a girl like you to a place like this?"

"I'm looking for someone," I said. "A man. Kalen Silverwind."

The spiky fairy wrinkled his furry snout and then shook his head without answering me. He munched a few more peanuts and then slid down off the bench. He waved back to me with one furry paw before waddling off into the market once more.

I sat on the bench for a while, twirling the empty skewers in my fingers. I thought about Stefano and the other College hunters again. What if they couldn't find Kalen, either? What if he got away with the wizards' book? What happened then? Evaine said that *The Gates of Avalon* was an important book, written by Merlin himself back when he founded the Castle. Was it dangerous?

I felt eyes on me and the warm tingle of someone's lust like an inverse chill along my spine. I looked up and spotted a man leaning against one of the tunnel's blackened buttresses. It was the one I had seen on my way in, with the bright violet eyes and short hair the color of twilight. I'm not being metaphorical when I say that his skin was golden – it shone like expensive silk in the myriad lights of the fairy market.

His iPod and headphones were gone, though I couldn't have told you where. His leather pants and coat were all skin-tight and the shirt he wore beneath was unbuttoned halfway down his torso to display an impressive expanse of lean caramel muscle.

Damn, he was hot. The purple-haired fairy man caught me staring and winked, just like when I first saw him at the market entrance. Then he looked pointedly down at my hands with those inhumanly colorful eyes. The skewers were gone from my fingers.

When I raised my eyes again, the fairy was twirling one of them between his long, slender fingers. When the hell had he taken that? With another wink, he dropped the skewer and then sprinted away through the market tunnels.

Hot as fuck and skilled enough to steal right out of my hands without me noticing? And arrogant enough to show himself? The man *had* to be Kalen Silverwind. And if he wasn't... well, I wanted to catch the guy anyway and get his phone number. I could think of all sorts of things to do with those nimble fingers.

I jumped to my feet and gave chase like a lioness after a gazelle. Or maybe more like a lioness running down a lion... But the handsome man who might have been Kalen Silverwind knew the fairy market much better than I did. He slipped between fairies and stalls without breaking his loping stride. Or even a sweat, it seemed.

But I bet he didn't count on my sex-enhanced speed. I had dropped off a little since taking Evaine to bed that morning, but still had plenty of power to run like a cheetah on crack. I wove between shoppers, bumping into a lot more of them than my quarry. I ran straight into the broad, rocky backside of some huge fairy. I wasn't sure if it was another troll or maybe an ogre, but didn't really care about species distinction right then.

"Watch it, bitch," the maybe-an-ogre rumbled like a rockslide.

I sprang up, planted one heel on his stony shoulder and vaulted over him. I just barely caught sight of golden skin and black leather vanishing around a tunnel corner and then landed down in the thick of the crowd once more. I had to catch Kalen before he got somewhere that he could use some kind of fairy trick.

I poured on the supernatural speed, skidding around a group of bipedal cats. One of them batted the tips of my hair as I raced past, but the others ignored me imperiously, as only cats can. Ahead of me, the golden-skinned fairy man leapt gracefully over a shopping cart of knockoff Gucci purses. The toad-faced fairy pushing it shouted after him and then flipped me off as I jumped his cart, too.

I was burning through my energy too quickly and was no closer than when the chase had started. Damn, he was fast. And good. The fairy looked over his shoulder and grinned at me through the crowd. My heart sped in a way that had nothing to do with our sprint but everything to do with the race. I wanted to win, and I wanted my unbelievably hot fairy prize.

In a flash of indigo hair and tight ass, my smirking mark vanished down a narrow side-tunnel. I skidded and grabbed onto the bricks hard enough to leave a few hairline cracks in the aging masonry, then sprinted after him along the shadowed corridor.

There was no sign of the market crowd in here. It was dark and the air smelled sharply of seawater. Or was it something else? There was a tang to the cold wind that I never smelled out on the Quay. The tunnel sloped away under me and was slick with water. Fine by me – it just made me run faster.

Without my sharpened senses, I would have missed him entirely. I caught only a faint glimmer of purple in the darkness and the dim silhouette of long, lean limbs just a few yards away. I was closing on him!

That was very nearly what killed me. It was only the hiss of cascading water that alerted me to the fall. I slewed to a stop inches from the crumbling edge of old brick and concrete. I wasn't sure how deep the pit was, but the fall was long enough that I couldn't see the bottom.

"Kalen Silverwind?" I called across the black expanse.

The fairy smiled at me. I could just make out the expression by the twilight glow of his eyes.

"Perhaps," he said, inclining his head slightly. "If so, then I'm afraid you have the advantage of me."

It sure as hell didn't look that way, but I intended to change that. He stepped back from the far edge of the pit, melting away into the shadows. About to escape.

I wasn't going to give up that easily. *He* had gotten across somehow. So I backed up a few hasty steps, sprinted and leapt. I poured molten hot sexual power into the jump, soared through twenty feet of cold, wet air and landed hard on the other side. Bricks cracked and fell away into the darkness, but I was already up and running again. Kalen let out a bright laugh of delight, turned on his heels and dashed ahead of me. I was so close that I could smell him, a scent like honey and clover.

But then he pulled swiftly ahead once more. After that jump, I was running on fumes. In another minute or two, I would be just another human woman, gasping and swearing as Kalen vanished underground. The tunnel sloped and now I was climbing against gravity and the flow of water under my feet.

Every breath burned in my lungs. By the time I staggered out into the next tunnel, I had lost sight of Kalen. This passageway was full of fairies again, wearing just as many colors and fabrics as those I'd seen before, but now I spotted a lot more spikes and chains in the mix. Through the smells of sweat, leather, seawater and old stone, though, I could still pick out the scents of clover and honey.

Got you, Kalen.

I wound my way between the market stands, walking quickly, but no longer running. Kalen thought he had lost me. Let him just keep thinking that. Tracking the slick bastard by smell ate up a lot less of my power than sprinting at thirty miles an hour.

The market stalls and blankets here didn't sell as many cell phones and movies, or crystal bottles and graceful fairy carvings. Kalen was in his own territory now, the deepest Unseelie shadows of the fairy market. Here, a big fairy with skin like obsidian and a girdle of battle-scarred chainmail sold axes, swords and knives at his table. All of them had jagged blades red with blood or rust – I couldn't tell which. A scorched-looking stall across the tunnel was heaped so high with bleached white bones that I couldn't see who or what was selling them.

I was getting stares, and the faces attached to those stares were considerably less friendly than the little peanut-munching hedge-hog guy. There was less fur down here – unless you counted the pack of ice-white wolf-things chained to a pitted steel ring in the wall – and a lot more thick scales and stony skin. The eyes fixed on me glowed red, yellow or balefire green. I ignored them all and focused on the scent of clover.

There. Kalen sat on an overturned crate that read *munitions* in faded stenciling, petting one of the silver-white wolves. It snapped at his fingers, but the fairy thief just laughed and pulled his hand back so fast that it left a faint golden trail in the air. The wolf sniffed and turned toward me, snarling. Kalen followed its black-eyed glare and grinned. He jumped lightly to his feet and darted down the nearest dark tunnel.

I gave up on walking and dashed after Kalen. Carefully. I didn't really think he would try the same trick twice – and how many bottomless pits could there be down here, anyway? – but I wasn't about to go rushing headlong into any more shadowy tunnels. I had more important things to do tonight than die and one of them had a fine, tight golden ass.

Unsurprisingly, Kalen was nowhere to be seen as I ran down the tunnel. But neither had I lost his scent, though it was mingled now with more of that sharper-than-seawater smell. Little green-brown fairies stood in a loose circle around a burning trash can. The tallest of them was only waist-high, but they all bulged with ropy knots of muscle. Their noses were thin and upturned to match their huge, bat-like ears. The goblins turned large yellow eyes on me and grinned to display lots of very sharp teeth.

"Pretty lady," one of them hissed like steam escaping a street vent.

The goblins spread out from their fire barrel. I slowed, then stopped as they filled the tunnel. I couldn't tell if the unpleasant smell came from their lumpy skin or the serrated red knives thrust through their belts. At least none of them had drawn their weapons yet.

Three more of the ugly little balls of warts and muscle shimmied up from god knew where behind me, hemming me in. And we had been off to such a good start with *pretty lady*.

"Look, if this is a mugging," I said, "you boys can forget it. I'm not as delicate as I look."

Trust an Unseelie thief to lead me into the only pile of fairies I wouldn't let gang-bang me. Well, maybe the one with the... No, not even him.

"Don't want money," hissed another goblin.

"No bucks," agreed a third.

"Hair so red," murmured a runty toadstool of slimy warts. His stumpy fingers caressed the hilt of his rust-colored knife. "We take hair."

"Okay, now that's going too far," I said. "Forget it, you snotty little creeps."

One of the goblins behind me jumped onto my shoulders and grabbed a fistful of my long hair. He yanked my head back with more strength than his warped frame suggested. I found myself yelping in pain and staring up at the dark bricks of the tunnel ceiling.

I heard the goblins rushing me and kicked out blindly. My foot impacted squirming flesh about as soft as a knot of tree roots. I kicked again, but this time I felt something crack under my heel and was greeted by a squealing, bubbling shout.

I reached behind me and grabbed the knobby wrist of the goblin on my back. I yanked him over my shoulder and jerked my hair out of his grubby fist, then held the writhing little bastard up like a badly behaved cat. I punched him in the nose, hoping it was as sensitive as it looked, but it just bent like rubber and sprang back into place. Fuck that, then.

The goblin made a great bowling ball, though. I pitched the fetid little fairy underhand into the charging mass of his friends. They scattered, burbling and hissing. One of them managed to regain his feet and ran at me, wrestling his knife from his belt. I kicked the goblin's hand before he could get a good grip, then planted another kick to the chest that sent him flying. He bounced off the curved tunnel wall and fell to the ground in a wheezing pile.

Another goblin jumped at me from behind, but I smelled him coming. I grabbed him out of the air by his long bat-ears. Those *were* sensitive, apparently, and the goblin screeched so loud that I barely resisted the urge to drop him to cover my own ears.

But I managed to keep my hold on the wriggling vermin and swung him like a club at two more goblins running toward me from the front. I sent them all sliding back on their asses before throwing the goblin in my grasp after them. He curled up on the wet black tunnel floor, hands cupped protectively over his ears.

"Had enough, boys?" I asked.

Evaine had taught me a lot meaner fighting tricks, but I really didn't want to get nasty over a hair fetish. The goblins were creepy bastards, but I had no particular desire to kill them. A full-blooded succubus would have done it, but I'm only half demon. Though the little fuckers had messed up my hair and I was tempted to at least break a few bones.

"Pretty lady," wheezed one of the goblins. "Powerful lady."

He pressed his forehead to the ground, repeating his praise. For a moment, I wondered if the goblins were going to start my own underground Lily Quinn cult. It might have been fun to be a goddess, but who had the time? I already had a job I liked just fine. But my would-be attackers only retreated into the shadows, dragging their injured companions away. I let them go.

The indigo-haired fairy leaned against the tunnel wall a dozen feet away. He hadn't been there five seconds ago. He waved and held up a wallet.

My wallet. I grabbed my ass, but the familiar bulge was gone from my back pocket.

"Lilith Quinn, hmm?" he said, brandishing my driver's license at me.

I put my hands on my hips, thrusting my lower lip out in a completely sincere pout. "You stuck your hand in my pants and all you grabbed was my wallet?"

"What do you want from Kalen Silverwind?" the fairy asked.

He straightened and fixed me with sharp, colorful eyes. I was reasonably certain that I had my thief, but if it would keep him talking and get me a few inches closer, I was willing to play whatever games he wished. Playing with him was a hell of a lot more fun than fighting off little green guys trying like fuck to steal my hair.

"I don't want Kalen so much as I want a certain book," I said. "I hear he stole it right out from under the wizards."

He eyed me carefully, but didn't stop smirking. "Very well, go on. I'm listening. And watching."

"I've got gold. Lots of gold," I said. I took another small, hip-swaying step closer. "And I want to buy the book. I'll even pay you a finder's fee if you can tell me how to contact Kalen."

"Oh really?"

He cocked his head at me, curiosity in his lilac eyes. Fuck, he was hot. What had Evaine said? As handsome as Oberon and as mischievous as Puck? Yeah, that sounded about right.

"Really," I answered. The smell of clover and honey was strong, heady. "Minus a little something for putting me through this bull-shit, of course."

"Kalen's looking for big jobs. Big scores. *Interesting* scores. Are you sure you can provide?"

"Yes. I've got plenty of money." I slid in another foot, narrowing the distance between us. I licked my lips and it wasn't just a sexy move. I really wanted this to work. "And I can be quite persuasive."

"Persuasive? Really?"

"Very," I said. "So can we stop playing this game, Kalen? I've got a much better one in mind."

He smiled and sketched a graceful bow. "Kalen Silverwind at your service. Or I will be, if you can *persuade* me."

Kalen closed the final feet between us and slipped one arm around my waist. I felt him push my wallet back into the rear pocket of my jeans. Probably light some cash, but I didn't give a shit right then. The fairy thief's clover scent enfolded me and filled my senses. I reached up, grabbed a handful of silky purple-blue hair and pulled the slick bastard down to my lips. Kalen laughed and then kissed me, deep and delicious and sweet. He didn't just smell like honey – he tasted like it, too. The tunnel vanished around us.

Chapter
FOUR

I wasn't being poetic when I said that the fairy market disappeared when Kalen kissed me. The tunnel literally vanished and then we were somewhere else entirely.

It was dark in this new place, but it wasn't the clinging shadows of the underground fairy market. Shifting light glowed up from the city through spreading windows and I heard music coming from somewhere below us. Through one open door, I caught a brief glimpse of a large bed, the covers neatly turned down, and a courtesy card on the nightstand bearing the embossed silver logo of the Bayline Hotel.

Kalen grinned as I gasped. He really liked keeping me on my toes, didn't he? Well, we were playing *my* game now and I intended to win. Kalen was already coming in for another kiss that I was all too happy to give. Our tongues twined and I felt the lust rising, growing inside him and warming me like fire. After that chase, I may have been just about out of sexual energy, but Kalen was going to give me more than enough to ensure his own capture.

I pushed Kalen back into the hotel room door and the fairy actually let out a musical little hiss of discomfort. He twisted and I let him press me against the door, pinning me there with kisses along my jaw and down my throat that made my whole body tingle. I licked the rim of one of Kalen's ears. It came to a delicate point that rose up from the indigo cascade of his hair.

I seized the collar of Kalen's coat and yanked it down off his shoulders. He gave a shudder of pleasure as the black leather hit the floor in a puddle of midnight and I suddenly understood why the fairy hadn't enjoyed being shoved against the door. Wings unfurled from his back, an elegant double set like those of a dragonfly. They were iridescent and turned the glowing city skyline outside into a colorful, lacy mosaic of light.

Gorgeous. I was already wet as the ocean, but something about the sight of those wings made my pussy absolutely gush.

"You like them?" Kalen asked. His tongue flicked over my lips.

"Yes," I said.

And I wanted to see more. I grabbed the front of Kalen's shirt and ripped it off his lean golden body. The silk tore easily and his eyebrows shot up as I threw it to the floor.

"Was that shirt magic?" I asked.

"No," he said. "Just tailored."

"Then I guess I owe you a shirt."

Kalen laughed and I bit his lower lip lightly as I raked my nails down his tawny chest. Kalen was slender and even smoother than his silk shirt. I gave a little growl of frustration when my questing fingertips encountered the waist of Kalen's pants. I felt his cock hard and long through the leather.

"I think I'll take that shirt now," he whispered into my ear.

Kalen stood back and I took a half step toward him, but the fairy raised one graceful hand, waving a finger mock-sternly and clicking his tongue at me. Then he snapped his fingers – I wanted those fingers inside me so badly that it made my knees weak – and they struck a spark in the darkness.

The bright little ember arced through the air and landed on me. I gasped and felt a crackle like static shock all along my body, then the crisp chill of air conditioning on my bare skin. I spun to find my clothes standing next to me, empty pants over empty boots. My shirt hovered above the lacy line of my thong, just visible over my jeans. My entire outfit floated beside me for a moment before apparently realizing that I was no longer wearing it and collapsed to the floor.

"Holy shit," I said, gaping. "Can you teach me that?"

I could think of all sorts of fun to have with magicking people's clothes off. Kalen laughed and backed slowly away. His wings rippled and sent prismatic fragments of light sparkling through the room. I stalked after him. The carpet was lush and thick under my feet. Bayline Hotel was expensive, at least eight hundred bucks a night. Kalen's thieving obviously paid well.

"So you want to buy the book?" he asked, gliding back toward the suite's bedroom. "Just how badly do you want it, Lilith Quinn?"

"Lily," I said. "And I want it bad enough that you better magic those pants off. Unless you want me to owe you a pair of those, too."

Kalen laughed again and kicked off his shoes as he passed through the door, with me chasing after him. He started on his belt and I sank down to my knees to wait patiently. Well, by *patiently*, I mean I licked my lips while grabbing one of my round tits and pinching the hard pink nipple in my fingers. I slid my other hand down between my legs and felt myself dripping wet. The lightest touch of my fingertips sent bright lightning bolts of pleasure racing through my body.

Kalen peeled himself out of his pants and then pushed a pair of clinging designer boxers down his long, long legs. The fairy's body was completely smooth. I don't just mean manscaped, but utterly hairless. His butterscotch skin was almost glossy and gleamed with reflected nightlight. I couldn't wait to lick every inch.

Especially Kalen's cock. It was as long, graceful and slender as the rest of him, promising to reach deep inside me. I sat back on my heels and trailed fingers down Kalen's stomach and then his lithe legs, everywhere but his dick. The golden length thrust out toward me invitingly and I blew a light breath over the flushed crown. Kalen's wings rustled like leaves and he let out a musical moan.

I slid my hands up and grabbed a double handful of lean fairy ass, then pulled him forward and parted my lips to accept his cock. I opened wide and swallowed inch after inch of smooth hardness until Kalen's dick nuzzled against the back of my throat. Thanks to years of diligent cock-sucking, I didn't have much of a gag reflex, so I could take him an impressive way down my throat. My tongue caressed Kalen's increasingly slippery length. Fuck dignity or propriety – I let myself drool hungrily down the shaft, getting my fairy thief nice and wet.

Kalen was beyond lust and the sexual energies built between us, heady and hot and surging through me. My blood pounded in my ears as I drank it in along with his dick, and my whole body tingled, aching with need. I thrust one hand back between my legs and shoved two fingers deep inside myself. My pussy pulsed with a fluttering heartbeat of desire as I sucked eagerly at Kalen's golden cock.

"Mmmm-nnn-mm!" I moaned with my mouth full. Roughly translated, that meant *fuck my face.*

My other hand remained on Kalen's taut ass and pulled him in, pushing his cock down my throat. I kept pace with my fingers between my legs and wetness ran along my bare thighs. The sensation of both sets of lips being parted at once made me feel open, spread and ravenous for dick. I curled my fingers into Kalen's flank, nails biting to leave a line of little red crescents for him to remember me by.

The fairy thief's head was thrown back and his lean muscles were tight with pleasure. A red-gold flush crept across his chest and cheeks.

"You're... amazing," Kalen panted.

I knew that, but it was always nice to hear. Sometimes I considered making myself a Yelp page so people could leave reviews. I was pretty sure Kalen would have given me six stars as I took his long cock deep down my throat and held him there, stretching out with my tongue to flick the tip over his balls. They were tight and hot, ready to blow.

I pulled my lips off of Kalen with a wet smack and slid my hand from his ass to close fingers around his slippery shaft. The fairy groaned and his wings rippled as I grasped and worked him. I curled my fingers inside myself and moaned, too.

"Show me how amazing," I said breathlessly. "Paint my body. Leave me creamy and dripping."

"By the Queen!" Kalen gasped.

Getting a fairy to invoke his queen's name was good, but the sudden gush of sticky white was better. Kalen's long body twitched and his dick bucked in my wet fingers as pleasure consumed him. Cum welled up and spurted in oozing lines across my face. I'd never seen anything like it: colors swam through the gooey mess, like veins of liquid opal dribbling down my cheeks.

Finally, Kalen sagged in relief, panting hard.

"Mmm," I purred. "Good boy."

I withdrew my slick, wet hand from my pussy and ran it up my chest to the iridescent cum cascading slowly down my skin. I swirled my fingers through it. Kalen's spunk smelled sweet, too, and I sucked one finger into my mouth. My eyebrows probably shot right up into my wild red hair.

"How much sugar do you have to eat to make it taste like this?" I asked.

Kalen's cum was so sweet I could have used it in my coffee. Hell, I wanted my next birthday cake covered in the stuff. Greedily, I sucked my finger clean and went back for more. I wiped shining pearlescent jizz from my face and licked it all up until all that was left on my skin was a faintly gleaming sheen. I sat back on my heels, licking my lips and seriously contemplating trying to lap up what had dripped onto the expensive carpet.

Kalen stared down at me with eyes that smoldered like violet embers in the shadowed hotel room and I considered grabbing him right then. We hadn't quite restocked all the sexual energy that I had gotten from Evaine, but fairies weren't as strong as vampires or werewolves. I doubted that I would need to be able to throw the couch at Kalen to catch him.

But it was the book that the College wanted. *The Gates of Avalon* was worth a lot more to the wizards than Kalen, though maybe that was just because they didn't know what his cum tasted like. Unless Kalen had magically hidden his stolen book away in the tight leather pants now sitting in a heap on the floor – which I supposed was a possibility – then he had secreted it away somewhere. If I was going to earn my gold from the College, I had to find out where. Maybe I should have asked before, but my mouth had been otherwise occupied. And a lady never talks with a mouth full of dick.

Besides, I was wet and ready, and I really wanted Kalen's long, sweet golden cock. I didn't think fairies shared my lust-sense – that's a gift from my succubus mother – but something of my desire must have shown in my expression. A roguish and slightly mocking smile spread across Kalen's face.

"Ah, now it *is* time for some of my tricks," he said.

The fairy thief dropped his elegant, long-boned hands between his legs. His cock flared with rosy light and swelled, rising swiftly once again. Beats the hell out of Viagra. When the glow faded, Kalen hooked one finger at me, silently commanding me to stand. I raised an eyebrow and slowly straightened.

"Tell me about a book called *The Gates of Avalon*," I said.

I sauntered the few short feet to Kalen and grabbed his cock. The fairy thief grinned as I stood up on my tiptoes. I lifted one leg high, almost into the vertical splits, and rested my heel on his shoulder. My toes nearly touched Kalen's beautiful wings. I angled his dick and guided it inside my wet slit. He slid easily into me, filling me. Kalen let out another musical moan and took my ass in deft golden hands. He pulled me closer.

"You were asking for me," Kalen said. "And now about the book. Then you know it was stolen."

"By you," I moaned.

I hooked my heel tighter over Kalen's shoulder, then began to rise and fall on the ball of my other foot. Kalen's cock speared deep inside me.

"Yes," Kalen said into my ear.

His dual pairs of exquisite wings stretched, unfurled, and began to flutter. At first, the movement was gentle; just enough to make the stirred air lightly stroke over my sweaty skin. But then the sound rose to something like the buzz of my favorite vibrator and wind tugged at my hair. My toes were no longer touching the soft carpet. We were flying.

Kalen held me close, sliding one hand up and the other down the back of my thighs, then pulling both legs around his waist. I didn't have the leverage to move, but I didn't have to. Kalen's narrow hips moved against me. His cock plunged into my pussy, churning pleasure and sweet fire inside me as his fingertips dug into my ass.

"What do you want with the book?" Kalen asked. The fairy thief ran his tongue along the rim of my ear. There was an odd edge of intensity to his voice.

"I... I just want to buy it."

I panted the lie again and punctuated it with a moan. Kalen's wings were an iridescent starfire blur as he turned me toward the window and the shining mosaic of city lights. I wasn't sure how many feet he was flying me up off the floor – I was far more interested in the smooth, slicked inches pounding into me. There was no way it was just his wings holding us aloft, not with me bucking in his slender arms.

"How're you doing this?" I breathed into one pointed ear.

"Magic." Kalen's fingers danced over my ass and then down to my slippery labia, spread open by his pistoning cock.

"More," I moaned.

One of his hands trailed along my spine and then curled into my hair, pulling my face up to his. His indigo eyes sparkled. Literally sparkled, as if they were cut from sapphire or amethyst.

"Who are you, Lily?" Kalen asked. "How do you know about me, about the book? If I had to guess, I would say... bounty hunter? But you don't carry any weapons. Not so much as a single willow wand or pinch of sulfur. You're no wizard, so how can you be a bounty hunter? The sorcerers trust none but their own."

Kalen's eyes were so bright that they eclipsed the glowing city skyline below. It was like staring into stars, brilliant and burning and beautiful. Evaine had warned me about this, about the power of fairy glamour. And that an Unseelie thief like Kalen would have absolutely no compunctions against using his abilities to get *exactly* what he wanted.

"So who are you?" he asked. "Tell me."

My heart fluttered and Kalen's dick slid smoothly in and out of my core. But Evaine told me something else: that Kalen's glamour probably wouldn't work on me. Succubae were mistresses of hypnotism – also spanking – and as the half-blood daughter of a lust demon, I was more or less immune.

I couldn't charm Kalen like a full-blooded succubus would have been able to, but neither could he charm me.

I grinned at Kalen and bit his lower lip. I locked my legs around his waist and used my superior strength to begin really riding my thief, driving myself down onto his cock over and over. Kalen groaned in musical surprise, but we continued to float smoothly, unperturbed. Not that I could say the same for the floor... My pussy left a wet, dripping trail across the expensive carpet as we drifted through the room. Kalen's balls were tighter, hotter and firmer against me with every hammering thrust.

"Where's the book, Kalen?" I asked. "Tell me."

"No. I'm not bringing that kind of power down on myself."

The College? Apparently, Kalen would steal from the wizards, but didn't want to stick around for the fallout. Smart man.

I grabbed Kalen's silky indigo hair and brought his face up to mine. I squeezed his dick inside me and felt wetness running down our joined bodies. I kissed slowly up his neck and Kalen panted. He seized my hips and tried to pull me close, but I was burning with our pleasure, with power and strength. Kalen might as well have tried to move a mountain. I held back, the crown of his cock just barely nuzzled inside me.

"The book is hidden," Kalen groaned.

"Give it to me," I said. I nipped the point of his left ear. "The wizards will go easier on you if I can tell them you cooperated."

"The College will never get the book back. I've already got a buyer. He hired me to get it and I will not violate our agreement."

I twisted my hips, caressing the head of Kalen's dick with my tight pussy. Wetness ran down his length and pattered to the hotel room floor.

"You're Unseelie," I said. "And a thief. You must break oaths all the time."

"Not this one."

Kalen's wings beat harder, vibrating our bodies against each other. He spun me away from the glowing window and grabbed my ass again. His nimble fingers played over the sensitive skin between my buttocks. I moaned and almost gave in, almost pulled myself down onto his long red-golden cock.

"Where's the book?" I asked.

"No," he answered.

"Who hired you, Kalen?"

"No!"

I heard the edge to Kalen's voice again, raw and hard and not just because we were both trembling on the tipping point of climax.

He really wasn't going to tell me. Was he that worried about ruining this deal?

My back hit the wall and Kalen leaned into me with all his slight weight and the thrumming beat of his wings. His cock pressed urgently inside me and my body responded. Kalen wasn't the only one who wanted this, who needed it. That need burned through me like wildfire and I dug my heels into Kalen's taut flanks. I impaled myself onto the Unseelie thief and he responded in kind, clutching my ass in both hands and spearing his dick up into my eager body.

I screamed and thrashed in his arms, hoping that the magic keeping us aloft was also enough to let Kalen catch me if he had to. I dug my fingernails into his shoulders as his cock swelled and then his sweet heat burst inside me. Kalen let out a moan that was half song and filled me. Fairy cum spurted and splashed into my pussy. Pleasure poured through me that felt... fizzy, effervescent.

The storm of sensations left me gasping, but I still heard the whirring hum of Kalen's wings change pitch. I tightened my legs around him with a start. If I wasn't careful with my sex-powered strength, I would shatter all of his ribs. But Evaine had painstakingly drilled control into me eight years ago, and even my startled responses were pretty measured.

Kalen simply alighted gently on the floor of the darkened hotel room. His skin was slicked in sparkling beads of sweat. I unclamped my legs and let them slide down over Kalen's slim hips, back to the deep carpet once more. His long cock slid free and opalescent rivulets of cream ran along my inner thighs. An honest-to-fucking-goodness magical creampie.

"Fine," I said as I swirled my fingers through the gleaming mess between my legs and left circular designs across my flushed skin. "If you won't give up *The Gates of Avalon*, I guess I'll just have to settle for your bounty. The College will have to get the location out of you themselves."

Kalen shook his head. "You were good, Lily. But I'm not talking to the wizards. They will never get me or the book. Don't come looking for me again, either. You won't find me."

"You really are an arrogant–" I began, but Kalen snapped his fingers and there was a flash of light.

It only took me a second to blink away the bright spots of color that swam across my vision, but by the time I could see again, Kalen was already gone.

Chapter FIVE

"What the fuck?" I asked the empty air where my bounty mark had just been.

I resisted the urge to kick the bed in frustration. I would only punt it through the wall and ruin the neighbors' evening. I've had plenty of men and women split after sex. That didn't bother me. I wasn't particularly big on cuddling, either, and had booted my fair share of lovers out of bed before they could start stammering their excuses.

But it was my job to capture Kalen. And more importantly, to return the book he stole to the College. There was gold and my reputation on the line. And what the hell? Kalen already had wings. Why the fuck did he get teleportation spells, too?

Sometimes life really wasn't fair.

I muttered a few more curses and stalked over to the bathroom. I cleaned up with one of the hotel's fluffy towels and then raided the minibar for a tiny bottle of expensive scotch on Kalen's tab. I took a couple of swallows while I poked around the suite, but Kalen hadn't left anything behind. Even the fairy's clothes had vanished along with him.

I really needed to learn that spell.

I finished the scotch, dropped the bottle into a discrete blue recycle bin under the sink, and got dressed again. I raked my fingers through my hair and inspected my reflection in a mirror.

When I checked the time, it was nearly two in the morning. Time flies when you do, I guess. I slipped out of the hotel room and into the brightly lit hall, memorizing the suite number before I set off. My only company was a few tastefully minimalist paintings under bright brass spotlights until I made it downstairs to the lobby. There, a short girl with a cute pixie haircut and nice cheekbones looked over the counter at me in surprise. I should have invited her up to eat my magic fairy creampie instead of toweling off.

Oh, well. To business.

"Hi," I said, approaching the check-in counter and reaching for my wallet. Kalen better not have stolen it again. "Can you tell me who's in room 924?"

The cute desk clerk blinked at me. "Good evening, miss. We really can't divulge customer information..."

I pulled the wallet out of my pocket and smiled, wondering if there was any cash inside. You can't really bribe people with a credit card. The clerk looked down at her computer and poked at a keyboard hidden below the polished marble counter.

"...But suite 924 isn't currently occupied. Would you like to book it?" she asked.

I slid my wallet back into my jeans. Of course Kalen hadn't paid for the room. Damn it.

"No thanks," I said. "You might want to send housekeeping up there, though."

The confusion on her heart-shaped face was adorable, but I walked quickly out of the Bayline Hotel before she could stick me with the bill. I passed through an etched glass revolving door, winked at the evening bellman and then strode swiftly away down the sidewalk.

After a block or two, I slowed and checked the GPS on my cell phone. I was at the east edge of downtown, miles from the Quay and my car. Kalen was an amazing lay, but he was really starting to piss me off. There's playing hard to get and then there's being an asshole.

It was late and there weren't many cabs out, but with a little persistence – and, of course, a pair of legs that went on for days – it didn't take me long to flag down a middle-aged driver. He even climbed out at the curb to open the door for me.

"Thanks," I said as I slid into the back seat. "Take me to the Quay, please."

The driver nodded and pulled his checkered yellow Prius out into the street. Fog rolled in off the bay, growing thicker as we drove west toward the coast. The tall red spires of the bridge jutted up from the silvery bay waters as we crested another hill. Other cars and late-night pedestrians were soft gray ghosts in the mist. Not that actual ghosts exist. Not that I knew of, at least.

Kalen hadn't said very much. Made plenty of lovely, musical noise, yes, but we hadn't talked a lot. My thief confessed to having stolen *The Gates of Avalon*, which was pretty brazen. About as brazen as walking – or flying, or apparating, or whatever – into the College library to steal a priceless fifteen-hundred-year-old book. Not just book. Tome. Maybe even grimoire.

Even if Kalen didn't want the wizards to find him now, that took balls. Big balls full of shiny, sugary fairy spunk.

Kalen had also admitted to two more things. First, that he already had a buyer. Hell, that someone hired him to steal *The Gates of Avalon* from the College in the first place. Kalen didn't just wake up one day with a craving to piss off the wizards.

And Kalen still had the book. He hadn't made the hand-off to his employer yet. He was worried about that meeting. Kalen knew I wasn't a mage and I got the distinct impression that he wouldn't have fucked me if I were. My fairy thief wasn't getting anywhere near Stefano and the other College bounty hunters. What could scare an Unseelie fairy with the power to vanish whenever and wherever he liked? The wizards? And besides the College, who the hell cared about *The Gates of Avalon*?

Kalen Silverwind was mixed up in something dangerous. Unsurprising, really... he *was* Unseelie. They lived for danger. But I remembered the sharpness of Kalen's voice as I asked about whoever had hired him. Was it possible Kalen could have gotten in even over *his* head?

My mark said I wouldn't see him again. Hmm... I knew where to find the fairy market and how to get in. Finding Kalen there wasn't easy, but it wasn't impossible, either. He was arrogant and slick, not stupid. So I doubted Kalen had stashed *The Gates of Avalon* behind a stall or planned to meet his buyer there at the market.

So where was it? Not the hotel room he had taken me to, certainly. That was just some place to whisk a gullible bounty hunter for a good fuck. What if Kalen had hidden the book in a magical fairy realm I could only access with pixie dust or something?

I clearly wasn't going to find *The Gates of Avalon* on my own. Kalen could have stashed it anywhere. Unless I developed psychic powers pretty damned quick, there was no way I was going to just stumble onto it. But eventually, Kalen would have to give up the goods to his buyer. If I could find out where that meeting was taking place, maybe I could swoop in to grab Kalen and the book together.

Same problem, though. Kalen had given me no more hints about where he planned to hand over *The Gates of Avalon* than where it was hidden in the meantime. All I knew was that Kalen was edgy and afraid.

I needed more information.

The cab pulled to a stop in front of a darkened coffee shop on the Quay. I paid the driver with a credit card – the cash was all gone from my wallet, but Kalen had left the plastic – and scribbled a sizable tip onto the receipt. Hell, I'm rich and driving a cab in the middle of the night is shit work. The guy deserved a treat. So I winked as the driver opened the door for me. He blushed adorably and hurried back out into the thick coastal fog before his evening could get any stranger.

The mist was heavy and silver in the moonlight. It swirled and eddied around me as I made my way back to the parking garage. When I climbed the stairs to my i10 – even at this hour, it wasn't the only car still in the garage – I didn't immediately get in. Instead, I leaned against the door and pulled my phone out of my pocket. I dialed Evaine's number and left a message.

"Hey," I said. "It's Lily. I found Kalen, but he didn't have the book on him. And then the fucker disappeared before I could bring him in. Anyway, if there's anything you can tell me about magical fairy hiding places, give me a call back. Or, you know, feel free to jump me at my house again."

I hung up and waited a few minutes, but my cell phone didn't ring and Evaine didn't appear. I might not see her again for months or years. She was mysterious that way. And sexy.

I tapped my phone against my lower lip, thinking. Evaine was my best source of information – when I could get in touch with her – but she wasn't my only one. I scrolled through my contacts and took a risk that he would still be awake at this hour.

Bingo. The line picked up on the second ring.

"Hey, Stefano," I said.

"Lilith?" asked the other bounty hunter. "What do you want?"

"Want? What makes you think I want anything other than to chat to a friend?"

"Right," said Stefano. "Just like yesterday, when you were asking me about the *Gates* job."

"Just like that," I agreed in a low purr. "But better."

He paused and there was still suspicion in the wizard's voice when he answered. But he *did* answer. Stefano's always had a hard time saying *no* to me. Emphasis on hard. I was pretty sure Stefano had a crush on me.

"I can be at your condo first thing tomorrow morning," he said with a sigh. "Seven o'clock."

That was awful early, but wasn't what caught my attention.

"Wait, you know where I live?" I asked. Now it was my turn to be suspicious. I never invited anyone there but Max and Evaine.

"The College keeps an eye on you, Lilith," said Stefano.

Of course they did. Even though I had passed their stupid test years ago, the wizards still didn't entirely trust me. I was half demon, after all. Still the enemy, more likely to end up being a bounty than turning one in.

No matter how often I proved otherwise.

"Hey, do you guys watch me on the scry network?" I asked. "Like when I'm in the shower?"

"I need to finish up some spells, Lilith. I'll see you first thing tomorrow," Stefano said.

"You do!" I said, laughing. "And I bet you jerk off watching me."

Stefano hung up. I took that as a big fat *yes*. I shrugged and pocketed my phone again. It was frustrating how little the College trusted me. I'd been working for the wizards since I was nineteen years old. But Evaine warned me about this kind of shit back when I first discovered what I was. No one was *ever* going to trust me.

And fuck the College and their magical cliques, anyway. They paid me and paid well. Screw the rest. Or, if I needed information, *I* would do the screwing.

Chapter
SIX

I made it home with just enough time to grab a few hours of sleep. I dreamed of Kalen flying above me, out of reach as he taunted me with a thick leather-bound book and his sweet, iridescent cum.

The alarm I had barely remembered to set the night before woke me up at half past six. I took a quick shower and got dressed, opting for a soft pair of yoga pants and a tank top. No bra, though. I planned on being topless soon enough and it felt nice to let the girls bounce free for a while.

I went to the kitchen, got out two wineglasses and checked the time: just about seven o'clock. Stefano would be arriving in five minutes. When he said seven in the morning, he damned well meant it. I'd never known Stefano to be anything less than excruciatingly punctual. I've met plenty of mages and not one of them are what you would call sloppy. Years of precision mixing potions seeps into everything they do. It has to.

Stefano Rossi was pretty much my favorite wizard. Well, maybe he tied with Dorian, who paid me when I turned a bounty in to the College. I chose a bottle of red wine – something tasty but not too strong – from the pantry and put it out on the counter next to the glasses. It was a little early for wine, perhaps, but I had plans for it.

Right on time, there was a knock at my door. I finished uncorking the bottle and went to answer. Stefano stood in the hallway and I smirked at him.

Stefano nodded to me. "Lilith."

"I didn't get a ring from the doorman," I said.

"He didn't see me. May I come in?"

I stepped back and gestured him inside. The drapes were open and slanting rays of silver-golden morning light splayed like fingers across the floor. Stefano entered cautiously, his dark eyes flickering between the windows and doors. Always on the lookout.

Other than me, the College employed seven more bounty hunters in the city, all of them wizards. Stefano is hands-down the hottest one. I didn't know anything about his parents except that they both used to live in Little Italy, but Stefano did not. If they taught their son the old language, though, I couldn't tell. Stefano had no accent, but all the rest was pure Italian sex: thick, dark hair and deep brown eyes. Stefano had a jaw that romance novels would call *chiseled* and wore a short, close-cut beard.

Education at the College didn't come easy or cheap. You think becoming a lawyer is expensive? Try telling your guidance counselor that you want to be a wizard when you grow up. So many of the younger mages have to work as apprentices and assistants to the older ones. But those who have the right skills and talents can earn a lot more as bounty hunters. At least until they learn how to turn their own lead into gold.

But even when Stefano gets that advanced, I don't think he'll ever retire from hunting. He's got that old-world honor and he takes his job seriously. Personally. So he trains hard. And that's why he's the only wizard in the city with six-pack abs.

Stefano was dressed for the job: black cargo pants that hugged his toned ass and one of those tight shirts that are made to breathe well when their owner gets sweaty, but mostly just ends up clinging like a second skin and showing off how much he works out. And to top – or middle – it all off, Stefano had an honest-to-goodness utility belt. Batman would have been jealous. Except Batman's belt rarely carried powdered silver and wolfsbane – all the little bits of spell that Stefano would combine to throw fireballs or cast shields. Hours of preparation so that a final chalk rune on the ground could unleash powerful, pent-up magic.

Eat your heart out, Batman.

I got by perfectly fine with my nice rack, hot ass, as well as sex-powered super strength, speed and senses… but I had to admit that the mage hunters were pretty good at their jobs, too.

I admired the view as I closed the door behind Stefano. Inside, I poured and handed him a glass of wine, which he took with an only slightly suspicious look. I *told* you Stefano liked me. Then I led him to the living room and gestured to the white leather sofa. The other bounty hunter did not sit.

"What do you want, Lilith?" Stefano asked. "You said this was about the missing book. Do you have a lead on it?"

I took a small sip of the dark red wine and watched Stefano over the rim of the glass. No matter what tests I pass, in his book, I'm still dangerous and untrustworthy. I'm the bad girl, the enemy.

"The real question," I asked with a smirk, "is what *you* want?"

I set my wineglass down on the end table and stepped in closer to put my hand on Stefano's chest. I felt the hard planes of his muscles beneath his shirt. The wizard stiffened at my touch and inhaled a sharp breath.

"Lilith, I shouldn't…" he said.

"No," I agreed. "You shouldn't. But you want to."

I closed a hand around Stefano's wrist and dipped one of his fingers into his glass. He sighed as I put it to my lips and sucked the tart red wine from his skin.

"Lilith…" he groaned.

Always so conflicted. Stefano knew he shouldn't be here, should not let me work my dark half-succubus magic on him, and definitely should not give up any of his information. But Stefano just couldn't say *no* to me. Still, I had to give him partial credit for not saying *yes* right away, either.

"I know what you want," I said.

I wrapped my lips around Stefano's finger again. I swirled my tongue over the tip, then bit lightly and tugged him toward the couch. This time, he followed.

I rewarded Stefano by giving his finger a low, slow suck, taking it all the way into my mouth before releasing him. I pushed Stefano back until he sat down on the couch. The front of his black cargo pants bulged and he almost moved to conceal his hardness, but I sank to my knees at the hunter's feet.

"You want me," I said in a low voice. "You always do. You can't help yourself."

Stefano's jaw was clenched to keep from answering, but the erection in his pants grew swiftly harder and larger. I nudged his knees apart until I could get close, then slid my hands under his shirt. I pushed the fabric up his body to reveal his sculpted chest and felt the muscles bunched beneath his skin. Stefano stared at me and took a long drink of wine, finishing the whole glass in a single gulp.

I ran my fingers through the dusting of dark hair across his chest, following the narrowing line of it down his stomach until I reached the buckle of his utility belt. I slipped my fingers beneath it, to the zipper of Stefano's pants. He drew long, deep breaths, trying not to groan, but I could hear his heart hammering against his ribs. I didn't need any supernatural senses to know how badly Stefano wanted me.

"I'm going to take your dick out and get it nice and wet," I said as I inched his zipper down. "And then I'm going to let you do something you've never done before."

Stefano tried so hard to keep stoic and silent, but he couldn't do it. His cock was rock-hard in his pants and hot even through the heavy cloth.

"What are you going to do?" Stefano asked.

I slid questing fingers down under his pants and sighed with pleasure at the weight of his dick against my palm. It was thick and heavy, throbbing with heat and need. I leaned in as I wrapped my hand around Stefano's shaft and let my breath play over the sensitive skin.

"I'm going to let you fuck my tits," I said.

Stefano's fingers dug into the couch and leather creaked. "Oh gods, Lilith."

His hips rose helplessly off the sofa, cock already straining up toward my breasts. I worked it free of his pants and Stefano gave out another reluctant groan. It grew louder and deeper in pitch as I sucked the big, flushed head into my mouth and traced my tongue over it. I tasted musky precum oozing from the tip. Stefano wanted me so badly...

I licked my way up and down his dick. It was silky soft over iron beneath, and soon gleaming wetly. But I had an even better idea. I reached out to grab my wine, then held it up.

"May I?" I asked.

Without waiting for an answer, I tipped the glass and slowly poured wine down over Stefano's straining cock. It ran along his olive skin in dark red rivulets. Wine dripped onto his pants and the couch cushions. Fuck it. I could get both dry-cleaned, if I needed to. This was far more important. I drank down what remained, tasting the fruity tang mixed pleasantly with the saltiness of Stefano's flavor on my tongue.

I sat back on my heels and peeled off my shirt. Stefano stopped breathing for a moment as I tossed it away over my shoulder. I raised my hands and cupped my breasts. They were so soft and smooth, just barely overspilling my curled fingers.

Stefano's wine-drenched cock twitched at the sight. The muscles of his arms and chest knotted as he struggled to maintain his composure. I pressed my fingertips into my breasts, dimpling the flushed skin. I squeezed them together and rubbed my palms over my nipples. The tiny nubs were already hard and blushing a deep, dark pink.

"Do you want them?" I asked. "Do you want to feel my soft tits on your dick?"

"Yes," Stefano answered, his voice rough with need.

"You want to cum all over them?"

"Yes, Lilith. I…"

Creamy white beaded at the tip of his cock and rolled down his shaft to mix with the ruby red of wine. I trailed one of my nipples lightly along the underside of Stefano's dick. The hunter groaned and dug his fingers deeper into the edge of the couch cushions.

Speaking of cushions… I leaned in and captured Stefano's hard cock in my cleavage. He was deliciously slippery, messy and hot thrust up between my tits. The dark, flared head jutted up from my breasts and I bent down to give it a lingering lick. And fuck, it tasted good.

I cupped my tits and pressed them firmly together around Stefano's dick. The smooth shaft stroked over my breastbone as I began to rise and fall, caressing him with the silky swells. I started slow, but the wine was slick and Stefano was so hot and hard that I couldn't keep my leisurely pace. I bounced my breasts up and down his cock, moaning a little as my skin tingled.

Stefano's tightened knuckles were pale and his hips lifted off the edge of the couch, thrusting in time with me. I felt his dick growing hotter and thicker against my chest. He stared down at my tits, at his cock between them, at my stiff little pink nipples and I knew he was close. The other hunter was already well past the point of no return.

"Lilith…" he grunted.

"Yes," I purred. "I can feel it, Stefano, how close you are. You're going to cum all over my tits, aren't you?"

I was at the edge, either. My pussy was a knot of blazing ecstasy. The scorching tingle spreading in a rosy flush across my chest shot down my spine in sharp jolts, too. But then I felt the spurt of semen at the hollow of my throat and I couldn't stop, either. I practically mewed with pleasure as Stefano fired huge, sticky lines of white across the tops of my breasts. It dripped and oozed down into my cleavage. Stefano's cock was so slick now that I had to press myself close, my cheek against his hard stomach, as I milked the last thick drops from him.

When I sat back, my breasts were liberally smeared in gooey spunk. It dribbled down my skin and a drop hung like a pearl bead from one of my nipples. Stefano's chest rose and fell rapidly as he fought to catch his breath. I was feeling strong enough to snap steel I-beams over my knee.

"So, what did you think?" I asked.

"Gods, Lilith," Stefano panted.

I laughed and went to the bathroom for a couple of towels. I tossed one to Stefano and used the other to mop up the mess he had made of my tits.

"I need information," I said.

Stefano finished cleaning up, stuffed his still half-hard cock into his pants again and stood. He sighed and rubbed one hand along his bearded jaw. Stefano didn't like giving me information, but the same sense of honor that made me such deliciously forbidden fruit also compelled him to answer my questions afterward.

"We haven't been able to find *The Gates of Avalon* on the scry network," he admitted reluctantly. "We've already tried. The High Magus has everyone pulling double shifts on the mirrors."

"Yeah, sounds like you've got the city pretty extensively covered in scry stones," I said with a nod toward my bathroom. "But I think the guy who stole the book is going to meet with his buyer soon."

"You know who took it? Who are they selling it to?" Stefano asked.

I winked at Stefano. I didn't share his sense of obligation or honor, and the other hunter knew it. Besides, I only had the answer to one of his questions.

"My thief is worried about this meeting going smoothly, I think," I said instead. "He might be taking precautions. Have you seen anything like that going on in the city? Extra wards or something? It wouldn't be Merlinic magic."

"What kind of magic, then?" Stefano asked. He shook his head when I didn't answer. "Fine. All of the College campuses and Castle keeps watch for violations of magical law, but I don't think anyone's reported anything like that in the city."

I frowned. Maybe I was wrong. Maybe Kalen was simply toying with me. A ploy, something to throw me off the scent... Kalen certainly wasn't above playing tricks. But if his worry *had* been a trick, I wasn't sure I saw the point. Besides, Kalen shook my tail just fine with his little disappearing act.

I bit on the tip of one finger while I thought, which Stefano seemed to find really interesting. He stared.

"Is there anywhere in the city that isn't covered by the scry network? Ka–" I stopped before saying Kalen's name. "The thief is pretty familiar with the College and your magic. He might know where you're blind."

"What are you going after, Lilith? Non-Merlinic magic, blind spots in the scry network? What's going on?"

"Come on, Stefano," I said with an admittedly adorable pout. "Just answer the question. Is there any place in the city safe from Peeping Tom wizards?"

Stefano colored a bit and he brushed self-consciously at the front of his pants. If they hadn't been black already, the cloth would have been stained dark with wine.

"There are a couple of places we can't watch," Stefano admitted.

"Each campus has their secured vault. They're so interwoven with wards and other protective spells that scry sensors don't work inside. Dorian has to check them individually every day."

I doubted Kalen was planning the meeting in a College vault for a few reasons. He didn't want to fuck with the mages unless he had to. And even if selling *The Gates of Avalon* right under the noses of the wizards that he had stolen it from appealed to Kalen's Unseelie sensibilities, what about his buyer? If they could just walk into the College that easily, I doubted they would have hired Kalen in the first place.

I gestured for Stefano to go on. "You said a couple of places."

"There's the penthouse at the hotel," he said with a heavy sigh.

"Bayline Hotel?" I asked.

"No. The Hotel Marquis. The penthouse suite at the top. We warded it against most types of magic the last time we hosted a meeting with the djinni. No one can use any kind of magic up there, and that includes scrying."

"What about fairies?"

Stefano looked a little confused, but he shrugged. "There's a tower in the Castle just like it set up for the centennial meetings with the fae king and queen. No magic in the world works in there: not Merlinic, djinn elemental, or even fairy."

I whistled. Those were some powerful wards. "Really?"

Stefano fixed his dark eyes on mine. "You think your thief might have hidden *The Gates of Avalon* at the Hotel Marquis or is going to sell it there?"

"No," I lied. "Why the hell would he go somewhere his own magic doesn't work?"

"Be careful, Lilith," Stefano said. "Your abilities are demonic in origin. They won't function in the penthouse, either."

I stuck out my tongue. "So good thing I'm not going there. Anywhere else my thief might be able to hide himself or *The Gates of Avalon* from the wizards?"

Stefano thought for a moment, then shook his head. "No, I don't think so."

"Well, since you didn't give me any directly actionable information, how about a different favor?" I asked with a grin.

No sense of honor, that's Lily Quinn. If I could get anything extra from Stefano, I would.

"What is it?" he asked.

"Have you got any iron?"

"So the thief *is* a fairy," Stefano said.

"I didn't say that," I protested.

Stefano raised one eyebrow, but opened a pouch on his utility belt and pulled out a handful of C-shaped black links.

"Just put these bands onto a pair of standard handcuffs. Make sure they have direct contact with your fairy's skin," said Stefano. The iron bands were cold and heavy as Stefano poured them into my hand. "Though I guess you really aren't going to the Hotel Marquis if you need iron to nullify fairy magic."

"See? I told you so. Now..."

I gave Stefano a light shove toward the door. Normally, I wouldn't have been able to budge a man of his size and strength, but I was all juiced up from fucking Kalen and then stroking a hot load out of a magical bounty hunter.

"Get out of here," I said. "I've got work to do."

Stefano grumbled half-heartedly but let himself be shooed from my condo. When he was gone, I grabbed my tank top, pulled it back on and then booted up my laptop. It didn't take long to find the Hotel Marquis' website. I blinked a few times at the price sheet, but didn't immediately see much of use. Of course, the anti-magic qualities of the penthouse weren't advertised. There was a phone number, though, so I found my cell and dialed.

"Thank you for calling the Hotel Marquis," answered a sweet female voice after the first ring. "My name is Yvette. How can I help you this morning?"

"Hi, Yvette," I said. "I'd like to book the penthouse suite for the rest of the week."

There were a few clicks on the other end and then Yvette spoke again. "I'm sorry, miss, but the penthouse is occupied tonight. It will be free tomorrow evening or I can book you another room."

"Sure," I said. I needed an excuse to be in the hotel, so I glanced at the price sheet again and shrugged. "Give me one of the executive suites."

"Of course, miss."

I made the reservation and wished I could claim the cost as a business expense, but I didn't feel like explaining what I did for a living to the IRS. As long as I managed to bring Kalen and the book he stole back to the College, I would still make a considerable profit on this job.

If he was at the hotel tonight… I hung up and tapped my finger-nails against the phone. Kalen hadn't bothered to book the Bayline Hotel room for us the night before, but that had been a spur-of-the moment thing. Kalen couldn't just appear in the Hotel Marquis' anti-magic suite like he had in the Bayline. Plus, I was pretty sure I ranked well below whoever had hired him to steal *The Gates of Avalon* in Kalen's eyes. Nice as the Bayline Hotel room had been, it wasn't a Marquis penthouse.

But there was no guarantee that Kalen would be there tonight. Maybe some rich businessman had booked the penthouse with no knowledge of its protections. Maybe Kalen would leave the city for his meeting. And the lie I had told Stefano had a grain of truth: agreeing to meet in a place he couldn't use his magic seemed like a risky move for Kalen. But the Hotel Marquis penthouse and to-night's occupant were at least worth checking out.

I picked up one of the iron bands Stefano had given me. Every lineage of fairies had their own quirks and powers, but they all shared a soul-deep aversion to cold iron. Stefano was right that if I found Kalen at the Hotel Marquis, I would be powerless and so would he. But as soon as I tried to drag Kalen out of the room, all bets were off, and I had no intention of letting the smug bastard vanish on me again.

The iron was rigid and brittle, but I had pliers, time to kill and several pairs of handcuffs.

Mmm. Handcuffs.

Chapter
SEVEN

I tucked my new iron-banded handcuffs into my jacket pocket. After a moment's consideration, I packed one of my guns, too: a neat black nine-millimeter. Even with the sexual energy Stefano and Kalen had given me, it was better to be prepared. My powers wouldn't work in the penthouse, anyway. Not that I was expecting much of a fight... but as far as I knew, gunpowder and lead would still do their jobs.

Just in case.

I'm rich, but even I had never stayed at the Hotel Marquis before. The old hotel was a spire of white and gold rising up above Gates Park, reflecting the red and violet of the swiftly setting sun until it looked like a great flower blooming over the bay. Even the stores and restaurants filling the rest of the high-rent block seemed a little in awe of the Hotel Marquis. Every other building was considerably shorter, as though kneeling in prayer at the hotel's feet. It couldn't have been more than twenty stories tall, but there had to be a zillion Marquis-sponsored building codes in place to protect the hotel's unobstructed view of the waterfront.

I left my car with the valet out front, along with a sizable tip to keep it nearby. I might need it again before long. A man in a smart red uniform held the door for me as I stepped into the hotel lobby. There was marble and crystal everywhere, all brightly lit and polished until it shone mirror-bright. Gold leaf, too – enough to pay the bounty on a small werewolf or middle-aged vampire, if I had to guess.

At the front desk, I checked in and accepted a slick black and gold keycard for the executive suite I had booked. I dropped it into my pocket and told the young man behind the counter that I didn't have any luggage. He nodded politely and probably figured I was there to screw someone expensive.

He wasn't entirely wrong, though I was more hoping to screw Kalen *over* tonight.

I went to the elevators and didn't have to wait long before one opened up and another uniformed hotel employee asked me where I was going. My room was on the twelfth floor, but...

"Penthouse suite, please," I said as I stepped inside.

The bellman nodded again, pushed the button marked with a number 19 and we began to rise. I really could have done that myself, but I supposed that sort of pointless luxury was great for impressing visiting CEOs and djinni. As we went up, the bellman's eyes dipped down to my cleavage, but he was courteous enough to raise his gaze swiftly back to safe levels.

The elevator slid to a smooth stop and a soft chime announced our arrival. The bellman touched the shiny black bill of his hat when I stepped out.

"Enjoy your evening, ma'am."

"Thanks. I will," I said.

The elevator closed once more and I was left alone in a private foyer with a green and gold compass rose inlaid in the slick marble floor. A crystal vase of white calla lilies stood on a carved mahogany table in front of a tall window with a dizzying view that looked south across the darkening city. I paused to take in the sight. This place made the Bayline seem like a roadside motel.

A pair of paneled walnut doors stood at the other end of the foyer. I contemplated the discreet card reader nestled above the right-hand doorknob. My key sure as hell wasn't going to open it. But if Kalen was here, he would be expecting company...

I knocked on the door and then stepped back, pressing myself against the wall beside the suite entrance so I wouldn't be visible through the peephole. To his credit, Kalen opened the door carefully, just a couple of inches to peek out. But unfortunately for him, I had already whipped my gun up and jammed the barrel into the gap before he could slam it shut again. I pushed through the door and Kalen gasped.

"Lily? How did you–?"

Kalen's violet eyes went wide as I shoved my way into the room and crushed my lips to his. The fairy still tasted like the best candy I'd ever eaten.

"Surprised to see me again, lover?" I asked.

"Yes," he answered in a tight voice. "And delighted. But you can't be here."

Kalen hooked one arm around my waist and snapped long golden fingers at me. When nothing happened, the fairy thief cursed in his own lyrical tongue.

"Magic doesn't work in here," I reminded him. "That was the whole point, wasn't it? The College couldn't find you. You or your secret buyer."

Kalen's fine brows knit together and he spun me in a smooth circle, back toward the door. "Lily, you *have* to leave."

I kicked the penthouse door shut with a bang and we slammed together into it. Kalen wore his coat once more, hiding his wings away. I grabbed the leather lapel in one hand and pulled Kalen close. His long body was lean and hard against mine. I pressed the barrel of my gun into his stomach, just above his belt.

"I don't think so," I whispered into his elegantly pointed ear. "Where's the book?"

Kalen shuddered in my grip. It was strange to feel the sexual power coursing through me, but not be able to use it. Kalen slid against me, struggling to escape, but without our magic, we were more or less evenly matched. I held Kalen fast and he fixed his indigo eyes on mine.

"No, you don't understand," he said with such intensity that my heart skipped a beat. "I'm not here to hide from the College. It's the only safe place to meet *him*."

This last word came out in a low, rough whisper. I felt Kalen's breath against my cheek and saw beads of sweat glittering along his colorful hairline. His hands shook where they held my hips.

"And even that's a gamble I can barely afford. You have to leave," Kalen told me. "Now."

"Not without you and the book," I said.

"Lily, this is dangerous."

"So am I."

Kalen stared at me, leaning in until I felt his lips brushing my own. I could hear his heart pounding. Or was that mine? My fingers tightened reflexively, curling into the leather of Kalen's coat. His sweet honey-and-clover smell filled my senses.

But then Kalen twisted and slithered out of his coat. Suddenly free, he sprinted toward the nearest window. The velvet curtains were thrown open to reveal their glorious view of the bay and the water was molten with the last red and gold of sunset. Kalen unfurled his long dragonfly wings.

I swore and flung the now-empty coat at Kalen as hard as I could. Black leather smacked into the fairy and snared around his wings. Kalen let out a musical hiss and had to stop to detangle himself. By the time he had freed his wings, I had launched myself at the thief and was tackling him to the lavishly carpeted floor.

I growled and jabbed him in the shoulder with my gun. "You idiot! This thing still works fine in here, you know. I could have shot you!"

"Better than failing my buyer," Kalen panted. "Lily, I'm begging you not to do this. Just go. We're running out of time. He will be here soon!"

I squirmed on top of Kalen. With some difficulty, I pulled the handcuffs out of my pocket and snapped them shut around his wrists. The fairy hissed again as the iron touched his skin, but it didn't seem to burn him or anything.

With Kalen's deft hands now bound, I holstered my gun again and yanked him upright. Kalen had replaced his torn silk shirt with a new one, but the fine cloth was damp with cold sweat and clung to his skin.

"Now," I said. "Where is *The Gates of Avalon*? I need to return it and you've racked up one hell of a late fee."

Kalen shook his head.

I ran a hand down his chest, feeling the lean, taut muscles beneath his shirt. I hooked a finger through his belt and tugged. In spite of everything, I couldn't help liking Kalen. The thief was confident, sexy and a great fuck, not unlike yours truly. Hardness pressed against my stomach as I drew him in close.

"Tell me and we can even have a little fun with the handcuffs before I turn you in," I promised.

Kalen groaned, but shook his head again. I frowned. What in the world could possibly frighten an Unseelie thief so badly? A day ago, I didn't think anything could shake Kalen. Or me. But now I shivered. Here in this room, I couldn't bend steel bars with my bare hands, sprint like a fired bullet, or heal my wounds. Kalen couldn't fly or vanish. Whoever he was meeting couldn't do anything, either. That was the whole point of the penthouse. We would be safe enough in here.

Right?

"You don't want to be here arguing with me when your buyer arrives, do you?" I asked. "Kalen, give me the book and I can get you out of here."

The sharp fairy's jaw tightened and there was something unbearably wild in his violet eyes. Something cornered and trapped.

"It's in the office," Kalen said so softly that I had to lean in to catch the words. He nodded toward a door. "On the desk."

I gripped Kalen's arm and walked through the door he had indicated, into a large and lavishly appointed office. A lamp with a stained green glass shade glowed on a wooden desk, illuminating a leather-bound book laid out on top. The book had to be six inches thick and the pages were rough, each yellowed around the edges with age.

"*The Gates of Avalon*," said Kalen. "The full and original text, as written by Merlin himself."

There was no title on the front, but the leather was burned with a pair of intricately twined dragons. They were somehow both crude and graceful, conveying a strange sense of age. I ran my fingers over the cover. It was cool to the touch and a little worn, but there didn't seem to be anything otherworldly about the book.

I tucked *The Gates of Avalon* under one arm and led Kalen into the penthouse's living room again. If I was going to get Kalen out of here, I needed to get that coat back over his wings. I found the heap of leather and threw it around his shoulders.

Kalen's handcuffs rattled and I grabbed his wrist, yanking his hands up where I could see them. Was he trying to break out of the cuffs? Kalen was doubly powerless in the penthouse and with iron against his skin. He was still an expert thief, though, and I suspected that ten seconds alone was all he needed to slip free. But Kalen wasn't trying to escape my handcuffs – he was just shaking so hard that the metal clattered.

"If you're so scared of this guy, then why the hell did you take the job?" I asked.

"He's not the kind of man one says *no* to," Kalen answered in a low voice. "We don't have long, Lily. He'll be here as soon as the sun sets."

"Right," I said. "Let's get you out of here."

Deep shadows were already filling the hotel room. I made sure *The Gates of Avalon* was secure under my arm and hauled Kalen toward the exit. I grabbed the handle and twisted, opening the door. Across the polished mosaic foyer, the elevator was sliding open. The bellman who had brought me up just a few minutes ago sat slumped in the corner of the open elevator, eyes cloudy and a rictus smile stretched across his face. Blood ran from his nose and ears.

Kalen wrenched himself away with a hiss as something dark slid out of the elevator. It moved with a liquid grace that hurt to watch. The shape was tall and as black as the deepest midnight. There were suggestions of long, lean limbs and flowing raven hair that swirled as though in a strong wind, but I didn't feel the faintest stir of air. The silhouette was blank of features, like it had been sliced out of reality. The only detail I could make out was a pair of glowing golden eyes that burned like fire. And they looked right at me.

"What the hell is that thing?" I shouted.

Kalen didn't answer. The faceless shadow strode slowly across the foyer with unearthly grace. The city nightlight streaming in through the window dimmed and died. Kalen staggered back with a cry. I couldn't spare a glance for him.

I yanked the nine-millimeter from my belt. I still held the book and couldn't brace my gun hand, but the silhouette was close enough that I didn't think precision was going to matter much. I pulled the trigger and my shot thundered. The gun's slide worked back and then forward again. An empty brass shell tumbled up through the air and then down onto the priceless carpet.

The shadow kept coming, not even slowing down. My bullet didn't draw blood or even pass straight through to crack against the far wall. It just... vanished, disappearing into the blackness of the silhouette as though down a hole.

"Oh, shit," I said.

"Lily, give him the book!" Kalen hissed from behind me.

I jammed the gun back into my belt and held up *The Gates of Avalon*. For a moment, I really considered hurling the book toward the shadow and then throwing the door shut. Had this been Kalen's plan? But I wasn't ready to give up the book that easily. Besides, where was there to run?

The shadow narrowed burning golden eyes at me. One feature-less black hand rose, reaching out. I pulled *The Gates of Avalon* tight to my chest.

"Go fuck yourself," I said. "This doesn't belong to you."

Kalen's faceless buyer moved so fast that all I saw was a streak of shadow hurtling toward me. I jumped back and the darkness slammed into the open door, against the wards.

There was a crash of sound. Or a sucking absence of sound... I wasn't sure which, but it left my ears aching. The entire penthouse shivered and rang like a struck bell. All around me, strange lines and glyphs flared all across the walls and floor, even through the empty air. They flashed with blue-white power like bolts of light-ning, and died just as quickly. The lights in the penthouse flickered and went out.

I stumbled and fell, nearly dropping *The Gates of Avalon*. In the doorway, the shadow had shattered, but wasn't gone. Graceful black tendrils swirled like ink in water around those scorching eyes. What the hell was it?

I jumped to my feet and spun to find Kalen crouching, slipping one slender hand free of his iron-banded cuffs.

"Hey!" I shouted. "What the hell do you think you're doing?"

"He's burned out the wards," Kalen panted. "He's too powerful. I have to get out of here."

I grabbed the dangling end of the handcuffs and was shocked to feel the metal dent under my fingers. Kalen was right. My strength was back. The wards were broken. I couldn't even guess how much power that must have taken.

I yanked Kalen close. It was a lot easier now. He didn't fall, but the leather coat slid off his shoulders again. Kalen's long wings quivered, making sounds like rasping autumn leaves.

Kalen closed his eyes. "King and Queen protect me."

"Until I get you back to the College," I said, "that's *my* job."

I searched desperately around the penthouse. The only exit was the door, where the swirling, bright-eyed black shadow was reforming, growing more solid by the second. Night itself was coming for us. Sweat cut cold, jagged lines down my spine. I hauled Kalen up to his feet and slapped the open bracelet of the handcuffs around my wrist.

"We're getting out of here together, Kalen," I said. "Do those wings still work when you're wearing iron?"

Some of the old pride and arrogance flared in Kalen's shining indigo eyes.

"Of course," the fairy said, but the twilight spark faded a little. "Though without my magic, it's more gliding than flying."

"Good enough. Hold this."

I shoved *The Gates of Avalon* into Kalen's hands and pulled him toward the nearest window. The sparkling sunlight on the bay was the only light left in the penthouse. I clenched my fist and hoped that *all* of the College's wards were burned out or I was going to break my fucking hand.

I punched the glass. It was thick, sturdy stuff this high up, but my hand slammed through. Pieces of glass like ice cubes sprayed from the window and wind whistled through the gap. Hot blood ran from my knuckles, where the glass had torn up strips of skin. But I figured that was a lot better than losing all of it to the thing coalescing in the door. The darkness had limbs again and that long, streaming black hair. It lowered its head, fixing its burning gaze on me.

"Take these off," Kalen shouted over the wind howling through the broken window. "I can teleport us out of here!"

"Teleport yourself, you mean." I grabbed onto the edge of the hole and yanked. The entire laminated pane of glass snapped and popped free of the window frame. "Not a chance, Kalen. Now get ready to jump!"

I flung the broken sheet of glass aside. It bounced across the floor and landed against the expensive couch. Kalen pulled on the handcuffs chaining us together. The air in the room was growing warmer. Strange, I thought absently. I would have expected colder. That seemed to be standard for the scary night-type monsters. But every breath was warmer than the last and tingled electrically in my breast.

The golden-eyed shadow strode through the door and into the penthouse. I smelled something sweet, sharp. Enticing. My heart pounded so hard I couldn't hear anything else. Even the howl of wind was muted by that racing red drumbeat. I heaved Kalen toward the empty window.

"Don't you let go of that fucking book!" I shouted.

If Kalen answered, I never heard him.

We jumped.

Wind shrieked around us and I clung to Kalen's shoulder as his iridescent wings unfurled like pulled parachutes. They caught the sunlight like otherworldly stained glass and then beat as hard as Kalen could manage. I couldn't hear them, but I felt the fairy's wings vibrating as they fought to keep us aloft.

We half flew, half fell toward the city below. The nearest rooftop was at least ten stories below. A distance we were closing alarmingly quickly. Kalen's whole body shuddered as he struggled to fly and hold *The Gates of Avalon* clutched against his chest. Sweat poured down his skin, drenching his shirt with the effort. Another tailored silk shirt ruined.

I craned my neck to look up at the window. The shadow stood in the empty frame, staring after us. I saw no sign of wings or anything else that would let him fly. We were safe, weren't we?

But the dark shape stepped up to the edge of the window and didn't hesitate. It leapt out and fell toward us.

"Kalen," I screamed. "Move your ass!"

The fairy twisted, turning to look, just before the shade slammed into us. It may have been a shadow – I could even dimly see the hotel through the silhouetted body – but he was solid enough that we began to plummet together in a wild spiraling corkscrew toward the street far below.

Dark fingers seized at me, one hand around my wrist and the other tangled into my long hair. I struggled to maintain my hold on Kalen, but then I was falling... I screamed as I dropped through the air, but only a few feet before I was jerked to a stop by the handcuffs. My shoulder popped and something inside it snapped like a rubber band. My weight yanked Kalen's arm down and I hung from him like a panicking spider on a thread of silk. Fresh blood ran over my wrist where the steel and iron bit into my skin, but the handcuffs held.

I thanked every deity in creation that I always invested in good quality handcuffs. Screw the cheap fuzzy ones.

"Lily," Kalen groaned. "I... I can't..."

The fairy thief gasped and beat his iridescent wings, but we were still dropping. The shadow clung to me. My fall had not dislodged it. Whatever this thing was, he was every bit as strong as me. Maybe stronger. I shoved and punched with my free arm, trying to throw off the shadow. It hadn't uttered a single word or made a sound since all of this began. My hand impacted something hard enough to jolt my bones, but the shadow was strangely yielding. Not soft, but somehow insubstantial.

Kalen's sleek body streamed with sweat. Rooftops and then windows raced past and the wind whipped my hair. He wobbled and we arced in the direction of the bay. No, the book...!

But then tears stung my eyes as we tumbled toward the water. The fading sunset gleamed across the quicksilver surface of the bay, blazing orange and red light. The shadow slithering up me froze, twisted and then... was gone, darkness shattered by the last glow of daylight.

There was no time to savor our strange victory. I slammed down like a ton of bricks on wet concrete. My right leg and several ribs snapped. Pain knifed through my body, but I managed to pull Kalen on top of me, cushioning his fall. More pain, but at least we were on solid ground again. On the back dock of one of the restaurants beside the Hotel Marquis, next to a dented and corroded trash bin, to be precise.

After a moment, Kalen rolled off me. My ribs and shoulder were healing swiftly, but Kalen wheezed and a trickle of blood ran from one high cheekbone. Groaning, I sat up and pulled *The Gates of Avalon* from his numb, trembling hands. I kissed the fairy's clean cheek.

"Good job," I panted.

Kalen sat up beside me and drew a deep breath that shook no less now than it had up in the penthouse.

"That... wasn't so bad. Just a shadow," I told him. "Nothing to be afraid of,"

"I'm not afraid of the shadow," said Kalen. "I'm afraid of what cast it."

Chapter EIGHT

Kalen really had done an excellent job, so it wasn't until early the next morning when I finally delivered him to the College. We had returned to my place to clean up and I made good on my promise to have some fun with the handcuffs, though I kept a close eye on Kalen to make sure that he didn't slip out of them again. Our late-night celebration of being alive had the added benefit of powering me enough to finish healing up the gashes left by our dive through the hotel window and the broken bones from the landing. Also to run down Kalen twice when he thought I was distracted by a mouthful of sweet fairy spunk.

Now Kalen and I waited in Dresden Hall. The ivy-covered old manor was the central building of the College, the sprawling center of study for the American order of Merlinic wizards. We were in the conference room that they call the *council chamber*. But I knew a fucking conference room when I saw it, even if the table was a big circular stone one engraved with runes that I couldn't read.

One of the wizards had carefully swapped out Kalen's handcuffs for a pair of inscribed iron manacles. The fairy stared at me sullenly, sexy even as he pouted. But I stood before the High Magus himself. He towered over me in stately antique black and silver robes. His face was carved with lines that seemed far too deep for his age. Vincent Myrdon was probably only in his early fifties, but his hair and trimmed goatee were almost entirely gray, with only a few streaks of darker color left. But the High Magus actually smiled as I held out the book.

"*The Gates of Avalon*," I announced, handing over the tome with far less gravity than Vincent accepted it. "Along with its temporary owner, Kalen Silverwind, fairy thief extraordinaire."

Kalen perked up a bit at the compliment and winked at me. I winked back. Vincent ran his fingers over the aged leather book cover and breathed out a sigh. I had flipped through a couple of pages the night before, in between bouts with Kalen, but I couldn't read any of it.

Vincent placed *The Gates of Avalon* carefully on the circular stone table. "You have the gratitude of the Castle and the College, Lilith."

"And of Avalon itself," said another voice, accented and lovely.

Evaine stood beside Vincent, though I hadn't seen her arrive. She wore a pristine white suit over a blue blouse. My teacher's pale ringlets were pulled up into a long ponytail that cascaded like a waterfall down her back.

She smiled at me. When I glanced through *The Gates of Avalon*, I may not have understood the words, but there were pictures, too. Or *illuminations* might have been the correct term. One of them showed a tall, long-haired woman in a silver gown standing on the surface of a lake. I swear she looked just like Evaine.

"Did you learn anything about who hired Kalen?" she asked.

"No," I admitted. "Some kind of... shadow came to collect the book. It vanished when we fell into the sunlight."

Vincent wrenched his attention up from *The Gates of Avalon* and turned his gaze on me. "Not many creatures can cast a shadow powerful enough to violate and destroy our wards. We must find out who did this. And why."

"Did Kalen tell you anything about this shadow?" Evaine asked.

I shook my head. "I tried to get more out of him, but no luck. And I used all of my most persuasive arguments, too."

"I suspect we will encounter Kalen's employer again," Vincent said. "But while the book remains here at the College, it will be under our best and fiercest protections. *The Gates of Avalon* will not be left unattended again."

"Why is that book so important?" I asked.

Vincent and Evaine exchanged a look I couldn't quite interpret.

"Among other things, it details the founding of the Castle by Merlin after the fall of Camelot," said the High Magus.

"The book also has much to do with the demons. After all, Merlin himself was a cambion," Evaine reminded me with another smile. "Like you. His father was a lust demon who fell in love with a human."

"Most importantly," Vincent went on quickly, "Merlin's book speaks of the Seal of Avalon."

"The what now?" I asked.

"The barrier – or *gate*, as it's known in the old parlance – was created by Merlin to seal the Nether, the realm of demons," said Vincent. He touched the cover of the book again, almost reverently. "The Seal was arguably Merlin's greatest accomplishment. Without it, mankind would never have risen from the Dark Ages. It protects our world against the depredations of–"

I could tell he only barely stopped himself from saying *your kind*. Just like I only barely stopped myself from kicking the High Magus right in his magical balls.

"–of succubae and other demons who would prey upon humanity," Vincent said with the faintest flush. He cleared his throat and continued. "Now they can only be summoned from the Nether by incantations taught to us by Merlin himself."

At this, the wizard cast another look at Evaine, who regarded him steadily. There was more to this story than they were telling me

– or wanted to discuss in front of Kalen – but then Dorian appeared in the entrance of the council chamber-slash-conference room.

The short old wizard carried a bundle of fabric that obviously weighed even more than the sizable *Gates of Avalon*. It clanked impressively when he sat it down on the table. Dorian unfolded the cloth covering to display the unmistakable sheen of gold bars.

Transmuting base metals into gold was one of the Merlinic mages' early achievements, but one kept wisely and carefully under control. Imagine the economic crash a few years ago times a thousand if that shit ever got out. It was easy enough to pay me and the other bounty hunters this way, though, and pay us well. It was more of a pain in the ass than direct deposit, but an inconvenience I was willing to deal with.

Hashtag magic-world problems.

"It's going for twelve hundred an ounce right now," Dorian said. "So after cleanup fees for the Hotel Marquis, you've got a little over a million dollars there."

Nice. I swept the gold bars into a sturdy sack I carried around for just this purpose. I would have kissed Dorian on his lined old cheek – and often did – but his boss was standing only a couple yards away. I didn't mind, but Dorian might.

"Thanks," I said instead. "What about the guy in the elevator? Is he okay?"

Dorian shook his head. "He died, I'm sad to say. By the time our people arrived, it was too late. His heart burst."

I sighed and turned to Kalen, who still waited to be hauled off to wherever the mages kept their prisoners.

"I suggest you tell them what they want to know," I said. "The College can protect you."

Kalen raised one elegant indigo eyebrow and didn't look entirely convinced. "One human is already dead, Lily. If I sell out my employer, do you really believe that even the College can keep me safe? No, I think I'll just wait this one out."

I shrugged. "See you around?"

"I'd like that," Kalen said with a grin.

"Maybe you get conjugal visits," I suggested.

Kalen winked and Vincent scowled dangerously. I laughed and hefted the bag up over my shoulder. I walked toward the door, my payday clinking musically with every step. But when I turned back to say goodbye to Evaine, she was gone.

LILY QUINN BOOK #3

The Beast WITHIN

Chapter ONE

I sat on the front of my car. The engine was still warm beneath me and I drummed my fingers on the hood. Every minute spent waiting put my target one step further ahead and me one step behind the rest of the bounty hunters.

I stared at the graffiti scrawled across the back of Golden Touch Auto, trying to bore through the concrete wall by pure force of will. That's not one of my powers, though. Maybe some other hunter has a spell for seeing through foot-thick reinforced concrete, but not me. Still, I had my own sort of magic. Being the half-demon daughter of a succubus meant that sex gave me inhuman strength, speed, healing and senses. A good fuck might make your day, but it turns me into a damned superhero.

Lily Quinn, at your service.

It felt like I was stuck there forever, each second creeping by like waiting for porn to buffer over a bad internet connection. But my phone assured me that only six minutes had passed before Max came jogging out through the back door of the garage and waved.

I've known Maxwell Ferguson since I was five years old. He lived two doors down from one of my foster families and was my first real friend. When that round of parents decided I was too much of a pain in the ass to keep – that sounds bitter, I know, but I honestly don't blame them – Max begged his own mother and father to adopt me. But they already had three sons and too many bills, so I moved on through the foster system.

Max and I remained close, though, and even after all these years, he's still my best friend in the whole world. He's always been there for me, no matter what I need. It's just a bonus that what I need is usually fun.

I stretched out across the warm hood of my i10 and tried not to look impatient. As Max came closer, wiping damp hands off on a paper towel, I spread my legs beneath my skirt. His stride became more like a stagger as he stared.

"Wow, Lil," Max said. "Are those even underwear? I've seen tea bags with more cloth."

"Cute. And true. Do you have time to come back to my place?" I asked.

Max's big heart hasn't changed since we were kids, but the rest of him has grown up quite a bit. He's never been a small guy, but now Max is over six feet of muscle, with sandy blond hair and dark blue eyes.

"My place is closer," he said.

"Even better." I sat up and hooked my fingers through Max's belt, pulling him in close to me. The front of his well-worn jeans were already impressively tented. "Ready to go?"

Max gulped and looked back over his shoulder toward the auto shop. "Uh, sure."

"Is it okay with your boss?" I asked.

"Sam won't even notice. Just let me grab some seat covers so I don't ruin your upholstery."

I slid my hand down to caress the growing hardness between Max's legs.

"Forget that," I whispered into his ear. "I can have the seats cleaned later. I want you *now*."

Grease-smudged is a good look on Max and the insistent heat inside me was turning swiftly into something deeper, wetter and in desperate need of being filled. If Max didn't get in the car pretty damned fast, he was going to end up getting fucked in the GTA parking lot. Again.

"You know that I'm going to be the one cleaning your upholstery," Max pointed out with a dimpled smile. "I'm the only guy you let work on your cars."

I winked. "Your hands are the only ones I want on my engine."

The same wasn't quite true of my body, but Max was my go-to guy when I needed a lot of power for a job. He knows what I like and always makes time to do it right. Plus, he puts out an unbelievable amount of sexual energy for me. If Merlin's seal wasn't keeping all of the full-blooded demons locked up in their own world, Max would have been a gold mine for succubae. A gold mine of cock. A cock mine...?

Obviously, I wasn't really thinking with my head anymore. I slid down off of the i10's gleaming hood and then towed Max by his belt. I led him to the passenger-side door and Max obediently climbed into my car.

"You're in a hurry," he said.

"A bit," I admitted.

"Let's go, then."

He buckled up as I slid behind the wheel, slammed the i10 into gear and peeled out of the GTA parking lot. We roared out onto Bayfront Boulevard and west toward Carver Street.

"You've got a new bounty, right?" asked Max. He glanced at my dashboard. "And to judge by how fast you're driving, it must be big. Or dangerous?"

"Both," I said. I threw the car into overdrive and shot past a line of trucks laboring their way up a steep hill.

"What are you after? Is this about that... shadow thing you saw at the Hotel Marquis last month?"

There was concern in Max's voice. Remember what I told you about his family? Max grew up helping his overworked parents raise his two younger brothers, and he did a good job of it. Living down in Southport, that often meant being protective, and even though Max never ended up my legal brother – which would have been pretty awkward about now – he's always included me in that protection. Which is cute... As big and strong as Max is, when I'm all charged up, I can bench press not only him but the cars that he works on, too. I don't need protection.

"No," I said. "The College still doesn't know anything about the guy who hired Kalen. Or if they do, they're not telling me. This job is something else."

"What then?"

"There's a werewolf in the city."

"And that's... bad?"

I nodded. "Werewolf hunts in high-density urban places get messy and complicated real fast. Most of the time, they attack rural areas, but here in the city, there are a lot more potential victims and witnesses."

"Shit," said Max.

"Yeah," I agreed. "So the College is offering a ton of gold to get this thing done. The bounty is big, but so is the competition. Especially now. The werewolf killed one of the College hunters."

Fortunately for everyone who wanted to keep their pants on, I was the only half-succubus in the city. Or in the entire world, as far as I knew. But I wasn't the only monster hunter. The College was a secret magical club – though they prefer the term *order* – of wizards. I freelance for the College, but they had their own bounty hunters. The mages are a pretty close-knit lot, and with one of their number dead, things were getting personal.

"What are werewolves?" asked Max.

"Seriously? You need to watch more horror movies, Max," I said. "Half man, half wolf. All monster. You know, like *Teen Wolf*."

"Ha ha. You haven't had me so tied up in bed sheets that I've never turned on the television. But what are werewolves *really*?"

Poor Max. Poor, lucky Max. He had just one toe in the world of magic and knew only enough to realize how little he knew. But I was grateful to have someone to talk to about the crazy supernatural fuck-fest that is my life. The wizards and I maintain a sort of truce, but we're not exactly close.

And that's why my friendship with Max is risky. If the College ever found out how much he knew, how much I *told* him, they would wipe Max's memory to preserve their secrets. Life is stressful enough without the general public panicking over monsters.

"Remember what I told you after all of the *Gates of Avalon* stuff?" I asked. "About demons?"

Max nodded. "They can't enter our world without being summoned, right? That's the point of the seal Merlin made."

"Right. Well, that doesn't stop the bastards from trying to mess with us."

"Like giving their blood to a human to create a vampire," Max said. He really did pay attention, and my boy was a lot smarter than most people gave him credit for. "Is lycanthropy anything like that?"

"A little. Vampires are willing and deliberate servants to demons, but werewolves are just agents of chaos," I explained. "Their change is a demonic curse."

"Do they transform during the full moon?"

I shook my head. "Not really. See, demons are lords of certain passions, like fear, envy, rage and so on. Things can get crazy during the full moon, which sometimes leads to the transformation."

"Okay," said Max. "So what's the truth behind the myth?"

"The werewolf curse hits whenever any of those dark passions are stirred. The cursed human changes and then they rampage. It's bloody and people die. And if anyone actually manages to survive being mauled by a werewolf, then they contract the curse. That much the movies get right."

"And you are going to hunt this thing down," Max said with a frown.

"That's what they pay me the big bucks for."

I signaled – hey, I'm not a *completely* reckless and shitty driver – as I turned onto Carver Street. The neighborhood was cheap and run-down, full of cramped apartment buildings and outdated duplexes with weedy yards. The sidewalks were cracked and patches of colorless lichen grew up through the damp concrete.

"Are you in any danger of catching the curse, Lil?" Max asked.

"Me? No," I answered. "I'm already half demon. Demon blood and curses can't infect me. But werewolves have some really nasty teeth and claws. They're sharp and they can still kill me."

"Silver bullets?"

I nodded. "They work... more or less. Usually less."

There was a nine-millimeter automatic pistol in my bag in the back seat, already loaded with a full magazine of silver rounds. Silver could hurt a werewolf, but I had to hit a vital target with it. Your average werewolf was six hundred pounds of solid muscle, fur and pure demon-cursed death. Putting enough silver slugs into the right spot wasn't easy.

"But the College is paying even more if I can capture this werewolf alive," I told Max. "His condition *is* a curse. The guy probably doesn't even realize what he's doing."

"Do you know his name?"

"Not yet," I said.

"So what happens if you manage to catch this werewolf?"

"That's a big *if*," I said. "But if I pull it off, curses can be lifted. I gather that it's a long and complicated spell. They do it back at the College, in some sort of special lab or tower or something that I've never been allowed to visit."

"Neat. That there's a cure, I mean."

"Any other questions?" I asked.

"None that I can think of," said Max.

"Good."

I yanked the steering wheel into a sharp turn and my car screeched through a broken gate, into the parking lot of Max's apartment building. The complex was small and paint peeled from the siding – being a mechanic at a crappy chain garage didn't pay terribly well and rents in the city were criminal. I had offered to buy Max a better place more times than I could count, but he never took me up on it.

I parked the i10 and climbed out. It was probably worth more than all of the other cars in the lot combined and there was an even chance that my hubcaps would be gone by the time I was done with Max. So I grabbed the bag that contained my gun from the back seat. There was no way I wanted to risk some stupid kid walking off with *that*.

Enjoying the sight of Max's jeans hugging his firm ass, I followed him up a set of mossy concrete steps to the third story. When we reached his apartment, Max unlocked the door and held it open for me. Inside was a small studio, with a kitchenette about the size of a closet instead of a real kitchen.

Which I supposed made the tiny room across from it a bathroomette.

The same couch that Max had bought after moving out of his parent's house still sat against the wall, with a battered coffee table in front of it. There was a nice big queen-sized bed, too, that had been a half-selfish gift from me the previous Christmas. It didn't leave room for much else in the apartment, though.

"It's a little late for lunch and early for dinner, but do you want me to make you something to eat?" Max asked. "You're pretty much always hungry, Lil."

Max had taken home economics twice in high school. He made a mean casserole and no one teased him for it because he took auto shop, too. Well, that and he had the body of a Viking warlord. All three had come in handy for me over the years.

I dropped my gear bag down on the coffee table. Max's meals were about the only home-cooked food I ever ate, but that wasn't what I needed today.

"Sorry," I answered. "Can't wait. The other hunters are nipping at my heels. Especially Stefano. You know how he is about werewolves."

"No, not really," Max said. He smiled at me and I wanted to lick his dimples. "Never met him. But let's get you powered up and back out there."

Max closed the front door, locked it, and pulled me close against him. His fingers followed the line of my spine down to my waist. His hands were so big that they nearly touched. Max leaned in and gave me a long, deep kiss that still tasted like his spearmint toothpaste.

Max's desire began flowing into me, filling me with the sexual power that my half-succubus heritage craved. I was in a hurry, but I needed a lot of juice to take on a werewolf. Max knew better than to just bend me over the couch and slam out a quickie. Sure, he could get us both off in a few minutes if he wanted to, but this was about giving, and Max had a lifetime of practice with that.

I inhaled Max's breath and sighed it back into him. I reached up to feel out his shoulders, tracing the familiar lines of muscles along his arms and chest. Max picked me up around the waist and carried me across the approximately foot and a half of open space in his apartment to the bed.

Gently, he laid me back and unfastened my skirt, then inched it slowly down my legs, planting kisses all along the way. I stripped off my shirt and bra while Max pulled away my already damp little panties. When I was naked, I stretched out across his bed and breathed in his scent from the sheets. My stomach fluttered with warm butterflies as Max's cock grew swiftly harder and more pronounced in his jeans.

"Damn, Lil," he sighed. "You're so beautiful."

"So are you," I said. "So get your fine ass naked and fuck me."

Max smiled and showed me his dimples again. He yanked the red and yellow GTA shirt up over his head and tossed it aside. It landed in the kitchen sink.

As Max began unzipping his oil-stained jeans, my hand drifted down between my legs. My pussy was slick and hot beneath my fingers. I drew glistening lines along my spread thighs and belly while Max kicked off his work boots. When he straightened, his cock towered over me, long and thick. Just how I liked it.

"Come here, babe," I purred.

I hooked a wet, shiny finger at him. Max obediently joined me on the bed. He took my wrist in one hand and sucked my dripping finger clean with a hungry groan. Heat bloomed between my legs.

"Lil, I want to taste more of you," Max said in a husky whisper.

He moved down the bed until he could press his face between my parted thighs. A hot flush raced up my spine as Max traced his tongue over the wet lines I had drawn across my skin, following them in and in. Every moment waiting for Max's mouth to reach my slit was agony and I found myself raising my hips and moaning.

"God, Max," I panted. "Lick my pussy!"

He's never once said *no* to that. Max dove in, his jaw slightly rough with a day's stubble. He kissed me – not a delicate kiss, but a deep, passionate dance of his tongue across my silky labia and then inside. Max cupped my ass and held me close. His breath was soft and warm against my sensitive flesh. It was only seconds before I was shaking on his bed. My hands twisted in the sheets and my pulse raced.

Max sucked my little pink clit into his mouth and teased it with his tongue until a hard knot of pleasure tightened inside me. He reached up to cradle my breasts in his hands and squeezed gently. Max's fingers found my nipples and tugged them quickly to hardened rosebud points. Jagged lightning bolts of sensation shot through my body and the searing ball of bliss between my legs felt too much, too big to contain inside me.

"Yes, Max," I cried. "Oh fuck, yes!"

I heard voices next door talking about heart medication. Max's neighbor on the other side cranked up her soap operas, trying to drown us out. But then I could barely hear anything at all – sex-powered super-hearing be damned. My senses, my whole reality, was ecstasy. I felt only pleasure, tasted and smelled only delight.

"Fuck me now," I moaned. "Put your big dick inside me."

I grabbed Max by the arm and hauled him up the bed, on top of me. Strengthened by the power he had already given me, I moved Max as easily as he had picked me up before. I reached between us and found his cock as hard as steel, and as hot as if just taken from a forge. I put my other arm around Max's neck, pulled him down to me and kissed him.

Max ran his tongue over my lips as the head of his dick pressed between my legs. His hips rolled forward and his cock slowly pierced me. Max eased his tongue into my mouth to twine with mine at the same gentle pace. My back arched and I wrapped my legs around Max's waist as he worked himself deeper into my body. I dug my heels into his buttocks and crushed my lips to his, un-willing and unable to take it slow. He so was hot and huge inside of me.

"Fuck, Lil," Max gasped against my mouth. "You feel amazing."

I wanted to tell him the same, but his hard cock filled and stretched me so gloriously that I couldn't seem to take a proper breath. Max drew back and slammed into me again, driving deep into my pussy. My world contracted down to Max's pounding cock and his strong hands on my breasts – a rose blooming in reverse until everything was a tight bud of furled, red velvet sensation.

Finally, I tore my lips from Max's and managed to moan out a few words.

"Fuck my ass!"

Werewolves were serious business and I would burn through a lot of power taking one on. I needed Max's cock in every hole. Plus, he's always been a fan of my ass and my panted demand drove a spike of his molten lust into me, enough to make me gasp.

Max pulled himself free of my gripping thighs and I braced my feet against his broad shoulders. He eased his thick cock out of my pussy and I whimpered at its absence. Wetness ran from inside me, dripping down the cleft of my ass. Max took hold of my ankles, one in each hand, and planted small kisses along my feet that tickled the arches.

"Do you want it back?" he asked.

"Yes!"

"In your pussy or up your ass?"

Max released one ankle and grabbed the base of his slippery cock. He touched the swollen head to my slit, then against the tight pink of my ass. I writhed agonizingly in Max's bed. I wanted him in both, but every moment of indecision was another second that my aching body remained empty. I reached down and slapped Max's thigh.

"Fuck my ass," I told him.

Max pushed my legs back. Good thing I'm flexible. He bowed his head and his tongue probed between the cheeks of my ass. Max worked me until he was sure I was wet and ready, his thumbs spreading slick pussy juices over the sensitive hole. I grabbed the sheets again and shoved my ass up at Max. I couldn't help the slutty whimpering noises I made and didn't really want to.

After what seemed like an eternity of licking and moaning, Max sat up on his heels between my legs once more. I slid my feet up over his shoulders.

"Fill my ass, Max!" I begged.

"Yes, Lil," Max breathed. There was another powerful surge of searing sexual energy from him.

Max nuzzled his cock against the clenched pink of my asshole and pushed slowly. My ass was well practiced, but taking a dick back there is never easy. It always felt amazing, though, as Max speared the first slippery inch of himself through, forcing himself into me. My taut muscular opening clamped down reflexively at the invasion and Max grunted.

"Fuck, Lil. Do you want me to stop?" he asked.

"Don't you dare," I gasped. "Give me more!"

Max pressed through my tightness and I urged him on with fingernails dug into his flanks that left red marks. The muscles of my ass tensed and rippled as Max sheathed himself in me. When I had taken his entire length, I came hard, milking Max's dick deep inside my body. He responded instantly and passionately, gripping my hips and pounding me in earnest. Sweat darkened his hair. Max was impaled inside me to the balls, his flexing thighs slamming into my buttocks with every thrust. He pulled out until the crown of his cock caught the tight ring of my anus and then hammered into me once more.

My pussy was streaming juices that drenched Max's shaft every time he withdrew and made sloppy, wet sounds when he pounded back into my ass. Through the sweet haze of blazing sensation – and driven on by it – I felt Max's cock growing hotter and thicker inside me. Faster and faster, closer and closer to the dizzying peak of pleasure.

"Max," I moaned. "Do it! Pour your cum into me!"

"Yes, Lil. Yes!" he groaned, almost as though in pain.

Max buried himself in my ass, his thighs trembling against my backside. He pressed harder and harder as molten heat gushed into me. Just as I had asked, Max filled me. He shot his load deep inside my ass and forced a wild, primal scream of pleasure up from my throat.

Shaking and sweating, Max collapsed beside me on the bed. His dick popped free of my ass as he rolled down to the mattress and thick, sticky cum oozed from my body. Max nuzzled against the side of my neck and draped an arm across my waist.

"That was amazing," he whispered.

"Yeah, you were," I told him. I sat up and flexed. Power coursed through my muscles. I felt ready to tear a truck in half. "Have you been practicing?"

Max shook his head. I punched him in the shoulder. Carefully.

"You should get yourself one of those girlfriends I've heard so much about," I said. "It's not right that I'm the only one who gets to cum like that. You're going to make some girl real happy someday."

Max laughed. "Thanks."

I had not forgotten the promise that I made to myself about having Max in every hole. He still owed on that. His cock remained long and hard where it lay against his firm stomach. I slid down through the tangle of damp sheets until I could straddle Max's legs and ran one finger along his length. His silky skin was wet with his cum and mine. I sucked my finger into my mouth and licked it all clean.

"We taste wonderful," I said.

Max gasped down a deep breath as I went to work on his dripping cock between my lips, tasting the muskiness of his semen and my tangier flavor. I licked every inch, from crown to balls, and savored it all. Heat rushed quickly into Max's dick once more. It's as reliable as the rest of him.

He threaded his fingers through my bright red hair and brushed it back from my face. I looked up at Max through my eyelashes as I sucked at the head of his slippery wet cock. I held his gaze, making him watch my pink lips wrapped around his dick. I cupped his balls in one hand and they grew swiftly tight in my grasp. Max couldn't stop himself.

"Lil, I'm going to–"

Max couldn't even finish the warning. His fingers tightened in my hair and his whole body went rigid. Hot streamers of cum flew into my open mouth and pooled on my tongue. I drank it down like cream again and again until the final drops oozed across my lips. Slowly, I sucked every one of them from Max.

I sat up, smacking my lips and grinning. I was full to the brim with Max's cum and, more importantly, the surging power of his lust. Enough, I hoped, to take on a werewolf.

"Damn, Lil," Max said. He sat and offered me a contented smile. "You're amazing. Was that enough? Was it what you needed?"

"Yeah. I'm ready to kick some furry werewolf butt now."

"Are you sure you can't stay for dinner?" asked Max. "You never eat anything but shitty takeout."

I stood and picked up my bag from the coffee table. "Sorry. I've got to get to work."

Max nodded and spanked my bare ass. "Alright, Lil. You go catch that werewolf."

Chapter TWO

I changed clothes at Max's place. My miniskirt and high heels weren't precisely great werewolf-hunting gear, so I swapped it out for cargo pants and a matching shirt of tight, breathable black mesh. Tight not because it looked good – which it did, by the way – but so that there was no loose cloth to snag on anything. I laced up a pair of sturdy boots and finally strapped a gun holster to my thigh.

Were you expecting a leather catsuit? Let me tell you something: I look sexy as fuck in those, but it takes forever to put one on. And even longer to take off, especially if you've been sweating at all. When this girl wants to get naked, she doesn't like to wait.

But I did sling a long leather coat over my badass ensemble – I didn't really feel like getting into another open-carry debate with the cops. I had permits for all of my guns, of course, but I still didn't like talking to the police if I didn't have to. It can be hard to explain why I've got pockets full of vampiric ashes or iron handcuffs without coming off just a *bit* odd.

"Be careful, Lil," Max said.

He handed me the knife I had set down on the kitchen counter. I drew it and checked the blade. Silver is too brittle to make knives out of and can't hold an edge worth shit, so the surface of my knife was blue-gray with a silver-based coating. I turned it toward the light and inspected the edge. The silver finish was prone to flaking, but my blade looked fine.

Satisfied, I sheathed the knife and stuck it in my boot. I smiled at Max.

"You don't need to worry about me," I told him. "I've got a magazine full of silver bullets and thanks to your mad sex skills, I can knock an elephant on its ass."

Speaking of ass, Max was still naked. I gave his muscular flank a sharp swat. He jumped and laughed nervously.

"Just... be careful, Lil," he said.

I left Max at his place – he assured me that he could get back to Golden Touch Auto on his own – and drove out to Gates Park. I stopped at a coffee cart in the north end of the park. It was four in the afternoon, but in my line of work, it's never too late in the day for an espresso.

While I waited for my drink, I pulled out my cell phone and opened up Fuzz Radio, a police scanner app. It was the best three bucks I ever spent. I slipped in a Bluetooth earpiece so everybody else in line didn't have to listen to the stream of police codes.

The old man behind the coffee kiosk handed me a red paper cup decorated with snowflakes. It never snow here in the city, even in December, but frigid winter wind off the bay whipped steam up from my cup. It smelled of sea salt and strong coffee. I paid and dropped a sizable tip into the jar, then carried my espresso down the street, clasping its warmth between my hands.

I sat on the curb beside a long hill of sandy grass that sloped away toward the gray ocean. The werewolf attacks had all been in or around Gates Park. Tor Lee had died just a few blocks from here, gutted and left floating in the cold sea. Poor bastard.

Tor had been a competent hunter and a good wizard, as far as I knew. We weren't exactly friends, but I wasn't glad to find out the guy was dead. And if my werewolf could take down a trained hunter so easily, that didn't bode well for the surfers and tourists that visited the park every day.

Even now, joggers bounced past me through the park, wearing tiny shorts and colorful sweatbands in utter defiance of the winter chill. They had no idea what horrors lurked in the shadows of their own city.

The College worked hard and cast a lot of memory charms to make sure that humanity could sleep soundly, believing that other humans were the worst threat they faced. If the police knew what was happening, could the College evacuate Gates Park? Would it matter? Werewolves were fast and terribly skilled predators, furiously fueled and driven by their demonic curse. Was there even a safe evacuation radius?

Well, if I could catch my werewolf and kick his furry ass all the way back to the College, then it wouldn't matter. I just had to find the monster. So I sipped my coffee and listened to Fuzz Radio for a few hours.

There were some 390 police codes, 507s and a 311. I had to look up the numbers. How did anyone get this shit done before smartphones and the internet? 390 was the police code for a drunk causing trouble. A 507 was a public nuisance, and 311 was indecent exposure. I finished my coffee and laughed as the 311 report escalated to a 288 – lewd conduct.

As the sun set and thick, wet gray fog rose up off the bay, an officer was suddenly shouting into my ear and I almost fell off the curb. I swore and turned down the volume.

"Dispatch, this is William 117, we have a 419!" cried a panicked male voice. "Repeat 419 and 444 at Gates Park south of the Bridge."

Hastily, I punched up the browser window and checked the police codes: human body and officer-involved shooting. Shit.

"Copy, William 117," said the dispatcher. "Backup is en route to your location. Can you describe the suspect?"

"It's a... a thing! I don't know," shouted the cop on the other end. His voice was high and sharp with panic. "Some kind of monster! It's heading south from Bridge Street."

"Please confirm, William 117. Did... did you say *monster*?"

They were playing my song in double time, but Bridge Street was too far away to run. Not without attracting a lot of attention with my sex-powered speed, at least. There were already going to be a lot of magical memory wipes before this hunt was over without me sprinting past witnesses at highway speeds. So I bolted back to my car, flung my empty coffee cup into the passenger seat, and then swerved out into the evening traffic pouring across the bay.

I raced my i10 between a minivan and mud-spattered pickup truck that didn't have its lights on, then made an illegal left turn down The Parkway: a narrow, curving road that winds a convoluted scenic route along the coast. To a chorus of honking and shouting from other vehicles, I floored it and the engine purred. The i10 was a high-performance machine and Max kept the sports car in perfect condition. It performed.

Gates Park was sinking quickly into darkness. The sun hadn't entirely set yet, but its glow was obscured to a flat silver disk by the thick evening fog. I caught sight of a huge, long-limbed shadow loping through the park just before it vanished into a stand of redwood trees. I slammed on the brakes and skidded to a stop beside the road – also illegally, but so what?

I jumped out of my car. The werewolf was out there. But so were humans. I inhaled the cold, wet air, sorting through the smells of the park with my superhuman demonic senses. Sea grass, salt water and decaying kelp, a trash can that needed emptying and... sex. I *knew* that smell. There was another indecent exposure turning into lewd conduct nearby.

Even pumped up on the power of Max's magnificent cock – he should have trademarked that thing – I still couldn't smell the werewolf. Not through the overlapping odors of what had to be thousands of dogs and their shit. Which damp fur and musk scent was my target?

But the sex… That hot, salty-sweet scent of hormones and human lust. If I could smell it, so could the werewolf. I breathed it in again and followed, sprinting through the mist. This part of Gates Park was mostly grass and jogging trails, dotted with patches of coastal ferns and redwoods. Very scenic during the day, but creepy and hard to navigate once the dark fog rolled in.

I leapt over a line of rusting trash cans. The smells of sex were strong now, but then there was something sharper. Fear. Was I too late…? A girl screamed and a boy's voice joined in, just as high and hysterical. Damn it.

"Hey!" I shouted.

I ran through a copse of towering redwoods and burst out onto one of the jogging trails. A pair of teenagers cowered behind a concrete bench, screaming and scrambling. The boy clutched his pants over his crotch and the girl was down to her bra and disheveled skirt. Both had gone pale and were trying to back away on shaking legs, staring in uncomprehending horror at the inhuman silhouette looming over them.

The werewolf was a nine-foot-tall nightmare of sleek fur and hard muscle. His coat was dark gray that lightened a shade across his chest and stomach. There were long arms and legs corded with muscle, twitching charcoal-colored ears, a bristling tail and pale brown-golden eyes that reminded me a little of my own. Those eyes were fixed on the petrified teens. Lips peeled back from a muzzle full of long, sharp white teeth that shone like bone daggers in the fading glow of sunset.

"Move!" I shouted at the teenagers. "Get the hell out of here!"

They were trying, but the kids were terrified and unsteady. I could pull my gun and put a few bullets in the werewolf, but unless I fired most of the magazine into his heart or head, it wasn't going to be enough. And shooting on the run – especially sprinting as fast as

I do – does bad things to your aim. It might take a whole load of silver bullets to stop a werewolf, but just one would fuck up either of the teenagers if I missed.

So I yanked my knife from its sheath and threw myself at the werewolf. He spun with inhuman speed and raked three-inch claws through the air. I was shorter, smaller, and just as fast. I slid beneath the claws and slashed back. My knife caught and sliced along the werewolf's thick forearm. The silvered blade sizzled as I cut into his thick gray fur. The monster howled in pain and fury.

I had his attention now. The two teenagers were finally on their feet and bolting away through the swirling fog. The werewolf snarled after them, but I jumped at him again, forcing the monster to turn his bright eyes on me once more. His snarl deepened into a bone-rattling growl of unearthly thunder.

My knife wasn't going to kill the werewolf, not unless I managed to put it through his eye or up into his heart, but I still hoped to take the wolf alive. Somehow. This monster was just some poor human inflicted with a demonic curse. But first, I *had* to slow him down.

The werewolf had other plans, though, that seemed to involve gutting me like a fish. He crouched and swung a massive paw at me, scythe-like talons extended. I hurled myself to the right, just fast enough to avoid the claws, but the werewolf's elbow caught me in the side and one of my ribs crunched under the impact. I grunted in pain and stabbed out again. A few inches of silvered blade sank into the werewolf's hip. By the time I wrenched it free, the wound was already starting to close. Silver slowed the healing process, but it was damned near impossible to stop.

I jumped over a lunging snap of his teeth and managed to tear a deeper cut across the werewolf's broad chest. Blood dappled the paler gray fur, but not much and not for long before his cursed body began to regenerate again. The werewolf's answer was a savage kick that seared four lines of blazing agony along my back and sent me flying across the jogging trail.

I slammed into the bench where the teenagers had been hiding hard enough to smash through the concrete like it was styrofoam. I fell to the ground in a jumble of jutting rebar, shattered concrete and shattered bones. The knife tumbled from my numbed and broken fingers.

Power flared bright inside me, surging to heal the slashes across my back and knit my bones together. I struggled to my feet and balled my healing hand into a fist just in time to punch the were-wolf in the snout as he snapped at me. The beast leapt away with a snarl, but was charging again in a heartbeat. Those murder-hook claws came at me and I tried to dive out of the way, but my lacerated back muscles were still healing and I couldn't move fast enough. The werewolf's claws hit hard and shredded right through my nice tactical shirt. And my nice tummy.

I'm pretty sure I screamed as I skidded through the wet grass, digging a deep furrow into the sandy earth. I clutched my stomach and blood poured out from between my fingers. There was something else, something rigid and sharp against my hand. Several of my ribs were broken... Had the werewolf snapped one of them in half? Was that the shards of my own shattered bones I felt?

No, whatever was sticking out of my side was smoother than that, the curve tighter. The force of the attack had broken one of the werewolf's claws off in my... Shit, was the fucking thing sunk right into the top of my pelvis?

With an effort that made me scream again, I shoved both feet up under the monster and kicked him away, then crawled toward the copse of redwood trees. Blood painted the grass red. I was burning through my energy fast and there was too much damage for even my supernatural healing to mend.

The dark shape of the werewolf loped after me, growling like an oncoming thunderstorm. My knife glinted on the ground twenty feet away.

Too far.

I rolled over onto my back and yanked the gun from my thigh holster, but my hands were slick with blood and my thumb slipped off the safety. The werewolf howled triumphantly and leapt at me, teeth bared.

I was fucked. And not in the fun way.

A gunshot echoed through the encroaching night and I stared. I still hadn't managed to turn off the safety on my weapon, and the sound was too deep and long for a handgun. The werewolf's howl became a snarl and bright blood spattered his thick fur. There was another crack of gunfire and a second hole appeared in his vast chest, blooming scarlet against the gray.

The werewolf threw back his head and howled again, this time in pain as well as fury. Steely fur rose in jagged hackles along his spine and he bared that muzzle full of deadly ivory daggers again. The other gun thundered a third time and the werewolf staggered, whipping his molten gaze back and forth between me and the thatch of misty redwoods. He snarled in confusion, pain and rage. Golden eyes glowed like flames in the deepening night.

And then the werewolf was gone. I caught just a glimpse of smoke-colored fur and bunched muscle before the wounded beast loped off into the fog.

My body was a raw knot of pain, but pain meant I was still alive. For now. I fell back against the ground and wondered who the fuck had just saved my ass. The cops? Not a chance. Lead would have bounced right off a werewolf. Those bullets were silver, like mine, but a hell of a lot bigger. So who...?

Stefano Rossi ran out from between the tall shadows of redwood trees. The other bounty hunter was dressed much like me, except... more. Where I carried only one gun and a knife, he wore a heavily-laden utility belt around his hips and a dozen pockets full of the tools of his trade: magic.

Stefano's dark eyes widened when he saw me on the ground. "Lilith?"

"The one and only," I said with a cough. "And the very bloody."

Stefano dropped to one knee beside me and raised the matte black bulk of his hunting rifle to his shoulder. He stared through the scope in the direction the werewolf had vanished, then lowered the weapon with an archaic oath.

"Curse this fog," he muttered. "Did you see where he went?"

"I was a bit occupied with keeping all of my insides, you know, inside," I admitted. I coughed again and tasted blood.

"You need help," said Stefano, now staring at my red-smeared midsection.

"Yeah," I agreed. "I'm sort of dying."

Hastily, Stefano slung his rifle, pocketed my fallen weapons and then scooped me up into his arms. He spent as much time in the gym as in the College library and didn't even grunt as he lifted me off the ground.

"The cops are on their way and this is a crime scene," Stefano said. "We'd better get out of here."

I sagged against his chest. My whole body felt cold, but I didn't have the strength to shiver anymore.

"Hey, this is your rescue," I said. Blood ran from the corner of my mouth. "You call the shots."

"This is way beyond any of my healing spells, Lilith. I have to take you to a hospital."

"Okay, never mind," I murmured. "I'm clearly the brains of this operation. No, Stefano. No hospitals."

Doctors tended to ask a lot of questions about claw wounds, bullet holes and all of the other boo-boos that came along with a career in supernatural bounty hunting. Besides, my powers were more than capable of closing up the gashes in my stomach. I just needed a little boost.

"Take me somewhere with a bed," I said.

Chapter THREE

Stefano buckled me into the passenger seat of a dented and mud-splattered truck that probably got about two miles per gallon around the city. He threw his rifle and belt full of gear behind the driver's seat, climbed in and gunned the engine.

Flashing blues and reds that definitely weren't Christmas lights glowed through the foggy night. They were getting closer, but Stefano turned the opposite way down the road and the sounds of police sirens faded behind us.

We drove a few blocks inland to a motel. I didn't catch the name – most of the neon was burned out and I was a little distracted by trying not to bleed all over Stefano's upholstery. To judge by the old stains, though, I wasn't his first leaky passenger.

When Stefano pulled to a stop in a parking lot, I could still see the towers of the big bridge glittering with lights over the motel's low, flat roof. We weren't far from Gates Park. I might have staked out the park for an afternoon, but Stefano had clearly been at it for considerably longer.

He jumped out of the truck and rushed to open the other door, pulling my arm around his shoulder while he slid me from the vehicle.

"A motel?" I asked. My feet hit the asphalt and I staggered. "You cheap bastard. What the hell do you spend your gold on?"

"Motel rooms have exterior access," said Stefano. He helped me stand. "Fewer questions that way. Especially when I'm carrying a woman covered in blood."

"Mmm," I agreed. The man had a point.

Stefano half carried me across the parking lot. I walked the other half, feeling pretty proud of myself. The motel had been painted brightly once, but years of sun and wet sea air had long since bleached away the color and cracked the finish in places to reveal the concrete beneath. Stefano helped me lean against the wall while he retrieved a key from one of his pockets.

He unlocked the motel room and picked me up again, carrying me inside like a groom and his wife on a really, really cheap honeymoon. Stefano kicked the door shut behind us and laid me out on the bed, then stripped off my coat and shirt. I winced. Not because being jostled around hurt... which it did. But this was a lot less sexy undressing than I was accustomed to.

My rescuer and rival grabbed some towels and water from the bathroom. He wiped away the blood smeared across my belly with surprising gentleness. When I was relatively clean, Stefano gave my tits a suspicious look.

The College of wizards continued the work of their founder, Merlin, to keep demons out of the world. To be fair, it seemed like a good idea. If you think vampires and werewolves are bad, pray you never meet the demons that create them. But someone managed to summon my succubus mother long enough to knock her up and presto, the world got Lilith Quinn. My powers are under control now, but the College mages still tend to glare at me like I'm about to start murdering puppies any second.

You know, it wouldn't hurt them to trust me a little more... Merlin's father was an incubus. The most famous wizard in history was a half-demon like me, and just look at what he accomplished.

Stefano's doubtful glare was probably supposed to be at my face, but his eyes didn't make it that far. Not that I could blame him. I still wore my sports bra, but even lying down, my breasts made a soft and inviting target. Stefano dragged his gaze away and unzipped a large canvas bag on the nightstand. He rummaged around for a moment and then found a pair of pliers.

"This is going to hurt," Stefano warned.

"Yeah, I figured."

Stefano pulled on some leather gloves and carefully prodded my side where the werewolf's claw was still lodged in my hipbone. I watched Stefano's face instead of the pliers or broken bit of werewolf jutting up from my skin. It was a much better view.

The wizard was a few years older than me, somewhere in his early thirties. Stefano had Italian olive skin and thick, wavy hair. His dark beard was cut close against his cheeks and angled jawline. Years of training and bounty hunting had hardened Stefano's body. A scar I had never noticed before ran in a pale line that curved down from his temple.

"Ready?" Stefano asked.

"Yeah. Let's get this–"

Stefano gave a sharp yank. I pulled a pillow over my face and screamed into it – a reflex I've developed through much more pleasant practice. There was one more blaze of agony in my side and then it was over.

"Fuck," I gasped when I dropped the pillow again.

Stefano placed the bloody claw into a small, stout black box and closed it firmly before removing his gloves.

"It's a good thing you're a cambion," he said. *Cambion* was fancy wizard-talk for a half-succubus like me. "Not many humans could have survived that. Even if they did, they would carry the curse. But you're…"

Already demonic. Stefano didn't say the words, but I knew he was thinking them. I groaned and blood welled up from where the claw had been. I had burned through too much energy fighting the werewolf and didn't have enough left to finish healing the wound on my own. Stefano pressed a towel to my hip.

"I've got to stitch you up, Lilith," he told me. "It won't be as neat as a professional job, but you're the one who doesn't want to go to a hospital."

"Forget it. I don't need the scars," I answered. "I need something else."

"What?"

With an effort, I sat up on the bed and brought myself face to face with Stefano. I kissed him deeply. Stefano's heart quickened – I felt the flutter of his pulse against our lips. I ran one hand down the mage's chest to the front of his pants. His cock stirred swiftly at my touch.

"Give me what I need, Stefano," I whispered.

I fumbled with his zipper. Most of my wounds were no longer open gashes, but my body was still struggling to recover from my thorough ass-kicking. I was as weak as a kitten. So Stefano put his hand over mine and helped me unbutton his pants. He kicked them off, along with his boots and boxers. I scrabbled feebly at Stefano's shirt until he pulled it over his head, revealing every inch of his hard bronze body to my ravenous gaze.

It wasn't easy, but I managed to strip my bra up and off. Stefano stared at my bared breasts, his brown eyes wide and his cock swiftly stiffening.

"Help me get my pants off," I said.

Stefano unlaced my boots and removed them, then worked his fingers under the waist of my pants and slid them down my legs. His hand lingered over my injured stomach and hip, the lines of the werewolf's slash red and angry against my pale skin. Trembling, I pushed his hand down to the waist of my black panties. Stefano's fingers closed almost involuntarily around the scrap of soft cloth and he dragged my underwear off, leaving me naked on the bed.

I needed Stefano. I grabbed his shoulder and tugged without strength. A wet swell of heat suffused me, a sweet tide of desire to wash away the pain. My hips rose weakly from the bed. The urge to spread my legs, to open myself was overwhelming. I *needed* this.

"Fuck me," I panted.

Stefano let me pull him falteringly down onto the thin motel mattress and up between my legs. His dick was growing as he stared at my body, bared beneath him. The wizard held himself up on one corded arm and closed his other hand over my uninjured hip. I raked my fingers along the muscles of his back and pulled Stefano closer, into me. My spine arched as the thick, solid heat of him pierced my pussy. Wet and ready, my body devoured Stefano's cock greedily.

"Yes," I gasped.

I felt it, the bright glimmer of golden light as Stefano sank himself deep into me with a long, low groan. Don't ask me how you can *feel* a glimmer. I just can. And fuck, it felt amazing. Stefano's desire poured into my body as the hunter began to pump himself in and out of me. The pain was vanishing with every second and pulsing pleasure filling me in its place.

I grabbed Stefano's taut ass. His cock was hard and long inside me, stretching me sweetly, but Stefano was moving gently, almost gingerly. Taking it easy on the poor injured girl. Kind of him, but ignorant. I slapped my hand down on Stefano's ass and he grunted.

"Stop being careful," I hissed into his ear. "Fuck me, Stefano!"

I dug my fingers into his flanks and delighted in the feel of toned muscles bunching under his skin as he did what I asked. His hips rolled faster and Stefano plunged himself into me. We filled the motel room with the sounds of bodies coming together again and again. His weight pressed against my clitoris, trapped and caressed between us as we writhed together. Strength and power built inside me and I wrapped my legs around Stefano's waist. I met him thrust for thrust and moaned into his ear with the ecstasy of it.

"Gods, Lilith," Stefano grunted. "You… you feel so…"

"You like it?" I purred. "You like fucking me, Stefano? Is it just because you think I'm pretty, or because of what I am?"

"Lilith…"

I tightened my legs around Stefano's waist, taking his cock deeper into me. I lifted my hips to accept the wizard's length until he could drive it no further into my pussy. Stefano's desire filled me, healed me and empowered me.

"Have you ever been tempted to summon a succubus?" I asked him in a low voice. "It's forbidden, but I know that it happens. You wouldn't be the first sorcerer to summon a lust-demon. To keep her bound in a circle of your magic, to take your dick in every hole, and then send her back to the Nether with your cum dripping out of her."

Stefano squeezed his eyes shut, but gave a long groan deep in his chest. He sat up on his heels and seized my ankles, spread my legs wide and held me there. The bed creaked ominously beneath us as Stefano began to slam his cock into my pussy with abandon. I grabbed the pillow again and screamed into it.

I knew Stefano would never violate the College's rules and that the wizards' punishment for summoning demons of any kind was steep. Stefano was too dedicated to the cause, to protecting the world from the evils of the Nether. But here I was: Lilith Quinn, half demon and acceptable to the College – if barely. Forbidden fruit that he could actually devour.

Stefano pounded me into the mattress and groaned aloud with every hammer-blow of his cock. Wetness ran down over his balls and splashed my thighs. Stefano wasn't being gentle with me now. He was taking me hard. If we had been on the second story of the shabby little motel, I'd have worried about him fucking me right through the floor and falling into someone else's bed. And still not stopping.

"Lilith!"

Only the wizards of the College insist on using my full name, but I liked it when Stefano growled it out in a low sound of pure, naked desire. He drove his entire weight into me with every thrust, oblivious of my wounds – which were long gone now – and plowing me as deep as he could.

"I'll be your demon whore, Stefano. Give it to me," I moaned. "Fill me with your cum, Stefano!"

"Fuck, Lilith…!"

Stefano slammed himself to the hilt inside me and his body became a rigid statue of trembling muscle. His cock throbbed, swelled and then pumped thick heat into my pussy. I twisted my clenched fists into the sheets and cried out with each boiling spume of spunk Stefano loosed inside me. Fuck the pillow. Fuck anything but the bonfire blaze of Stefano's desire shooting into me and setting my nerves on fire.

At last, Stefano's ragged breath began to even out and he released his grip on my ankles. Limply, my legs fell to either side, but not because I was weak anymore. My belly was smooth and unmarked again. There was no sign of the claw slash that had nearly disemboweled me.

Stefano pulled himself slowly out of me and his cum ran from my pussy, down my ass to puddle on the bed beneath me like a sixth Great Lake. Well, at least the cheap motel room was probably pretty used to this kind of abuse. Stefano pushed damp hair back from his face and his dusky skin gleamed with sweat. I stretched out across the rumpled sheets, feeling wonderful.

"Just what the doctor ordered," I sighed.

Chapter
FOUR

Unfortunately, the motel room shower was far too small to share. I claimed it first, on account of a last few smears of blood and a lot more cum oozing from between my legs. It took me long enough to wash that I didn't leave Stefano much hot water, but I promised to make it up to him later.

Now, before you roll your eyes and call me a dumb-ass for not carrying a grocery bag full of condoms with me at all times, you should know that cambions are effectively immune to all disease. The same power that Stefano gave me to heal that deep werewolf claw wound deals with any disease in short order.

And I can't get pregnant, either. Not easily, at least. I'm like my mother that way. It's not just the Seal of Merlin and the College's strict rules that keep the world from being overrun by hot half-succubae. Creating a cambion is... complicated. Even before Merlin locked the demons away, their children were extremely rare.

While Stefano sputtered and swore in the cold shower, I tried to get dressed. My cargo pants were a little dirty from getting knocked on my ass and one knee was torn out. It could have been worse. My shirt was a complete loss, though. The whole thing was shredded beyond repair and not in a sexy way.

I tossed the remains of my shirt into the trash can and rummaged through Stefano's luggage. He had a lot of it. There were dozens of cases full of ritual crystals, scrolls, incense, vials, oils and powders. Finally, almost as though packed as an afterthought, I found a duffle bag of clothes half stuffed under the bed. I stole one of Stefano's plain black t-shirts out of it.

"Can you take me back to my car?" I called through the open bathroom door.

"Why?" Stefano asked as he turned off the water.

"I need new clothes," I said. "And we should talk about this job. Do we have time for that?"

"What time is it?"

I glanced at the clock on the nightstand. "About eight o'clock."

Stefano pushed the plastic curtain aside and stepped out of the shower. His dark hair and beard were slicked wet and water trickled down his muscular body. His cock hung invitingly between powerful legs, just a wink and a kiss away from waking up again. I thought that I might need a cold shower myself.

"Alright," Stefano muttered to himself. "I hit the werewolf with three silver nitrate hollow points. That's two-thirds of a gram of silver each..."

I'd already used the last clean towel, so the other hunter pulled his clothes on over wet skin, making them cling enticingly to his hard body. He stepped out of the bathroom, grabbed the yellowing pad of motel stationery and jotted down some numbers. And by *some*, I mean that they would have given even a mathematician a major headache.

"The werewolf shouldn't be strong enough to hunt until ten o'clock tomorrow morning. Give or take a few hours, depending upon his metabolism and stimuli," Stefano said after double-checking his work.

"So... we have time to talk?" I asked.

Stefano nodded.

When we were both more or less decent and I had reclaimed my weapons, Stefano led me back out to his truck. It was late by now and there wasn't much traffic. The police seemed to have finished up and Gates Park was quiet once again. I guided Stefano down The Parkway to where I had hastily stopped my car. There was a parking ticket under the 110's windshield wiper, proving that no matter the hour or what supernatural shit was going down, cops always made time for the important stuff.

"Hold on a second," I sighed. "I need to call Dorian."

Stefano leaned against the hood of his truck to wait. It was a big utilitarian thing that looked more than a little out of place in the city. But to judge by the mud caked into the wheel wells and a few sizable dents in the body, Stefano actually took his truck off-road.

"I know a guy who can take care of that for you," I said, gesturing to one of the deeper dings. "He can probably get you a good deal, too."

Stefano just scowled at me. I guess Max wasn't getting any new customers today. So I took out my phone and swore. The screen was a spiderweb of cracks. It must have broken during my fight with the werewolf. I sighed again and dropped the stupid failure of technology back into my hip pocket.

"Can I borrow your phone?" I asked.

Stefano considered my request for a moment, then nodded. He pulled out a thick block of black metal and tossed it to me. I caught it, looked down and groaned. I held up the ancient flip-phone accusingly.

"What the hell is this?" I asked.

"My phone."

Stefano didn't look even slightly embarrassed. His cell phone had to be ten years old. At least. I've told you before about how archaic the wizards are and not a word of it is exaggeration. I supposed that I was just lucky that Stefano even owned something as newfangled as a cellular phone at all.

I flipped the antique phone open and wasn't surprised to see that Stefano hadn't programmed it with a single contact.

"Do you know Dorian's number?" I asked.

Stefano nodded. I dialed the number that he recited, frowned for a moment – I hadn't used a phone like this since high school – and hit the green *send* button. I put the flip phone to my ear and waited. While it rang, I wondered how ancient the telephone that would answer was. Stefano was a kid compared to some of the elder wizards of his order. I imagined Dorian's phone with a yellowed ivory handle, silver numbers on the rotary dial and probably a cord wrapped in dusty cloth.

After seven rings, I finally heard Dorian's slightly creaky voice on the other end of the line.

"Good evening, Lilith."

How did Dorian know it was me? There was no way the old wizard had caller ID. Even if he did, I was using Stefano's phone. I chalked it up to magic – which was exactly what I needed now.

"Hi, Dorian," I said. "I need a little cleanup."

I heard the rustle of papers over the line. At least, I thought so. The speaker on Stefano's chunky cell phone was truly shitty. Dorian asked me for details.

"Two kids saw our werewolf tonight," I reported. "Seventeen or eighteen years old. They might be in police custody now, but I'm not sure. I didn't get their names."

"We'll find them," Dorian assured me. "By morning, they will remember nothing of consequence. Anything else?"

I considered. "A cop saw it, too. Dispatch called him *William 117*, I think."

"We'll take care of it."

"Thanks, Dorian. You're the best."

Dorian laughed like a rusty door hinge and hung up. Praise all the gods and spirits for the College's magical abilities. Without them, monsters would overrun half the world and the remains of humanity would be hiding under their collective beds. And the wizards' anal-retentive need for order and secrecy kept me out of prison for the work I did on their behalf. I appreciated that, too.

I tossed back Stefano's phone and told him to choose somewhere to eat. I was starving.

"We're not far from Little Italy," he said.

"Lead on."

I followed Stefano in my 110 for a few miles, until he stopped at a narrow building with an Italian name scrawled in flickering green neon across the front. I parked behind Stefano's truck and grabbed my bag from the back seat before going into the restaurant.

A black-haired young waitress smiled at Stefano with a familiarity that suggested he was a regular. She gave me a much more skeptical look, though, and raised one eyebrow. Wearing a guy's shirt is sexy and all, but it's more of a *let-me-make-you-breakfast-to-thank-you-for-last-night* kind of thing, and somewhat less of a *let's-go-out-in-public* move.

I took note of our table and went to the ladies room. I swapped out Stefano's t-shirt for one from my bag. I removed my pants, too, and pulled on a pair of shorts. Monsters make messes, so I always pack a change of clothes or two, but I hadn't brought extra shoes, so the boots stayed. The outfit would probably get me another raised brow from the waitress, but at least the clothes were mine. Well, the shirt was an old one of Max's, but that practically made it mine.

So looking a bit like a Metallica groupie, I returned to the table. Stefano caught his shirt when I threw it and I dropped into the booth across from him. The separators around each table were tall wooden walls, thick with shellac that bounced the orange restaurant lighting back and forth between them.

The waitress was there a moment later – with the expected dirty look at me – to take our drink order, but Stefano and I both knew what we wanted.

"Linguine alla carbonara with pancetta," Stefano said

The man knew his pasta. Or so I assumed. I had no idea what he just ordered.

"Ice cream," I demanded.

"One scoop or two?" the waitress asked.

"Eight."

She blinked at me a few times, then scribbled on her notepad. "I'll uh... get you a banana split. That's got three scoops."

Mmm, bananas.

"Eight scoops of ice cream?" Stefano asked when the waitress had gone.

"Hey, I punched a werewolf in the face tonight. I earned it," I said. "Are you worried about my figure?"

Stefano traced the figure in question with his eyes and finding nothing at all wanting, shook his head. My weird super powers ran on sexual energy, but they seemed to eat through a lot of calories, too. Anything less than about six thousand calories on a work day left me starving. So when Lily Quinn wants ice cream, she fucking gets ice cream.

"So let's talk about this hunt," I said. I lowered my voice in case our waitress was the nosey type.

"Why?" asked Stefano.

"Because I just about got my guts carved out by that werewolf. It would have killed me if you hadn't shown up. You put three high-caliber silver rounds in him. We hurt him, sure, but that thing is still out there. He's licking his wounds right now, but he'll be back."

"Yes," Stefano agreed.

"My plan was to beat our werewolf up, put enough silver bullets into him to knock him out and hopefully back down to human. Then probably stuff him in my trunk and sit on it until the College arrived," I said. I spread my hands with a shrug. "But you saw how well *that* was going. So what about you? What's your plan?"

Stefano was quiet and I wondered if he was going to answer me at all. Finally, he sighed.

"The same as Tor Lee's. The College has treated a cell at the Tower with silver to contain the werewolf, so we can lift the curse, but we need to get him there. I've prepared a teleportation spell to do the job, but it's a difficult incantation and can't all be done ahead of time. There's a certain amount of work that needs to be completed at the site. The werewolf ripped Tor apart before he could finish."

That made sense – Merlinic magic was complicated. It involved a lot of chemicals, herbs, runes and incantations. I had a hard time imagining a werewolf just standing still and letting a wizard chant at him.

"In rural areas, I usually clear anyone else out of the hunting radius," said Stefano. "I can inscribe my spell circle and wait until the werewolf is close, then finish the casting. When I'm the only human in scenting distance, the werewolves always come after me eventually."

"Ballsy," I complimented the other hunter.

Stefano shook his head. "But here in the city... There are too many people, too many things to hunt and kill besides me. I just haven't been able to pin this werewolf down long enough to finish the job. Tor got close, but..."

"But nothing's working this time, is it? You set up shop in that motel and I'm guessing you've been there a while."

Stefano fixed me with his dark eyes. "I *want* this bounty, Lilith. I've never given up the hunt for a werewolf. Never. If you're trying to talk me out of it so you can grab him on your own, you're wasting your time and mine."

The words came out in something awfully close to a snarl. Stefano was a good enough sorcerer to graduate from bounty hunting to more serious magic, but for some reason, he stuck with it.

"Hey, I'm not trying to steal anything out from under you," I assured him. "I'm suggesting we work this thing together."

Stefano's brow furrowed deeply. "What?"

"You've got the magic. I've got the ass-kicking skills. But neither of us have been able to manage the job alone."

"I've captured more than two dozen lycanthropes," Stefano objected stiffly.

"Yeah. But if I understand this correctly, you bait the trap yourself and count on the time it takes a werewolf to hunt you down to finish your spell. Right?"

"Right," said Stefano.

"But there are too many other tasty morsels in the city. You can't guarantee that the werewolf will come to you."

Stefano drew a deep breath and nodded slowly. "Werewolves are ruled by their passions and those passions can be... unfocused. One scream or backfiring car and he's gone, chasing it down."

"So you need someone to get and keep his attention while you cast your teleportation spell," I said. "Sounds to me like you need a partner."

Stefano drummed his fingers on the tabletop and watched me carefully. Did he still think the half-demon temptress was trying to trick him? His brown eyes were intense. It was hot, but I had to admit that I was curious. Stefano had a thing about werewolves. I didn't know what kind of thing, but he had been known to drop out in the middle of other hunts and trek all the way across the world after one.

"Fine. I'll work with you on this, Lilith," Stefano said. "You've already helped a great deal, actually. Part of my problem has been not knowing where to find the werewolf until too late. I simply can't move fast enough."

"I've been using a police scanner, but had pretty much the same problem," I admitted. "So how did I help with that?"

"There's a spell that can predict where the werewolf will be. I can divine his future location, but the ritual requires a part and piece."

"Isn't that... redundant?" I asked.

Stefano graced me with the ghost of a smile. "That's just what the literature calls it. Casting a divination requires a bit of hair or fingernail clipping from the intended target."

"Fingernails? That's sexy magic," I said with a smirk. "But how hard could it be to find some hair?"

"Do you know how many people walk their dogs through Gates Park?" Stefano asked. He rolled his eyes. "Hours of casting and I ended up scrying on some wolfhound's lunchtime dump."

I laughed. I'd had my own complaints along those lines. But now we had a werewolf claw, the one Stefano pulled out of my side before fucking me back to health. That was a hell of a fingernail clipping.

"You kept that claw, right?" I asked.

"Yes. It's in a warded ebony case with the rest of my gear," he said. "Safe."

"So what now?" I put my chin in my hand and smiled across the table at Stefano. "Partner?"

"When we're done here, I can use the claw to cast a divination spell. It'll take a few hours, but we'll know exactly where to find the werewolf. Then we can corner and teleport him to the College."

"But you still have to cast the teleportation without getting your face ripped off, right?" I asked.

"Right."

"How much time will you need for that?"

"Fourteen minutes," Stefano answered. Precise as ever.

I sucked down a deep breath. "That's a long time to tangle with a werewolf. That thing just about killed me in less than five. First, though, we need to know where we're going. But that's your area of expertise, so let's eat and then you can take me to your sanctum."

Every wizard has a sanctum, a safe and protected place where they do their magic. I'd never seen one before and had to admit that I was curious what Stefano's might be like. Even after eight years working for the College, I hadn't witnessed much magic close up.

But Stefano started, half jumping to his feet and banging into the table. Our silverware bounced across the top.

"No!" he snarled.

"Okay then," I said, holding up my hands in surrender. "Wow, easy there."

Stefano sat again and flushed beneath his close beard. He leaned back and straightened his fork on the tabletop.

"Sorry," he apologized shortly.

"No, it's fine," I said. "I get it. I'm not a wizard. I'm not one of you guys."

"This whole thing is… difficult," said Stefano. He rubbed his eyes. "I brought everything I would need to do my magic in the field. I can work in the motel room."

I nodded. I should have expected something like that. I'd even noted how much magical gear Stefano had in his rented room. I guess I just got a little too excited.

"Lilith, we don't even share our sanctums with other wizards, as a general rule," said Stefano. "That's like inviting someone into your bedroom. It's private and it's personal."

I didn't mention the bedroom he and I had just shared. I have *some* tact. So I sat quietly until the waitress returned with Stefano's pasta and my banana split. She seemed a little reassured by the awkwardness hanging in the air between us and smiled at Stefano. He stared down at his meal without apparently noticing her at all. The waitress' smile faltered and she retreated once more.

Despite her apparent dislike of me – or perhaps because of it – the waitress had doused my banana split in a truly impressive amount of fudge, strawberry sauce, caramel and whipped cream. I popped three cherries into my mouth and bit down until the skins finally burst. Sweetness flooded across my tongue. Then I grabbed my spoon and attacked the mountain of ice cream.

Stefano watched me eat with an expression I couldn't quite read. I almost stuck my tongue out at him, but the wizard was still feeling touchy. And not in the sexy way he had been back in his motel room. It wasn't long before my curiosity and natural aversion to silence got the better of me.

"So what's your deal with werewolves?" I asked.

Smooth, Lily. So much for tact.

Stefano stopped with his fork halfway to his mouth. His pasta was wound in a huge ball around the tines, dripping with creamy sauce. Apparently I wasn't the only one who had worked up an appetite.

After a moment, Stefano stuck the knot of linguine in his mouth and chewed without relish. I didn't think he would answer, but then he put down his fork and drew a deep breath.

"When I was seventeen, my parents took me hunting up in the mountains," said Stefano. Each word was slow, reluctant. "My dad and I shot a couple of quail. Mamma cooked them. That kind of thing. But on the second night, something followed us back to our campsite. Tracked us. It was a werewolf."

"Oh." I was really starting to regret asking. "Look, you don't have to tell me about this, Stefano."

"No, it's fine."

Stefano rubbed one hand against his temple. Did he feel guilty for coming down on me about the sanctum thing? If so, he didn't need to make it up to me. Not with this story.

"Everything went... crazy," he said. "I think I got a shot off, but I'm not sure. My dad had his gun and told me to run. Mamma grabbed my arm. She was... covered in blood. We ran. We made it back to the truck and I heard my father screaming as we drove away."

Stefano paused, picked up his fork and wound noodles around it again. He bit and chewed mechanically. I didn't say anything.

"My mother was bleeding because she had been bitten," Stefano went on. "I don't know when it happened. But the curse doesn't take long to go into effect. She was scared, angry. She changed before we made it halfway back to the city."

"Fuck," I breathed. I hadn't meant to say it.

"She lost control of the truck, slammed into a tree. My head just about went through the windshield." Stefano brushed hair away from his temple to reveal the curving scar I had noticed before. "My mother... the werewolf was pinned by the steering column. That was the only thing that saved my life."

"What happened?" I asked.

"She was all... fur and claws and fury. She didn't even recognize me anymore. There were still some guns in the truck. I emptied them all, fired every single bullet we had, but they were only lead. It wasn't enough to kill her.

"In the end, I was just standing there, watching her claw at the steering column and wondering when she would finally kill me. But... she was trapped long enough to calm down, I suppose. Or maybe there just wasn't enough blood in her brain to sustain her rage. But she changed back into my mother."

I let out a breath I hadn't realized I was holding. "Did the College cure her?"

"No," Stefano said in a flat voice. "I was just a scared kid. I didn't know anything about magic or the College back then. I only knew my mother had become a monster. So I slit her throat with a skinning knife."

I choked on a mouthful of ice cream. Stefano didn't seem to notice. He twisted his fork between thumb and forefinger.

"A little while later, a wizard showed up. Her name was Sylvia. She doesn't hunt anymore. I'm not sure how long I just... stood there, covered in my mother's blood. I think Sylvia asked me about what had happened, but I only wanted to know one thing: if there were more werewolves out there."

"What did she say?" I asked.

"Yes. Sylvia was supposed to wipe my memory, but she took me back to the College first. Vincent Myrdon told me that they could have saved my mother."

I winced. "Ouch."

"He wasn't blaming me. The High Magus said if I was willing to work and study hard, then I could learn how to hunt werewolves. How to stop some other kid from having to... do what I did."

"I... I'm sorry." It was such a stupid and inadequate response, but I didn't know what else to say. "We'll stop this one, Stefano, before he hurts anybody else."

The wizard just nodded and returned his attention to his pasta. I resumed shoveling ice cream into my mouth as fast as I could. I felt *really* bad for Stefano, but a girl's still got to eat.

"So how long's this divination going to take?" I asked when I was down to running my fingers around the glass dessert bowl and licking caramel sauce off them. Stefano seemed to find this process intensely fascinating.

"I uh... that spell takes about five hours to cast," he answered.

"Alright. Let's pay and get started."

I picked up the bill for dinner. It was the least I could do.

Chapter
FIVE

I needed more than the contents of one hastily packed bag, so I promised to meet Stefano back at the motel in an hour. I made a quick trip out to my condo to take advantage of a real bathroom and my own shampoo. When I was done in the shower, I got dressed again and stuffed some more tactical blacks into my bag. I packed a few extra magazines of silver ammunition, too, which ate up most of my supply. Getting silver bullets isn't easy and I didn't exactly keep an arsenal of them around. Luckily, werewolves weren't common.

One last thing. I grabbed a spare cell phone from my desk. It wasn't as nice as the one the werewolf had destroyed, but I had no intention of using Stefano's antiquated brick again. I packed a charging cord in case the battery was low, zipped up my bag and went back down to my car.

It was nearing midnight by the time I returned to the motel. Stefano opened the door and kindly lowered his huge revolver when he saw that it was just me. He locked the door behind us and set the chain. Not that it would stop a werewolf, but I appreciated Stefano's paranoia. It mirrored my own. We knew what was out there prowling through the night.

"Don't touch anything," Stefano said.

He sat down at the warped little motel desk. There was a lot to touch... Every flat surface was covered in hobby and tackle boxes. Each plastic compartment was full to the brim with weird magical reagents, more than I could possibly name. The motel room was a riot of strange smells: burning stone, metal and herbs. I really hoped no one thought we were cooking meth or something and called the cops.

Stefano had a piece of parchment laid out on the desk and was carefully inscribing a knot of runes in fine red ink that looked suspiciously like blood. The black box containing the werewolf claw sat beside him, along with a heavy pair of leather gloves and steel tongs. I guessed Stefano really didn't want to accidentally get stuck with that thing. After hearing his story, I didn't blame him one bit.

"Need a hand with any of this?" I asked.

Stefano glanced up at me. "Do you know how to mix a Leyden's tincture?"

"Unless that's a martini," I said, "nope."

"Just get comfortable. This is going to take a while."

I sat down on the bed. I don't spend the night with men and I wasn't particularly looking to start a new tradition, but it was late and being pummeled through concrete by supernatural beasts tends to tire one out. So I piled up the pillows, leaned back and closed my eyes. I might even have slept a little, but Stefano's magical prep work involved a lot of mixing things in clinking glass beakers and chanting over strange-smelling concoctions in a language that definitely wasn't Italian.

Briefly, I considered renting another room nearby. There was no way this craphole was sold out on a weeknight. But I was still curious. I'd never been this up close and personal with Merlinic magic. Most wizards cast their spells behind locked doors, either in their sanctums or the laboratories of the College.

I got up and paced across the room to Stefano again. He had stopped chanting for the moment and I looked over his shoulder. He tensed, but I didn't touch anything. I did point, though.

"What's that?" I asked.

"A bowl."

"Yeah," I agreed. "But it's weird."

"It's carved with ogham runes."

"And it's dirty."

"It's supposed to be," Stefano said. "It was buried under the earth for a fortnight in a circle of standing stones."

"Oh." I studied the incomprehensible jumble of magical paraphernalia and pointed to a vial. "Hey, I know that one! That's gold."

Stefano set down a clay crucible. I didn't see any fire or burner on the desk, but the contents of the crucible smoked gently.

"Yes," he said through gritted teeth. "Because it's already too late to divine where the werewolf will be tonight. I need to find out where he'll be tomorrow, during the day. Gold shows us where he'll be at noon. Silver for midnight."

"That's pretty specific. And arbitrary. Why not at dawn and dusk?" I asked. Something else occurred to me. "Hey, what about time zones? Do they matter? What if you were trying to divine where to find someone in France?"

"Lilith, can you shut up?" Stefano asked. "I really need to concentrate on this."

"Yeah. Sorry."

I retreated to the bed once more – where I did my magic – and sat to watch. Quietly. But while magic is truly intricate and involved, it gets quickly boring if you're not the one doing cool wizard shit. So I broke out my new cell phone and chopped up some digital fruit with an imaginary sword.

————

Despite all the chanting and clanking, I eventually fell into a restless doze. When Stefano shook my shoulder, I woke with a start. My hand shot out instinctively and I grabbed his wrist. Stefano's dark eyes went wide.

"Lilith, stop!" he gasped.

Stefano's legs buckled and he sank to his knees. Several hours had passed since he first brought me here for a medicinal fucking, but I hadn't used up all that energy yet and for a second, I worried that I had broken his wrist. Like I said, I don't sleep over and wasn't used to anyone else waking me.

I released Stefano. "Are you okay?"

"Gods, Lilith." He inspected the damage and gave me a suspicious look, but seemed to decide that it truly had been an accident. "Nothing broken. But that's going to leave a bruise."

"Sorry," I said.

I was having a really hard time staying on Stefano's good side tonight.

I rubbed my eyes and checked the cheap digital clock on the nightstand. A little before five in the morning. Stefano's supplies were sealed up and stacked neatly beside the door. The motel room still smelled of sulfur and sage, but the magic was over. For the moment.

"You found the werewolf?" I asked, sitting up. "I mean, where he's going to be?"

"I did. Come look at this."

Stefano watched me climb out of the bed and then gestured to the bathroom. There was still one magical instrument that hadn't yet been cleaned and packed away. Stefano's dirty iron bowl sat on the counter beside the sink. I glanced down at what looked like muddy water. Other than a thin layer of mist clouding the surface, I didn't see anything interesting.

"What am I looking at?" I asked.

Stefano stood at my shoulder and peered down into the bowl, too. "At noon tomorrow – today, that is – he'll be in an apartment, asleep on the bed. I think this is where he lives."

"You can see the place?"

Stefano nodded.

"Do you know where it is?" I asked.

"No," Stefano admitted. "The divination spell only shows me an image."

"Hold on a second."

I ran back to the bed and grabbed my phone off the pillow. I had three bars – plenty for some research. I pulled up a local rental website.

"Okay," I said. "Describe the apartment to me."

"Small. One bedroom, but nice," said Stefano.

"Are there windows?"

"Yes. He's at ground level." Stefano cocked his head and stared into the bowl of murky water. "I can see a building across the street. A library, I think, but I can't read the name from this angle."

"You *would* recognize a library. What about the interior?"

"Hardwood floors, probably only a few years old. There are claw marks in them now, though. The wood is birch."

"Birch? You can tell just by looking?" I smirked at Stefano in the bathroom mirror. "Of course you can. Anything else?"

"There are bars on the windows," he reported. "But they're nice, too. Wrought iron."

I typed in some keywords and showed Stefano my search results. He squinted at the phone screen.

"That might be it," he said. "The second one."

I checked the address. "A brownstone at the other end of Gates Park. It's an older building, but the interiors were renovated last year. Brand-new birch flooring."

"We don't have a unit number," Stefano pointed out.

"I think I can work around that. What about our werewolf?" I asked. "You said that he was asleep. Does that mean he is... or will be... human?"

"Yes."

"A sleeping human. If I find out which apartment is his, can we sneak you in there to cast your spell before he wakes up?"

Stefano considered, but then shook his head. "No. Teleportation isn't a simple or quiet spell. That's part of how I attract a werewolf's attention during rural hunts. Even then, it's tricky. Teleportation requires a lot of real-time incantations. Unless our werewolf is in a coma, he's going to be aware of what I'm doing. And angry. Most demonic creatures have an instinctual hatred for Merlinic magic."

"Hmm," I said. "Well, distracting a human is a lot easier than wrestling with a werewolf for fifteen minutes."

"Fourteen minutes." Stefano corrected.

I regarded Stefano in the mirror and trailed my lips up along the side of his neck. The other bounty hunter stiffened and grabbed the edge of the bathroom counter hard enough to turn his knuckles white.

"I think I can keep him busy and off your back," I told Stefano in a low purr. "Human men are so much more pliant than a fully transformed werewolf."

I ran my fingers through Stefano's thick brown hair and gently pushed his head down toward the bowl again.

"So, what does our guy look like?" I asked.

"Naked and sweaty. The curse is hard on its victim," Stefano told me in a slightly strained voice. "He's tall. It's difficult to determine exact numbers when lying down, though I would estimate at least six feet. Caucasian, but very tanned. There's a definite line from wearing trunks. He probably spends a lot of time at the beach."

"Can you see his face?"

"He'll be lying face-down, so no."

"This future-tense stuff is weird," I said. "What's his hair like?"

"Shoulder-length and blond. I have no idea if it's his natural color or not. I can't tell his age with precision, but to guess by his physical condition... young. Maybe in his early twenties."

"Great," I said. "So this will be happening at noon. On the dot?"

"Yes. If we don't manage to capture him then, I'll have to repeat the ritual with silver to catch him at midnight."

"He can kill a lot of people in that time. Nothing in between?" I asked.

"That's how divination magic works. And next time, he may not be human," said Stefano. He rubbed his eyes. There were dark circles beneath them. "This could be our only shot."

"You need some sleep," I told him. "I'll wake you up in... say, six hours?"

Stefano consulted his watch and jotted down some calculations against the dose of silver nitrate he had used on the werewolf.

"Yeah," he said after a moment. "Sleep. Sure."

Stefano stumbled out of the bathroom and to the bed. I noticed that he set the alarm on the clock out there, too. Habit? Or did Stefano still not entirely trust his cambion partner? I smiled as he stripped out of his shirt and dropped onto the bed. Poor Stefano just didn't quite know what to make of me. He threw an arm across his eyes.

The mage made a pretty damned hot sight draped across the bed. I lounged in the bathroom door and contemplated the soft heat blooming in the pit of my stomach.

I had known Stefano Rossi for years. Not as long as Max, but Stefano was a rookie hunter back when I first got started. We had bumped into each other on plenty of jobs, at the bounty board or in bed – usually when I wanted information. But I didn't spend much time with him. We'd certainly never had dinner together. This was kind of... fun. Stefano was a little on the serious side, but mostly in an intense, sexy way.

I slipped across the motel room to the bed.

"Hey, Stefano," I whispered. "Are you asleep yet?"

"Almost," he groaned. "What is it?"

By the time Stefano managed to get his eyes open, I was already on the bed, straddling his waist. He stared at me on top of him and his breath quickened.

"Lilith, what are you...?" Stefano started to ask, but I ran my hands down his chest, through the light dusting of dark hair there. Stefano broke his question off with a low groan.

I flicked open his pants with expert ease and slid my hand inside. Stefano's cock was already hard as one of the iron rods he used in his magic. I leaned down against him and crushed my lips to his, tasting another deep moan as I curled my fingers around his length.

"Well, *part* of you is certainly awake," I murmured.

Stefano's hands found my hips and held me close. His fingertips dug into my ass through my shorts with mute but eloquent need. I yanked my shirt off over my head and disheveled hair spilled across Stefano's shoulder in soft copper rivers. I licked the rim of his ear.

"Do you want me to stop?" I asked.

"No..." The word came out in a low moan. "Gods, no. Don't stop, Lilith."

Stefano shoved my shorts and panties down, nearly tearing them in his haste, and then his hands raced back up my thighs. One cupped my ass, but Stefano pushed the other between my legs. I grew slick under his touch and the heat flared inside me. Stefano's fingers traced the soft, wet contours of my pussy with the same studious care that he had shown with his spells.

I slipped my hand down into Stefano's pants again and worked his cock free of its confines. It towered against my belly, silky to the touch and burning with his desire. I stroked Stefano slowly from root to tip, twisting my palm over the sensitive crown with every caress. Sweat broke out across Stefano's olive skin and his breath came faster. His grip on my ass tightened and the fingers playing over my entrance were suddenly spreading my pussy open and plunging inside, burying themselves in me. I bit into Stefano's chest and tasted salt as his touch penetrated me.

"More," I gasped.

Stefano's cock twitched in my hand at the plea and he slid a second digit inside me, alongside the first. I rocked my hips, fucking Stefano's fingers as he explored my velvety tightness. I pressed my face into the hollow of his shoulder to muffle the loud sound of my cries.

When my body quieted once more, I sat back and took a few deep breaths. I released Stefano's cock and grabbed his wrist, withdrawing his sopping fingers from my pussy. I held his hand up between us, locked my eyes on Stefano's, and then slowly sucked one of his fingers into my mouth. I tasted the wet tang of the pleasure he had given me and loved it.

Stefano swallowed hard. I turned his hand and fed the mage his other dripping finger. He sucked every trace of me from his skin and then licked his lips.

"It's good," he breathed.

"You like it?" I asked with a grin.

Stefano nodded mutely. I leaned back astride him and dropped my fingers between my legs. I rubbed my pussy until my hand was slicked, slippery and wet, then reached down to grab Stefano again. He groaned and his hips rose, thrusting his dick into my grasp.

I jerked Stefano's hot length. The skin was smooth and his cock subtly ridged beneath. My touch left Stefano glistening with wetness. The wizard's bearded jaw clenched against louder sounds as I stroked him. Lust burned through him like wildfire.

"Damn," Stefano said in a strangled voice.

"Damn?" I asked. "Or damned? Do you like your little demon whore?"

Stefano loved being goaded just as much as I loved doing it. He grabbed my hip and shoved his fingers into my pussy again. There was a loud wet sound as he forced a third digit up between my legs, stretching my tightness. Stefano's palm pressed hard against my clitoris and my legs began to quiver.

"Do you want to be damned?" I whispered.

"Fuck," Stefano gasped into my ear. "Lilith...!"

My mind and body were consumed by the blaze of pleasure. I couldn't think, but I didn't have to. I pumped Stefano's cock urgently, pushing us both up and over on instinct. Seriously, if you put a broom in my hand while I'm cumming, I will jack it off. Probably make it cum, too.

Stefano's fingers curled inside me and his dick throbbed in my grasp. White-hot spunk fountained from him, splattering into liquid pearls against my stomach. Thick drops rolled down my skin to pool in my navel. So much heat inside me and all over me... I couldn't help the sharp scream that tore up from my throat and doubtlessly annoyed the hell out of any neighbors.

Sagging back into the bed, Stefano withdrew his fingers from me. I released him, too, and ran my hand through the sticky mess, down to rub cream-covered fingers against my dripping pussy. Stefano watched me intently even as his eyes began to drift shut.

"What was that for, Lilith?" he asked in a voice thickened by fatigue.

"Nothing," I said. I slid off the bed. "Now get some sleep. I'll wake you in the morning."

Stefano mumbled something and barely managed to get his pants zipped up again before rolling over. By the time I threw the blankets over the exhausted wizard, he was fast asleep. Stefano's magic was complex work and with his personal vendetta against werewolves, I doubted he had slept much in the past week. The death of his family drove Stefano, and it drove him hard.

I toweled off and dressed quietly, then pulled on a new pair of cargo pants from my bag and Max's old t-shirt. Stefano didn't even stir when I took the room key off the nightstand. Silently, I slipped out of the motel. My partner needed his rest. He had a teleportation spell to cast tomorrow and neither of us wanted him to fuck it up.

Chapter
SIX

If I were really honest with myself, I could have used a little more rest, too. But it was getting close to dawn and after nearly snapping Stefano's wrist like a celery stick, I didn't want to nap – or wake up – anywhere near him. And besides, we've already talked about my feelings on sleeping over. Once the fun is done, so am I.

I lingered quietly outside Stefano's motel room for a while, fiddling with my backup cell phone, but then grew quickly bored. I crossed the cracked asphalt to my parked i10, unlocked the door and slid into the driver's seat. I had to download Fuzz Radio to my new phone and pair the Bluetooth again, but soon the car was full of the chatter of police codes and harried dispatchers.

I didn't hear any more codes for shootings or dead bodies, though. Stefano's bullets must have been doing their job keeping the werewolf on his ass. Maybe our guy was already at home, collapsed sweaty and naked in his bed after a night of rampaging. Not a bad mental image, but it still wasn't enough to keep me entertained until morning.

There still were hours to kill before I woke Stefano up again. I drummed my fingers on the steering wheel. Most of the bars and clubs had closed hours ago, so I decided to head back to my condo and pick out something sexy for seducing a werewolf. Leather, maybe...

I pulled the iio out of the motel parking lot and into the street. Fog shrouded the silent pre-dawn. It lay like a thick silver blanket over everything. Mine wasn't the only car on the road, but I felt strangely alone as I drove through the ghostly city. The electric engine purred softly as I accelerated up a steep hill. At the top, I should have been able to see across Gates Park and to the bay beyond, but the whole world was an ocean of cold, soft gray. To the east, the fog glowed gold and silver with the first pale touch of the rising sun.

Near Gates Park, I stopped at a red light and flipped on my turn signal, waiting for an early-morning jogger to finish crossing the street. She tugged on her dog's leash and waved apologetically as the fuzzy little beast paused to sniff a patch of weeds. I waved back.

Movement caught my eye – a faint shadow sliding through the fog that I was sure the jogger couldn't see. Without the sexual energy Stefano had just poured into me, I would have missed it, too – the sleek gray-against-gray of a fully transformed werewolf loping through the thick mist.

What the hell was going on? Stefano's silver nitrate was supposed to have hours left on it. And the werewolf wasn't rampaging, just as Stefano promised. He moved on all fours, slowly and with his long snout low to the ground. Sniffing. Tracking.

Tracking what? What could be interesting enough in the riot of smells filling Gates Park for the werewolf to be following...?

"Shit," I hissed.

The werewolf was following our scents back the way I had come, back toward the motel where Stefano was sleeping. Helpless. I had to warn him. I grabbed for my phone, but dropped it and swore again. Stefano's number wasn't programmed into the new phone and I sure as fuck didn't have it memorized.

I gunned the i10's engine. The jogger on the sidewalk shouted and yanked her dog away from the road as I threw my car into a skidding u-turn. My tires squealed on damp asphalt and I raced down the street after the retreating werewolf. Blasting through a red light, I tore along the road toward the motel. I could just make out the long limbs and steely fur ahead of me, dashing through the shadowed pre-dawn with his nose to the grass.

Was that the scent of my blood he was following? I had certainly lost enough of it. I struggled to remember how far Stefano carried me after coming to my rescue. Fuck, I'd bled all over his truck, too...!

Distractible. Stefano said the whole problem with werewolves in the city was that they weren't focused.

So I pounded my fist against the i10's horn and it blared a long, shrill note out into the dark pewter morning. In front of me, the lupine silhouette snapped his muzzle up from the ground. His golden eyes met mine and a cold shiver slid down my spine as the werewolf turned to face me.

"Fuck," I breathed. "Now what?"

I didn't have long to consider. The werewolf whirled toward me and charged. Not as fast as he had moved when he just about gutted me, but fast enough. I yanked on the steering wheel and swerved left, down The Parkway as the monster gave chase.

My headlights were useless in the fog and I had power enough to ace an eye exam at a hundred yards, so I shut them off. Hurtling north along the narrow, windy road at sixty miles per hour was far from legal, but right now, a speeding ticket was the least of my concerns. I needed every second and every advantage if I was going to play tag with a werewolf.

I had 427 well-maintained horsepower and I let them run. The i10's engine growled and I shot along The Parkway. How much had Stefano's silver nitrate slowed the werewolf down? Could I outrun him?

Patchy sea grasses and redwood trees reared up out of the fog and then vanished as I raced past, hurtling through Gates Park and toward the ocean. The road beneath my wheels rose swiftly and steeply, winding up into stony cliffs that overlooked the sea. The huge shape of the werewolf ran after me through the wet, dark morning. Waves crashed and roared below us.

I came around another curve and almost lost control of the car on the slick pavement. I wrenched the i10 back into my lane, but my rear view mirror was full of a storm of gray fur and sharp teeth. I was ahead of the werewolf, but not by much, and his claws had far better traction on the wet pavement than my tires. The Parkway was rising again and the drop on my left side grew disturbingly sheer. Black water churned eighty feet beneath me and I slowed around another hairpin curve. I hesitated for only a moment, but it was too long.

The werewolf leapt and then slammed down with a bone-jarring thud onto my i10. A massive paw crashed through the windshield and I shouted. Glass and metal flew as huge claws cleaved my dashboard in half. I jerked the wheel and stomped on the brakes. The werewolf snarled and slid over the front of my car, tearing three-foot-long furrows into the hood and then flying off across the asphalt. He flattened a rusting streetlamp and left a serious dent in the cliff road's metal guardrail before finally skidding to a stop. In a single pounding heartbeat, the werewolf was back on his blade-clawed paws. And this was *weakened*?

Thick fog eddied around us. The werewolf threw back his head and howled. Blood ran down my face from half a dozen shallow wounds. They were already healing closed, but how long would my power last if I had to go another round with this monster? Stefano wasn't here to back me up this time. The werewolf's tongue lolled red and wet from his fang-filled mouth as he regarded me.

Twin beams of blinding white light fell over us as an early-morning tech commuter honked at my car, stopped diagonally across both lanes of The Parkway. The other vehicle crunched up onto the inland shoulder, trying to squeeze around me and the driver shouted in Spanish. The werewolf whipped his head toward the new prey and howled.

The other driver screamed in terror and stomped down on the gas. My rear fender gouged a long silver line into the side of his car as he struggled to get away. Spinning tires threw gravel up into the misty morning air, but he was stuck, wedged between my i10 and the steep slope. My werewolf bunched his powerful gray legs beneath him and tensed to pounce. If the monster went after that other car, he would tear it open like a tin can and the driver was going to be blood soup.

I pounded on my horn again and shouted through the shattered windshield. "Over here, you big furry bastard! Come and get some!"

The cold, salty ocean wind tore my words away. The werewolf wasn't listening. So I slammed my foot down on the accelerator. My i10 growled and surged into motion, pointed right at the beast. I had less than a second to brace myself before six hundred pounds of supernatural muscle collided with a ton and a half of sports car.

You might think the car would win the altercation, but the werewolf only slid across the asphalt and we slammed into the guardrail, distending the already bent metal. I swore again and struggled to keep from spinning out as we hit. The steering wheel wrenched and I nearly tore it off trying to keep control of the car.

With his car no longer hemmed in, the other driver floored it, tires screaming on the slick Parkway, and vanished into the fog again. Which left me alone once more with a pissed-off werewolf and the uncaring ink-black ocean. Great...

I kept the front bumper jammed against the huge wolf, pinning him to the guardrail. For a moment, I thought of Stefano's mother there, trapped in the wreckage of her car. But the werewolf brought his claws down into my front fender and wrenched. Half my bumper flew and scattered sparks as it spun out across the road.

Corded arms snapped out over the crumpling metal of the i10's hood and one massive, gray-furred paw lanced through the shattered windshield. I hurled myself sideways into the passenger seat. Scythe-like talons sliced through my seat belt and tore deep gashes into the leather upholstery where I had just been.

I threw my i10 into reverse. The werewolf's long muzzle split open and showed off deadly sharp teeth in a feral smile as the car pulled away. He tensed himself to leap at me once more.

But I had already thrown the i10 into drive again. Blood-tinged sweat poured down my skin. The damaged engine groaned, but Max had done his work well and the car leapt back into motion. Blue-white smoke flew from my burning tires as they struggled for traction. But then they caught and the vehicle shot forward like a silver bullet at the werewolf.

We smashed together into the guardrail and the remains of my hood crunched as the car rammed into the barrier with the werewolf still only halfway up. Tearing metal shrieked and the railing gave way.

I planted both feet on the brake. My i10 fishtailed wildly. The werewolf snarled and grabbed onto the front, trying to hold on as the vehicle lurched to a stop, but his own huge mass worked against him. His sharp claws sheared through tortured steel and he flew out, off my car and fell. The huge gray shape twisted in the empty air and plunged toward the churning ocean. There was a distant splash and then the werewolf was gone.

"Go home," I panted. The swirling fog closed in once more, obscuring the water far below. "Please, just go sleep it off."

Chapter
SEVEN

Carefully, I climbed out of my car. Both of the front wheels were spinning over empty air and I used my sex-powered strength to heave the 110 onto the road again. With all four tires back on the pavement, I inspected the damage.

It was pretty ugly. All of the windows were broken and the driver's side wheels were tilted at unpleasant angles. The hood was a mess of shredded metal and ripped cables. I tossed my torn-up front fender into the trunk and pounded out the worst dents with my fists.

When I slid into the driver's seat again and tried the engine, it whined piteously. An awful lot of my 427 horses were lame now, but the 110 groaned and then lurched into motion. I patted the steering wheel.

"Good girl," I said.

I drove slowly through the lightening morning fog. There was no way I was going to manage anything over thirty miles an hour, so I stuck to surface streets. My rudimentary efforts to smooth out the damage were... well, rudimentary, and I got more than a few weird looks from the first wave of commuters. But at least I no longer had a werewolf clinging to my hood.

I limped the i10 back out of Gates Park and up to Golden Touch Auto just as the sun was cresting the eastern horizon. The windows of the little concrete shop were dark and still displayed the plastic *Closed* sign, but I recognized Max's truck in the parking lot.

The rolling metal door of one repair bay was open and Max stood inside, cleaning a row of spark plugs laid out on the workbench. When he heard the grinding of my engine, he turned and ran into the parking lot.

"Holy shit, Lil," Max said as I climbed out of my trashed car. "What happened? Are you okay?"

"Yeah," I said. "I'm fine. Just played a little demolition derby with a werewolf this morning."

Max threw his arms around me and gave me a long, tight hug.

"So can you fix it?" I asked when he let go.

Max walked a slow circle around the i10, frowning. "You really did a number on her, Lil. I can repair it, but it'll take a while. Shit, are these claw marks?"

"Yeah," I admitted modestly.

This job was going to challenge even Max's skill and he would probably have to work on it in his off time. I would tell him not to and he would ignore me, claiming that it was fun.

I grabbed the rear fender and dragged the car into the garage. Max threw a green tarp over it.

"I don't want any of the other guys asking questions until I get some of the body work done," he said, then jerked a thumb over his shoulder at the dented steel workbench. "Want a key to the loaner?"

I made a face. "Eww. No thanks. I'll get a cab back home and dust off the Alfa Romeo."

"Are you hurt? Do you need anything else?"

Max picked a piece of safety glass out of my hair and brushed his fingers gently down my cheek. I had gotten a little banged up in the crash, but nothing that my half-demon healing couldn't deal with. I took Max's hand and kissed the palm.

"I'm good. You can keep your pants on... for now," I said, then glanced up at the clock. It was about six in the morning. "I'm kind of surprised to find you here already. I expected to wait a while. The shop doesn't open for another hour."

Max nodded. "Sam texted me last night and asked me to come in early to talk about something. I thought I'd get in some work before he got here. Besides, I couldn't really sleep."

"Why not?"

Max just smiled at me, showing off his dimples, and didn't answer. Girlfriend? Surely Max would have told me when I teased him about it earlier. I would pry it out of him later, but right now, I had to get back to Stefano.

———

I pulled into the motel parking lot once more. I had stopped by my place again to pick up my other car and finally grab that change of clothes – still all in black, but this time a tiny leather skirt and vest that I left zipped down low.

I parked between a couple of outdated economy cars and set the alarm on the Alfa Romeo. Quietly, I unlocked Stefano's motel room. The wizard was still in bed when I closed the door behind me, but no longer asleep. His wavy brown hair was mussed, though, and there were pillow lines embossed across his skin.

Stefano blinked at me and lowered his revolver. He yawned.

"Where the hell were you keeping that?" I asked.

"Under the pillow," Stefano answered in a sleep-husked voice. "Where were you?"

"Playing the world's worst round of bumper cars against our werewolf," I admitted. I locked the door behind me and perched on the corner of the desk.

"You what?" Stefano asked. The other hunter jumped to his bare feet, eyes wide. "Lilith, what the hell happened?"

"The werewolf was tracking my blood trail, I think, and heading back here. I couldn't warn you, so I had to lead him off and then sort of dump him in the ocean."

"Did... did you kill him?" Stefano's voice was as tight as a guitar string.

"No. He was still sick from your silver, but that fucker is tough. I really, really hope he's crawling back home to take that nap you saw in your bowl."

Stefano dropped heavily onto the edge of the bed and blew out a long breath. "Gods, Lilith. Are you okay?"

"Yeah." I pulled my feet up onto the desk chair and wrapped my arms around my knees. "Hey, Stefano...?"

The wizard looked at me. "What?"

"You said you saw our guy asleep in his bed at noon. Alive. Was it even possible for me to kill him?"

Stefano closed his eyes and sighed. He nodded. "Yes. You could have killed him."

"But what about what you saw? What about the magic?"

"You'd have created a paradox. It would have been... bad."

"Is this like a time travel thing? A paradox that would unravel the whole time-space continuum if we change the future?"

Stefano shook his head. "No."

Oh. I was kind of disappointed.

"But if we changed the future I divined, then the spell would backfire," he said.

"Backfire?" I asked.

"If you had any talent for magic and a decade to study, I might be able to explain it to you, but let's just say it would be bad," Stefano said. His tone was curt, but not unkind. "That's why we're not going after him until noon."

I wasn't sure what constituted *bad* in a wizard's book, but after everything that had happened in the last day, I was in no hurry to find out. I checked the time.

"Fine with me. I'll buy breakfast," I said. "I'm starving. Is that teleportation spell good to go?"

"Almost. The cinquefoil needs to be ground fresh."

"Get that ready," I told Stefano. "I'll go do my makeup. I've got a werewolf to seduce."

Chapter
EIGHT

At noon, Stefano's truck was parked in front of the Lorenzo Public Library. A few dozen students sat on the library stairs, all checking their phones and ignoring unopened reference books in their laps. An older man – their teacher, I supposed – looked on with a resigned smile. It was hard to contend with Wikipedia. For some information, at least. The kind of information that I worked with didn't exactly have a wiki page.

I sat in the passenger seat of the truck, watching the brownstone across the street. Stefano held several rolled parchments in his lap and had a bandolier of vials draped across his chest: a wizard ready to do battle. He wore a long leather overcoat that almost managed to hide it all.

"I'll text you when I get an apartment number," I said. "Once I'm in, give me five minutes to get our guy distracted."

"Five minutes? You think that you can get into his pants that quickly?" Stefano asked.

I winked. "Are you kidding? He won't even be wearing pants. I'll leave the door unlocked. Keep quiet as long as you can."

"Be careful, Lilith."

"Yeah. You, too."

I kissed Stefano's cheek, then waited for a break in traffic, climbed out and trotted across the street. The fog was long gone by now and the day was bright, if still cold enough to make Stefano's coat unobtrusive. In my high heels and leather miniskirt, however, I got several whistles and catcalls – one from a student sitting in front of the library. The kid's teacher shouted at him and I waved to them both before vanishing around the corner.

The brownstone's security door stood open this time of day and the neighborhood was nice enough that it didn't make me suspicious. There was another door in the hallway hung with a wreath and the words *main office* stenciled underneath, but a sign perched in the window informed me that the staff was out for lunch. So I made my way further down the hall, high heels clicking on the wooden floor.

I picked a door. Both the knob and the lock were old, worn. They hadn't been replaced for at least a decade. This was the home of a long-time resident. Probably not my werewolf, who was a young man that couldn't have moved out on his own more than a couple of years ago. But with any luck, this apartment belonged to a nice nosey neighbor.

I knocked and waited. The door opened and an elderly man peered through. His eyes just about fell out of his head when he caught sight of my cleavage.

"Hi there," I said, offering a little wave. "I'm here to visit my brother, but I don't remember his apartment number. Can you help? He's tall and blond, like a surfer."

"Dominic?"

"That's him," I said with a genuine smile. It was good to have a name instead of just calling him *the werewolf* or *the monster*. It made him feel more... human.

"Down in number seven," the old guy told me. "Is that boy alright? He's been looking poorly for days. When I see him at all."

"Yeah. Dominic's been sick. I came over to take care of him."

"Hey, can I call you if I get sick?" the neighbor asked as I turned away.

I laughed and gave him a wink back over my shoulder. It wasn't a bad line.

I paced down the hallway. Number five, six... I stopped in front of apartment seven and pulled out my phone. I texted the number to Stefano and reminded him to give me a few minutes. Then I tucked the phone into the pocket of my vest again and knocked.

"Dominic?" I called out.

I had to shout his name twice more, but then I finally heard a muffled thud from inside the apartment and the door opened. A tall young man stood in the doorway. He blinked sleepily at me and rubbed his dark-circled eyes. I guessed that being stabbed, shot, run over and thrown into the ocean tired out even a werewolf.

Aside from that, though, Dominic looked... good. He was taller than Max, but leaner and had the tanned, toned body of someone who spent a lot of time outside. His sun-bleached blond hair was damp across his shoulders. In human form, his eyes weren't yellow, but a nice olive green.

Dominic clutched a sheet around his narrow hips, leaving his chest bare. There were no signs of Stefano's shots anywhere across his bronzed skin and not so much as a bruise from my car slamming into him. Say what you will about demonic power, but it's hard to beat the health plan. Dominic was sweating, though, and I saw the white lines of scars along his ribs, just above where he had wrapped the sheet.

"Hi, Dominic," I said. "Can I come in?"

He blinked slowly and his gaze drifted up and down my body.

"I... uh... Do I know you?" he asked in a rough voice.

"I'm Lily. Don't you remember? We met last night."

Strictly speaking, that was true. Dominic shook his head, still looking confused, but stepped back from the door.

"You *do* seem kind of familiar," he said. "Um, sure. Come in."

I went inside and closed the door behind me, but didn't lock it. Dominic peered around his small, nicely furnished apartment as though he thought he might find some answers written on the walls. A surfboard leaned in the corner of his living room and there were several paintings of beach scenes. Dominic's eyes lingered on the floor. The birchwood – just like Stefano said it would be – was rough in places with claw marks that looked a lot like the scars along Dominic's side.

"Sorry…" he stammered. "I uh… I don't remember last night very well. Or anything this week, actually."

Dominic raised his free arm, bicep bunching nicely, and scratched at his tousled thatch of golden hair. I wondered what it would take to occupy both hands and get him to drop that sheet.

"I bet, the way you were drinking," I said with a laugh. "Not that I can talk. I only remember bits and pieces, too."

I advanced on Dominic, swinging my hips. I slid the zipper of my vest down another inch. Dominic cocked his head in bewilderment, but the corners of his mouth quirked upward in a dazed smile. I was close enough now to touch my fingertips to his lean stomach and walk them slowly up his abs and smooth chest.

"I was hoping you could jog my memory," I said softly.

"Um… okay…"

I slipped my hand from Dominic's chest to his shoulder and stood on my tiptoes to kiss him. He started a bit, but then I felt the smoldering heat of lust kindle inside him. I had Dominic's interest. Now I just had to keep it long enough for Stefano to get in here and cast his teleportation spell.

The sheet fell around Dominic's feet. He was a little slow and confused at first, but didn't disappoint. His hands came up to grasp my waist and pull me close. I felt hard heat pressing against my stomach. He was tired, not dead, and his lust swelled swiftly into hot passion that I couldn't help but answer with my own. Everything between my legs went wet and warm.

Dominic let me shove him backward through an open door and into the bedroom. I had studied the apartment layout during my research. I knew exactly where we were going and was in a hurry to get there. And not just because Stefano was going to arrive soon.

Clothes were strewn haphazardly around the bedroom. I wasn't sure if Dominic was a naturally messy young man or if it was a result of his suddenly chaotic and confusing life. There were claw marks scratched into the hardwood floor in here, too.

I kept my hand over Dominic's hammering heart and kicked the bedroom door shut behind us. He had stripped the bed to conceal his nudity and the fallen sheet was still tangled around his feet. Dominic wobbled and I gave him a shove. He tumbled back onto the mattress and stared up at me, bemused. His dick lay heavy and tempting against his stomach. I unzipped my vest the rest of the way, then peeled away the layer of leather. My breasts spilled free and Dominic's cock sprang up to attention.

I stepped out of my high heels and reached up under my skirt to pull my panties off down my legs. They were wet and Dominic's eyes flew wide. I didn't want to spend the extra few seconds it would take to shed my skirt, so I crawled up onto the bed with it bunched around my hips.

I crawled on hands and knees along Dominic's body. My tits bobbed and he watched them like a cobra watches a snake charmer. I bent low and trailed my nipples up his long, bronzed legs. Goose-bumps rose on his skin and by the time I reached his crotch, Dominic's need made his cock throb like a second heartbeat. I caressed his length with the soft spheres of my tits.

"Oh my god," Dominic groaned.

"Remember anything yet?" I asked.

I heard the front door open and soft footfalls in the living room. Stefano. I was hardly at full power yet, but enough to hear much better than your average human. At least, I *hoped* normal human hearing couldn't detect Stefano's entrance.

"No," Dominic groaned. "I... I don't remember... but I want to..."

I crawled along his taut body, brushing my nipples over his flat stomach and making us both sigh in pleasure. I added little kisses to my journey up Dominic's long frame. His skin was warm. More than warm – hot, like he had just come in from the sun. Sexual energy sizzled off him and it felt... amazing. There was something different about it, something primal and dangerous. Bestial, yes, but more than that.

I could feel the demon in him.

Or maybe it was the demon in me, recognizing one of its own. My body burned with desire and my pussy streamed with every touch. I didn't bother moving slow anymore. I wanted Dominic inside me and I sure as hell didn't want him to notice what was going on in his living room.

I pounced on Dominic and crushed my lips to his. He let out a muffled groan and his body stiffened as I straddled him. Dominic's cock strained between my legs, hot and insistent against me. The room was cold, but the places where our bodies met were fire. I fell and then Dominic was sliding inside me, entering and filling me. Wetness ran in hot lines down his cock and along my trembling thighs.

I moaned against Dominic's mouth and bit his lower lip, teasing and inviting. He moaned back and I breathed it in. Dominic rose to my invitations. His tongue dove into my mouth, tasting and exploring me, while his fingers pressed into my thighs and then raced up to hold my waist. Dominic pulled me down and his hips flexed, plunging himself into me.

"Yes!" I threw my head back, tossing my hair and letting my loud cries fill the bedroom.

I smelled Dominic's sweat and masculine musk, but there was sulfur and saltpeter from the living room. I heard charcoal scraping over the floorboards as Stefano traced his spell circle and the drumbeat of Dominic's heart as he fucked me.

Dominic cupped my ass and I bounced on top of him. His cock drove into me, deep and hard. He pulled me down to him and buried his face against the side of my neck, his eyes falling shut. I felt lips on my skin, kissing, and then teeth biting into tender flesh. I gasped as the pleasure jolted through my body.

"Oh... oh, fuck," I moaned.

My voice shook as Dominic pounded himself up into me. I braced my arms on the mattress to either side and held on. My whole body went tight and exploded with ecstasy. Orgasm poured through me and forced a scream of pleasure from my throat. I'm sure it was a little distracting for Stefano, but I just couldn't help it.

"More," I said.

I swung a shaking leg off and crawled up beside Dominic in the center of the bed. I pressed my face into the mattress and pushed my ass up into the air. He was on his knees in an instant, sliding behind me and grabbing my backside in both hands.

"Who the hell are you?" he groaned.

I had told him my name, but that wasn't really what Dominic was asking. He wanted to know what was going on, why a strange redhead was in his house and throwing herself at him for no apparent reason. Those were dangerous questions. I needed Dominic to focus on me. I arched my spine and brandished my ass.

"Spank me," I told him.

Dominic decided – and quite correctly, in my not-so-humble opinion – that smacking the fine butt offered up to him was far more important than any questions. His hand cracked down on me and I gasped at the sharpness of the blow, then moaned as the edge of pain warmed into pleasure. Dominic slapped my ass twice more before he couldn't wait any longer and sank his cock into me again. Wetness slicked my skin.

A voice... I heard Stefano chanting. I didn't understand the words, but I didn't have to. I just had to keep Dominic from hearing them.

"Fuck me deeper," I cried. "Harder!"

"I... I can't believe I don't remember you," he groaned.

"Fuck me!"

Dominic grunted and hammered himself into me, pounding us into the mattress. His body blazed with heat and energy. I took it all and felt how wild he was, how close Dominic was to losing control and falling right over the edge into the tidal force of his lust. I was full of power, pleasure, of hard cock, but something in the back of my mind shrieked a warning. Dominic was losing control...

"Oh god," he said. The words were low, nearly a growl. "I... I feel..."

Dominic let out a long groan that rose and changed until it became a lupine howl. His hands grew larger, the fingers longer and I felt the tips pressed into my skin with bright pricks of pain. Claws. Dominic was transforming. We were about to give a whole new meaning to the term *doggie style*.

I twisted as best I could – which wasn't well, with Dominic gripping my hips and ass – and stared. He threw back his head, eyes squeezed tightly shut. His sleek surfer's body was covered in fine blond fur that grew swiftly thicker and darker as I watched, until it was that terribly familiar smoky gray color.

I gasped and squirmed in Dominic's bed. Shit, Stefano had warned me to be careful and I had even told Max about the demonic passions that cause werewolves to change. I was the daughter of a succubus – I should have known better than anyone about the passion of lust.

The rest of Dominic was growing, too. His limbs were becoming longer, thicker before my eyes. Dominic's face elongated, teeth lengthening to sharp white points in his muzzle and his sooty gray ears twitched in the direction of the door. I had to keep the werewolf focused on me and keep his lust from tipping over into bloodlust. The desire to fuck had to outweigh the urge to hunt and kill, or Stefano didn't stand a chance.

Dominic was too tall to fuck me on my knees anymore. The werewolf pinned me against his huge gray chest with talons curled around me, his hands so large now that the claws touched about my waist. I could take it as hard as any human man could give it to me, but *all* of Dominic was growing. His demon-wolf cock had easily doubled in length and thickness. It plunged impossibly deep into my body as he held me against him.

"Fuck!" I screamed.

I writhed on the end of the werewolf's monster cock and felt it twitch inside me, the bonfire of his lust rising. I had to keep him here, like this. But my pussy was reflexively tightening, instinctively trying to halt the ruthless invasion of my body. And with the power Dominic had given me, I was like a warm, wet vice. The werewolf snarled dangerously deep in his throat.

"More," I demanded in a low, sultry voice. "Fuck me hard."

I moaned and leaned back into Dominic. I willed myself to open, to take every inch of his steely length. His snarl turned into something huskier and Dominic began to move inside me. Not gently – he drove himself into me with swift blows. I can't say that it didn't hurt. The werewolf took me mercilessly, with all of the hellish passion of his demon curse.

His huge cock filled me entirely and then some. My nerves and my voice screamed out with pleasure and pain as Dominic speared me on his dick. I clawed wildly for purchase, for some handhold against the savage pounding. I sank my fingers into the wolf's fur as his taut thighs banged into my ass. His pelt was surprisingly soft under my touch and I held on for dear life.

"Fuck me," I whimpered.

Dominic seemed to be filling my entire body. I cried out again, but this time in pure pleasure as the orgasm poured through me. I squirmed and writhed on the end of Dominic's towering cock, moaned as he stretched me. Beneath us, the bed creaked and then finally collapsed with a crash under the weight of a fully trans-formed werewolf fury-fucking his half-demon prey.

We slammed to the ground and Dominic dropped me into the broken bed. I rolled over as the werewolf surged up to his feet, his sharp claws gouging new furrows into the hardwood floor. His long ears twitched in the direction of the door again and Dominic's nose rose toward the ceiling, nostrils flaring. He sensed Stefano and his spell. A deep, terrible growl rumbled through the werewolf.

"No," I gasped. "I'm not done with you!"

I grabbed Dominic's wrist. It was as big around as my bicep and even with my sex-powered strength, the werewolf just about yanked my arm from its socket as he pulled away. But I had his attention.

"Fuck me," I commanded.

I spread my legs wide, an invitation that few have ever resisted. Dominic's long body tensed and his ears laid along his skull, torn between the need to rip out my throat and the primal desire to ravage my exposed, vulnerable pussy. I threw my head back, thrust my soft tits up at him, and let out a loud, slutty moan.

Dominic seized me again. He hooked sharp claws through my skirt and pulled, slicing the leather and tearing it away. When I was naked, Dominic threw me back until I hit the wall and pinned me there with his massive weight. The werewolf's cock stood out from the thick gray fur of his powerful body, its length still glistening and wet from my pussy. I twined my legs around Dominic's hips and he plunged himself up inside me again. I screamed. His cock was huge and he wasn't gentle. The sexual energy that poured from him was raw and wild, healing me and keeping me strong even as the werewolf savaged my body.

"Don't stop!" I cried. My voice was raw from screaming. "Fuck me, damn it!"

Dominic leaned against me and his claws sliced deep gashes into the wall behind us. The monstrous wolf panted and growled as he pounded himself into me. But to be fair, so did I.

My pussy was so fucking full of dick, stretching me and stroking every inch inside me. How much more time did Stefano need? I had no idea. I had lost all sense of time. My whole world was sharp claws, thick gray fur and fourteen inches of cock hammering into my streaming slit.

"Is... is that all you've got?" I moaned.

I wound my arms around the werewolf's neck and met him blow for blow. I put every ounce of my supernatural strength to use. I squeezed and milked Dominic's demon-cursed cock with all my might. He didn't hold back and neither did I.

His growl rose to an otherworldly howl and his jackhammer rhythm faltered. I wasn't prepared and I convulsed, gasping, when Dominic loosed himself inside me like a fucking fire hose. The torrent of cum filled and then swiftly overfilled me. Slick wetness gushed from my pussy and ran in rivers along my ass. Heat and pain and blazing, glorious pleasure consumed me. I came hard, screaming and rising with the creamy tide pouring into my body.

Werewolves are not kind or delicate lovers. When Dominic was done flooding my pussy, he dropped me to the floor and stood over me like a predator over downed prey. His breath rasped, deep and rough while I lay twitching and whimpering on the scarred hardwood. Cum gushed from between my limp legs, oozing out into a spreading puddle of white. Dominic's tail swept in a slow arc, side to side as he regarded me with burning golden eyes.

Stefano's voice rose outside the door. The werewolf spun and his claws flexed like a row of scythes. His smoky muzzle peeled back from dagger teeth in a terrible demon grin.

"No," I groaned. "Stefano..."

Dominic hurtled toward the living room. The door and its frame exploded outward in a shower of splinters. Fucking the werewolf had consumed just as much power as I could take from him, but I heaved myself to my feet and ran through the hole in the wall that used to be a bedroom door.

The rest of the apartment was nothing like I had left it. The coffee table and its burden of surfing magazines were shoved out of the way, back against the wall. Stefano knelt in the center of the living room, at the heart of several interlocking charcoal circles twined with runic symbols. Strange herbs burned without fire and filled the room with a sweet scent. The air itself felt strange, too, electrically charged and somehow thin, as though we stood on the top of a mountain instead of in a sea-level apartment.

Dominic didn't seem to appreciate the skilled magic at work, though. Steely hackles rose along his back like bristling iron blades and his eyes burned with demonic fire. The werewolf snarled and launched himself at Stefano.

I ran after Dominic, grabbing and managing to snatch a handful of tail. He lurched and slowed for only a fraction of a second, and then his fur slipped out of my grasp.

"Stefano!" I screamed.

The wizard didn't look at me. Instead, he stared at Dominic and held up his hands. Was Stefano... surrendering? If so, the werewolf didn't care. He pounced toward the charcoal circles with sharp claws extended. Dominic was going to rip Stefano apart, just like Tor Lee.

I whirled, searching for a weapon, for that revolver Stefano had brandished at me twice already. Where the fuck was a gun when I needed it?

Stefano spoke a single arcane syllable and the charcoal sigils exploded with brilliant blue-white light. Magazines, a few coasters and a can of surfboard wax drifted up into the air. I couldn't see Stefano or Dominic through the blaze of light. I shouted at them and threw my arm across my stinging eyes.

And then the light was gone and so were Stefano's runes and circles. Pale winter sun streamed through the window. There was no sign of Dominic except a new set of claw marks scratched into his floor. Stefano dropped his hands back to his sides, smiling.

I had never seen a smile like that on the other hunter's face, not even after I fucked him.

Stefano finally turned to me and stared. I must have been quite a sight – naked and trembling, werewolf spunk streaking my legs from crotch to ankles. I could only imagine what my hair looked like. I thought I felt a stir of lust from Stefano, though I was ready to admit that my senses were pretty blasted. I might have been wrong.

"Wow," Stefano said. "Lilith, are you okay?"

I drew a deep, shuddering breath. "I think this takes the walk of shame to a whole new level, but... yeah. I'm good."

"We better clean up and get back to the College," said Stefano. "I'd be surprised if the neighbors haven't already called the police."

I laughed shakily. "Or at least animal control."

Chapter NINE

Three days later, I knocked on Max's apartment door. There had been plenty of time to recover from my supernatural fuck-fest with Dominic, but I still felt like I was walking funny. I juggled the pink bakery boxes to my other arm and was digging through my pocket for the key when the door swung open. Max's eyes widened and he pulled me into a tight hug.

"Lil!" he said. "I'm glad you're alright. I was so worried. Did you get your guy?"

"We got him."

"We?" Max asked.

He let go and gestured me inside. I set the boxes down on his coffee table and dropped onto his threadbare couch. Max sat next to me.

"Stefano and I took him on together," I said. "I fucked Dominic until Stefano could finish his spell. It was close, though. I told him that if we ever have to do this again, we're switching jobs."

Max chuckled. "Dominic? That's the werewolf's name?"

"Yeah. Stefano teleported Dominic off to a secure cage somewhere at the College and the High Magus is working to lift the werewolf curse. It's a long and complicated spell, and the College is really curious how Dominic got cursed in the first place... But he's going to be okay."

"Will Dominic remember any of this?" Max asked.

"Some. He doesn't remember what happened while he was transformed," I said, repeating what Stefano had told me. "But the College can't do much about the memories that remain. The demonic nature of the werewolf curse makes Dominic more or less immune to memory charms."

"Just like you," Max said with a nod. "What are they going to do once he's cured?"

"Keep an eye on him. Hopefully, Dominic will understand the importance of keeping the secret." I sat back and laced my fingers behind my head, staring up at the ceiling. "Stefano and I split the bounty, minus cleanup fees. He really earned it. The wizards can do some truly amazing stuff."

"Well, it *is* magic."

"So is what I do," I said. "But that was... something else."

Max squeezed my knee. He was a warm, comfortable weight beside me on the couch. Max didn't understand, not truly. But he was good at listening.

We sat in silence for a few minutes. Finally, Max leaned forward and nudged the pink boxes on his scuffed old coffee table. The smells of fresh dough and hot sugar filled his tiny apartment.

"So what's this?" he asked.

"Donuts. I wanted to thank you and the GTA guys for taking care of my car. But when I showed up, they said you were gone."

Max's face turned red and he ran his knuckles along one cheek. "Yeah... That's what Sam wanted to talk to me about. When I left with you the other day, I was sort of in the middle of pulling a transmission for a client."

"So?" I asked. I remembered what had to be dozens of visits I had paid to Max at work. "You said it would be fine. We do it all the time."

Max shook his head. "I guess that was the last time, though. Sam finally fired me."

"What? That sucks," I objected. "Want me to talk to Sam? I'm sure I could convince him to change his mind."

"No. It's okay, Lil. This would only happen again. I doubt Sam will ever think me being your booty call is more important than his business."

"Only because Sam doesn't know how fine the booty is," I said, then sighed. "He has no idea how much you've done for me."

"And we can't exactly tell him."

"I could give you some money," I suggested. "Just until you get back on your feet. I mean, you earned it almost as much as Stefano did."

"No way, Lil."

I knew Max would say that. He always did. So I put an arm around Max's shoulders and kissed the angle of his jaw.

"Well, you'll figure something out, a smart boy like you," I said. "You'd make a great porn star, you know. And in the meantime, I brought two dozen donuts to share with the garage, but fuck those guys. Let's get sick on way too much sugar and watch bad movies."

Max laughed and grabbed the remote, but by the time the television flickered on, I had already forgotten about movies and donuts. My gaze slid from the television to Max's profile and then down to his lap. There were other ways to cheer up my best friend.

LILY QUINN BOOK #4

Chapter ONE

The winter cold cut right through the ivy and brick of the College. Even inside Dresden Hall, I could just about see my breath. I shivered and wondered if the wizards had some kind of magic to deal with the icy chill or simply didn't worry about such mundane things. I wrapped my arms around myself and studied the wall. But the bounty board that hung in the huge – and did I mention drafty? – foyer of Dresden Hall was mostly cork. There were only a few notices posted. I sighed, tucked my hands into my pockets and checked them all.

Let's see... A pack of goblins had taken up residence in the basement of the museum of modern art. Goblins were gross, tenacious and rubbery little bastards that didn't really hurt anyone. They smelled terrible and the last ones I dealt with had an unhealthy obsession with my long red hair.

Pass.

But that was the best bounty available. I looked up at a brown clay doll skittering across the top of the corkboard. Its features were rough and the whole thing was no larger than my hand. The homunculus belonged to Sabra, one of the other College hunters, and regarded the sparse postings with skeptical black glass eyes.

I was beginning to think that I'd go after the goblins out of sheer boredom when I heard footsteps behind me in the hall. I turned and waved to Dorian Vandi. The old sorcerer was short, balding and the only one in the entire College who smiled when he saw me. I guess I couldn't blame the others for some prejudice, though. I *am* half succubus, after all, and the wizards have been fighting against demons since Merlin's day.

"Hello, Lilith," said Dorian.

I've tried more times than I can count to get him to just call me *Lily*, but the wizards are obsessed with true names and that kind of thing. They don't do nicknames. I pointed to a slender roll of parchment in Dorian's hand.

"Please tell me that's a new bounty," I said.

Dorian nodded and found a few free pins. There were plenty of them clustered unused around the corkboard's edge.

"Is it for whoever tried to steal *The Gates of Avalon*?" I asked.

"We're still looking into that," Dorian admitted, shaking his head. "We have questioned Kalen Silverwind repeatedly, but the fairy is proving remarkably close-mouthed on the issue."

"You should let me take a run at Kalen."

"You already did, before you turned him over to us."

I grinned. "Yeah. And it was fun, even if I didn't get much out of him."

Dorian's bushy gray eyebrows furrowed. He selected an open patch of cork – there were plenty of those, too – and smoothed the page he was holding out onto the bounty board.

"Why actual paper?" I asked. "I know that you guys have at least heard of email. Stefano even owns a cell phone. Couldn't you just send out a group text or something?"

"Parchment and books on actual shelves can't be hacked or intercepted," Dorian answered with a small smile.

"Maybe. But they can still be stolen," I reminded him. "Or else you wouldn't keep questioning Kalen."

Dorian blushed through his beard and managed to prick his finger with one of the pins. I watched over the old wizard's shoulder as he finished posting the bounty. Sabra's homunculus scrambled down the corkboard for a better view.

"So who's the target?" I asked.

"A German nix," said Dorian. "A slippery fellow who escaped us some years back."

"Adähr," I gasped.

I stared at the parchment. I didn't even need to read the name written in Dorian's neat handwriting. I recognized the picture at once. Thick black hair, secretive smile, shimmering sea-blue eyes... I shook my head, trying to clear it. Eyes did *not* shimmer in a black-and-white sketch.

"Yes," said Dorian. "I suppose you would remember him. Adähr has returned to America, it seems."

"Back to his old tricks?" I asked.

Dorian nodded. "Haunting all eight bridges and robbing any pedestrians unlucky enough to tempt a nix."

"Any drownings?"

"Not yet. And we would like to stop Adähr before that happens. He's not been very careful with his powers, either, flaunting them in front of his victims. The cost of memory alterations has been considerable."

A shiver slid down my spine that had nothing to do with the cold of Dresden Hall. In fact, I suddenly felt rather warm. I stuffed my hands into the pockets of my jeans.

"What's Adähr even doing back here in the States?" I asked. "I thought he was in Europe."

"He was," Dorian answered. He smoothed out the poster and stood back. "And the Castle posted quite a bounty for his capture. In fact, they believe that Adähr fled to America again because their own hunters were closing in."

"Slick bastard."

Sabra's homunculus dropped down off the bounty board to the floor at our feet and scuttled off to find its mistress. Sabra would have her army of clay men staking out the shadows of every bridge in the city by dinnertime. I eyed the black and copper of Stefano's spell-card tucked in the corner of the board. Within the hour soon, every hunter in town would be alerted to Adähr's return and on the prowl.

"We'll catch him this time, Lilith," Dorian assured me.

I might have growled a little at that. I didn't want the other hunters to catch Adähr. *I* wanted to do it.

"It sounds as though you 'ave some history with the nix," said a new voice. It was deep and beautifully accented in French.

I turned to find a new wizard in the hallway, standing next to a polished suit of armor. He was a tall, handsome man in his forties. The dark stubble along his cheeks was just short of a beard. He wore a long black overcoat with an ornate silver cross pinned to the lapel. I had seen that sigil only a few times before – the mark of the Castle.

"Good afternoon," he said. "My name is Remy Saville."

He removed a worn, wide-brimmed leather hat and inclined his head to me. Remy's hair was a deep mahogany color and tied back from his face in a neat tail.

"He's a hunter from the Castle," Dorian supplied. "Remy, may I introduce Lilith Quinn? She works for the College as one of our bounty hunters."

Remy fixed hard gray eyes on me, then took my hand and kissed it lightly. I shivered again and couldn't help a bit of a sigh. I've always had a weakness for that old-world charm. Something else I blamed Adähr for.

"It's a pleasure to meet you, Lilith," Remy said.

"What's a wizard from the Castle doing all the way over here?" I asked.

"Pursuing Adähr. I 'ave been tracking the elusive nix for several months. Fleeing across the ocean will not save 'im from justice."

"You'll have to beat me to Adähr if you want to bring him in," I countered.

One of Remy's eyebrows rose and he inspected me carefully. I cocked my hips to let him get a good long look and felt his interest like heat from a flame. But the French hunter's lust was restrained, well-contained and controlled.

"I 'ave reviewed all of the magi in your city," Remy said. "You don't match the name or description of any of them."

"No one said I was a wizard," I told him with a smirk. Suddenly, icy Dresden Hall was positively smoldering.

"Fascinating," Remy murmured. "I 'ave never before met a hunter who was not one of our own."

"As far as I know, I'm the only one."

Remy inclined his head to me again. "I would very much like to hear more. Tomorrow morning, I begin my hunt for the nix. But tonight I would consider it an honor if you would agree to dinner with me, Lilith. I 'ave many questions for you."

Dorian glanced back and forth between us, then shrugged and made his way down the hall the direction he had come, inspecting the polished armor and shields minutely. I cocked my head toward Remy.

"Dinner sounds great," I said. "Six o'clock?"

Remy's other eyebrow shot up. "That is... quite early."

"I'm expecting a long night," I said with a wink. "And I'm eager to get started."

The French hunter smiled at me. "Then I greatly anticipate our dinner. And perhaps we will share something sweet for dessert."

Chapter TWO

I drove straight home. There wasn't much time before my dinner date with Remy Saville and I badly needed to change my panties. Between news of Adähr's return to my city and meeting Remy, I had soaked right through them. So I stripped out of my clothes, threw them in the laundry basket and took a quick shower.

When I was done, I padded into my bedroom on bare feet with a towel wrapped beneath my arms. The toy boxes under the bed called to me. They were full of the kinds of toys that were brightly colored and sometimes made noises, but which you would certainly *never* want to give to a child.

I resisted the temptation to fuck myself silly, though. If I played my cards right, I was willing to bet that I could get a handsome Frenchman to do it for me. And if I did say so myself, the deck was pretty well stacked in my favor.

So I dried my hair, put on some makeup, and slipped into a slinky little red cocktail dress that was sure to make Remy's mouth water. I inspected the results in the mirror, winked at my reflection, and grabbed the keys to my Alfa Romeo. I threw them and my cell phone into a beaded purse. I don't really like carrying purses, but I didn't want to try secreting a handful of necessities in my dress. There wasn't a handful of extra space available.

As the sun sank down into the ocean, I drove across the city toward the bayfront. The day had been cold enough that there wasn't much fog and the last shards of sunlight glittered in pink and silver on the water.

I parked in front of the Hotel Marquis just before six o'clock and tossed my keys to the valet. I didn't go into the hotel itself, but a restaurant next door called The Green. Whoever named it wasn't being even slightly literal. I couldn't see a single bit of green inside that wasn't on someone's salad plate. Everything in The Green was clean and white – including the pants, shirt, and starched apron worn by a clean-shaven young man who escorted me to a small table in one corner.

Remy was waiting for me. He stood at my approach, circled the table and pulled out my chair. I wasn't sure yet if Remy was being chivalrous or sexist, but decided to give him the benefit of the doubt. I sat down.

"It's a pleasure to see you again, Lilith," he said.

I smiled and Remy seated himself once more across the table. I could have said the same. The French hunter looked unbearably hot. He had swapped out his traveling clothes for a neat slate gray suit that matched his eyes. His cheeks remained rough with dark stubble, though.

"Are you staying over at the Marquis?" I asked.

Remy nodded. "It's a favorite when conducting Castle business in your country."

"Is that what we're doing?" I picked up a menu and looked over it at him. "Business? Should we be up in the penthouse suite with the wards?"

"Those wards are still being reconstructed, I am told. I also understand that you 'ad something to do with their destruction. That is… impressive."

I just smirked at that. I didn't often get the chance to be mysterious around the wizards. The College didn't trust me very much and kept a close eye through their extensive scry network. I didn't have many secrets from them, but they told me only what they wanted to.

Another server in crisp whites came by to take our order. Remy selected a bottle of twenty-year-old Chateau Latour to go with my braised lamb. When the waiter inclined his head and retreated again, I looked at Remy.

"You've traveled a long way to hunt down Adähr," I said. "What, doesn't the Castle trust the College to do the job?"

"The Castle 'as great faith in our American cousins," Remy answered politely. "But the Saville family 'ave served the Castle as hunters for generations. It is my job to stop Adähr and I *will* carry out that duty, no matter the cost."

There was a deep but restrained intensity to this final statement that made me press my thighs tightly together beneath the tablecloth. Remy took this job seriously. He steepled his fingers on the table and watched me closely.

"So what's Adähr been up to since he left?" I asked.

"The nix 'as made his way across Europe, like the highwaymen of old, following the rivers. Over the last year alone, Adähr's stolen an estimated five hundred thousand euros."

About a million dollars. Not as much as a Wall Street broker, but that was a lot of wallets and jewelry. Adähr had been busy.

Remy fell silent when the white-clad waiter returned with the Chateau Latour and measured a little out into a glass. The French hunter inhaled the bouquet, took a slow sip, and then nodded an approving dismissal to our waiter. Remy poured me a glass of wine.

"Worse is Adähr's lack of concern for how many humans witness 'is abilities," he continued. "It 'as caused considerable 'eadache for the Castle".

Dorian mentioned something like that, too.

"Had to fix a lot of memories?" I asked.

Remy nodded with a small smile. I took a sip of the wine he had selected. It was dark, rich and I caught the scents of wood and leather.

"Catching Adähr 'as proved... difficult," Remy admitted. "The nixi are – if you will forgive the saying – slippery creatures. They are elemental beings, much like the djinni, and never venture far from water if they can avoid it. It is the center of their strength. Nixi can control any body of water or disappear into it entirely. Isolating a nix from such a ready and plentiful source of power is a challenge, to say the least."

"Yes," I agreed. "Adähr's a hard man to catch."

"It will take a hard man to catch 'im," Remy said.

"And are you a hard man?"

I peered over the rim of my glass at Remy, down in the direction of his lap, but sadly, the table was in my way and x-ray vision isn't one of the powers that sex gives me. Strength, speed and healing, yes. And even heightened senses, too, but no vision beyond the standard spectrum. No flight, either. Too bad – that would have been pretty damned cool.

"Let us say simply that I am experienced," Remy replied evenly. "My skills 'ave never disappointed before."

I smirked at him, but Remy didn't drop his gaze. English may not have been his native tongue, but the Frenchman certainly knew his way around a double entendre. I looked forward to putting his claims to the test.

Our meals arrived and Remy raised his glass to me. I mirrored his toast, then took another sip of wine and licked my lips. The other hunter leaned closer, ignoring his food.

"And what of you, Lilith?" he asked. "Why does a woman like you hunt monsters?"

"The money's good," I pointed out. That wasn't the real reason, of course, but the paycheck didn't hurt.

"Very," Remy agreed. "And a great deal of danger. Your life, as I understand it, is dangerous enough. You are the daughter of a demon. A succubus."

"Did Dorian tell you that?" I asked.

Remy nodded. "Cambions are rare, to say the least. And even with the writings that Merlin left behind, the Castle still knows so little about you, Lilith."

"I'll have to talk to Dorian about giving out my personal information," I said with a sigh, but then smiled across the table. "Did you ask about my parentage before or after the dinner invitation?"

"After. I was already quite... intrigued," Remy answered. He regarded me with his hard, steel-colored eyes. "You are something of a mystery, Lilith."

"Oh?"

The lamb – especially paired with the wine – was delicious, but I pushed my plate away. Beneath the table, I slipped my foot from my shoe and ran it up along Remy's calf.

"I 'ave never before met one of your kind," he said. His voice remained even despite my toes moving further up his leg. "And I am surprised to find you in the employ of the College, rather than 'unted by them."

"I've proved myself to the High Magus... More or less. And I always end up getting my man."

Remy kept his expression cool until my toes were running along his inner thigh. Then he let one dark brow rise a fraction of an inch.

"And Adähr?" he asked.

"Adähr was my first job," I admitted. "I was young and he got away from me. But now he's back in my city and I've got a second chance. I *will* catch Adähr this time."

"Perhaps. There will be stiff competition."

Remy refilled our wineglasses. The French hunter's hands were absolutely steady, even as the muscles of his legs bunched under my toes. I slid up another few inches and found his package thick and heavy against my questing foot. Not quite hard yet, but growing swiftly.

"I have an edge," I said softly.

Remy took a long drink of wine. "You know Adähr."

"I've hunted him before."

"And so 'ave I," Remy reminded me. "More recently and for far longer than you."

"I have my tricks."

"I'm certain you do. Your beauty is certainly enough to leave mortal men stunned and 'elpless in your wake," Remy said with the ghost of a smile.

I traced the swelling length of his cock with my nimble toes and Remy calmly took a sip of wine. His composure remained unshakable as my foot curled against him. Impressive. Sometimes a nice experienced man is just what a girl needs.

"My abilities are... special," I said. "I do need something to fuel them, though."

Remy's accented voice dropped to a deep basso rumble. "And what is that?"

"I could show you," I suggested.

The older hunter inclined his head once more in a short nod. "I would like that. I 'ave always wanted to study a cambion in person. There is much to learn from you, Lilith."

"I'll be a good teacher," I purred.

Remy insisted on paying the bill and then stood, smoothly adjusting his slate-colored jacket over the thick bulge in his pants. He pulled out my chair and I took his offered hand. I rose and Remy escorted me out of The Green, down the sidewalk to the Hotel Marquis. The sun had set and the hotel glowed blue and silver with tasteful spotlights all along the waterfront.

The etched glass doors slid open and Remy guided me across the gold and marble of the hotel lobby. A pair of well-dressed businessmen attempted to follow us into the elevator, but Remy shot them a look and held the button until the doors shut, leaving us alone. Remy wound a strong arm around my waist, pulling me close. He inhaled the scent of my hair and I felt his breath on the back of my neck.

"There are stories of the succubae," he said, lips brushing my ear. "That the lust demons can bring mortals to the edge of climax with nothing more than a kiss."

I turned in the circle of Remy's embrace and his arms tightened around me. His jaw was rough against my cheek as I pulled the French hunter into a long, deep kiss. His tongue traced my lips lightly and they parted before him. Feverish heat flashed through me as Remy dove sinuously in. Being French kissed by an actual Frenchman is an experience I highly recommend.

I would have torn open Remy's pants and fucked him right there – the mirrored walls reflected infinite copies of us and that was a *lot* of sexy – but the elevator slid to a stop and chimed softly while I was still drowning in his kiss. Remy kept his arm around my waist and led me down the hall. His pace was easy, unhurried. A younger man might have rushed me to the nearest bed, but Remy remained composed. At least, if you didn't count the massive tent in his pants. Personally, I counted that in his favor.

Remy unlocked a slick black door with a keycard and escorted me into his hotel room. The lights were on, but turned down low, surrounding us in their dim amber glow. Well-worn leather cases with scarred brass buckles sat on the desk and there was a trunk beside the couch that filled the suite with rich herbal scents. There was a wooden box, too, that seemed a little small compared to the array of other magical accoutrements. But the top was seared with the same cross that Remy had been wearing on the lapel of his coat when we met, and closed by an heavy iron latch. I was pretty sure I didn't want to touch that.

I took a step away across the hotel suite, into the door of the bedroom. Remy watched me with those hard gray eyes as he unbuttoned his dinner jacket and draped it over the back of a chair. Remy said he didn't know much about cambions and I looked forward to educating him.

I ran my hands up the door frame, caressing the polished wood, and let my hips sway in time to the hot throb between my legs. Remy's fingers slowed and actually fumbled in unknotting his tie. The bright golden glow of lust flared inside him and my own desire rose in immediate answer.

"Come here," I purred.

Remy pulled his tie free with a hiss of silk and it fell to the floor as he strode across the thick carpet to me. I turned in the doorway and bent over. My dress was short when I stood, but doubled over, it slid up enough to reveal the soft globes of my ass and the brief black lace line of my thong. I love that dress – it really puts the *cock* in cocktail dress.

As I straightened, I ran my hands up my calves, my thighs, and up under the hem of my dress. I moved up further, peeling the clinging red fabric away over my head and leaving myself clad only in high heels and underwear. The rest of my body was bared before Remy. His strong fingers combed through my long hair and then trailed lightly down my spine.

"I 'ave never seen a creature so lovely," Remy said in a low voice.

I slipped away again, through the door and into the bedroom. Remy followed, raking his gaze over me. I curled my finger, gesturing him closer. When Remy was near enough, I slid my hands under the collar of his shirt and yanked it open. Beneath, the French hunter's chest and stomach were hard and as sharply defined as if they had been chiseled out of granite.

No, I corrected myself. *Chiseled* was far too crude a word. Remy's muscles were sculpted and molded by decades of training and combat. I pushed his shirt off his shoulders and my fingers lingered on a pale line of scars that angled down over one toned pectoral.

"*Loup garou,*" said Remy.

That was French for *werewolf*. A mark like this meant Remy had been bitten by a werewolf. So he had gone through the curse – and the cure.

I ran my fingers over the firm knots of his abdominal muscles. There was another scar just below Remy's navel. The hunter took my wrist gently.

"Vampire." Remy guided my touch to the matching scar on his back. "She ran me through."

I hooked my fingers through his thick leather belt and pulled it open.

"Is that all she did to you?" I asked.

Remy gave me a grim smile and stepped out of his slacks when I pushed them down. Before I could strip him any further, Remy cupped the back of my head in one large hand and ran the other along my side.

"You, on the other 'and, are flawless," he noted.

Remy said it like a compliment and his rich French accent made everything sound like poetry, but I wondered. Did Remy think me less of a bounty hunter because I had no scars? But if so, it did nothing to dampen his desire for me. Remy's lust burned like a bonfire as he traced the delicate, lacy lines of my underwear and finished undressing me, laying aside the wet tangle of lace on the dresser. Remy's trapped cock strained insistently in his fitted boxer-briefs, but still the French hunter didn't hurry.

Remy guided me gently down into his bed, back against the pillows. He pressed me into the covers with the hard, unyielding weight of his body. I felt his mouth against the sensitive flesh just beneath my ear and then nibbling a tingling path along the side of my neck. Remy's lips and tongue explored my skin and left blushing bites all across the pale curves of my breasts that seared like burning embers of pleasure.

I arched my back and eagerly pushed my tits into his mouth. Remy's tongue was *amazing*. I actually whimpered a little when he prowled further down my body on hands and knees like a stalking tiger. But then Remy's deft hands were between my thighs, parting them. His fingers brushed over my pussy and then in, spreading me like the pages of a book.

"You told me you wanted to learn about cambion powers," I moaned.

"I am," said Remy.

His cheek was rough against the soft skin of my inner thigh, and his mouth was hot. Remy's nimble tongue slid over my slicked labia and made my breath come in sharp gasps. It slipped warm and wet inside me. Remy kissed my pussy with every bit as much skill and desire as he had my lips.

I curled my fingers into Remy's dark hair and pulled him tight against me. The pleasure jolted through my body and I squirmed, bucking my hips and pushing up toward him. Remy's tongue stirred sensations through me, liquid and hot and racing along every nerve. I wrapped my legs around Remy's neck, squeezed my eyes shut and came with a long, loud cry.

When I pried my eyes open again, the Frenchman was sitting up, propped on one elbow and licking his lips. My whole body burned with need and I grinned at him.

"My turn," I said.

Remy let out a deep, pleased sigh as I pressed my hand over the bulge at the front of his fitted trunks. I sank my teeth into the waistband, then tugged the cloth down and away. Remy's freed cock jutted out toward me with commanding desire. I closed my fingers around his thick base and the hard length pulsed with heat in my hand. Remy's sigh became a low groan when I sucked the head hungrily into my mouth.

The hunter reached out and stroked my hair back from my face, watching me wrap my lips around his dick. Remy caressed the nape of my neck and then my shoulders. I shuddered with electric jolts of pleasure and let out a moan muffled by my mouthful of cock.

Remy's powerful lust surged and sexual energy flowed from him in a smooth, measured stream. It filled me with a molten golden glow that I was always a little surprised wasn't visible.

I plunged my head down onto Remy's cock and swallowed him deep. I swirled my tongue along his length and licked at the heavy weight of his balls. A bead of sweat rolled down Remy's chest and I swear even his groans were accented. I pulled my mouth off him when I ran out of air and threw my head back, whipping my hair like a flaming halo. I gasped for breath.

"And this is what empowers you, Lilith?" Remy asked.

I nodded and licked my lips. The French hunter's taste on them was musky and masculine. And it was delicious. Wetness dripped down between my legs.

"Do you require sex?" Remy trailed his fingers along my spine to cup my ass. "As the succubae do?"

"Need sex? No," I said. I squeezed his cock gently. "All I *require* is passion, lust. But what I want..."

I caressed the length of Remy's dick and loved how it made his jaw tighten. He seized me around the waist with one corded arm and flipped me onto my back beneath him. The urge to spread my legs before him was overwhelming and Remy slid smoothly between them. His cock brushed the slicked, sensitive pink of my pussy, making me moan and my hips rise up to meet him. I locked my legs around Remy's waist and he sank his dick into my body, filling me.

"Yes," I moaned. "Yes!"

Remy moved slowly, rolling his hips and pumping himself into me in long, smooth strokes. The muscles of his back flexed under my heels. I laced my fingers into Remy's thick mahogany hair and pulled him in for another of those famous French kisses. His tongue danced skillfully over mine, matching the pace of his dick inside me. Ecstasy pulsed through my body and felt almost like being fucked from both ends.

I let Remy bear me down, willingly drowning in the storm of sensations that he loosed inside me. But still I wanted more. I grabbed Remy's hands and pulled them against my chest. I gave an encouraging squeeze. Remy nodded once and clasped the softness of my breasts together. He pinched the sensitive nipples between long fingers and they stiffened to rosy peaks.

I released Remy's wrists. The French hunter clearly knew what he was doing... Actually, that was a bit of an understatement. Remy Saville played me like a fucking violin. His hands and lips moved over me with swift certainty. And if I was a violin, then Remy was a master musician. Every time he changed angle or pace inside me, rich new pleasures boiled through my body.

Remy leaned back on his heels, holding one of my legs out and kissed the inside of my ankle as the fingers of his other hand danced over my clit. My metaphors failed me utterly and there was nothing musical about my screams. I moaned like a whore as Remy Saville fucked me. I grabbed onto his taut thighs and the world exploded in brilliant fireworks of desire.

"God, you can do this to me all night," I panted.

"Perhaps I will," said Remy.

The sheets were a damp, twisted mess beneath us. Every time Remy plunged his cock into me, more wetness streamed down my skin. I bit my lip – hard – to silence myself and simply listen to the slick sounds of Remy driving himself into me. But I was hardly content just to be an audience to his admittedly impressive skills. I dug my heels into Remy's flexing buttocks and used the leverage to bring my hips up, meeting his thrusts and taking him to the hilt. He grunted and hammered his dick so deep into me that spots of color swam through my vision. I raked my nails over Remy's hard chest and felt the other hunter's heart pounding beneath my fingertips. I had to restrain myself to avoid giving him new scars with my nails. Though maybe Remy would have liked that...

"I want you to cum," I moaned.

It wasn't a request. I squeezed Remy's cock deep inside me and milked his length urgently. He gasped and the flow of his sexual energy became almost frenzied. No matter how experienced and controlled any of us are, we all lose it when we're at that peak of pleasure and feel the fall coming.

I pulled Remy deep into me, his balls impacting heavily against my pussy. They felt hot and full. Remy spoke with an effort and his voice was raw with naked need.

"Where do you wish me to finish?" he asked.

Still so polite, even now. I slowed my rolling hips just enough to keep Remy from blowing and trailed a circle over my tummy, tracing my navel with one finger – a soft, smooth canvas for him to paint.

"Right... here," I said.

I gave Remy's cock another rippling squeeze that sent more wetness cascading down over my ass to soak the bed sheets. The French hunter groaned and slit his eyes shut against the surge of helpless ecstasy. He was skilled and experienced at sex, but so was I.

Remy only barely managed to yank his dick out from the tightness of my body in time. A ribbon of cum splashed against my hip before I could seize his pulsing cock. Remy's breath sawed and deepened into a loud grunt as I stroked his slippery shaft. White poured across my belly and pooled in my navel, then ran like spilled cream along my sweat-slicked skin. Remy stared and the sight coaxed another long spurt from his tightened balls that splattered all across my stomach, throwing pearly droplets up onto my breasts.

I sat and pulled Remy easily into another long kiss. He was still bigger than me, but now I was a hell of a lot stronger than him. Warm drops of Remy's spunk rolled down my skin and made me shudder in pleasure. The other hunter drew a deep breath and nodded his approval.

"Very impressive," he admitted.

Chapter
THREE

Remy started a shower and then joined me under the stream of hot water. He slid a soapy washcloth over my skin, working strong fingers into the knotted muscles of my shoulders. His hands were just as amazing here as they had been in the bedroom.

"I'm surprised you don't know more about us," I said, punctuating the statement with a pleased sigh. "I mean, Merlin was a cambion, too. And he founded the Castle, right?"

"Yes. But Merlin charged us to defend humanity from the torments of 'is father's people. Our histories are dedicated more to Merlin's magical teachings than 'is cambion abilities. Which, if you are any example, must 'ave been considerable."

I laughed. It was hard to imagine Merlin fucking his way across Europe. But if the first wizard had been anything like me, I was certain that it had happened. I turned under the pouring water to look up at Remy. He ran the soapy cloth over my wet breasts in slippery circles, leaving iridescent bubbles beading my skin.

"I don't know much about Merlin's father," I admitted. "No one ever talks about him."

Remy's touch slowed across my belly, gently and leisurely scrubbing away the thick white mess he had left there.

"Merlin's father was a powerful incubus," he told me. "Perhaps the greatest demon of all the Nether. They called 'im the Lord of Lust in those days. And Merlin inherited much of that power."

I sighed and my breath made steam eddy around us. "For me, it was my mother. She was a succubus. Apparently, some wizard summoned her and got her pregnant. They never caught that guy."

Remy scowled at that for a moment, but then the French hunter went back to smiling and pulled me close against him.

"But you 'ave inherited great power, as well," Remy said. "From your mother and your father. I must confess to being surprised that Adähr ever managed to escape you at all."

Water slicked Remy's dark brown hair back and streamed down his hard body, but the sudden surge of heat inside me had nothing to do with sharing a shower with a delicious Frenchman. I hoped that my skin was too pink for Remy to see that I was blushing.

"I was young," I said. Did that sound defensive? "Adähr was my very first bounty."

"Ah," Remy answered. He draped the washcloth over the wall of the shower and picked up the shampoo.

"I thought I was being so damned smart," I said with a sigh. "Adähr was holding up everyone with a Rolex along the waterfront, and the police were going crazy trying to catch him at it. So I filled up my wallet with as much cash as I could scrounge up and hung out around the bridges."

"Baiting the trap." Remy seemed skeptical, though. "But the bridges are too close to water for you to catch a nix that way."

I leaned back against his broad chest as the French wizard began to work a handful of shampoo through my tangled red hair. It smelled like vanilla.

"I wasn't trying to catch Adähr. Not yet," I said. I smirked over my shoulder at Remy. "Just bug him. I bought one of those GPS tags for finding your keys. They were still pretty expensive in those days, but I figured it was worth the price. I stuck the tag in a plastic bag to keep it dry and sewed it into the wallet lining."

Remy rubbed his strong fingers through my hair and massaged the scalp beneath. I sighed again, this time in pleasure. Most men don't understand how heavy a head of hair like this can be.

"And did the nix take your bait?" Remy asked.

"Yeah. I was about ten steps out onto the bridge when Adähr confronted me. He kissed my hand and demanded everything I had. I demanded his phone number. He gave me a bogus one and I gave him my wallet. Then he jumped off the bridge."

"A clever ruse," Remy said. He sounded impressed. The thick weight of his cock pressed against my backside. "Why didn't it work? Did your technology fail?"

I closed my eyes as Remy angled the shower head to rinse the shampoo from my hair. Hot water and scented white foam slid down my body as I bit out an answer.

"No. The GPS tag worked just fine until Adähr found and broke it a few hours later. But by then, he was far enough from the water and I was already closing in on him."

"And where did you find the nix?" Remy asked.

His rich, accented voice still sounded casual, idly curious. But the Castle hunter had just fucked me deliciously and my senses were hyper-alert. I heard Remy's heartbeat speed, felt it where his chest pressed against my back. I looked up to find him watching my reflection intently in the shower's glass wall. His gray eyes were narrowed thoughtfully. The view was extremely sexy, but I knew exactly what he was doing.

Remy Saville was pumping me for information. I've pulled the same trick far too many times not to recognize pointed pillow talk. Son of a bitch… That was *my* trick!

With Adähr back in the States, Remy gave up his home field advantage. I might have lost the nix eight years ago, but I still knew the city better than the French hunter did, and where Adähr might go. Starting his hunt tomorrow, my ass. Remy had already begun.

"I caught up with Adähr at the arena," I said, keeping the smirk off my face by sheer force of will.

"Arena?" asked Remy.

"In uptown. They hold concerts there sometimes."

That much was true, at least. None of the rest of it was, though. Remy's fingers trailed up and down my spine. It was bluffing time.

"But that night, the game was football," I said. "The American version, I mean. Not soccer. But I guess Adähr doesn't care what sport is on the menu, as long as he can bet on it."

Remy's reflection nodded. "Yes, Adähr 'as a tendency to lose as much money as 'e steals. Our nix enjoys taking risks. But a sporting stadium... A good place to corner a nix, if one could keep 'im away from the sprinkler systems."

"That's what I thought. But like I said, I was young. I wasn't careful enough. Adähr recognized me and ran. I lost him in the crowd. Maybe he made it to the watering system or a drinking fountain. I never did find out."

Remy's hand lingered on my ass for a moment, then reached past me to turn off the water. He stepped out of the shower and took a towel from the rack. I let out a sincerely regretful sigh when he wrapped it around his waist.

"But you were close, Lilith," Remy said. "Close enough to badly frighten Adähr and send 'im fleeing back to Europe."

"Not enough to stop him from starting the same racket all over again," I answered with sincere irritation. "Adähr is a slick bastard."

Remy gave me a shrug that did nice things to his broad, muscular shoulders, and held out a towel for me. I hadn't forgotten that the French hunter, too, was a slick bastard. I smiled brightly at Remy and accepted the towel. Slick or not, there was no way I was going to let him beat me to Adähr. I had a score to settle with the nix. *No one* gets away from Lily Quinn.

Briskly, I rubbed myself down with the soft hotel towel until I was dry and my skin glowed pink. When I straightened up from patting off my feet, I found Remy watching my backside with a contemplative expression. The front of his towel was distended imposingly. I cupped my hand over the growing length of Remy's cock through the cloth and winked.

"I'd love to stay," I said. "But the other hunters are going to be sorting through every drop of water in the city. If I want to get to Adähr first, I better move."

Remy inclined his head in mute agreement, hiding a smile that I caught in the foggy bathroom mirror. I gave his dick a firm squeeze and enjoyed his deep sigh. He reached for me, but I was full of bright sexual power and slid away easily. Remy was left holding only my towel. He followed me back into the bedroom, where I began scooping up my clothes, but didn't try to grab me again.

"You are an impressive woman, Lilith," Remy admitted. "I 'ave never met another like you. And if the world is lucky, I never shall."

I smirked at him as I pulled my dress back on. "Who says we're done meeting each other now? I'm sure you'll see me again before this job is finished."

Chapter
FOUR

I stopped by my condo to change into a new dress and underwear. They didn't cover a whole lot more than what I had worn to dinner with Remy, but instead of black and red, now I dressed all in blue. I applied fresh makeup, too, and combed out my hair. When I was done getting dressed, there was nothing else to prepare.

Nixi weren't vulnerable to much except being separated from water. Adähr could control or vanish into any water that he could see. You won't find a nix in the desert. Or if you do, he's going to be *really* grumpy.

Outside the windows, the sky was dark and stars shone between fingers of silver clouds. Before leaving again, I paused at my computer to check the arena website. I was right – there was a football game tonight. Our team was playing against Denver. Good. The game would draw a crowd large enough to keep Remy Saville busy for a while. If I judged the French hunter correctly, he was already on his way across the city to the arena, following the "lead" I had given him.

In the meantime, I just needed to snag Adähr out from under all of the other hunters. Fast. Remy was right about one thing, though

– I knew Adähr. I had eight years to obsess over the nix and how he got away from me the first time. The truth was more complicated than I had told Remy. And a lot more embarrassing.

I took the elevator back down to the garage and slid into my Alfa Romeo. The i10 was still a shredded heap from tangling with a werewolf last month, tucked away in a storage unit when Max wasn't working on it. I pulled out onto 12th Street and drove southwest, in the opposite direction of the arena.

The best lies were those with a grain of truth. Adähr really did like to gamble, but not on sports. It wasn't the arena where I had finally discovered the nix eight years ago. I took the freeway south, past Francis Port and didn't even need to check my GPS. I could see my destination from half a mile away.

The House of Diamonds looked like it belonged in the heart of Las Vegas. It was the biggest, flashiest and brightest building in the entire city. The massive hotel-casino was a thirty-story cylinder of colorful glass and light like some giant's huge cocktail. It lit up the night with miles of neon and a dozen spotlights pointed skyward, twirling their beams in eye-catching aerial dances. There were even nightly fireworks shows that annoyed the rest of the neighborhood to no end, but the House of Diamonds made too much money for anyone to stop the casino from doing exactly as it pleased.

I pulled into the House of Diamond's parking structure – a building that almost rivaled the casino for size – and locked up the Alfa Romeo. It was growing late by now and most of the casual gamblers were heading back home, but there was still a considerable crowd streaming in through the long line of doors. Every pane of glass was etched with the casino's name in bold block letters and a row of shining gold diamonds beneath.

Inside the casino was a whole world of lights, noise and smoke. Slot machines chimed and played little snippets of songs as octogenarians threw away their pensions one nickel at a time. Blackjack and poker tables were islands of relative class among the slots, but even there, most of the patrons were locals looking for cheap thrills and enjoying the endless happy hour.

Up on the third floor were the first roulette wheels and craps tables. Here, I noted a couple of suits and cocktail dresses mixed in among the muumuus and Hawaiian shirts. Better, but still not what I was looking for. So I kept climbing up through the casino, past restaurants, bars and lounges. Cigarette smoke and beer gave way to the sweeter smells of cigars, martinis and good cologne. I moved through the crowd of well-dressed gamblers, searching, but I didn't see Adähr. Not yet.

The tables on the sixth floor of the casino were finished in emerald felt and spaced widely enough to give some illusion of privacy. Servers moved between them, taking drink orders and returning swiftly with frosted glasses, then setting them down beside stacks of colorful chips. Tall stacks.

This was more like it. The clothes here were tailored and expensive, the conversation muted. These were the serious gamblers and their high-stakes games.

Money flows in. Money flows out. That was what Adähr had told me once. *Just like the tide.*

Time to ride the waves, then.

I went to the cashier and bought ten thousand dollars in chips, immediately flagging myself as a high roller. Before I had gone ten steps with my bright, shiny new chips, a man in a smart black suit with the House of Diamonds logo stitched onto the breast approached, offering me something to smoke or drink. I turned down the cigar – as much time as I spend with my lips glued to someone else's, I just can't stand smoking – but accepted the drink. When I had selected a blackjack table and sat down, a short hostess was dropping off my Stiletto: a delicious concoction of bourbon, amaretto and lime juice.

As I pushed a few chips toward the dealer, I took a drink. I was working, but thanks to Remy's attentions, I had no concerns about having too much alcohol. It's actually a little hard for me to get drunk. As long as I'm pumped up on sex, my liver is kind of stuck in overdrive. If it's been a day or so since I last got laid, I *can* get drunk. But that doesn't happen very often.

I lost three hands and two thousand dollars inside of the first fifteen minutes. Blackjack really isn't my game. I'm more of a poker girl – and not just because Daniel Craig was the hottest Bond in... ever. I can read people pretty accurately, as well as distract them, and bluff like you wouldn't believe. But blackjack is more or less a game of odds, not much better than any of the slot machines down-stairs.

This blackjack table was right in the center of the room, though, and offered me the best view and access to the rest of the floor. The moment Adähr appeared to gamble away the fruits of his day's thieving, I wanted to be ready to jump his ass.

So I kept playing blackjack. And kept losing.

I tapped my cards. "Hit me."

"Are you sure, miss? You're showing fifteen," the dealer pointed out. He wasn't really supposed to be helping me, but my cleavage works absolute wonders.

"Sorry, I always get *hit me* confused with *spank me*," I said, wink-ing. "Never mind, I'll stay."

My table filled quickly with other players, mostly men more eager to win me than the game. After about an hour, a dozen drinks and twice as many date requests, I was ready to get up and start walking the casino floor. There wasn't much above me except hotel rooms, but maybe Adähr was slumming it down on one of the lower levels. I had a hard time imagining the nix sitting in front of a slot machine and pounding cheap vodka, but I had misjudged him before.

Then I smelled it: petrichor, the scent of fresh rain. It was at once clean and earthy, both sharp and smooth. I closed my eyes and just inhaled, following my nose. When I looked again, I saw him.

Adähr stood at one of the roulette tables, setting down an impressive stack of chips. At a glance, the nix appeared human. He was tanned and long-limbed like a swimmer, wearing a pair of expensive gray slacks and a neat navy shirt unbuttoned at the throat. Adähr's tousled black hair was a little shorter than the last time I had seen him, but his eyes were the same pussy-watering blue; one of those amazing sapphire shades that you just know *has* to be designer contact lenses.

The nix's eyes were natural, though, and rose to meet mine from across the room. Even through the smoke, perfume and cologne, I sensed the change in Adähr's scent. No longer petrichor, but the electric smell of a brewing storm. He recognized me.

Adähr darted a sea-blue glance down at the roulette wheel, at the ball bouncing and whizzing across it, then back to his chips, stacked up on red. His gaze flicked to me again and then the doors. If Adähr left the table now, he would forfeit his bet. And that was making him hesitate.

I jumped up to my feet, ignoring the dealer telling me that I had actually won. The man in the seat beside mine rose and slid in front of me, smiling beneath his lustrous mustache. His suit was expensive and professional, marking him as a rich out-of-town business executive. Probably blowing his bonus at the tables after closing some multi-million-dollar deal.

"Looks like your luck is finally turning," he said with a wink. "Stay and let me buy you a drink. The night's still young, honey."

"I'll ride your mustache all the way back to wherever you came from later," I growled. "But right now, get the hell out of my way!"

I could have picked the guy up and flung him after Adähr like an overdressed javelin, but that was a really good way to get the police involved. Fortunately for us both, the mustachioed executive stepped back, blinking at me as I took off across the casino.

At the roulette table, Adähr had made his decision. With a sigh and then a smirk, the nix turned away from the still-spinning wheel and sprinted for the closest exit. Remy had poured plenty of lust into me, so I was running well under my top speed. But racing like a rocket-powered gazelle across a crowded casino was about as smart as hurling businessmen and luckily, nixi are no faster than humans. On dry land, at least. Within twenty strides, I was already closing in on Adähr.

But the handsome blue-eyed bastard didn't share my compunctions against using supernatural powers in public. A host walked out from behind the bar, balancing a tray of fresh drinks on one hand. He was too far away to reach, but Adähr didn't need to lay a finger on the man.

With a glance, the nix sent the cocktails flying, splashing and toppling their glasses. Alcohol and colorful garnishes spilled onto the shocked-looking host and the nearest poker table. Shouting players jumped to their feet and back from the spreading puddle – right into my path.

I swore and started shoving my way between ruffled gamblers and the dismayed host, who was trying to assure everyone that he had no idea what just happened and that the House of Diamonds would certainly cover any cleaning expenses. A white-haired old woman with more wrinkles than my bed sheets at the end of a work night scowled as I pushed past, and then my heel came down on a fallen martini glass. It snapped under my weight and I slid, reeling and swearing.

I didn't fall, but only because I grabbed onto the closest solid object: the frowning lady. She shrieked, smacked me with her purse – which she was somehow still holding – and I stumbled away.

By the time I was steady on my feet again, Adähr had vanished, but I didn't see a fountain or anything else wet outside. The room opened into an elevator lobby. One set of metal doors was sliding shut and the 'up' arrow glowed above them. I had done my homework and knew exactly where the fucker was going.

Shit.

I pounded on the button, ignoring the cranky old woman's equally cranky old husband shouting after me and demanding to know why I had groped his wife.

"Come on. Come on!" I muttered under my breath.

I was hardly the first to perform this same elevator-summoning ritual, and just like those who had come before me, it did absolutely no good. Adähr must have taken the only elevator already on this floor. Where the hell was a wizard when I needed one? The *up* button continued to glow steadily, serenely unaware of my fury. I briefly considered breaking it, but that would only get the attention of casino security.

So I ran for the stairs. No one comes to a casino for a workout – at least, not one that doesn't take place between the bedsheets – so the concrete stairwell was plain and narrow. But more importantly, it was empty. I took the steps three at a time, hurtling myself up them so fast that wind whistled in my ears. Five, ten and then fifteen stories blurred past, my heels ticking a rapid staccato against the stairs.

I burst through the rooftop door hard enough to make the steel slam back into the wall. It was wet up here, too, but this time, I was ready. Cold wind whipped my hair and raised goosebumps across my exposed skin.

A huge blue pool dominated the House of Diamonds' roof. A sign posted on the gate notified me that it had closed hours ago, but on the other side, the water shone brightly with submerged lights silhouetting a single swimmer.

Adähr.

My heart raced and I wiped my sweating hands on the hem of my dress. I pulled off my high heels – they had caused me enough trouble already – and jumped over the fence. I landed lightly on the far side, between a pair of empty lounge chairs. I slid one in front of the closed gate, in case anyone else decided to break the rules tonight. I didn't want to be disturbed.

Adähr sat in the glowing water, naked and grinning at me. His clothes lay in a heap at the pool's edge. The nix wasn't swimming at all, or even treading water. He simply floated in the pool as casually as sitting in a chair.

With this much water around, Adähr had every advantage and he damned well knew it. If I tried to grab the nix now, he would just melt away into the pool and it wasn't as though the water spirit needed to breathe. So unless Adähr decided to climb out of the pool and pour himself into a jug for me, I was out of luck.

So why was I even here? Why had I followed him to the roof when I already knew the chase was over? But I couldn't give up on catching Adähr that easily. Water sparkled in the nix's black hair and his white teeth flashed in a grin.

"Lily. You let your hair grow," he said.

"You cut yours." I wrapped my arms around myself and shivered. "But you really haven't changed at all, have you?"

"Why would I?"

I had no answer for that.

Adähr's grin widened into something so sharp that it could cut. "I should have known that coming back here would mean facing you again. I'm looking forward to it. And I would bet that you are, too."

His voice was accented, but much less so than Remy's. There was just a thin Teutonic edge to Adähr's words, slightly cold but so confident in his superior position that it made me feel like a teenage girl on my first hunt all over again.

Adähr leaned back in the pool, spreading his arms across the surface of the water as he regarded me. I swallowed against the tightness in my throat. I was an idiot... What did I think I was going to do? Drag the nix out of his casino without ever coming close to enough water for him to just vanish? I was stronger and faster than Adähr, but even I couldn't catch water.

"What are you still doing here?" I asked. "You could be down through the pipes and long gone by now."

Adähr laughed lightly. "And miss seeing you again? No, I don't think so. I'm in no danger here. But you... Lily, even with all of your demoness powers, you can't fly. It would take so little for me to fling you off this rooftop. Yet you remain."

He was right. It was a hell of a fall. The nix had a whole pool full of water and I couldn't do much if he decided to use it against me. Ever tried to punch water? I was outclassed by a long shot. As soon as I saw Adähr in the pool, I should have cut my losses and left the House of Diamonds. I still didn't move, though. I stayed there, standing at the edge of the pool.

"I want to catch you," I admitted.

The nix shrugged elegantly and the water rippled around him. "You never could before, though your attempts were... delicious."

"I was young," I said. "I've gotten better."

"You were good, Lily, even then. Why don't you jump on in and show me just what *better* is like?"

Adähr's blue, blue eyes practically glowed in the deepening night. The lights of the pool illuminated his naked body and picked out every lean muscle in silver and sapphire. All around Adähr, the water began to swirl and then churn. Tendrils rose up from the pool's surface like liquid icicles. Shining with refracted light, the shimmering tentacles grew longer and thicker until they curved out, reaching for me.

I still didn't leave the rooftop, even as the first slithering tentacle of water twined around my ankle and then slid along my leg. The pool had probably been warm during the day, but the House of Diamonds had turned off the heaters for the night and it was cold now. It raised goosebumps as the sinuous liquid limb caressed my skin.

The touch felt strange... Adähr held the water in shape with his will, wet but not dripping. His control had gotten better since our last encounter. The clear water was strong but flexible, firm and as smooth as the coils of a snake spiraling up my leg.

A tentacle slipped across my shoulder and caught the zipper of my dress, dragging it slowly down until I felt chilly night air against my bared back. Another shining silvery-blue tendril slid under my dress and helped the first peel the garment away. I shivered and gasped on the edge of the pool in nothing but my underwear.

Adähr's smile was hungry as his azure gaze swept along my body. A cool tentacle flowed up my leg and trailed over my lace-covered pussy. I shivered again and whimpered as cold water mixed with my own wetness. The tendril wound through my thong and yanked it away, leaving me naked beside the pool.

"Glorious," said Adähr. "You're even more beautiful than I remember, Lily."

His coils of water tugged at me, pulling me closer to the pool's edge. The nix's impossibly blue gaze was possessive, his grin predatory. Water slipped over and around me, curling across my skin and making me tremble. My knees were weak.

"I should leave." My voice was no steadier than my legs.

"You won't," Adähr assured me.

I lifted one foot to step out of the puddle of my clothes, but the water encircled my ankle like a rope. Adähr's impossibly smooth tentacles tightened around my wrists and thighs. The faintly luminous water rippled and my stomach jumped into my throat as it raised me off my feet, up into the cold, clear night air. Far below, lights sparkled across the city as though the stars had fallen out of the sky and landed at my feet.

Adähr closed the fingers of one hand and his flowing tendrils lifted me up until I hung suspended above the pool. The silvery tentacles stretched and lengthened as they held me, tips moving slowly over my ass and the feverishly flushed skin of my breasts. Water caressed sensitive flesh, making me whimper and my nipples rise to stiff pink nubs. I arched my back and spread my legs.

"You've never been a patient woman, Lily," Adähr said in his cool voice. "Have you been waiting long for me?"

"Eight years," I moaned.

Adähr gave me that predatory smile again and his eyes shimmered like light through water. He floated back in the pool, regarding me. Adähr's cock lay against his stomach, long and hard, yet still somehow lazy. The nix knew he was going to get exactly what he wanted from me. That I was going to give it to him.

One of Adähr's liquid tentacles glided further up, brushing over my pussy. The tip was fine and slid easily between my legs, into me. I squeezed my eyes helplessly shut and gulped down a desperate breath. The air was still chilly, but the swelling desire made me burn inside. I couldn't tell what was wetter, me or the tendril made of actual water.

What the hell was I doing up on top of the House of Diamonds? I couldn't fight Adähr out here, not like this. Maybe I could break my way out of his magically controlled water and escape, though... But then what?

Adähr's tentacle slithered deeper into me and I couldn't think anymore. It twisted and began to expand as the nix streamed more water and opened me slowly. I tensed reflexively at the strange feeling of liquid rushing and moving purposefully between my legs. I gasped and the other coils of water tightened around my body, holding me while I squirmed.

Adähr raised his black eyebrows at me and I felt more heat, this time in my face as I blushed. I took a deep breath, smelling the pool and petrichor, and tried to get myself to relax in the slick grasp of Adähr's tentacles. But my heart hammered and I couldn't be still. It just wasn't an option when a long, curling cock of water was surging up into my pussy. I writhed uselessly against Adähr's wet tentacles. The tendril didn't thrust, but rippled all along its length inside me, sending waves of sensation crashing through my body. I moaned.

"What was that?" Adähr asked. "I can't hear you, Lily."

I bit my lip. I was determined not to give Adähr the satisfaction of hearing me beg. The nix smirked and the slippery tentacle slowed its churning inside me until it only fluttered tauntingly there. My moan became a whimper.

"No... Adähr, don't stop," I said.

The nix watched me writhe with bright eyes. He lifted one hand and hooked a finger, making the tendril stroke slowly, lazily deep inside my body.

"Please! Make it fuck me!" I cried.

"Very well, Lily," said Adähr.

The tendril piercing me pulsed and became almost opaque with bubbles as the water began to churn in my pussy. I threw my head back and my whole body shook with need. Wetness gushed from my slit and along the surging tentacle of water. Adähr just streamed it back up into me, fucking me with my own juices.

"Yes!" I moaned.

Adähr's other magically controlled tentacles tugged my limbs, holding me spread-eagle above the pool. The nix watched me without moving, not once reaching for the hard length of his dick where it lay stretched out along his lean stomach. He loved watching me squirm.

And squirm I did when I heard the rustle of water and felt another tentacle pressed against my ass. This tendril was thin at first, too, just a thread of water that smoothly inserted itself. I stiffened, but only for a second before another wave of pleasure rippled out from my pussy. The water penetrating my ass moved, making me reward Adähr with a slutty moan.

"You like that, Lily?" the nix asked. "Do you want more?"

"Yes!" I cried.

So Adähr gave me more. Another tentacle of water reared up before me like a serpent and then thrust its cold, heavy length into my mouth. Whatever magic the elemental nix used to make water dance to his will made it soft but firm enough to force my lips apart.

For a moment, my body resisted this new intrusion, but I wasn't drowning, so I threw back my head and welcomed the cool, slippery weight pushing itself down my throat. I could even feel the swell of a large, blunt crown like a real dick.

Adähr held me spread open and filled every hole until my cries of pleasure sent bubbles up through the liquid cock fucking my face. A dozen other tendrils wound and coiled over me now, around my legs and waist, throat and breasts like rope bondage. But no ropes could move like Adähr's water tentacles. They slid across my skin and squeezed softly, caressing me even as they imprisoned me.

The tentacle in my ass was growing and moving, plunging in counterpoint to the water pulsing in and out of my pussy. They didn't just ripple inside me now, but surged like waves crashing on the shore. I could feel them pressing against each other from deep within me, doubling down on the thrusting sensation that sent me screaming over into climax once more.

The water grew warmer inside me, almost like flesh and blood cocks penetrating me front and back, from top and bottom. I didn't know if it was the addition of my streaming wetness, the heat of my body, or maybe Adähr himself. Was it conscious, or some side effect of his own arousal? The nix's smell was powerful, the scent of a storm and the sharp ozone of striking lightning. It was the smell of danger, of excitement.

I could have torn my way out of Adähr's tentacles. I don't know how far I would have gotten before he grabbed me again, but I was aglow with sexual energy. I could run. I didn't *want* to run, though. I wanted to cum. Even more than that, I wanted to catch Adähr. I needed to. If only I could figure out how...

When the storm of pleasure and confused shame had abated enough that I could open my eyes once more, I found Adähr much closer. I was descending into the pool without the slightest splash. My hair fanned out across the surface, bright red against blue. Adähr's tentacles of water remained coiled around me, but they were invisible, submerged in the pool and distinct from the rest of the water only by the force of the nix's will.

A sudden current through the pool swept me into Adähr's arms. The tendril of water withdrew from my mouth as he pulled me in. Adähr was sleek and strong against me. Not as strong as I was, but the nix's power over me was nothing that simple. His exquisite blue eyes demanded my attention and held it there.

Adähr combed his long fingers through my hair and curled my wet red locks around them. He tugged at me, pulling my head back. Adähr kissed me and I accepted his tongue with the same eagerness and shame as the liquid cock he had poured down my throat. He didn't release his possessive grip of my hair as he kissed me. Adähr's fingers tightened and almost didn't let me up when I had to gasp for air.

"Tell me what you want, Lily," he whispered. His voice was soft, but the nix wasn't even slightly out of breath. "Just beg and you can have it."

I didn't want to answer. I bit my lip resolutely and said nothing. Adähr laughed. The sound was a musical hiss like driving rain. The tentacle of shaped water slithered out of my pussy, leaving me gasping at its sudden absence. I grabbed Adähr's shoulders hard enough to make the nix grunt.

"Play fair," he admonished me. "Or this game ends."

"And you call any of this fair?" I panted.

Adähr smirked and his eyes sparkled. "Just tell me what you want, Lily, and I'll give it to you."

"Fuck me!" I moaned. My face, my whole body burned. "God, please fuck me!"

The nix nodded in satisfaction and my moan grew louder as he yanked me down onto his hard cock. After the cool and yielding water, it was like being fucked with hot iron. But the liquid tentacles were still there, one throbbing languidly up my ass as the others pulled at me, slamming me onto their master's dick.

"Adähr!" I screamed as the ecstasy rose up and closed over me.

Underwater sex is a lot more awkward and difficult than it looks in the movies... unless you're fucking a nix. Adähr held me effortlessly in the water, fighting neither to remain afloat nor to hold his position in the pool. Hundreds of gallons of water pushed me against him, pulling and maneuvering my body for Adähr to ravage.

He pumped his cock deep into my pussy and the colder length of his wet tentacle rippled inside my ass. Hot and cold, in and out. I clawed at Adähr's smoothly muscled back and came hard. Water churned all around us as though in a storm.

"Yes, Lily," Adähr said in a low voice. "I always remembered this. I remembered you."

His dick pistoned faster and faster into me. The nix's slick water tentacle wasn't just fucking my ass – it thrashed wetly inside of me, wildly stroking Adähr's cock deep within my body. It felt amazing. Probably for him, too.

I dug my heels into the small of Adähr's back and urged him on. His dick was swelling inside me. Now he was finally panting, breath rasping in my ear with every thrust of his magically twinned cocks up my pussy and ass.

"Do you want it?" he asked. Adähr's voice was rough with pleasure, but it still remained even and cool. "Tell me you need my cum, Lily."

I was a fucking cambion. Short of somehow breaking the Seal of Avalon and returning full-blooded succubae to Earth, I was the closest thing in this realm to a demoness of lust. Adähr should have been the one begging... But he didn't have to and he damned well knew it. He held all the cards.

"Give me your cum, Adähr," I begged. "Pour it into me! Fill my pussy!"

Adähr kissed me when he came, crushing his lips against mine as his cock became a rock-hard pillar inside me. His heat flooded me and I felt every pulse gushing into me, the texture so much thicker, richer and hotter than water. I parted my lips to scream in climax and Adähr's tongue invaded my mouth, stifling my cries.

Finally, the geyser of cum abated and Adähr released me. The watery tentacle in my ass thinned and then slid away, vanishing into the rooftop pool once more. I splashed, suddenly back under my own control.

"I win again," said Adähr.

"Maybe this round," I answered, but the words sounded weak, even to my ears. The nix *had* won. Again.

"And many more rounds to come," he said. "You'll be back, Lily. But for now..."

The water eddied around me and then a pair of thick tentacles lifted me out of the pool, depositing me on the cold concrete beside my discarded cocktail dress and soaking panties. Adähr's warmth leaked from my pussy and left pale blue-white streaks down my wet thighs.

"What the fuck–?" I started to ask, turning back toward the nix. *He* was kicking *me* out?

But the pool was already empty. Adähr was gone.

Chapter
FIVE

Compared to dealing with Adähr, getting away from the House of Diamonds was a breeze. Still, I had made a bit of a scene on the casino floor and had to duck a few security goons. I traded my phone number to a bartender who let me slip out one of the casino's staff doors.

Finally, I made it back to my car and drove home. After a walk of shame up to my condo, I rinsed off in the shower and went to bed. But I only managed a couple fitful hours of sleep. My encounter with Adähr kept replaying in my head, making me want to grab a vibrator from one of the boxes under my bed and scream with both frustration and pleasure.

Not long after dawn, I gave up on sleep. I slid out of bed, pulled on a pair of jeans and a t-shirt, then did what I always do when I feel like crap: I went to see Max.

I drove across town before rush hour started and parked the Alfa Romeo outside his small, run-down apartment building. There was a gate around the parking lot, but it had been broken since long before Max moved in. I climbed up the cracked, mossy stairs to his door and knocked hard enough that my knuckles left dents in the rust-spotted metal.

I took a deep breath and blew it out in a sigh. Losing control of my strength was a bad sign.

The deadbolt turned with a loud rasp. I was still charged up – for all the good that had done me last night – and could already smell Max on the other side of the door: warm and cottony from his sheets, and sleepy. Yeah, sleepy has a smell. It's a nice one that I would have enjoyed if I weren't so fucking angry about Adähr.

The chain rattled and then the door opened to reveal my best friend framed inside like a prize: tall and well-muscled, with sleep-tousled blond hair and denim-colored eyes. Max wasn't dressed yet, wearing only his boxers and the cloth was still a little rumpled from sleep. He smiled, though, and gestured me inside.

"Morning, Lil," he said, stifling a yawn. "If it is morning…"

"Just barely. Sorry, Max."

He shrugged and closed the door behind me. "Hey, your insomnia is my insomnia. What's wrong? You didn't use your key."

I touched my thigh, feeling the jagged bulge of the key ring in my pocket. Max's house key was right next to mine on it.

"Damn it," I said with a sigh. "Sorry. I forgot."

Max gave me a quick hug and then went to the tiny kitchenette to turn on his coffee maker. It was one of the few decent appliances in his home – a Christmas present from me, of course.

I watched my half-dressed best friend pull a pair of mugs down from the cupboard, enjoying the sight of muscles bunching and releasing beneath his skin. But even that view wasn't enough to make me feel any better.

I flopped down onto the threadbare couch. The coffee table was littered in classified ads and Max's cheap laptop sat open on top of them. Cheap laptop? Hmm. I would have to fix that next birthday. I nudged the computer with one foot.

"Job hunting?" I asked.

"Yeah."

"Any luck yet?"

"Not really," Max admitted as the smell of coffee filled his apartment. "Mechanics are a dime a dozen. But hey, it's leaving me lots of time to work on your 110. I'm more interested in what's got you so upset. What's going on, Lil?"

I scowled. "First off, you are *not* a dime a dozen. And what's pissing me off is Adähr."

Max poured two cups of coffee, then stirred a ton of cream and sugar into mine. Just how I liked it. He carried the mugs carefully and set them on the battered table before sitting next to me on the couch.

"Adähr?" Max asked. "Isn't he the water... guy... that you were after on your first job?"

"Yeah, that's him."

"Why are you worried about him? Didn't he run back to Germany last time?"

"Adähr's in the city again," I said. I eyed the coffee Max had made me, but I didn't trust liquids very much at the moment. "Now half the College is going to be hunting him. A French wizard even followed him over from Europe. But *I* want to be the one to catch Adähr."

Max looked at me, furrowing his blond brows. "Why, Lil? You've got plenty of money. Why does it matter if anyone else catches this guy?"

"Because... because he's the one that got away! God, Max, I was so young and stupid back then. I had just finished all of Evaine's training. I was ready to dazzle everyone, to show the College what I could do."

"And you did, Lil," Max said gently.

"No, I fucked it up. I was so excited to go after Adähr. I even liked how his name sounded: *a dare*." I barely resisted the urge to kick Max's coffee table across the room and through the opposite wall. "Adähr was my first... everything. My first job, the first time I really got to use my powers, my first fuck–"

Max gave me a mildly offended look. "Your first fuck? Hey, what about me?"

"You don't count," I said.

I poked Max in the side to let him know that I was joking, more or less. He sighed and smiled at me, gracing me with his dimples. Max *was* the first guy I ever had sex with, but he and I grew up together and he was always there for me. Always. It was different with Adähr.

"Alright," said Max. "So Adähr is... special to you."

I snorted. "Yeah, but don't you tell him that. I don't think I've ever met a man more full of himself. But the worst part is, he's kind of earned it. Remy – that's the French hunter – has been after Adähr for almost a year and never caught the slippery bastard."

"I thought you liked slippery," Max teased.

"Well... yeah."

"So what happened last night?"

"I found Adähr at the House of Diamonds again, just like eight years ago. But I didn't come any closer to catching him than I did back then. Fucking nix! I... I want to punch Adähr in the crotch. With my crotch."

Max laughed and I shot him a scathing glare. He fell instantly silent and looked apologetic. Still smiling, though.

"I just can't get Adähr far enough away from water," I said. "Just one stream or leaky pipe and he's gone. What if one of the wizards figures out how to catch him before I do?"

Max sat back in the couch cushions and laced his fingers behind his head. His gaze followed the wisps of steam rising up off our untouched coffee.

"Well," Max said. "What did you do last time? I know you got close enough to spook Adähr, but you never told me much more about it."

I leaned against Max's side and nudged him unsubtly until he draped one arm around me.

"I was too embarrassed," I confessed. "I still am, kind of."

"You don't have to tell me if you don't want to."

"It's okay." I sighed and buried my face against Max's shoulder. "I had this plan all worked out, how I was going to be the sexy bait and let Adähr rob me, then track him down and slap some cuffs on him."

"That's not what happened, though."

"No. I mean, yes... at first. The robbing part went fine. Adähr even gave me his phone number. A fake one, but still... Anyway, I followed him to the House of Diamonds, that big casino. Adähr didn't seem to know about the tracker I had planted on him and didn't ask any questions. We just gambled and drank and fucked like crazy in his room while the rain poured outside."

"You remember the rain?" Max asked.

"Yeah, I do," I said with a sigh. "Because when I tried to slap the cuffs on Adähr, he just grinned at me and dove right off the balcony, into the storm and vanished in the rain. He knew exactly who I was and what I wanted. He was playing me the whole time."

I shifted on the couch, resting my cheek more comfortably against Max's big shoulder. His bare chest was soft and warm and inviting. I accepted the invitation and let my hand wander over his muscles.

"To be fair," said Max, "you tried to play him, too."

"Hey, whose side are you on?"

Max squeezed my arm. "Yours, Lil. Always."

"Adähr got everything he wanted from me," I said. "And I had to go back to the College empty-handed. No one's ever been able to manipulate me like that, Max, and I've never forgotten about it. I want to be the one to catch Adähr."

My hand found its way down to Max's lap and his cock pressed heavily against my palm. He was already half hard and it took only a few light brushes to bring him the rest of the way up, now jutting thick and flushed through the open front of his boxers. I curled my fingers around Max's dick and couldn't quite get the tips to touch as I began to pump him slowly, meditatively.

"Uh," said Max. "Should we move this over to the bed?"

"Move what?" I asked.

Max gestured to his lap.

"Oh, this," I said. "It helps me think."

"You seem really upset by all this, Lil."

"Shush. I'm trying to concentrate."

Max nodded and settled back again, lightly stroking my shoulder. I rested my cheek against his naked chest. The heat of his cock in my hand and the steady drumbeat of his heart helped soothe my frayed nerves. I gave Max a little squeeze and moved my fingers faster up and down his length. I smiled as his heartbeat sped.

"Are... are you in love with Adähr?" Max asked after a moment.

My hand stilled and I stared up at Max. His jaw was tight and his cheeks quite red, but he didn't make a sound or push his hips toward me.

"In love?" I repeated. "Are you crazy? I'm half demon."

"Even demons fall in love sometimes," Max reminded me.

I shook my head and his dick pulsed with need in the circle of my fingers. Slowly, I resumed stroking and Max sighed quietly, almost inaudibly.

"No," I said. "I haven't fallen for Adähr. It's just... he was my first job and I failed. I've always hated that. Hated how powerless he made me feel."

I slid my hand down the front of Max's boxers to cradle the solid weight of his balls. He let out a long, controlled breath, trying to keep it quiet. Max didn't want to disturb my concentration, I supposed. I ran my fingers back up along his cock. His smooth skin was hot under my touch.

"You know, Adähr seems to think I'm pretty obsessed with him, too," I said thoughtfully.

"You are," Max groaned.

"Maybe a bit," I admitted. "But what if I can use that to my advantage?"

The seed of an idea was taking root and it made my pulse speed. My hand raced faster over Max's long dick, too. His heartbeat went from drumming to galloping and then thundering in my ear as I stroked him. Max's breath grew rougher until he was panting and lust boiled off of him, filling me with more warm golden energy. It felt like swallowing the sun.

"Give me what I want, Max," I said.

It was nice to be in control again, if only for a moment, not being played by either Remy or Adähr. And Max did exactly as I asked, finally letting out a long, loud groan as his thighs tensed like steel bars. His dick pulsed in my grasp and thick cum surged up hard enough to fly into the air. White streaks splattered his stomach and began rolling like liquid pearls along Max's abdominals.

I milked out the final pale drops from my friend's cock and they spattered down just above the waist of his boxers. I admired the sight of his painted six-pack, but it looked too good not to taste. So I leaned in and lapped my way along Max's chest and abs, licking up the sticky cream. I saved his slippery dick for last, taking it deep down my throat and drinking every drop of cum.

Every drop. Hmm... I sighed contentedly and licked my lips. Max panted and stroked my hair.

"Uh... so did that help you think?" he asked.

I kissed Max on the cheek.

"Yeah, it did," I told him. "I've got a game plan."

"Do you have time for breakfast?"

"I just ate." I pointed to his dick. "But I could go for some pancakes."

"Sure. Give me a minute to mix them up. Want syrup?"

"On the pancakes or on you?" I asked.

Max laughed. He rose, tucked his cock back into his boxers and then went to the kitchenette. I grabbed my now-lukewarm coffee and followed Max. I sat on the counter, sipping my coffee while he pulled flour, sugar and coconut oil down from the old cabinets.

"It's better for you than butter," Max said, nodding toward the coconut oil. "And tastes better, too. Lil, can you pass me the milk?"

I opened the refrigerator with my foot and held the carton out to Max. When he reached for it, though, I pulled back a few inches.

"Hey, I thought I helped," Max protested. "Why am I in trouble now?"

"Guys like you are *not* a dime a dozen," I said with a mock-stern glare. "Really."

Max gave me a dimpled smile. "Thanks, Lil."

"Have you ever thought about opening your own garage?"

"Sometimes. But that would take a whole lot of money that I don't have. There's work on your iıo that I've had to put off because I can't afford the right tools. And a shop? Commercial rents in this city are crazy."

"Don't you dare let that stop you," I said. I finally handed over the milk. "I'm pretty sure we can find you at least one investor."

Max's brow furrowed as he measured out the milk for pancakes. "You think so?"

"Yeah, I do."

Chapter
SIX

After finishing breakfast with Max, I went back to my condo and spent the rest of the morning on the phone. First, I called Stefano and asked if he was looking for Adähr.

"Yes," said Stefano. "He's the best job in the city right now."

I could barely hear the other hunter over the rush of wind and what sounded like the grumble of a laboring engine. I turned up the volume on my phone and put a finger in my other ear.

"Adähr's the *only* job in the city," I pointed out. The only one worth doing, at least. "Where are you?"

"I'm covering the north end of the bay. I think Clio's down in the south."

"You two are coordinating?" I asked, surprised.

"Of course not," Stefano said loud to make himself heard over what I supposed now was the noise of his boat. "But I pay attention to what the others are doing."

"Have you been watching me?"

"Uh... recently?" Stefano said. "No. Only one of us can use the scry network at a time, you know."

I didn't know that. Interesting.

"So who's using it now?" I asked.

"That hunter from the Castle. He's been snapping up pretty much all of the available time slots."

"Remy Saville?"

The French hunter must have figured out that I had lied to him. So now he was scouring the citywide magical surveillance network to find Adähr. I smirked. That's what Remy got for trying to pump Lily Quinn for information. And it was nice to have the scry network trained on someone other than me for once.

"You've ah... met him?" Stefano asked.

"Yeah. Do you know if anyone's hitting the bridges?"

"Besides Adähr?" Stefano sounded sour. "Redmond, I think. I found an arrow in the water earlier this morning."

I put the phone on speaker and checked the feed from Fuzz Radio, my police scanner app, filtered by neighborhood. I couldn't search just the bridges, but the police in Gates Park alone had reported twenty-three robberies with no suspects in custody. And two accounts of a man carrying a bow and shouting in an unknown language. That wasn't exactly a crime, but he was making the tourists nervous.

The College would have swept those reports quietly under the rug by lunchtime, but they sounded a lot like Redmond chasing after Adähr – and failing to capture him. Even the wizard's spell-enchanted arrows couldn't catch water.

"What about Griffith and Doyle? Where are they?" I asked.

"I'm not sure," said Stefano. "I've seen a few of Sabra's homunculi prowling around the drainage outlets, though."

"But aren't they made out of clay? How're they standing up to the water?"

"Not all homunculi are made of clay, you know. Besides, I think Sabra puts a water resistant finish on all of them. Her constructs wouldn't serve the College very well if they just dissolved every time it rained."

"Yeah," I agreed. "And what about you?"

Stefano didn't answer right away. I leaned into the window. It was still early in the year and bitterly cold outside, but the sun was out and the glass was warm against my back.

"Come on, Stefano," I said. "It's not like I can steal any of your magic tricks. I'm not a wizard. Just tell me what I shouldn't waste my time with."

There was another moment of silence. At least, Stefano wasn't talking, but I heard seabirds squawking and squabbling nearby. Finally, he sighed.

"I spent the last two days enchanting a net that should be able to catch the nix even in his liquid form," Stefano admitted grudgingly. "I've been trolling for him all day, but I can't follow Adähr's movements fast enough."

"Join the club," I muttered. I paced across the condo to my bedroom. "Thanks, Stefano. I owe you one."

"You're not going to tell me your strategy for nix?"

"Nope," I answered cheerfully. "But give me a call when you've got a free evening and some clothes that you don't mind getting ripped off."

I ended the call while Stefano was still sputtering for breath and dropped my phone onto the bed. I've always had that effect on him, and always loved it. Don't worry – whenever Stefano gives me information, I make it worth his time.

And Stefano's a big boy. He can handle himself, even around me. I've seen his magic in action and it's... amazing, to be honest. I may be dismissive of the wizards when I'm annoyed at them, but I would *not* want to fuck with the College.

I went into my closet and packed a suitcase. When I finished loading it up with everything I needed, it would have been impossible to lift without my sex-powered strength. But I still had plenty of that, so I put the suitcase next to my phone on the bed – which creaked ominously – and returned to the closet. I closed the safe and then searched through my underwear drawer.

"What should I wear?" I muttered to myself. "My slutty panties or my *really* slutty panties?"

When I had answered that pressing question, I chose a little dress so dark blue that it was almost black. It was a bit longer than the one I had worn the night before, but made up for the extra hem with a plunging neckline. Even Adähr could drown in the cleavage I was showing off.

As the afternoon darkened into evening, I listened to the police scanner. Robbery reports from the waterfront were slowing down. I guessed they would spike again as full night fell, but for now, Adähr seemed to be done with the day's thieving. Unless Redmond or one of the other hunters had managed to catch the nix, Adähr would soon be off to gamble away everything he had stolen. It was all part of the game for him.

I heaved the suitcase downstairs and into the trunk of my Alfa Romeo, then got behind the wheel and pulled out of the condo's garage. Outside, the sunset was a deep violet, dotted with a few faint stars and streaked in magenta clouds. The bay was a soft silver lake of fog, but I drove away from the water, back to the House of Diamonds.

The casino was already ablaze with neon that rivaled the setting sun for gaudy glory. A bright-lit billboard advertised cheap drinks and huge payouts. People streamed through the doors, far more than late last night. There were a pair of cable cars out front, stopped on the steel rail inlaid in the road to release a fresh batch of chattering tourists.

I parked my car and then carried my suitcase into the casino. A concierge in a red jacket stepped out from behind the counter as soon as I came through the door, offering to summon a cart and bellhop for me.

"No thanks," I said. Unless the casino staff spent a *lot* of time in the gym, none of them would be able to take my bag for me. "But I could really use your help with something else."

"Of course, miss," the concierge answered, smoothing out the diamond-embroidered lapels of his suit jacket. The gold name tag affixed there read *Kono*. "What do you need?"

"I'm looking for a man I met here last night. Tall, with black hair and blue eyes that you would never forget."

Kono nodded. "Ah, yes. Mister Adähr."

The arrogant bastard wasn't even bothering with a fake name. I bit my lip and tried to look earnest.

"Is he... here tonight?" I asked.

"Mister Adähr arrived not long ago and went up to his room," the concierge said.

Perfect. I hadn't been sure if Adähr had a room at the hotel, or just used the casino. But it made sense – the nix could transform himself into water, but not his stolen possessions. He had to keep his clothes and money somewhere. Preferably somewhere with a sturdy door.

"Which room is he in?" I asked.

I gave Kono my best puppy eyes. And a good view down my cleavage, just in case. He hesitated.

"I... really can't give out that information, miss," he said.

Wow, a casino employee with actual integrity. Didn't see that one coming. Maybe I should have, but I covered my dismay with a bright smile.

"Maybe you can call up to his room?" I suggested. "Adähr and I had so much fun last night. I think he'd like to see me again. But if he says no, I promise I'll leave without a fuss."

Kono nodded slowly. "That... sounds reasonable. And who may I say wishes to see him?"

"Lily."

"One moment," the concierge said.

He stepped back behind his desk, checked his computer and dialed the phone. He waited and then cleared his throat.

"Good evening, Mister Adähr," Kono said in a crisp, professional voice. "There's a young woman named Lily here to see you."

There was a second of silence on the other end of the line, but my ears were still plenty sharp enough to hear Adähr's answer, even over the chatter of voices and tinny music of slot machines.

"Let me talk to her," he said.

"Yes, sir." Kono gestured me closer. "Mister Adähr would like to speak with you."

My stomach flipped and I didn't have to fake nervousness as I took the receiver from the concierge's hand. I put it to my ear.

"Lily," said Adähr. "You're back."

"I... I need to see you again," I stammered.

There was a moment of silence over the phone. Finally, Adähr answered. "You've got something planned."

"Yes, but it's not what you think. Don't hang up. I just want to talk to you. I need to show you something."

"Hmm."

The long syllable was thoughtful, but I heard Adähr's breath quicken. He was curious.

"We can meet wherever you want," I told him. "You pick."

"On the shore of the bay–" Adähr began.

"No," I interrupted. "Not there."

"And why is that?" Adähr asked. His voice was still smooth, but there was a sharp edge of suspicion there, too.

I hesitated, eyeing Kono. The concierge had stepped back a little to create the illusion of privacy, but I knew he was listening. Adähr might not have cared about revealing himself to humans, but I did... if only because the College's cleanup and memory wipes came out of my pay.

"On the bridge today, there was a guy with a bow," I said slowly. "His name is Redmond. There are two more... like him out on the bay. They're watching all of the waterways. And you know Remy Saville..."

"Yes," Adähr hissed. "I do."

"He's here in the city, too."

"Interesting. Thank you for the warning, Lily."

"So… can I see you?" I asked.

"I'm up in room 1615."

Adähr hung up. I replaced the phone in its cradle and glanced over at Kono. He was too professional to betray any judgment of the strange conversation. The concierge only inclined his head and asked if there was anything else he could do for me.

"No," I said. "Thanks for your help."

I slipped Kono a discreet hundred-dollar tip. He really had been quite helpful and it never hurts to be friendly with a good concierge. Kono's smile appeared genuine, so I gave him a wink as I picked up my suitcase again and headed for the elevators.

I shared the ride up with a handsome older couple that whispered to each other about whether or not I would be offended if they invited me back to their room. I wouldn't have been – in fact, I was flattered – but I was about to be *very* busy. So I just blew them a kiss when they got off on the tenth floor.

Alone in the elevator, I resumed my nervous fidgeting. This was my one shot. If I screwed things up now, I could lose Adähr forever.

Two floors later, the elevator stopped again and I stepped out into a wide, richly carpeted hallway. I made my way down the hall to room 1615. The door wasn't quite closed and swung open at my gentle push. Inside, the lights were all turned off, but the hotel drapes had been pulled back and the uncovered windows were full of the multicolored glow of the city below. I shut the door firmly behind me.

The hotel room wasn't just nice – it was lavish. I doubted Adähr had paid for it, though. He threw a lot of money around the casino and I guessed the House of Diamonds had offered him the upgrade. It was in the casino's best interest to keep their high rollers close and happy. Smart move.

There was a wet bar with a dark granite countertop. Wallets, cash, jewelry and watches lay in a glittering heap beside the sink like a dragon's horde in miniature. There had to be several thousand dollars sitting there. And that was only one day's worth of the nix's thieving.

"Adähr?" I called quietly.

I heard water bubbling and smelled petrichor. Carefully, I set my suitcase down and followed the clean scent of water. The air was warm and heavy as I stepped into a bathroom the size of Max's entire apartment. There were windows in here, too, that ran from floor to ceiling and looked out over the city. Lights flickered to life as the sun vanished below the western horizon.

I caught Adähr's reflection in the long wall of mirrors set behind widely spaced double sinks. The nix lounged in a sunken bathtub large enough for at least four people. Adähr's black hair lay wet against the back of his neck and his blue eyes were the brightest things in the dimly lit room. The tub's jets churned hot water and steam around him.

Adähr looked at me in the mirror and smiled. "You came back to me."

I walked toward the oversized bath, my heels clicking on the marble-tiled floor.

"You were right," I told him.

Adähr sat back and draped his arms across the edge of the tub. His grin was a white crescent in the shadows.

"Right?" Adähr asked. "And what was I right about, Lily?"

"Me. Everything I want," I answered in a quiet voice. "You were my first, did you know?"

I reached up to slide the strap of my dress off one shoulder. Adähr's long, lean body glistened wetly, as though oiled for display. The nix watched me with his cool blue gaze. How good was my poker face?

"Your first what?" Adähr asked. His tone was coldly taunting. "Tell me, Lily."

"My first lover. The first man I was ever with. I was so young," I confessed. It was some truth, some lies and everything Adähr wanted to hear. "I didn't know what I was doing. And when I'm with you, I still feel like a teenage girl. I'm lost all over again."

I slipped the other strap off my shoulder. Adähr remained still. No tendrils of water snaked out to help me this time. My dress slid down my long legs to pool on the cold floor and I stood naked before Adähr like an offering. In the end, I had chosen no panties at all.

"What do you want?" Adähr asked.

"You," I said.

The nix sat unmoving, surrounded by gently bubbling water. Steam rose and clung to my skin in sparkling liquid beads. My stomach fluttered.

"Come, then," he said. "Show me."

Adähr hooked one long finger at me and I stepped down into the marble tub. Hot water swirled around my legs and then the rest of my body as I sank down into it. I pushed through the bath between us until I reached Adähr. The nix's arms remained spread across the tiled ledge as I pressed myself against him. I slid my hard nipples over his slick skin and let out a soft mew of pleasure. He reclined on an angled seat that ran around the huge bathtub's edge. I placed my knees on either side of his legs and nuzzled at Adähr's neck, kissing and licking. I tasted salt on his skin more like the ocean than like sweat.

"May I have you, Adähr?" I whispered into his ear. "Do you want me?"

Usually when I asked that, it was teasing. A taunt. But now I let the questions come out in a hungry whimper. Adähr's cock responded, rising even more swiftly in answer to my words.

"Yes," he said in a low growl. "You will have me."

Adähr pulled me into his arms and kissed me. His tongue danced against mine and I tasted the martinez he had drunk before I arrived – a mix of gin, sweet vermouth, curacao and bitters. But beneath that, he tasted of rain.

I plunged my hands into the swirling water. Adähr's dick was so hard and long that the tip nearly jutted up from the churning white bubbles. He was even hotter to the touch than the water around us. Adähr grabbed my ass and squeezed, finally breaking the kiss.

"I couldn't stop thinking about you all day," I said.

"What did you think of doing to me, Lily?"

I sank down under the water in answer. The tub's jets rushed in my ears and bubbles obscured my vision, but Adähr knew what I was doing. His fingers cupped the back of my head and guided me unerringly to his dick. I parted my lips carefully around the crown to keep the water out and filled my mouth with his hard heat.

Adähr's grip tightened in my wet hair as I sucked his cock. I splashed with every bob of my head, but the nix let out a groan so low and loud that I heard it even underwater. Encouraged, I devoured Adähr's wet length again and again. I ran one hand along his inner thigh until I felt his taut balls against my fingertips. I squeezed and rolled them gently and heard another groan of pleasure from Adähr.

At last, my chest burned too much and I had to release the nix's cock. I broke the surface of the water and threw my head back, slashing a scarlet arc through the air with my wet hair. I gasped for breath.

"Very good," Adähr said. "You really have gotten better."

"You like it?" I asked.

The nix nodded, but caught my arm before I could dive down once again. He pulled me into his lap, fixing me with his glittering cerulean gaze.

"I want you," he said.

"Then take me," I moaned. "God, please fuck me!"

I wrapped my legs around Adähr's waist and rubbed myself impatiently along his hard cock. He didn't have to grab himself – eddies of the swirling water moved to his will, positioning the head of his dick against my pussy. Then Adähr pulled me down onto him, filling me in one sudden stroke. The invasion of my body was fast and hot.

"Yes!" I cried.

Adähr held my ass in a tight grip, the water taking my weight as he moved me up and down on his cock. I rocked into him, not stifling a single moan every time the nix impaled me. He kissed me hard, stealing as much breath as though he were pushing me under the water once more, drowning me in sensation.

"You came back to me," Adähr whispered against my cheek as I rode him. His breath was cold and I smelled the storm brewing inside him.

"Yes," I whimpered. "I came."

I did cum, there on Adähr's cock. The nix dug his fingers against the softness of my ass and yanked me down onto his dick, forcing himself deeper and harder into me. We were whipping the water into a frothing vortex all around us. Desperately, I clung to Adähr as the pleasure built and exploded through me. My hands slipped on his wet skin, drawing red lines across his shoulders and chest. My voice rose and echoed through the tiled room.

"Oh, fuck!" I screamed out. "Adähr!"

The nix seemed to like hearing his name on my lips. His cock throbbed inside me and his grip became almost painful. Adähr surged to his feet, shedding water in every direction.

"What–?" I started to gasp.

But Adähr was already shoving me down over the edge of the tub, pressing my breasts into the cold, hard marble. My hair coiled in a coppery puddle beside me. Adähr's dick was gone from my pussy and I whimpered in protest.

"I want your ass," he said.

One hand remained heavy at the small of my back and I felt the slick head of his cock brushing against my ass. Adähr selected one of the bottles lined up along the window and flicked the cap off. It went spinning and rolling away across the tiles. Adähr upended the bottle of lavender-scented body wash and it splattered me in thick purple drops.

"Yes," he said in an icy voice. "Ah, Lily... My lost little huntress."

The nix's hands were all over my ass, slicking my buttocks and the cleft between them until they were slippery and shiny. Adähr admired his work for a moment by the colorful light of the window and then brought his palm down to crack loudly against my ass. I let out a surprised cry.

"Do you want it?" Adähr asked. "Do you want me to put my cock up your tight little ass, Lily?"

"Yes!" There was no lie in that moan.

The nix's finger traced the shallow valley between my cheeks and then pressed the tip to my ass, rubbing in teasing circles. I pushed back against him and made the water around us seethe.

"Is this what you wanted, Lily? Is this what you dreamed of all these years?"

"Yes!"

I reached behind me and grabbed my own eager, tingling ass. My skin was so slippery with lavender soap that my hands just slid. Adähr laughed low in his throat at my show of desperation and spanked me again, then held me firmly still.

"Patience," Adähr told me.

I whimpered and bit my lip. The nix seized my hips and I felt his cock slipping and rubbing against my ass. Just when I was about ready to turn around and pounce on Adähr, he finally shoved himself hard up into my ass.

My fingers splayed across the marble tiles and I gasped at the sudden intrusion spreading me open. Adähr grunted at my tightness, but another deep thrust buried his dick all the way inside me.

His hips came to rest against my buttocks and his balls brushed the empty wetness of my pussy.

Adähr moved in smooth, swift motions, hammering his hard cock into me and making the bathroom echo with the overlapping wet sounds of our bodies coming together. The nix's thickness filled me, stroking and stirring my depths. It wasn't long until I was panting and moaning on the edge of climax again. Before I could fall over that precipice, though, Adähr pulled me down into the water once more, submerging our bodies. He held me to his chest and I felt his lean muscles bunched against me. The nix ran his tongue along the rim of my ear.

"I'm not done with you yet, Lily," Adähr said.

He reached around me to caress the wet curves of my breasts, rolling the nipples between his fingers and teasing them up into hard pink buds. Then his hands moved down, grabbing my thighs and spreading them wide. Adähr moved in the sunken tub until I was angled toward one of the rumbling jets. Not straight on, but what did that matter to a nix? The hot water instantly obeyed his every whim.

Wet heat rushed over the sensitive softness of my labia, making my pussy tingle under the stream of bubbles. Adähr's cock kept moving smoothly in and out of my ass as the jetting water assaulted my clitoris. I let him hold me there, let him pull me down into the sea of sensation and willingly drowning in it.

Brilliant colors arced and exploded across my vision and I almost didn't realize that they weren't because of what Adähr was doing to my body. It was the House of Diamonds' nightly fireworks display flashing through the windows. Red and green and gold reflected across the polished marble.

"Oh god, Adähr," I cried. "Yes! I want to cum. Please, make me cum!"

The nix held me spread open before his liquid onslaught and pounded his cock deep up my ass. I twined my arms back around

Adähr and held on as I went tight, squeezing and gripping his dick to bring him over the edge with me.

He pressed his face against the side of my neck, biting into the delicate skin there to mute a loud groan of pleasure. I screamed wordlessly as thick liquid heat fountained into me. It sprayed so deep and hard that it felt almost like I had swallowed the nix's load. The flood of molten cum pumping up my ass sent me hurtling over the peak of ecstasy. I thrashed against Adähr, splashing so much water in the throes of passion that it was like another firework of blue and silver.

Droplets pattered down around us as I finally descended once more. Adähr guided the warm rain out of the air with a gesture and back into the bathtub. I leaned against him, struggling to slow my racing heart. Adähr withdrew himself from me and freed a small cloud of pale spunk from my overfilled ass. I stretched out in the hot water.

Adähr rose, cock hanging long between his well-toned legs, but didn't step out of the sunken tub.

"You said that you had something to show me, Lily," he said. "Was this it?"

I shook my head. "In the front room. It's in my suitcase."

"Show me."

The nix stood back and waited for me to climb out of the water first. I wrapped myself in a towel. Adähr flicked his fingers and the water streaking his skin leapt obediently back into the bathtub with a splash.

Adähr followed me through the hotel suite, always keeping himself between me and the still-steaming tub full of water. He nodded to my suitcase on the bar. I drew a deep breath and un-zipped it. I pulled out a small stack of clothes and set them aside, then looked over to Adähr. He stepped closer, cold blue eyes going wide as he took in the sight of the gold bars. Millions of dollars' worth.

"I want to leave," I told him.

Adähr turned back to regard me. The nix's expression was difficult to read, but the air in the hotel room suddenly smelled charged and stormy.

"I want to leave with you," I said. "You were the only one who ever got away from me, Adähr. The rest... they paid well."

The nix inspected the neat rows of gold bars and I wound my arms around his waist. The final volley of fireworks launched from somewhere on the roof of the House of Diamonds and erupted into flaming sparks against the ceiling of clouds. The reflection of sparkling colors danced across the polished gold laid out before Adähr. My bet was on the table.

"There are seven other bounty hunters in the city," I said. "All working for the College. You can't stay here, Adähr. But when you leave, I want to go with you. I don't want it to be another eight years before I see you again."

The nix reached out to touch the smooth gold, perhaps to assure himself that it was real. It was. I had emptied my safe of every ounce. There was still a lot of money in my bank accounts, but I couldn't drain those without attracting attention.

"We can go wherever we want. Anywhere in the world," I whispered. My hands dropped from Adähr's waist down to the stirring length between his legs. "Las Vegas. Atlantic City. Paris. Or Victoria Falls, if you want the water. I don't care, as long as I can come with you."

"The wizards will be angry," said Adähr. "You belong to them."

"Not anymore." I stroked the nix's cock lightly. "I'm yours. All yours, for as long as you want me. The College is going to be furious, but I don't care. You're worth the risk."

Adähr sighed in pleasure, though his sapphire eyes remained transfixed by the gold.

"We can catch a boat out of the city," he said. "A cruise to someplace far away from here."

I shook my head. "Stefano's still out there. Clio and Sabra, too. I don't even know where Griffith and Doyle are, but it's a solid bet they're watching the water. If we get anywhere near a boat, the other hunters will be all over us."

"Including Remy Saville," Adähr said. His hard accent made the name sound like cracking ice. The nix finally peered over his shoulder at me. "But you have an idea. Don't you, Lily?"

"I don't want any of those other hunters to catch you, Adähr. So we fly. First thing in the morning, we get a ridiculously expensive charter flight to wherever you want. The College would never think to search for you on an airplane."

The nix actually looked shocked, as though he had never even considered such a thing. Which, I supposed, he hadn't.

"An airplane?" Adähr asked. "I don't own a passport. I didn't come to your country by any method so pedantic. But my methods won't get me past customs."

"With this much money, we don't have to worry about customs or anything else. We'll get a private plane and no questions. We can go wherever we want, do whatever we want."

"But on a... plane?"

The hotel room was full of the smell of an impending storm again. I dropped my towel to the floor and pressed myself against Adähr's bare back. I stood on my toes and trailed my lips up the nix's neck to his ear.

"It's a gamble," I admitted quietly. "On me, on the plane. But I'm all in. Are you?"

Adähr gave me a wicked grin.

"Get dressed," he told me. "We're hitting the tables. I'm feeling lucky tonight."

Chapter
SEVEN

We didn't sleep that night. Adähr and I gambled and fucked and drank until dawn. The nix didn't seem any more affected by the endless stream of alcohol than I was, unless you counted how hard he got when doing shots out of my navel. By morning, I could barely walk and we had lost nearly a hundred thousand dollars, but I was smiling as we left the House of Diamonds.

We drove toward the water. The airport was located on a blocky peninsula built out into the southern bay. It was a sprawling tangle of terminals and runways that did its best to look graceful with a lot of glass and white arches. But the whole thing still looked more like a whale in a wedding dress, if you ask me.

Adähr regarded the airport with an expression of brittle distrust, but seemed reassured by the proximity of the cold waters of the bay. We drove past the commercial terminals, all crowded with travelers even this early in the morning. Instead, we parked close to some of the smaller private terminals, down at the far end of the rectangular peninsula. There were no crowds and no metal detectors here.

Good.

I collected the suitcase full of gold from the Alfa Romeo's trunk. Adähr would have preferred to carry it, but my luggage was too heavy for the nix to lift. There was a *lot* of gold in there. But the night before had left me power enough to carry my car out to the plane if I wanted, though I doubted it would fit in an overhead compartment.

"Which one is ours?" I asked.

"Number twelve," said Adähr. "Signature Flights. What about your car?"

"Fuck it. You should see what I did to the last one. Werewolf."

Adähr laughed. He hooked an arm around my waist and pulled me close as we walked to the small building bearing the neat white-on-silver sign of Signature Flights. The doors slid open at our approach and I smelled something that wasn't the wet scents of Adähr and the bay.

Burnt herbs, leather and wood.

Remy Saville stood in the center of the empty Signature Flights lobby. The French hunter was dressed for work once more, in his long traveling coat and the leather hat pulled low over his steel-gray eyes. In one hand, he held the wooden box I had seen in his room, the one with the cross sigil of the Castle branded into the top.

Remy raised it, placing his thumb against the box's intricate black iron catch.

"Adähr," he said. His accent turned the name into a leonine purr. "At long last, you are mine."

The nix swore acidly in some language much older than German and leapt back, shoving me toward Remy. I was still shocked and off-balance from finding the other hunter here at all and we fell together into a tangle of limbs. My suitcase crashed to the floor, cracking the tiles. The strain was finally too much and the seams split, spilling lacy underwear and gold bars in every direction. Our fall jolted the wooden box from Remy's hand, too, and it spun away across the lobby.

Adähr was off and running in a heartbeat, bolting out through the terminal door. So much for loyalty. I wrenched myself free and struggled to stand.

"What the hell are you doing here?" I shouted, kicking at Remy. He slid across the gold-strewn floor on his back. "How did you find Adähr?"

"I didn't find 'im," Remy panted as he rolled to his feet. "When I realized that you 'ad lied to me about the arena, I knew that you 'ad some other plan. So I watched you through the scry network. It is already well-attuned to you, it seems, and I found out where you were going."

I jumped up. "Fucking wizards! I hope you enjoyed the show, you pervert."

Remy grabbed for the wooden box he had dropped. I kicked a bar of gold and it cracked against his questing fingers. He pulled away with a snarl.

"And 'ow exactly did you think you would catch a nix 'ere?" Remy growled. "This airport is surrounded by water!"

Fuck, he was hot when he was angry. That didn't stop me from being royally pissed, though.

"I was about to get Adähr onto an airplane!" I shouted. "Thirty thousand feet up with a closed plumbing system. Until you screwed it all up!"

I snatched Remy's wooden box and shook it at him.

"What the hell is in here?" I asked. "Some kind of magic to help you catch Adähr?"

"*Oui*," Remy said, lapsing momentarily back into his native language. The other hunter lunged for me, but I was far too fast for him now and slipped out of reach, toward the terminal door. "What are you doing? You are no wizard, Lilith. You can't use that!"

I was already whirling away and sprinting out of the terminal. Adähr had a huge head start on me, but thanks to last night, I was faster than even a panicked nix and I ran after him. Adähr fled not back through the parking lot, but out across the tarmac and toward the open water of the bay. If he touched that water, he would get away. If I was lucky, Clio would find him and collect the bounty. More likely, Adähr would just be gone.

Fuck that. No way I was letting Adähr escape me again.

Whatever Remy had done to clear out our terminal for a clean takedown had kept the nearby runway empty. So I let the power Adähr himself had given me course through my muscles and ran. The light-studded asphalt was a blur beneath my pounding feet. Adähr risked a glance back and saw me closing swiftly in on him. The nix didn't slow. In fact, he was picking up speed. I guess he didn't trust me anymore. Smart man.

The fleeing nix grabbed an unattended luggage cart, heaved and swung it into my path. I coiled my legs beneath me and leapt over it, landing hard enough on the other side to leave cracks in the tarmac. Adähr was a hundred yards from the water's edge now, but I was only thirty behind him.

Wind roared overhead, tugging at my hair and clothes. The thunder of turbines was deafening. Remy may have been able to shut down a single small terminal, but not the entire airport. The great white underbelly of a commercial airplane raced toward me, landing gear extended. Adähr staggered, but I was the one right below the incoming plane. Shit.

I threw myself to the side, skidding so fast that my shoes left tracks of melted rubber across the asphalt, and out of the way of the massive wheels descending toward the runway. But the gale-force winds of the huge turbines could overturn cars stupid enough to be in their way. Sex might give me the strength to flip a car, too, but it doesn't make me weigh as much as one.

The windstorm yanked me right up off my feet and hurled me spinning through the air. I flew, fell and then finally slammed to the ground so hard that I felt bones break. Groaning, I rolled with the impact, my sex-fueled powers already pulling my shoulder back into place, but I was too far behind Adähr now. There was no way I could reach him before he made it into the bay. My mark was at the edge of the runway and the water in front of him swelled, arcing up toward its master.

"Adähr, stop!" I called out.

The nix hesitated for just a fraction of a second, looking back at me. His blue eyes were dangerously dark and even over the stink of airplane fuel and the burnt rubber of landing gear, I smelled the sharp storm-scent of Adähr's rage. Cold seawater curved behind him like the huge, bared claws of some immense oceanic monster.

"What are you doing, Lily?" Adähr shouted across the tarmac. "I thought you wanted to run away with me. You lied to me!"

"And you were going to live happily ever after with me? I know you better than that, Adähr," I said. Every muscle inside of me was knotted, trembling and ready to move. But he was too close to the water. "You would have fucked me and had your fun until the gold ran dry, then just jumped out another window."

"You played me!" Adähr hissed.

He curled his fingers and the churning blue-gray claws of water stretched toward me, but I brandished Remy's strange wooden box. I had cushioned its fall as best I could and it was a little scuffed, but otherwise intact. I had no idea what was inside or how to use it, but Adähr didn't know that. I hoped.

"Not another inch," I told him. "Or I'll open this. I'd rather take you alive, Adähr, but I'll settle for blasting you into a puddle."

The water arcing toward me froze and Adähr's glittering sapphire eyes narrowed. I put my thumb over the box's iron catch.

"What is it?" Adähr asked.

"The Eye of the Sun. A fire djinn gave this spell to the wizards a thousand years ago. It can turn an entire sea into nothing but dry gray dust. Just imagine what it could do to a nix."

Adähr frowned, but didn't look convinced. "The Castle wizards are cowards. They would never kill me."

"Remy has been hunting you for a year." I kept walking slowly, holding up the box. I was moving through the shimmering shadow of Adähr's sharp-tipped hooks of water. "The Castle is done with your shit. They're done cleaning up after you and your tricks. It takes months to prepare the Eye of the Sun spell and more gold than your entire bounty, but stopping you is worth any price."

The nix grinned rakishly at me. "But you can't use their spells, Lily."

"Really, Adähr?" I matched his smirk with my own. "You want to bet on that? I've had eight years to get ready for this."

"I know what you are Lily, and you're no wizard."

"You've heard of Merlin, right?" I said. The best lies had a grain of truth. "The greatest sorcerer the world's ever known. And he was a cambion. Half demon, just like me."

Adähr's smile vanished and his glare was as icy as a blizzard. I thumbed up the latch of the branded box and turned it toward Adähr.

"I can open this and trigger the spell faster than you can drown me. So drop the water and step back from the edge," I told him. "Or I'll burn you and half the bay away to bare earth."

"You wouldn't kill me," Adähr insisted. "You're bluffing."

"I'm done playing with you."

Adähr tensed, but then sagged. The water splashed back down into the bay.

"I thought I had you. You were mine," he said in a small voice. "I thought you loved me, Lily."

I grabbed Adähr by the shoulder and pulled him away from the water. Once we were a safe distance from the bay, I took a pair of handcuffs out of my pocket – I told you I didn't want to go through a metal detector – and closed them around Adähr's wrists.

"Love? Come on, Adähr," I told him. "I'm a cambion. I don't fall in love."

Chapter

EIGHT

A few hours later, I was making my way down one of the wide corridors of Dresden Hall, past the silent ranks of empty armor emblazoned with twining red and white dragons. The head of the College, High Magus Vincent Myrdon, walked along beside me.

"You caught him this time," Vincent said.

I guess that was supposed to be congratulatory, but the wizard still sounded like the school principal lecturing me for wearing too short a skirt. Again.

If Dorian was the perfect image of the kind but bumbling old wizard from some kids' movie, then Vincent Myrdon was more like the grand vizier trying to take over the kingdom. The High Magus was tall and severe, with steel-gray hair and a silver-streaked auburn goatee. He wore stark black robes that made me think of a judge and didn't invite anything like familiarity.

I put my hands in my pockets, not sure why Vincent was talking to me at all, but I couldn't stop a small grin from curling my lips.

"Yeah," I said. "I caught Adähr. It's finally done."

The High Magus nodded in apparent satisfaction. "On behalf of both the College and the Castle, I thank you. Adähr has been incarcerated and Dorian will meet us in the council chamber with your compensation."

"I thought the Castle was paying for Adähr," I said.

"The Castle will reimburse our expenses."

I gave Vincent a sidelong look. "You guys can make your own gold. So how exactly does reimbursement work?"

"It's complicated," he said. "But the details of magic have never been of interest to you."

Translation: none of your business, demon girl.

We arrived at the council chamber. The thick wooden door swung open, but I was pretty sure the iron gargoyle knocker was eyeballing me as I followed Vincent through. Dorian stood at the circular table inside, laying out gleaming gold bars on the inscribed stone surface.

"Hello, Lilith," he said. "Six and a half bars for Adähr's capture. Well done."

"Thanks, Dorian."

I hesitated, then went ahead and gave Dorian a quick kiss on the cheek. It didn't matter if our boss was watching. After all, it wasn't caution or playing it safe that had finally caught Adähr. From the doorway, Vincent cleared his throat and Dorian shuffled away, blushing furiously.

"The Castle hunter came to see me," Vincent said.

"Remy?" I asked. "Did he get that box back?"

"Yes," answered Vincent. "Zane returned it to him when Adähr was brought to the College."

"What was actually in that thing, anyway?"

"A variation on an ancient mariner's spell. It would have contained the nix in a water-tight seal for several hours."

"Neat. What did Remy want?" I asked. "To complain about me?"

"On the contrary. You made quite an impression. His plan was clever, but not as clever as yours. Remy Saville sends his compliments."

I almost tripped, even though I wasn't walking. Was that a smile on the High Magus' face?

"Thanks," I said as I collected my gold from the round table. "Well, give Remy my compliments right back. He was good, too. On the job and in bed."

Vincent blinked. He certainly wasn't smiling now. "...What?"

I grinned and headed for the door, leaving Dorian and Vincent to manage the aftermath of Adähr's capture. I was done worrying about the nix. There were more important things to think about now, like what to do with my brand new gold. I could always wait for the market to swing in my favor and get even more money for it, but I wasn't sure I wanted to do that. After all, there was a certain auto-repair business looking for investors...

LILY QUINN STORY #5

Max's
LONG NIGHT

Max's
LONG NIGHT

The restaurant sat in the middle of downtown like a diamond in its setting – shining, beautiful and way outside my price range. But Lily picked the place and I really couldn't decline her invitation. Have you ever tried saying *no* to Lilith Quinn? I dare you.

On second thought, don't. You might get hurt. Badly.

The name of the restaurant was something long and French that I couldn't pronounce. A young woman in a fitted black vest opened the door at my approach.

"Uh, thanks," I said.

The woman smiled and closed the door behind me before too much of the February cold could get through. Inside, dinner was in full swing and well-dressed couples sat at every table. There was nothing metaphorical about the diamonds sparkling at their throats and ears. I saw cufflinks that cost more than I made in a year. Back when I had a job at all.

I felt more out of place in that restaurant than I ever had as the only guy in my high school home economics class. In my tailored suit, I *almost* would have blended in... but my jacket was still balled up in the passenger seat of my truck and my shirt sleeves were still rolled up to my elbows. I didn't dare pull them down, either, and not just because I didn't even own a pair of cufflinks.

Behind something that looked suspiciously like a polished mahogany podium, the host – or in a restaurant like this, I suppose he was a *maître d'* – inspected me with a raised eyebrow.

"Uh, hi," I said. "I'm here to meet Lilith Quinn."

His eyebrow jumped up a little higher, but he just inclined his head and escorted me back to a small white-draped table beneath a tall, narrow window. I'm sure the view outside was great, but my eyes didn't make it that far.

Lily was already seated at the table, of course, and she looked gorgeous. She wore a long, clinging black dress with no sleeves and a matching black silk choker around her neck. Her red hair cascaded over one shoulder like something on fire.

"Sorry I'm late, Lil," I said. "You look amazing."

I sat down into the chair opposite Lily and she smiled brightly, waving off my apology. She's never been much for formalities. If Lily picked this restaurant, it wasn't to impress me or anyone else. And to judge by the delicious smells coming from the direction of the kitchen, Lily had chosen well. Some restaurants get to mark up their prices on ambiance or location alone, but this didn't seem to be one of those.

Lily turned the dazzling force of her smile on the maître d'.

"Would you mind having someone bring that wine now?" she asked. He nodded and left. Lily returned her attention to me. "What kept you, Max? I hope you weren't working on the i10. And where's your jacket?"

The suit had been a gift from Lily, who insisted that I should have at least one. And I've told you how hard it is to decline her. I have to pick my battles with her and save each *no* for something important.

"Not the i10," I answered quickly. "I left early to make sure I got here on time. I just got sort of... held up."

Lily leaned across the table, making her perfect breasts squeeze softly together in the confines of her dress. My pulse doubled and I felt the animal instinct to dive right into that silky cleavage. Instead, I tore my gaze away just as Lily ran one finger along my jaw and held it out.

It was smeared in black and I flushed.

"Looks like grease to me," she said, mockingly skeptical.

I had spent ten minutes scrubbing my hands, but cheap gas station soap wasn't up to the challenge of car grease. And it had just made a hopeless mess of my dirty cuffs. I sighed and knew I was blushing.

"There was a minivan stuck on the side of the freeway with a flat tire," I admitted. "They didn't know how to change it and couldn't afford to call someone. I'm really sorry, Lil."

"Don't be, Max. Most people would have driven right by."

I had no idea what to say to that – except perhaps to point out that I had ruined my expensive tailored jacket – so I kept my mouth shut. Lily held up her smudged finger like she wanted to lick it clean, but carefully wiped it with her napkin instead. I unfolded my napkin, too – which had been sculpted into some kind of origami flower – and rubbed at my chin until there was enough black on the cloth for me to hope there was none left on my face.

Yeah, fat chance.

"You really didn't need to take me out," I said.

Lily smirked. "Don't be stupid, Max. It's Valentine's Day and I don't have a boyfriend. You don't have a girlfriend. This way, neither of us has to be alone tonight. Besides, we have to celebrate finding a place for your new garage. Even though it's a rat-trap. You're going to be fixing that building up for months."

"Hey, it was cheap," I said, then hesitated. "You know, relatively."

"I would have given you more money."

"Loaned," I answered firmly. "I'm going to pay it all back. With interest."

Lily narrowed her eyes at me. They're an exquisite hazel color that's almost gold, especially by the flickering light of the candle burning at the center of our table. Remember what I said about picking my battles with Lily? Well, this was one of the important fights. There was no way I was letting her just buy me a garage.

So I stared right back until Lily finally smiled and relented. Sort of.

"Why don't you have a girlfriend?" Lily asked. "You're smart. You're handy. You're really hot. You can even cook."

She ticked items off on her fingers like a shopping list. I shifted uncomfortably in my seat and wasn't sure what to say. My relationship with Lily was weird, to say the least. She's been my best friend ever since we were kids, but we also sleep together. A lot. So it always feels strange when Lily grills me about my sex life. She *is* my sex life.

"I don't know, Lil," I said. "It just... never works out."

"How long since the last time you had a date? Six months? No, longer than that. What was she...? A nurse, right?"

I shook my head. "A phlebotomist. I met her at a blood drive. Why don't you have a boyfriend or girlfriend, Lil?"

"Are you kidding?" Lily said, laughing. "And what exactly would I tell them about myself? About what I do for a living?"

She had a point. Strictly speaking, Lily isn't human. She's a cambion, the daughter of a succubus and a human father. That means that sex gives Lily superpowers she uses to hunt monsters. I'm not even supposed to know about that, but I was there when she found out what she was. Lily's never kept any secrets from me, but I had a hard time imagining her explaining her life to anyone else.

"I could get a dog," said Lily, resting her chin in one hand. "Or maybe a cat. They don't give a shit about what time I come home."

Our waitress appeared beside the table and introduced herself as Courtney. She had deep brown eyes and a thick black puff of hair held back from her face with a headband. Courtney opened the bottle of wine that Lily had requested – which was labeled in more French – and poured us each a glass.

"Thanks," I said.

Courtney smiled at me. "Are you two ready to order?"

"No, not really," Lily answered. "We haven't even looked at the menus yet."

"In that case, let me suggest the fresh salmon with balsamic and maple glaze," said Courtney. "It's Juliette's specialty."

Lily made a pleased sound and nodded. Courtney turned away to take care of another table and I caught my friend watching the waitress go. Well, that might have been an understatement – she was practically falling out of her seat as she stared at Courtney's retreating ass.

"She's cute," Lily said. "Want to ask her out?"

I paused in the middle of raising my wineglass. "What? I... uh... She probably thinks we're here on a date. She doesn't know we're just friends."

"So inform her otherwise."

"Don't you think that might be a bit... awkward?" I asked.

"If you don't tell her, I will."

"You really don't need to worry that much about my love life."

"Well, one of us has to. You're a great guy, Max. You deserve a great girl."

"Thanks, Lil. So um... how's work?" I asked, trying as quickly as I could to change the subject.

"You mean working for a secret cabal of wizards as a monster hunter?" Lily said, dropping her voice conspiratorially. She grinned. "It's okay. There was a bounty to go take out a chupacabra. You know, the goat suckers? But I think I'll let Redmond have that one. Or maybe one of Sabra's homunculi – they don't even have blood. But a bounty just went up a couple of days ago for a wyvern spotted hunting along the coast."

"Wyvern?"

"It's kind of like a dragon," Lily said. "But smaller and dumber. It's poisonous, too. I'll drive out there tomorrow and see if I can catch it."

"Poisonous? Can it hurt you, Lil?" The question came out a little sharper than I intended and I covered my dismay with a long sip of wine. It was good – sweet and a little citrusy.

"Nothing I can't handle."

"So... there are dragons?" I asked. Lamely, I'll admit.

"Hell yeah," said Lily.

I might have mentioned that she's not very formal.

I took another swallow of wine. I wasn't sure if Lily was exaggerating, but I doubted it. At least, not by much. I knew for a fact that my best friend tangled with vampires, and I was still trying to repair her car because a werewolf had ripped it open like a sardine can. So it wasn't a stretch to believe that there were dragons out there somewhere, even if I had never exactly seen them on the news. The wizards that Lily works for make it their business to keep monsters out of our lives. And Lily was their best bounty hunter. I'd be lying if I said I wasn't damned proud of her.

"How's Evaine?" I asked.

Lily's mentor was a strange woman. Hauntingly beautiful, yes, and profoundly knowledgeable about the supernatural world, but strange. It was Evaine who taught Lily what she was, who told her about fairies, spirits and demons. Those are all real, too. Evaine also taught Lily how to fight with everything but nunchucks and chainsaws. And chainsaw nunchucks, I suppose.

"I saw her about three months ago, when I was after that Unseelie thief," Lily said. "She asked about you, too. That was before you lost your job."

"It's okay, Lil. That wasn't your fault."

"Yes," she said. "It was. Which is why I wish you would let me just give you the money for the new garage."

"Not a chance."

We stared at each other across the candlelit table for a moment, then Lily suddenly smiled brilliantly.

"Hey, I almost forgot," she said. "I brought you a present."

"What? Lil, no," I groaned. "It's not my birthday yet and we just did Christmas."

Another *no* used up. And I was a hypocrite – on the floorboard of the truck were a dozen white roses that I really shouldn't have bought while I didn't have a steady paycheck. But after I stopped to help out with the tire, they slid off the seat and onto the grease-stained floor. By the time I made it to the restaurant, I was too embarrassed to give her the ruined flowers.

Not that they would have been nearly good enough for Lily, even before. Ever since she started bounty hunting, Lily's had a lot of money. A *lot*. The wizards pay her in solid gold and she says that they also make sure the IRS doesn't come asking questions. I'm not certain if that means Lily doesn't pay taxes, but it definitely means she tries to spoil me. I don't think she has anyone else to spend her money on.

Lily opened her purse. It wasn't very big, but that didn't mean I wasn't about to try out another *no*. Just last year, Lily tried to give me a fifty thousand dollar watch.

The box Lily pulled from her purse now was small, red and tied with a white ribbon. Lily slid it across the table to me. It was light and rattled when I gave it a gentle shake. I frowned.

"There better not be a car key in here," I said.

Lily smirked. "It's not a key. Though you should let me buy you a new truck. You've had that one since high school."

"I'm not getting rid of that truck, Lil. That's where we... uh... you know."

I'm not particularly shy – I've known Lily too long for that. But despite its many dents and repairs, that truck was still special to me. It was where I lost my virginity with Lily and where we discovered exactly how special she was.

"I didn't say to get rid of it. Just get a new one for work. The Truck–" Lily gave it proper noun status. "–can go into a gallery or something, where it belongs."

I had a hard time imagining what sort of gallery that would be and figured that Lily was joking... but I never quite knew with her. She tapped the box.

"Now I'm getting impatient," Lily said. "Open."

I untied the ribbon and pulled off the lid of the box with one eye squeezed shut, afraid to see cufflinks that might actually blend in at the restaurant. But what lay on the little cushion of pink tissue paper inside was a shiny lavender remote control.

It was small enough to fit comfortably into the palm of my hand and had two sliding controls. They were labeled *min* at the bottom and *max* at the top.

"Um, what is it?" I asked. "A garage door opener for the My Little Ponies dream mansion?"

Lily laughed and kicked me playfully beneath the table. Then she leaned forward, forming that magnetic cleavage again. She lowered her voice until I was more reading her perfect red lips than hearing her words.

"One of those sliders controls the vibrator in my pussy," Lily whispered. "The other is for the one in my ass."

I almost dropped the remote. You know, I really thought I was beyond surprise when it came to Lily, but she never ceases to amaze me. There was a lump in my throat nearly big enough to match the one rising in my pants.

Choking, I yanked the control down under the table, out of sight. Of course, in the dim golden mood lighting, there was virtually no chance anyone could have seen it in the first place... But it still felt like Lily had erected a huge neon sign over my head that screamed *pervert!*

"Lil!" I hissed. "What the hell?"

"What? Don't you like your present?" Lily teased.

The remote felt heavy and red-hot in my hand. I risked a peek down at it, but I had no idea which slider went with which vibrator. Both were at the bottom of the control in what I assumed was the *off* position.

"So are we... uh... done with dinner then?" I asked in a strangled voice.

"What? We haven't even ordered yet. Go on, give it a try. Please?"

I could never say *no* when Lily needed me, so I squinted at the remote. Which one to use first? I put my thumb over the slider on the right and pushed up gently. There was a subtle clicking sensation as the control moved and turned the vibrator on. Lily leaned back in her seat and gasped softly. God, she's beautiful.

"Have you two decided on dinner?"

I jerked my thumb off the remote with a start and stared guiltily at Courtney. The waitress smiled at us and Lily winked. Her cheeks were flushed a delicate rose color as she addressed Courtney.

"I'm in the mood for something special," Lily said.

I held my breath and pushed the first slider all the way to the top. Lily's pupils dilated wide and dark, but she showed no other outward sign of the vibrator buzzing inside her. I could almost hear it, though, a buzz like bees busy at work making honey. Which was ridiculous... there was no way I actually heard the toy over the hum of conversation and clinking dishes, but my imagination was going wild. I thought of the vibrator inside Lily, her tender pink pussy making its own sweet honey. But for all I knew, I had turned on the one in her ass.

"I bet that you have excellent taste," Lily was saying. "I think I'll have that salmon you suggested."

Courtney offered up a bright smile. "Wonderful. Don't worry, you're going to love it."

"Oh, I'm going to love a lot of things tonight," Lily said, her voice falling into a seductive purr that made my cock throb.

Courtney looked between Lily and me.

"Sounds like you two have a long night ahead of you," she said. "You're a cute couple."

"We're not… together," I blurted.

Both Lily and Courtney stared at me, blinking. My face was flaming and I nearly dropped the remote control again. Lily recovered first and laughed.

"That's right," she said. "Just a pair of single friends out enjoying Valentine's Day."

Lily emphasized *single* with a small nod toward me. Courtney's smile wobbled, but she didn't look upset. In fact, her cheeks seemed to have darkened a shade. But she turned to me.

"And you, sir?" Courtney asked.

"Huh? What?" I stammered.

Her fine black brows arched. "What would you like?"

"Um…"

"For dinner," Lily said.

"I'll have the salmon thing, too," I told Courtney.

She suppressed a giggle, but only barely. I wanted to bang my head on the table. Anything to end the torment. Courtney walked away to take our order to the kitchen and Lily watched her go again, then turned back to me with a grin.

"That wasn't so hard, was it?" she asked. "Or is it… hard?"

I felt Lily's foot against my leg again, but not kicking me this time. Her stocking-covered toes slid up my leg, past my knee and traced along the inside of my thigh. I clenched my jaw so tight that my teeth ground audibly.

"There's still another one in the back," Lily said softly.

I almost asked what she meant, but then her toes caressed the bulge tenting my pants and my hands tightened reflexively. Plastic creaked in my fingers.

Oh, yeah. The remote.

Taking a deep breath, I did my best to ignore Lily's toes rubbing along the agonizingly confined length of my cock. I pulled the first slider down to half – the one controlling the toy in her pussy, apparently – and waited a beat. Lily opened her mouth to object and I jammed the second control up to full.

A sharp gasp escaped Lily's parted lips before she could snap them closed. I darted a nervous glance around the restaurant, but each table was an isolated pool of candlelight. Couples were absorbed in one another's company and paying absolutely no attention to us.

I stroked the second slider, moving it up and down. The vibrator's speed rose and fell as I envisioned my cock stroking in and out of her ass. Lily's hands were steady as she lifted her wineglass and took a sip, but her eyes were wide and bright in the dim light.

Lily can handle public play... mostly. She shifted in her seat, instinctively pressing her body back as if she could push against something already buried deep up her ass. I swallowed hard. Was this going to be the time Lily finally lost it and started moaning for everyone to hear? Not that I would let it stop me from getting her off, of course.

I brought both of the vibrator controls down to a low, soft thrum inside Lily and enjoyed how she wriggled in her seat. Then, beneath the tablecloth, her toes curled against my dick as I pushed both sliders slowly, firmly to the top. Lily's hands twitched and her fingers tightened around her salad fork as she came.

"All ready for me, I see," Courtney said.

Damn, she sure was quiet. The waitress placed a pair of small, stylish salads in front of us.

"Is there anything else I can do for you two?" she asked.

Lily grinned up at her, though she was breathing hard and her voice was a little rough. "We're just wonderful."

"Excellent. I'll be back soon with the main course."

Lily panted as Courtney retreated and finally dropped her fork to the tabletop again. I stared at the crumpled ball of metal. Lily's foot must have fallen out of my lap at some point, but I didn't care.

Knowing I had made her cum hard enough to make her control slip just about made me cream my pants.

We had hardly touched our salads before Courtney returned with the salmon. Not because she didn't give us enough time or because Lily didn't have a salad fork anymore, but because my hands were tucked beneath the table with a thumb on each slider, alternating the buzz of pleasure between Lily's ass and pussy.

"Here you are," Courtney said, setting down two new plates that smelled absolutely delicious.

"I'm cumming," Lily announced.

Courtney blinked. "I... I'm sorry?"

"I'm coming back here," Lily corrected herself. "This place is wonderful."

"Excellent," Courtney said. "Maybe I'll get to take care of you two again."

I brought both sliders down warningly, trying to keep Lily from saying anything naughty to our very polite waitress. Low, but not off. Lily would kill me if I quit on her now. I was in this until the batteries died. But I kept them on low and saw Lily concentrating, almost straining to feel the paired vibrators inside her. Not that it stopped her at all.

"Oh, I'd like you to take care of me," Lily purred.

If Courtney caught the subtext, she was too professional to let it show. She turned away with another bright smile and headed off in the direction of her other tables.

"Lil!" I hissed.

"What?"

"Are you *trying* to get us kicked out?"

Lily just laughed. Yeah, that wasn't going to get through. I tried desperately for another tactic. Lily could do whatever she wanted to me, but Courtney hadn't signed up for my sex-crazed best friend's attention.

"And... I thought you wanted *me* to ask her out," I said.

"I do," Lily answered. "But don't tell me you're not just dying to see me lick your warm white spunk out of that gorgeous ass."

I really hadn't been thinking about that, but now I couldn't stop. I shook my head and grinned across the table at Lily. It was *on*. So I jammed both vibrators to high, stuck the remote in my pocket and began to eat.

Lily gasped and then picked up her undamaged fork. She could manage only slow bites, never taking her eyes off me. I sort of expected them to be out of focus, but Lily's green-gold gaze was sharp. She held my gaze like a cobra hypnotizing its prey. Every delicate bite of her food, chewing and then swallowing only heightened the sensation.

I supposed that some men were intimidated by that hard golden stare. And I'd be lying if I said that I wasn't too, at times. I wasn't exaggerating about Lily being able to kill me. I'm not a small guy and ten years of working on cars have given me a few muscles here and there, but Lily could crumple me up and toss me across the restaurant just like that fork if she wanted to. And early on, before she learned to control herself, Lily did pretty much exactly that. Without Evaine's intervention, I would have spent most of my senior year of high school in a body cast.

Lily wiped her full lips with the corner of her napkin and then smoothed it across her lap again. Not that it stayed there. She was squirming too much for that. Lily and I watched one another through the candlelight. We probably looked like any other love-struck couple in the restaurant, I realized with a flip in my stomach. But our table was different. I doubted any of the other diners were on their ninth orgasm.

I saw Courtney approaching this time – thank god – and managed to wipe the goofy grin off my face before she arrived.

"Would you two like some dessert tonight?" Courtney asked.

"No, thanks," Lily said in a tight voice. "I have something else in mind."

"Alright. Let me get these out of your way."

Courtney collected our plates and retreated once more. Lily cocked her head at me. She seemed to have more or less recovered from my vibrating retribution.

"How was your dinner?" she asked.

"Great. I think."

"You think?"

"Honestly, I have no idea," I confessed. "I didn't taste any of it. I was rather distracted by... you know... you."

Lily frowned. "Max, you could have stopped long enough to enjoy dinner. I didn't bring you out just to get me off."

"You're a lot more important than food, Lil."

"That kind of sweetness is exactly why I don't need dessert."

Courtney unobtrusively dropped off our check and Lily snatched up the little black leather folder before I could even try to reach for it. She tucked a few bills inside and I saw at least two with Benjamin Franklin's face on them.

"You don't have to pay," I protested.

"Don't worry about it, Max. Just consider it profit sharing. You're the one who charges me up for at least half of my jobs."

Half? I think I blushed at that. "Okay, Lil. Thanks."

"Speaking of thanks, I'm going to the little girls' room. Meet me there in two minutes."

Now I was definitely blushing. "In... in the ladies' restroom?"

"Yeah." Lily stood and threw her napkin at me. It was damp and smelled faintly of her pussy. She leaned close to whisper into my ear. "You made me soak right through my dress. I owe you for that, Max."

I wasn't sure if that was gratitude or a threat.

"Lil, someone's going to see us!" I said.

"What? I tipped well. And maybe you can give Courtney your tip, too. But if you're not there in two minutes, I'm starting without you. And I won't bother staying quiet this time."

A threat, then. An astonishing, delicious threat that made my cock ache. Lily stalked off and I wasn't the only one watching her go. It's difficult not to stare at a woman like Lily Quinn.

Only too late did I realize that I probably should have asked if Lily wanted the vibrators off, but she was too far away now and I wasn't going to yell *that* across the restaurant. So I sat still, staring at the clock on my cell phone and willing myself not to bust through the zipper of my pants.

At exactly the two-minute mark, I stood. At least, I meant to. Lily was as good as her word. She really would rub herself off in a restaurant restroom. And if anyone caught her at it, Lily would just bribe or charm them, or else give everyone the wet, slippery finger and walk out with her head held high.

But in reality, it took me another full minute to nerve myself up. Working Lily's little remote like the world's sexiest video game all through dinner had gotten me hard enough to drive nails. I needed to get moving, though. I thrust my hands into my pockets as I rose from my chair. There was still a pretty massive bulge in the front of my trousers, so I hurried and hoped that no one would notice in the low light. Luckily, I'm not Lily and didn't attract the same attention.

The bathrooms were at the end of a short hallway near the kitchen and there was no one outside to watch me hesitate at the ladies' room door. My pulse raced, but the longer I stood out here, the more likely it became that someone would see me. I pushed the door open a tiny crack and squeezed my eyes shut.

"Lil...?" I asked quietly.

The door swung inward so fast that I nearly fell. My eyes flew open to see Lily grabbing me by my tie. She hauled me inside.

"The batteries just died on me," Lily hissed. "I need you *right now*, Max."

If my heart was racing before, then now it hammered double time as Lily dragged me toward the row of sinks. A line of tasteful recessed lights glowed above the mirror.

"What if there's someone in here?" I whispered.

"I don't care. Hold out your hands."

I craned my neck, trying to look under the stall doors, but Lily was all done being patient and quiet. She pulled the slinky black skirt of her dress up around her hips, showing off her thigh-high stockings and the drenched lace of her panties. My heart threatened to stop entirely when Lily planted one high heel on the edge of the counter and slid her sopping wet thong to the side.

"Hands out," she repeated in a low gasp.

Utterly shocked and utterly captivated, I stared at Lily's pussy. Her pink lips were shiny and so very wet. And then they were parting and Lily gave a long, low moan as sparkling lavender plastic spread her dripping slit. I stuck out trembling hands just barely in time to catch the slippery vibrator as she squeezed it out.

"Oh my god, Lil," I breathed.

I was raging hard and felt my pants straining to contain my cock. Another curve of shimmering purple appeared at the entrance to Lily's ass, forcing the tight pink hole open and then sliding through. I didn't dare move a muscle as her moan rose and the second small vibrator fell out to join the first in my cupped palms. My hands were shaking.

"Do you uh... want them back?" I asked, struggling to form a single coherent thought.

"I said they were your presents," Lily said. "You can put them in me again some other time, when we get new batteries. But right now, I want that dessert."

Lily stepped down from the sink and fell to her knees. I fumbled the slick vibrators into my pocket as she yanked down my zipper and pulled out my aching cock. Just the feeling of freedom made me sigh much louder than I meant to. The suit pants were tight – one of the selling points for Lily had been how they showed off my ass. My dick twitched, basking in Lily's attention. I swear she can make me harder simply by looking. But any harder and I was going to blow. I couldn't stop myself from groaning as Lily grabbed the base of my cock, making smooth twisting motions as she began to stroke me.

A quiet sound echoed through the bathroom, a gasp that seemed far too shy and shocked to be Lily's. I stared down the line of stalls. One of the doors was closed, but I didn't see any feet beneath...

I could no longer focus on the rest of the room as Lily licked up and down my shaft, slicking every inch nice and wet until my flushed skin glistened under the lights. Then she took me in her mouth, starting with her lips gently pursed. Lily pushed her head forward, making my dick slowly penetrate them and slide over her tongue.

God, it was so hot inside her mouth. My eyes wanted to squeeze shut with pleasure, but I didn't want to miss the sight of Lily's lips wrapped around my cock. My hands curled into fists at my sides with the effort. It was a good thing the vibrators and remote were safely in my pockets or I would have crushed them in my grasp.

"Holy shit, Lil," I whispered as softly as I could manage.

I reached down to run my fingers through her flame-colored hair. It was soft and thick, the kind of hair you could write sonnets about. I was crap at that sort of impressive stuff, though, and Lily might have taken it... wrong. So I slid my hand down the back of her neck to her bare shoulders and Lily gave a little purr. Not a *grab-my-hair-and-fuck-my-face* sort of sound, but more of a *thanks for the encouragement, but you just stand there and enjoy this.*

I've had a lot of practice reading Lily.

She kept her grip firm and her tongue stroking all along my cock, not neglecting a single inch. With her mouth and hand, Lily coaxed me quickly up to that precipice that had been threatening all through dinner.

I was grateful. Lily's taken hours before. Literal hours spent just slowly, slowly sucking my dick until she's ready to make me erupt like a volcano. It was always well worth being dead tired at work the next day, but I doubted we had hours until one of the customers or servers came in.

Well, Lily was getting a massive load, anyway. Ignoring my entire dinner to remotely toy with Lily's perfect pink holes had started my balls boiling a long time ago.

"Lil!" I gasped in warning.

She sucked harder, faster, and didn't bother to quiet her moans. My cock stuffing Lily's mouth was the only thing keeping her cries from ringing loudly off the tiles. But even muffled, Lily's voice became more urgent and she drooled down my length. I gathered her glorious copper-colored hair back from her face and just couldn't stop myself anymore. The molten ache inside me built to a crescendo, overwhelming all my senses.

"Yes, Lil!" I grunted. "Ah, fuck...!"

I could no longer hold still. I thrust my cock deep once, hard, and the hot-sweet rush poured out of me, into Lily's waiting mouth. Her tongue and lips worked me expertly through cresting waves of pleasure, but there was too much. A white line of cum oozed from the corner of her mouth and along her cheek.

"Wow," I panted.

"You always make me the best desserts, Max," Lily said as she sat back, licking her lips and grinning.

She stood and smoothed her short dress down once more, then sniffed the air almost delicately. Grinning, Lily grabbed a folded paper towel from one of the discreetly placed dispensers. To clean up, I thought, but then she opened her tiny purse and took out a pen instead. I looked over her shoulder as I stuffed my still half-hard cock away into my pants again. Lily was writing... my name and phone number?

"Uh," I said. "What's that for?"

Lily winked at me in the mirror, then stepped away to slide the paper towel under one of the polished black stall doors.

"Give him a call sometime, Courtney. You won't be sorry," Lily said. "And I love your perfume."

For a moment, nothing happened, but then a pair of neat black shoes lowered to the floor and a trembling hand reached down to pick up the paper towel. I wondered if it was possible to die of embarrassment.

"Oh god, Lil," I groaned. "Did you drag her in here or something?"

"Me? No," said Lily. "I think Courtney came to the restroom for the normal reason."

"And we trapped her in here?" I raised my voice. "Courtney, I'm *so* sorry!"

Now we were definitely going to get arrested for indecent exposure or... or something. But Lily laughed, smacked her lips loudly and gave me a shove toward the door.

"Unless you want to walk out of here together and advertise to the whole restaurant what we just did–"

"No thanks," I said.

"–then why don't you go back to the table? I'll be there in a minute."

Lily gave me a light push that sent me staggering. I pulled open the restroom door and slipped out, then hurried down the hall. I passed a waiter in a neat red bowtie and wondered if he had seen me exiting the ladies' room. If my face got any hotter, it would reach the ignition point.

I waited at the table for just under three minutes. I know because I checked the time every ten seconds. Had Courtney reported Lily and me to management? Maybe I could argue that I had gotten Lily drunk and forced her into the whole thing. It didn't matter if I was barred from the restaurant – it wasn't like I would ever be able to afford to eat here, anyway.

But then all the fates decided to give me a break just this once and Lily came sauntering through the tables toward me.

"Ready to go?" she asked.

"Yes," I said. "Now. Quickly."

Lily giggled at that, then finished off what was left in her wine-glass and stuck an extra hundred into the bill folder sitting on the table's edge. She took my arm and escorted me toward the door.

We almost made it out clean, too, but then I spotted Courtney emerging from the kitchen. At least it was her turn to nearly drop something – five plates of gourmet food – as she caught sight of me. I mouthed *I'm so sorry* again just before Lily swept me out through the door.

The February night was cold and dark. Clouds filled the sky, but were thin enough that the moon shone through and turned the edges into celestial etchings of pearl. Wisps of fog filled the streets, too, as though even the silvery clouds had come down to Earth for a romantic Valentine's Day.

Lily grabbed my arm and leaned against my shoulder. "Where are you parked?"

"Uh, down the street," I said and waved vaguely in the right direction. I couldn't afford to waste money on valet parking, though it might have been funny to see my old bucket alongside the expensive Jags and Teslas.

"Let's go for a drive," Lily said. "I haven't been in the truck for years. I'll pick up the Alfa later."

We walked together a few blocks to the truck. I unlocked the passenger side door first, wrapped my oil-stained jacket around the mangled rose bouquet and stuffed them both behind the seat. Then I offered Lily my hand and helped her up into the cab. It can be an awkward climb in high heels and a dress. With Lily's half-succubus superpowers, though, the gesture probably seemed pretty stupid.

Lily leaned over and unlocked the other door for me. I got in and started the truck, proud of the smooth purr that came from beneath the hood. It rumbled like a tiger instead of coughing like the sick dog you might expect looking at the exterior. Lily smiled and patted the dashboard.

"You take good care of it," she said.

My pride climbed up another notch. Not just because Lily noticed the work I put into the old truck, but because she knew her cars well enough to hear the difference.

"Where are we going?" I asked.

"I don't care." Lily kicked off her high heels and put her feet up on the dashboard. "Just... drive."

I shrugged and pulled out into the road. It was well past rush hour, but downtown traffic was thick. So I drove away from the restaurants and nightclubs, moving south through the city along the coast. When we got off the freeway, I cracked my window open to breathe in the cool salt smell of the sea. On Lily's side, the water stretched out flat and black, too dark to see much. At least for me. Lily could probably count the fish swimming out there.

"She's going to call you," Lily said suddenly.

"What? Who?" I asked.

"Courtney, our waitress. I bet she's going to call you."

"We're lucky she didn't call the manager, Lil," I said. But I was smiling. And blushing. "You uh... didn't talk to her when I left, did you?"

"No. Courtney scampered out right after you did. She didn't say anything, but she still had that paper towel."

"...Really?" I shook my head. "Lil, why the hell did you do that?"

"Suck you off in the bathroom or give Courtney your number?" she asked.

"Um..."

"You deserve a nice girl and a nice time, Max."

"Thanks, Lil," I said. "You know, sort of. You just about gave me a heart attack back there."

"Only one?"

"Three or four," I admitted.

The darkened coast rolled past outside. There were buildings on the waterfront, but not many lights. The piers and wharves that jutted out into the ocean were old, cracked and covered in patches of moss. Abandoned.

"Hey, this is Southport," said Lily, a little surprised.

She was right. I hadn't meant to take us down here, but without any other destination, I was driving us back home. Well, what used to be home when we were kids. Southport wasn't the worst place to grow up, but it was bad enough that neither of us lives there anymore.

"Do you miss it down here?" Lily asked.

"Sometimes," I said. "You made high school pretty exciting."

Lily laughed and unbuckled herself. She slid along the bench seat and up next to me, leaning her head against my shoulder. One of her hands rested on my thigh.

"Seat belt," I reminded her.

"I'm so charged up right now that I could fly through the windshield and be just fine."

"That doesn't mean I want to see you get hurt," I told her.

Lily stuck her tongue out at me and sat back, but her fingers stroked lazy circles along my thigh, moving slowly, agonizingly upward. I was rock hard in seconds, of course. Lily's lips brushed my ear and sent shivers racing down my spine.

"If you don't want to wreck the truck, I suggest we park," she whispered.

She didn't need to tell me twice. I took the very next turnout – a short, pitted strip of asphalt that ended in a sandy patch of grass overlooking the dark midnight ocean. There was a sign attached to the railing that probably used to post some interesting tidbit for tourists, but sun and time had bleached it out into a blank white rectangle.

"How's this?" I asked.

"Perfect," Lily said.

She cupped her hand between my legs and grinned at my loud sigh of relief. I unfastened my seat belt and pulled Lily to me, caressing the softness of one breast as I leaned in to kiss her. She opened her mouth and moaned against my lips. Even if I had paid attention to dinner, there was no way it was half as delicious as Lily's kiss. I could taste her desire, her excitement.

At least, I felt like I could. I've known Lily a long time and gotten pretty good at reading her. I think it's as close as I'll ever come to understanding how Lily drinks in lust, how it makes her feel. It must be amazing.

I felt for the zipper of her dress. It was tiny and hard to get a grip on, but if I can rebuild a transmission from scratch, I could deal with a dress. I managed to slide it down and Lily shoved the slinky black fabric around her waist to reveal the creamy curves of her tits.

Looking wasn't enough. I pushed Lily back along the seat and pressed my face between her breasts. For a second, I just reveled in the silky feel of her skin against my cheeks, then turned my head and bit gently. Lily gasped, arched her spine and grabbed double handfuls of my hair as I tugged lightly at her slippery, wet nipple with my teeth. I took the soft swell of her other breast in one hand and squeezed, my thumb flicking over the hardening pink peak in time with my tongue. I didn't want anyone to feel neglected.

Lily squirmed beneath me, but she was just stripping her dress and panties down off her hips. She kicked the tangle of cloth across the floorboards, leaving herself in only the black choker and thigh-high stockings. I groaned in pleasure at the sight.

"You're so beautiful, Lil," I told her. My lips brushed her breast as I spoke.

"Show me," she said.

Lily seized the front of my expensive shirt – the one she had bought me – and tore it off. By the end of the night, there would be nothing left of my suit.

I was okay with that.

As quickly and gracefully as I could manage – which wasn't very – I pulled off my pants. One of my shoes got kicked up on top of the dashboard, but I had far, far more important things to worry about. Lily lifted her legs up until her toes touched the roof of the truck's cab, then spread them before me. She reached between us and grabbed my dick, eliciting another low groan from me. I pushed my hips urgently forward and let Lily guide my cock into her.

God, her pussy was so hot. So tight and so wet. Lily can take it and take it hard, but I worked my length into her slowly, inch by inch with each roll of my hips. When I was buried to the hilt inside her, Lily let out a small squeak and then a long sigh of satisfaction.

I held myself up on my arms, watching her beneath me as I began to move myself out and then back into her body. Lily's red hair was strewn across the seat, all around her like a burning halo. Her soft tits bounced hypnotically when I started off with small, shallow thrusts, then more and more as I hammered my cock deep into the velvet heat of her.

Lily threw back her head and let out a high, breathless scream as she came. Her already tight pussy squeezed even more, making it difficult to move. But I don't work out for nothing. My fingers gripped the edges of the seat, my knuckles turning white as I pounded into Lily hard enough that wetness squirted in molten drops across her parted thighs.

Despite the cold sea wind blowing through the window, by the time Lily fell limp beneath me, sweat rolled down my skin. I slowed my thrusts and watched her face. Lily smiled as she opened her eyes again.

"I want to do it in the back," she panted.

I sat, rebalancing my weight so I could reach down and cup Lily's rounded ass. I gently spread the smooth cheeks. She was dripping wet and I used the tip of one finger to rub the slick juices over her tiny anal hole.

"I mean in the back of the truck," Lily said with a laugh.

"Oh."

As well as I know Lily, I still manage to get it wrong sometimes. I felt pretty damned stupid, but Lily just leaned up on her elbows and kissed the tip of my nose.

She started to wriggle out from under me, making her body rub deliciously against mine, but I wrapped one arm around her waist. I lifted Lily with me and sat again, pulling Lily into my lap with my cock still buried inside her. Lily whimpered and pressed her forehead into my shoulder as she began instinctively to ride me.

"Not yet," I whispered into her ear.

Ignoring Lily's answering moan – which wasn't easy – I grabbed the door handle and pushed it open. I held her against me – again, not easy as she rocked herself on my dick – and slid out of the truck. Standing now, I hooked my arms behind Lily's knees, holding her up so she could concentrate on the fun part, and cupped her ass in my hands. Her stockinged feet crossed at the small of my back.

"Max..." she moaned.

I stood on the grassy hill overlooking the sea, holding Lily close. I lifted her an inch or two, paused for one heartbeat and then dropped her back down onto my cock. A little higher and then a longer fall, pounding pleasure deeper into Lily's body.

"Oh fuck, oh fuck," she chanted.

The cold night didn't stop the sweat from trickling along my spine. Not because Lily was heavy; she's tall, but slender, though when she's all charged up on how much I want her, Lily can pick me up, too. Hell, I've seen her lift a car with one hand.

No, it was the effort of not blowing my load with every thrust into Lily's lithe body, not flooding her pussy with cum like I so badly wanted to. I knew I couldn't get her pregnant, but she was moaning so much. I wanted to make Lily feel good for as long as I possibly could. I never wanted to stop.

I held Lily still and hammered myself up into her. Hot wetness ran down my dick and over my balls, spattering the grass at my feet.

The sound of our bodies coming together again and again was just as loud as the hiss and rush of the ocean. I panted hard into Lily's hair as I clutched her against me, smelling her and feeling her so intensely that it made my heart ache.

My cock throbbed, pulsing in time inside Lily's slick heat. Shit, if I didn't stop soon, I wasn't going to be able to avoid shooting her full of cum. So I focused on walking, carrying Lily to the back of the truck while she writhed sensuously on the end of my dick. I shifted her a little so I could lower the tailgate with one hand, but then I needed both. Lily whined adorably as I lifted her off my cock and set her down. Wind whipped her brilliant hair around her.

"Hey, not finished," she protested.

"Just... hang on a second," I panted.

I climbed up into the bed of the truck, where I kept a set of tools in a big diamond-plate box. How do you think I changed that mini-van's tire? The jack and iron that come with a car are pretty much universally shit.

One of the things in the toolbox was a quilted pad for when I need to move something delicate or work under a car out on the road. I spread it over the corrugated plastic of the truck bed, then turned to Lily again and patted the makeshift blanket. She crawled up into the truck.

"Lay down," she commanded.

I had no desire to use up a precious *no* against that order, so I laid on my back across the blanket and let Lily straddle me. She held my hard, wet cock in one hand and sank onto it with a moan.

"Now," she breathed. "Just lie back and enjoy."

I crossed my arms behind my head, but there was nothing leisurely about Lily when she began to ride me. It was a fucking rodeo. She steadied herself against my chest and her nails bit into the skin there as she moved on top of me, rocking and twisting her hips with every deep thrust. Even when she held still, she squeezed and milked my dick inside her.

Her pussy was all tight, soft silky wetness around my cock. Lily's breasts were flushed a bright rose color with the heat of her pleasure. I clenched my teeth against the surging sensation and desperately grabbed Lily's ass, trying to slow her bouncing, grinding dance atop me.

But as I may have mentioned before, when she's all powered up on lust, Lily's a hell of a lot stronger than I am. I couldn't stop her, and I didn't really *want* to stop her... Not if Lily didn't want me to stop.

"Cum for me, Max," she moaned.

"Yes, Lil!"

The tight heat in my balls poured instantly into Lily. My hands tightened on the firm flesh of her ass as the tidal force of orgasm rushed through me, echoing the waves surging and crashing below. One thick liquid pulse after another gushed into Lily, filling and then overfilling her pussy with white until we were both soaked.

She rolled off of me and lay panting beside me in the bed of the truck. One of her legs was still draped awkwardly across mine, but we were too boneless to care. Hesitantly, I inched my hand over until I found Lily's and threaded my fingers through hers.

"No fucking way," she said.

I blinked. It wasn't the first time we had held hands, though I admit that it didn't happen often. Still, it wasn't that big a deal... was it?

Then I heard it – the rasping hiss that I thought was the ocean, but it was growing louder. Closer? Something dark moved above us, little more than a shadow slithering across the racing gray and silver clouds. Lily leapt up to her feet, all languor gone from her body. She crouched like a tigress about to pounce.

"You've got to be kidding me," she said. "Here?"

The shadow swooped lower and I could just make out the angular spread of wings. A... bat? No, it was far too large and getting larger.

Lily sprang out of the truck with such force that the whole thing bobbed and the suspension squealed in protest. She flew up into the dark night, colliding with the shadow, and they plummeted together into the grassy headland. I saw a long tail covered in blue-black scales twisting around Lily, but then they were skidding away down the sandy slope.

I jumped up – much slower than Lily had – and stared. The thing coiling itself around her was about the size of my truck, but much longer and thinner, with a serpentine body and two vast, thrashing wings. There were a pair of legs, too, each ending in clawed feet that were busily tearing deep furrows into the grass. A frilled, pointed head darted out at Lily and split open into a huge, fang-filled maw.

Lily balled her fist and punched the wyvern in its long muzzle. Its head snapped back, but then whipped around to glare at her, dark eyes glittering with animal malevolence. The wyvern's tail lashed out, wrapping around Lily and yanking her down to the ground.

"Oh shit," I said. "Oh shit, oh shit...!"

I tore open the toolbox again. I try to be prepared. Prepared to change a tire or give Lily the best sex I know how, sure – but pre-pared to fight off a big flying monster? Fuck. I wondered if I should get a gun rack and start packing a shotgun or something.

Maybe a rocket launcher.

Right now, though, Lily was wrestling with a wyvern and I needed a weapon. Pressure gauge? No. Chains? Not really. Road flare? WD-40? Motor oil? Tire iron?

Tire iron! I grabbed the steel cross and the flare, too, then leapt out of the truck. Lily had pulled herself free of the wyvern's con-stricting tail and seized one of its deep blue frills. The beast let out a cry that sounded like a nail being dragged over metal and kicked at Lily with one of those stout, powerful-looking legs. She spun gracefully aside, avoiding the hooked claws, but the monster's heel slammed against her stomach, sending Lily skidding back. My guts twisted in a painful knot, but I made myself suck down a cold breath.

"Hey!" I shouted. "Hey, you big bastard! Over here!"

I struck the flare across the side of the truck. Red flames spat from the end and I waved the tire iron threateningly. At least, I hoped so.

"Max, no!" Lily cried. "What the hell are you doing?"

The wyvern swung its thorny muzzle in my direction and shrilled deafeningly once again. Tucking its leathery wings tight against its side, the monster charged toward me with its long tail arcing up over its head. There was even a huge, sharp stinger on the end, like some massive scorpion. Now what?

Lily moved so fast that her nude body was no more than a white blur. She lunged at the wyvern and slammed her fist into its face. Slender naked girl, big scary monster; you think she would bounce right off. But the wyvern reeled and tumbled to the ground in a writhing knot of teeth and spines.

Lily leapt astride the beast, wrapped her arm around its twisting neck, and yanked it back until I heard a sound like a tree snapping in a storm. The wyvern let out one last gurgling hiss and then Lily dropped its limp body to the ground. I held up the flickering red flare like a torch.

"What... the fuck?" I panted.

"That wyvern's been hunting hikers and snorkelers all along the coast," Lily said. She stood naked and gleaming with sweat in the crimson light. "Boy did it ever pick the wrong prey tonight."

"Is it dead?"

I couldn't quite dispel the horror-movie image of the creature surging back to its feet in a final death lunge and stabbing Lily with that huge stinger. She kicked the wyvern's head. It wobbled, but the body didn't. The head clearly wasn't attached to the rest of the wyvern. Not in any way that counted.

"Yeah, it's dead," Lily said. "I'd better call the College guys to come clean up. We don't want anyone else seeing this thing."

Good idea. It was creepy as hell. So I put the tire iron away and grabbed a big blue tarp from my toolbox. I threw it over the dead wyvern and used a few rocks to weight the corners against the wind. When I was done, Lily was just replacing her cell phone in her purse.

"Thanks, Max," Lily said when she saw the tarp. "The College will have some wizards here in twenty minutes to collect the body. Apparently they use the stinger venom and scales in some of their spells. They're going to pay me a little extra for that."

Lily toed the sputtering flare from where I had set it on a patch of sand and put her hands on her bare hips.

"That was pretty dumb, though," she said. "Running at a wyvern with a road flare and a tire iron."

"Uh, yeah," I admitted. "Sorry. Can we just chalk it up to adrenaline?"

"Dumb," she repeated. "But brave."

Lily reached out and squeezed my cock. It was as hard as though I hadn't cum in days.

"Should I chalk this up to adrenalin, too?" she asked.

My heart still beat like a drum – which really *was* adrenalin – but I had to admit that seeing Lily in action, going toe to toe with a two-ton monster, was amazing. And she had been naked the whole time...

"Come on. I've got to get you out of here before the College shows up," Lily said. She grabbed my wrist and hauled me back to the truck, then bent over the tailgate and brandished her pale, perfect ass at me. "But first, victory sex!"

"Uh... what?" I asked.

Lily winked at me. Her hazel eyes were bright and mischievous. "And victory sex goes in the butt."

I didn't know that about victory sex. But Lily was the monster-killing badass, so I trusted her authority on the matter.

———

Lily had me wait in the truck about a mile down the road while she spoke to the College wizards. When she was finished, Lily gave me a call and I picked her up beside the faded old lookout sign. She was dressed again as she climbed into the truck and we drove back out of Southport.

"Did they wonder what you were doing out here in a dress?" I asked.

Lily laughed. "Nope. I don't think anything that I do surprises the wizards anymore. Especially when it comes to me and slinky evening wear."

I laughed, too, but then we drove in silence, not even bothering to turn on the radio. We made our way up along the coast again with the windows rolled down, listening to the wind and ocean until the sounds of the city closed in around us once more.

"Well, that was an interesting..." I trailed off. It wasn't a date. "An interesting night. Thanks for dinner, Lil. And... and the rest."

"It was fun," said Lily. She set her elbow in the open window and her chin in her hand. "You know, Max, you helped with that wyvern."

"I did?"

"Hell yes. You help me with my job all the time. I don't suppose you would accept part of the reward gold?"

"I don't think that fucking my incredibly sexy best friend entitles me to any money," I told Lily. I pulled the truck to a stop in front of the restaurant and turned in my seat to look at her. "I'd do that anyway."

"Yeah, I know," Lily said. "And you know what else?"

"What?"

"This was the best Valentine's Day that I've had in years. I even got roses."

"You uh... saw those?" I asked.

Lily leaned in close until her soft lips brushed mine. My heart hammered. It always does.

"Smelled them as soon as I got in the car," she said.

"You're kind of... hard to shop for," I stammered.

"Max, you never need to buy me a thing. You already give me the best present in the world. Every day."

"I do?"

"You're the best friend I could ever ask for, Max. I'm still trying to pay you back for that. However I can. Now go on home and wait for Courtney to call."

Lily gave me a long kiss, and then climbed down out of the truck. I stayed until the valet brought her car around and Lily got inside. She waved to me one last time as she pulled away from the curb. I put the truck into gear and then drove the opposite direction, heading home.

"Happy Valentine's Day, Lil," I said.

For more stories by
Natalie and Eric Severine,
visit us at **LLStories.com**

www.ingramcontent.com/pod-product-compliance
Lightning Source LLC
Chambersburg PA
CBHW030517120726
47904CB00005B/1505